INNOCENT EMPLOYMENTS

Innocent Employments

ROGER BEARDWOOD

THE BODLEY HEAD
LONDON   SYDNEY
TORONTO

For Françoise

British Library Cataloguing
in Publication Data
Beardwood, Roger
Innocent employments.
I. Title
823'.9' 1F   PR6052.E1/
ISBN 0–370–30129–3

© Roger Beardwood 1978
Printed in Great Britain for
The Bodley Head Ltd
9 Bow Street London WC2E 7AL
by Redwood Burn Ltd, Trowbridge
set in Monophoto Baskerville
by Keyspools Ltd, Golborne, Lancs.
First published 1978

There are few ways in which a man can be
more innocently employed than in getting money.

Samuel Johnson

All fiction is a fusion of an author's experience and imagination. In this book a few celebrities are named, and even assigned walk-on parts, as are some real hoteliers, restaurateurs, head waiters and barmen. But the world in which they move is imaginary; so are the characters populating that world.

My characters' flesh is paper, their blood is ink; and if they seem to live that is an example of imagination's power. If any bears the name of a living person that is the result of a growing paucity of names in an era of rising population.

Roger Beardwood
Biarritz, France
1978

I

> The form of gambling known as business looks with
> disfavour upon the form of business known as gambling
> *Ambrose Bierce*

In my speech to our firm's last annual dinner I observed with some asperity that accountancy had never achieved the status and dignity it deserved. To be sure, the services of accountants are increasingly in demand, thanks to the ceaseless outpouring of legislation and regulation from Washington, and no prudent businessman makes a major decision without consulting a member of our profession. But our image, to use a term I dislike, is still that of book-keepers, to which the adjectives desiccated or dried-up are frequently applied. This complaint was received with some laughter and cheers, since I stand six feet two inches tall and weigh 210 pounds, despite a daily squash game and the unremitting exhortations of my wife. After the laughter had died down I added that when we were not described as desiccated we were accused of indulging in 'something called creative accountancy, and though my physical appearance attests to my love of good cooking this does not extend to treating arithmetic as one of the culinary arts'. This brought another roar of laughter, through which I heard cries of 'What about Equity Funding?' and 'Don't forget Penn Central'.

I would like to be able to say that our firm has never been involved in such enormous scandals because its ethics and vigilance are of a higher order than those reigning at some other firms – which, indeed, they are. But simple truth compels me to admit we are not among the Big Eight of our profession, a description that always makes me think of Detroit's more bloated products. We are, perhaps, one of the twenty largest accounting firms in the United States, and as such are not subjected to the temptation of auditing companies so structurally complicated that management can bury its peccadilloes with little fear of early discovery. No, our speciality is the conservative company, bank or individual in need of personal attention and the imprimatur of a firm that has been in the profession for almost a century without once being involved in an unseemly dispute with a regulatory agency.

Even our offices reflect this innate conservatism; not for us the style I call chequebook modern, but three converted brownstones in Murray Hill, decorated and furnished in a manner hinting discreetly at a long past and longer future. Our name – Kemble, McKenzie and Horton – is engraved on a small brass plate, and some older clients who visit us complain that we are hard to find. They also complain that the steps from the street to the front door are hazardous, but I do not think we have lost any clients, either figuratively or literally, because of these difficulties. Even if we have, they are outweighed by the new clients who feel that to be accepted by us is tantamount to their joining a club with particularly restrictive criteria.

At one of the cocktail parties my position requires me to attend a brash young man from one of the Big Eight – Peat Marwick Mitchell & Co., I think – observed that my firm had evolved what he called 'a very successful marketing strategy'. Resisting the temptation to address him as 'young man' – he was in his early thirties, whereas I am forty-eight – I replied mildly that our 'marketing strategy', as he chose to describe it, had grown organically out of the history and character of our firm, which was founded in London by my great-grandfather, William Kemble, who emigrated to the United States in 1887. The young man smiled sardonically, and retorted, 'Sure. But it's still a great gimmick.' That night I recounted the exchange to my wife, Nancy, as we savoured a post-prandial cognac. Her comments disappointed me.

'But Charles,' she said, 'you know as well as I do that you didn't buy the brownstones until 1962. All that old family retainer atmosphere is a lot of hogwash.'

There are times when I think Nancy has been tainted by the prevailing cynicism of our era. Even so, I replied patiently. 'My dear, your memory for dates is impressive, but I would like to remind you that our firm has been in existence since the last century. Our way of conducting ourselves has nothing to do with the date on which we actually occupied our offices; it has everything to do with our traditions, and our offices are a reflection of them.' I forbore to point out that those traditions helped to explain why we were sitting in the living-room of a duplex on Park Avenue, drinking a more than passable John Exshaw, and planning to visit our son at Phillips Andover the following weekend. Long experience with wives – Nancy is my third, and in many ways the best – has shown me that observations of that nature are open invitations to verbal warfare.

I don't want to give the impression that Nancy and I do not get on together. We do, and even if our *badinage* strikes outside observers as being abrasive we know that her testing of my attitudes, and mine of hers, proceeds from the great respect we have for each other. Even so, some of her frequent criticisms cut deep, and impel me to rebut them in ways that may appear oblique. I must admit that my speech to the assembled partners of our firm was inspired in part by Nancy's describing me as 'a pompous penpusher labouring under gross delusions of adequacy'. The next day I asked the research department to provide me with a sampling of quotations dealing with accountants, and when this arrived on my desk the following week found that her attitudes towards my profession were all too common.

But that late-night conversation with Nancy had another consequence more important than the speech. As I have said, our firm is buoyed by its traditions, and one of them is that every spring we give a reception for our clients and, to be frank, those whom we hope will join that select group. For many years – from 1962 until 1972 to be precise – we held this function in our offices. But though the roster of our clients remains select, it has outgrown the partners' room, and since then we have held the reception at Twenty-One. There are those, I know, who profess to scorn '21', holding it to be a restaurant that serves ego rather than food, and contending that the Kriendler and Berns families, who own and run it, are mere first-generation Americans who have arrogated to themselves the role of Manhattan's social arbiters, allocating the socially prominent to highly visible tables and the obscure to obscurity. But I have never found the Kriendlers and Bernses to be either whimsical or unrealistic; I myself have always been able to sit where I wish, and either Jerry Berns or Pete Kriendler has usually found time to say a word or two. This mark of their personal esteem has nothing to do with the custom I and my partners take to '21', as I stressed to Nancy when she described the ambience as 'spurious and meretricious'. At the time we were having an after-theatre supper upstairs, and I was able to point to several newspapermen stretching their expense accounts. Incorrigible as ever, Nancy replied that Mr Berns and Mr Kriendler were always attentive to 'those who can burnish the legend in the public prints', and nodded towards Cy Sulzberger of the *New York Times*.

But to return to our reception. We held it, I recall, on one of those mid-April days when New York glitters with sun, and the city's financial problems are belied by the opulence of the stores and the cheerful flapping of flags in Rockefeller Plaza. Outside '21' was the usual clutter of double-parked limousines and gossiping chauffeurs; inside, the receptionist, Chuck Anderson, was rationing smiles and handshakes. I've always had a warm spot in my heart for Chuck, and think he has one for me. Certainly, he was particularly cordial that evening, and took me personally to the elevator. 'Don't worry about a thing, Mr Kemble,' he said. 'It's all ready. You got any problems, just give me a call.' By design, I was slightly early, and the waiters and bartenders were still fussing over the room. One of the many nice things about '21' is that the staff remember regular clients like myself – '21' calls us 'friends of the house' – and I did not have to ask for the Bombay martini on the rocks.

Before the first of the guests arrived I reviewed the invitation list. Now it is a curious fact that most people think accountants are obsessed by figures and fairly oblivious of culture and history, but I believe my reactions to the list disprove popular misconceptions. The list was in alphabetical order, of course, and as I read through it the impression was of a who's who of American business. But something about four of the names stuck in my mind, and I read through again, only half-consciously starting on a second Bombay martini, which one of the servitors had placed by my side with '21' unobtrusiveness. 'Acheson, Peter,' I read, and 'Rusk, Henry'. They were no challenge: Acheson and Rusk had been two of the most able Secretaries of State since World War II – more able, in my view, than Dr Kissinger. I read on. 'Eden, Jacqueline.' Eden? The surname, of course, of Winston Churchill's Foreign Secretary and successor as Prime Minister. 'Jobert, Michel.' Jobert was harder; yet it was a name I half-remembered. Yes, Jobert had been France's Foreign Secretary under President Pompidou. I glanced at my watch and it was, let me say, a fine example of the horologer's art rather than one of those ugly, fashionable digital affairs. Five minutes to go before the first guest was due to arrive. I looked at the notes for my speech, and decided to add a few graceful, humorous words about the unlikely statistical freak that had brought together in the same room four people who bore the surnames of eminent Foreign Secretaries.

While I was composing this extemporaneous addition one of my partners walked in. John Williams is a great-nephew of the McKenzie who joined my forebear in the early days of the firm, and as such is rather more familiar with me than his rank justifies. He is a plump young man in his middle thirties who tends to parade the solidity of his home life – he lives in Westport, Connecticut, where he is a pillar of community organisations – and a somewhat suspect dedication to our firm's traditions. If that sounds sour I don't mean it to be; but John's interpretation of tradition is that the firm was founded by innovators, and the current generation should stress that aspect of its history rather than its timeless nature. I'm among the first to agree we should move with the times; but I am adamant that in the process we should not abandon, or even dilute, the commitment to quality and ethics upon which our success has been founded. Recently John had been urging us to accept an engagement – that is the accounting profession's jargon for contract – with a small conglomerate that owns a substantial interest in Nevada gambling. He had even infiltrated the president of this company, a Mr Nagel, into one of our monthly luncheons. Against Mr Nagel I held nothing personally: he turned out to be quiet, civil, and unobtrusive, and to share many of my own views on the state of society. But, as I told John afterwards, Mr Nagel would almost certainly be happier with one of the larger, less discriminating accounting firms. 'After all,' I said, 'his company does depend for forty per cent of its profits on a casino, and I don't think that's the kind of business to which our firm should give its audit certificate.'

Emboldened, perhaps, by the Mouton Cadet served at our luncheon, John did not accept that statement for what it was: a closing and locking of our particular door. 'Hell, Charles, don't you see you're turning away two hundred thousand bucks a year? Maybe more? I tell you, Nagel is going places.'

'To the same places, no doubt, that Jimmy Ling and some other conglomerators have already gone,' I retorted.

'Well, some of us think that two hundred thousand bucks a year should not be turned down lightly,' said John. He added, ominously, 'And there are more of us every day.'

That I doubted. In every organisation as large as ours – we have twenty full partners – there are bound to be a few dissidents, generally the younger men who may have been promoted a little too fast for their own good. But I believe very firmly that when the issues are presented fairly and squarely – in other words, when the chips are down – most will see where their best interests lie.

On that April evening, mellowed by the weather and by two excellent martinis, I was in a conciliatory mood, and so was John. 'Are you going to give us one of your famous speeches?' he asked.

'You can count on me,' I replied. And then I mentioned the strange coincidence that four of our guests bore the surnames of former Foreign Secretaries.

Conciliatory though he was, John raised doubts. 'Don't you think they're tired of people ribbing them? For Christ's sake, if your surname was Eisenhower don't you think you would have run out of replies to the obvious question?'

'I don't intend to make a major issue out of this,' I answered. 'All I want to do is to stress the statistical improbability of four people with such names being in the same room. And after making that point – lightly – I shall draw a parallel with accounting and accountants, and their mistrust of statistical freakishness.'

'You're the boss.'

That statement needed no comment, and I turned to the task of greeting the arriving guests. After hosting many parties I have become adept at this skill; but it is one demanding considerable powers of memory and tact. For a start, one must remember the name of every guest, or at least appear to. My own technique is to name in stentorian fashion those guests I do recognise, and to greet those I do not with a resounding 'Sir'.

John Williams has, predictably, suggested that it would be easier for everyone if guests wore lapel badges emblazoned with their names. 'Easier, no doubt,' I retorted, 'but hardly the kind of thing we should do. Can you really imagine Baron Guy de Rothschild wearing a lapel badge? Or David Rockefeller?'

'They don't come to our parties.'

'No, and they never will if they have to wear lapel badges.'

Even so, I wished that Acheson, Jobert and Rusk bore some distinguishing marks; even Jacqueline Eden was a problem, since I had no idea whether she was young or old, tall or small, fat or thin.

Then I saw Mark Edwards, one of our brighter young men; he will make partner before he is forty, of that I'm sure. Mark knows everybody, or claims to, and I beckoned to him. 'Have you noticed, Mark, that we have four famous names in the room?'

'Only four, sir? I thought they were all famous in their way.'

'No, I mean we have four guests who bear the names of famous Foreign Secretaries: Acheson, Rusk, Eden and Jobert. I want to mention them in my speech – an interesting statistical improbability.'

'But you can't put the faces to the names, is that right?'

Mark is too quick sometimes. 'Exactly. They've obviously been invited by some of the other partners.'

'Yes and no. They're on Mr Murchison's list; but I invited them.'

'You?'

'Mr Murchison said he was tired of seeing the same old faces, and asked me to find some new ones.'

Irregular, extremely irregular; but this was not the time to say so. 'Well, as they're your friends, perhaps you would introduce me.'

Mark steered past Bobby Sarnoff, late of RCA, who was talking to Andrew Heiskell, chairman of Time Inc., neatly avoided old J. J. Chetwynd, who becomes more garrulous with every passing year, and led me towards an animated group in a corner near the bar. At the centre of it was a tall, slim young woman with shoulder-length black hair, dark eyes in a pale face and, at this moment, a smile on her full lips.

She held out a firm, cool hand as Mark explained who I was. Once again I launched into an explanation of how unlikely it was to find an Eden, Rusk, Acheson and Jobert in the same room. 'Yes, but Eden is really a very usual name,' she said. I noticed that her voice was low, and her accent slightly Southern. 'But if you are looking for improbabilities, I can add another: one of my stocks is Avon.'

'One of your stocks is Avon?'

'Yes.'

There was a long silence. Mark broke it. 'Jacqueline is a securities analyst. She means that one of the stocks she follows is Avon.'

A harsh voice broke in at my ear. 'And if you still don't get it, Anthony Eden became the Earl of Avon.' I turned and looked; it was one of the journalists we are forced to invite every year.

'Thank you,' I said. 'I am quite aware that *Sir* Anthony became *Lord* Avon. I happen to be of British ancestry myself.'

'Well, don't worry, you're getting over it,' the fellow said, laughing immoderately and seizing a Scotch and water – not his first, by a long way – from a passing waiter.

Fortunately, Mark interrupted the conversation before it could become a verbal scuffle. 'Here's the second of your quartet – Henry Rusk. Investment banking, sportsman, Harvard and Oxford. Anything more you want to know?'

Rusk was tall – taller even than Andrew Heiskell (why does Time Inc. seem to specialise in very tall senior executives and very small, almost dwarfish editors?). 'Dean Rusk is no kin of mine,' he said in a deep, rumbling voice. 'Thank God. I don't like his politics.' I introduced Jacqueline Eden to him. 'Your namesake wasn't much good either,' he said. 'First he gets the British into Suez. Then he pulls out at a word from Washington. We should have shown the Gyppoes a thing or two – the world would have been different if we had.'

Those were, I suppose, acceptable sentiments in a city sympathetic to the cause of Israel, but somewhat unfashionable and unwise in an age when any tinpot country was encouraged to throw its weight around – provided it was poor and run by a dictator.

Mark, who is youthfully liberal, was quite clearly torn by his sympathy for Israel and dislike of armed, or any other, intervention in another country's affairs. Wisely, he chose to move off in search of Peter Acheson, while Miss Eden and Rusk and I agreed that it was, indeed, a difficult world, and becoming more difficult. Rusk, I noticed, was drinking champagne from a long-stemmed glass with a tulip-shaped bowl. 'Krug, '59,' he said. 'Can't stand this rotgut stuff they pour into you at cocktail parties. They know me here – break out a bottle as soon as they see me. Of course, it's an expensive taste. Suppose you're glad there aren't too many guests like me?'

I was saved from answering by the arrival of Peter Acheson, a plump, smiling man with receding hair and eyes gleaming behind thick glasses. He didn't look like Dean Acheson, whom I have always thought was one of our better Secretaries of State, and when he spoke any family connection seemed unlikely: although his grammar was good, his accent was Queens. When I asked whether many people remarked on his bearing a famous name, he laughed. 'Oh, sure, and they wonder how a guy like me could let the family down. Fact is, the family name used to be something else back in Bosnia, or wherever, but the first of us on this side of the water changed it. The story is, he owned some stock in the Atchison, Topeka and Sante Fe, but got the spelling wrong. Got the right company though – the shares did very well.'

'Are you in Wall Street?'

'Kind of. I'm a commodities dealer. Blame me when you can't afford to buy a pork belly.'

When Mark introduced Michel Jobert, he turned out to be as unlike his namesake as possible. Pompidou's Foreign Secretary is a dark, tiny man; this Michel Jobert was fair, tall and massive, with huge hands and thick neck. His voice was oddly out of keeping with his appearance: light, gentle, and marked by a French accent only a little less obtrusive than Maurice Chevalier's. He was, he said, a *pied noir* – the child of French parents themselves born in Algeria.

'People think of us *pieds noirs* as farmers, and I look like one, is it not so? But my father was a banker and money, thank God, you can take with you. It was the farmers and the vineyard owners I was sorry for. They lost everything, everything they had worked for. I tell you, that de Gaulle, he sold them out, right down the river. No, I am not an admirer of Monsieur Michel Jobert. He is a Gaullist.'

Jacqueline Eden, I was surprised to see, was tense with anger. 'But aren't you in favour of freedom for colonial peoples? You French ran Algeria for yourselves. You gave nothing to the Algerian people.'

Jobert looked down at her. 'On the contrary, we gave them everything, and since we have left, they have ruined it. In all the colonies it is an old, old story. The Europeans bring civilisation, technology, prosperity. Then a small group of natives, saying it is the people, agitates to get us out. Then, when we go, what happens? The small group of natives takes over – in the name of the people. But the liberals think that is all right. For them, it is good; if the exploitation is done by a man with a black skin, it is excused and explained. But a white man who rules wisely and well – he is a rogue.'

Rusk gulped another glass of champagne – his fourth in ten minutes, according to my account – and looked at Jobert with a tight smile. 'Well said, *mon cher*. Well said. I don't know what the French is for "putting the natives in their place", but you've done it.' He turned to look at Jacqueline Eden. 'And a very charming native, too.'

Suddenly, everyone in the group was talking simultaneously. Out of the cacophony words and fragments of phrases emerged: 'colonialism and racism ... nonsense ... liberal arrogance ...' Acheson's glasses, I noted, had misted over. The journalist, dazed either by the noise or by drink, stood in silence, not even lifting his Scotch to his lips.

A hand tugged at my sleeve, and I turned to see old J. J. Chetwynd. 'Charles, you've been neglecting me,' he said, his old man's voice quavering. 'But now you're glad to see me, right? I can rescue you from this gathering of the intellectuals. They remind me of my children, always quarrelling about matters that don't concern them, and not seeing what is going on under their eyes.'

I felt a sudden wave of affection for old J.J. and looked around the room for a celebrity who would make his day. 'You're right, J.J.,' I said. 'You always are. Now let me introduce you to somebody you ought to know, Howard Stein, chairman of the Dreyfus Fund.'

When I left them, J.J., the manufacturer, was telling Howard, the professional investor, what was going to happen in Wall Street.

By then it was time for my speech, and the head waiter started to tinkle a glass with a knife. My partners, well trained, did the same with their glasses, and soon there was virtual silence.

'Ladies and gentlemen, first our thanks for being here tonight. Every year, I try to make this little speech into an occasion for saying something about what interests us most, the trend of business. Tonight, I want to start with a phenomenon that Ambrose Bierce identified many years ago: "The form of gambling known as business looks with disfavour upon the form of business known as gambling ..."'

Business was founded, I pointed out, on probabilities, but the executive who made statistical probability his guiding light could be missing opportunities. 'Here tonight, for example, by sheer coincidence are four people bearing the names of famous Secretaries of State – two of them American, one of them French, and one of them British. Now what, I ask you, is the likelihood of their all being here in the same room tonight, and all of them being in Wall Street? But in one way, they run true to form: like their famous namesakes they all hold strong political views.'

On the whole, I think, my speech went over well. The congratulations of my partners I discount; they are on my side, or should be. But the applause lasted a little longer than either politeness or Twenty-One's drinks could account for, and when Mike Bergerac, chairman of Revlon, came to congratulate me I felt that all those hours of writing and rewriting were justified.

I was not so sure about the wisdom of having drawn attention to Jobert, Acheson, Rusk and Miss Eden. From their corner came the sound of raised voices, and a curious crowd had gathered round them. Even Mark, I noted, was gesticulating, and opening his mouth rather wider than usual. No, 'the Foreign Secretaries', as I had come to think of them, were definitely not a good influence. Separately, each was probably sound enough. As a group they were a force. Yet they held a certain attraction for me, even though it was hard to explain. I had a feeling I would be seeing them again and that not before too long.

2

> 'Wherever fighting's the game,
> Or a spice of danger in grown man's work,'
> Said Kelly, 'you'll find my name.'
> *Joseph Ignatius Constantine Clarke*

'Charles Kemble is a bore,' said Jacqueline Eden.

'A goddamned bore,' said Henry Rusk.

'Well, he's an accountant,' said Michel Jobert.

'Like hell he is,' said Peter Acheson. 'He's just fronting for the crowd. I doubt whether he can do his own tax returns.'

'Still,' said Jacqueline, tilting her wine glass, 'he did say one bright thing. Admittedly, it was borowed from Ambrose Bierce: that quote about gambling and business. I've always felt that Wall Street was a casino by another name, and that all the professionals are croupiers who go to good tailors.'

'Cynicism,' said Henry, 'but it appeals to me.'

'And to me,' said Acheson. 'What do you think I do all day except guess which way the commodities markets will jump? Oh sure, I can dress it up with research, and even find a respectable name for it, the free market. But, come down to it, and it's pure gambling. Still, it buys baby new shoes, and daddy the occasional lunch.'

He looked round the Perigord, on East 52nd Street, one of the few expensive French restaurants in New York where the staff actually speak French. The captain glided over and asked, 'Is everything all right, *monsieur*? Will there be liqueurs – *petits digestifs*?'

'There certainly will,' said Henry. 'A large vintage port for the lady, and three of those 1894 Armagnacs. And don't tell me you don't have them, because I know you have.'

'*Certainement, monsieur, tout de suite.*'

For a few moments, there was silence. Jobert gazed at the heavy white tablecloth, and crushed a Gauloise into the ashtray.

'You know, I have been thinking. We all seem to agree that the world of finance is a respectable casino. We all seem dissatisfied within our lives, is that not so?'

He looked round. Jacqueline avoided his eyes.

Henry replied, 'I'm not arguing. Go on.'

Peter sighed. 'Yeah, I guess I am.'

'Well,' said Michel, 'I have a proposition. We've all made a certain amount of money, but we're still on the treadmill. We still go to the office every day. We still have to live in this monster of a city. We still work for somebody else. So should we all go to live on a desert island? No! We should make money *and* have fun. It can be done, assuredly. Let us treat it as a game, and the money we make or lose as a way of keeping score.

'I am divorced, for the second time. *Ma petite amie* may be a little sorry to see me go, but she will find consolations. You, Henry, are also divorced. You, Peter, too. And you, Jacqueline – you have no ties, is that not so?'

She nodded. 'But I still don't see what you're suggesting.'

'I do,' said Peter. 'What he's saying is, let's cut loose, and play the game as it should really be played, with no holds barred, and in some place that's better than this stinking city – which means almost any place.'

'Oh, great, just great,' said Henry. 'You mean give up everything, and become rich hippies – barefoot boys from Wall Street?'

'Give up? I say nothing about giving up. I say we use our capital and our skills to compete against each other for the rest of the year. Henry is in investment banking; so he can play that game. Peter is a commodities dealer; let him play that. Jacqueline is a securities analyst; there are plenty of rich Europeans trying to find a safe home for their money. Me, I am a foreign exchange dealer. It is a game one can play anywhere, usually with other people's money.'

'I like it, I like it,' said Peter. 'I like it so much I'm gonna have another of these Armannacs.'

'*Cher* Peter,' said Michel, 'a summer in Europe would do you good. At least you would then know that the word is Armagnac – pronounced a-r-m-a-n-y-a-c.'

'And a little failure might make you less arrogant,' said Jacqueline. 'What does it matter how Peter says it, so long as people know what he wants?'

'But in France they would *not* know.'

Henry drained the last of his Armagnac, signalled for more, and cleared his throat. 'Some of what you say makes sense, Michel. Frankly, I'm feeling pretty frustrated down there on the street. A summer in Europe would suit me fine. And the thought of cutting you down to size is pretty damned good.'

'You're pretty smug yourself, Henry,' said Peter, 'I wouldn't mind showing you a thing or two myself.'

'Well, as it's time for hostilities to show,' said Jacqueline, 'let me say that Michel is a racist, you, Henry, are a stuffed shirt, and you, Peter, go on so much about your immigrant grandfather that I suspect you're a genuine Acheson, not a fake one.'

'So, we are agreed, then?' asked Michel. 'None of us would go into business with each other, but we might go into business against each other and the world? Then I propose some simple rules:

'First, we all start with the same stake – a quarter of a million dollars.

'Second, we can make money any way we wish, as long as it's legal in the country in which we do it.

'Third, the Game starts at exactly midnight on the agreed date, and ends at exactly midnight six months later.

'Fourth, the winner is the one who has made the most money, counted in dollars. His prize is a quarter of everyone else's winnings.

'Finally, the Game must have an umpire. I propose Kemble.'

'Kemble?' said Henry. 'Kemble? You must be out of your mind. He'd have a heart attack if you suggested it.'

'No, you're wrong,' said Peter. 'It's the kind of game he'd play himself, if he had the guts. He's a bore because he's bored. Under all that pomposity is a dreamer. Through us, he can live a little. We'll all send him postcards from romantic places.'

Henry leaned back in his chair and lit a short, torpedo-shaped cigar. 'I'm not saying I'm going along with any of this.

But suppose, just suppose, I did. How serious are the rest of you? You, Michel. You talk about a quarter-million stake. Do you have it?'

Michel reached into an inside pocket of his coat, took out an envelope, and handed it to Henry. 'Open that.'

Slowly, Henry slit the envelope with a knife, looked at the paper inside, and raised his eyebrows: 'A treasurer's cheque for a quarter of a million bucks, for credit to the account of Michel Jobert.' He handed the cheque to Jacqueline, and said, 'Well, that's serious money. Did you bring it to impress us, or to convince us, or what?'

'I brought it because, whether you three join the Game or not, I'm going to play it. Your competition would add the spice. Without you, I would be playing against faceless rivals. Still fun, but not quite the same fun as throwing darts at a face instead of at a number.'

'Count me in,' said Peter. 'When do we start?'

'Just a minute,' said Jacqueline. 'We've had a cocktail each, three bottles of wine for the four of us, and so many huge *petits digestifs* that I've lost count. Let's meet a week from now, after we've all thought it over. If we still say yes let's invite Kemble and meet for dinner – then let's start on the first of July.'

Outside, rain was falling heavily. As Peter ran after a taxi the off-duty sign suddenly showed and he slipped in a pile of dogshit. 'Yes, count me in – Armannacs or no Armannacs,' he shouted.

3

> We need some imaginative stimulus, some not impossible ideal such as may shape vague hope, and transform it into effective desire, to carry us year after year, without disgust, through the routine-work which is so large a part of life.
>
> *Walter Pater*

By 6.30 the rain had stopped, and Jacqueline walked the five blocks north from her office in the General Motors Building to her apartment overlooking Central Park. The air smelled fresh, and a gusty wind shook the leaves of the trees so that they shimmered in the pale sunshine. Under the canopy of her building the old doorman, Mike, greeted her with an accent unchanged since he left County Cavan forty years before. 'Good evening to you, good evening, Miss Eden. It's turning out fine, to be sure.'

The elevator operator, a younger version of Mike, asked, as though it had been a daring feat, 'And were you after walking home, then, Miss Eden? Sure, and it's a treacherous night for it.' Jacqueline wondered, not for the first time, whether there was an elocution school for Fifth Avenue doormen where they were taught a limited number of phrases, or whether they all talked like that because they hoped for bit parts on television.

Her apartment on the ninth floor was bright, welcoming, and clean; even so, there was a scuttle of roaches as she opened the kitchen door, and she reached, with a sigh, for a canister of Raid. Should she have a Scotch after all that lunchtime drinking? No. A bath first, then a Scotch, and half an hour to relax before going out to meet Dick Trelford. As she undressed in her bedroom, with the sun streaming through the double-glazed windows, she wondered what she really thought about him. Intelligent? Yes, within limits. Good looking? Yes, if one liked blond, slightly puppy-fattish men who seemed younger than they were.

Jacqueline looked at herself in the full-length mirror as she stepped out of the bath. Breasts small, but firm and high; long, tapered legs; fine-boned ankles and elbows. Not bad for thirty-two. Hell, not bad for *twenty*-two; and too good, perhaps, for Dick Trelford, or anyone remotely like him. And that, she thought, was her problem, or one of her problems: she was never attracted to available men. Yet she could not – would not – have another affair with a married man. She remembered too well the anguish of phone calls that never came, of hurried couplings before the last train to Scarsdale, of seeking out obscure restaurants where neither he nor she would run into friends. No. Never again.

The trouble had started, she thought as she towelled herself dry, when she rebelled against life in Charleston, South Carolina. Her father was a doctor, a kindly man who was an unconscious racist; to him, it was unthinkable that the blacks for whom he cared at a quarter of his normal fee, or no fee at all, should want one day to be able to pay their way like white folks. Her mother, who had married at eighteen, saw blacks only as servitors, or as extras in a never-ending soap opera set in the Old South. As for her only sister, two years older than Jacqueline, she was cocooned in a romantic fantasy in which she played the leading role as a Southern belle whose beauty gave her the pick of the eligible young men. Perhaps because her eyes were dazzled by the dreams, her choice was far from impeccable; her husband was a hard-drinking Mississippi plantation-owner who whored and gambled until he crashed his car while drunk, and now sat at home, half-paralysed and surly.

Of the many analysts Jacqueline had consulted, only one had said anything that seemed to her remotely sensible: 'You made your own career because you are frightened of marriage. You fall in love with married men because you are frightened of marriage. And why are you frightened? Because you saw your parents' marriage as stifling, and your sister's as a mistake. There is a term in logic for what you did, and it is fallacy of composition. You see two marriages, and think they represent all marriage.'

At first, Jacqueline was proud of her independence: proud

of forcing her parents to send her to Smith, and then to Columbia, proud of finding a job unaided, even more proud of rising through the ranks of Wales, Newton, until she was one of the best-paid securities analysts in any New York stockbroking firm. She was still proud; but when her father died, and left her a totally unexpected $300,000, a vague dissatisfaction became specific. Was she to do nothing for the rest of her life except go to the office, write reports on companies, and drift in and out of affairs, knowing how they would end before they started?

Jacqueline looked at herself in the dressing-table mirror: hair shining, eyes large and lustrous, mouth full and soft. 'Yes,' she thought, 'you look like an adorable, warm girl. But there's something cold inside, something waiting to be warmed, brought alive. And you won't find it or him in New York City.'

Henry disliked Wednesday evenings. By custom, they were put aside for dinner with his mother. Each week, he found less to talk to her about; and the food was wretched, too, exactly the kind of peasant pap one would expect from his mother's maid, an Irish farm girl who had emigrated to New York fifty years before and stayed with the Rusks ever since. Week after week, Henry invited, almost begged, his mother to have dinner at a restaurant. She always refused, and always gave the same reasons: 'But Henry, we can't talk privately in a public place. And the prices!' He never quite found the courage to say that if she would move out of a ten-roomed apartment on the East Side that now housed only two old women, she could afford to invite all her friends to the Pierre three times a day.

That night, lit by the last of the evening sun, the apartment seemed gloomier and more cavernous than ever. A small wood fire burned in the grate of the drawing-room; above it, a white marble mantelpiece held a collection of silver-framed family photographs, and a particularly hideous ormolu clock. Henry, at forty-two, felt apologetic as he helped himself to a stiff Scotch; his mother, of course, would never run to Californian champagne, let alone Krug. She looked at him anxiously from bright blue eyes. 'You're not drinking too much, are you, Henry? Your eyes look a little puffy to me. It runs in the family, you know.'

'What? Drunkenness or puffiness?'

'Henry, jokes like that are quite all right between you and me; but I hope you don't speak like that anywhere else. I meant puffiness, of course. No, drinking has never been a weakness in our family, on either side.'

'But I thought that Uncle Basil...?'

'Yes, he was a very sad case. But it was the war, you know. He was shot through the head.'

'Mother, you know as well as I do that all he had was a light scalp wound, and that came from being hit over the head by a military policeman during a brawl.'

'That's what he *said*, Henry, but he was far too modest to let us know what really happened. It had something to do with saving a woman's honour.'

'I didn't know that women who went to public dance halls in 1917 had any honour to save.'

'When you're in this mood, Henry, we'd better talk of something else. Tell me about the bank.'

'Oh, it goes on.'

'And are they treating you well? I must say, they should have made you a director by now.'

'By their standards, I'm a mere stripling.'

'Times have changed, Henry. Your father was president at thirty-eight.'

'Yes, Mother, but the family owned the bank. That made a difference.'

'Henry, you are in one of your cynical moods. You know as well as I do that nepotism was always shunned by the family.'

'All right, Mother, all right. Let's just say that it didn't do any harm to be the founder's son, right?'

Dinner was dreadful: chemical-tasting prawns in a bottled pink sauce of peculiarly glutinous consistency, followed by lamb chops that appeared to have been cooked with a blowtorch, and new potatoes boiled until they were close to disintegration. Only the dessert was passable: cheesecake from the delicatessen. The wine did nothing to help. It might have been a Gallo reject designated for use as industrial alcohol until rescued by his mother.

The elderly Irish maid hovered, her false teeth clicking as

she waited for a word of praise. It came. 'Very good, as usual, Peg,' said Mrs Rusk.

A faint pink suffused Peg's parchment skin. 'Ah, sure, ma'am, it's nothing but plain cooking.'

'And that's the best, isn't it, Henry?' Mrs Rusk looked at her son, who was trying to stifle a belch.

Henry managed a smile, and muttered, 'If you say so, Mother.'

She was, he estimated, worth not a cent less than two million dollars, yet lived with a parsimony that suggested she was about to join the ranks of the indigent at any moment. George Bernard Shaw had reflected that even if money couldn't buy happiness, it was nice to be miserable in comfort. He had not met Mrs Rusk.

The ormolu clock whirred and struck ten with extreme slowness. By unspoken agreement, it was time for Henry to go. As always, he and his mother had spent three hours saying nothing; he thought he could even detect a glint of relief in his mother's eyes as he rose, stooped to kiss her surprisingly unwrinkled cheek, and headed for the door. Could she find him as much of a chore as he found her?

Still hungry, he walked briskly to Twenty-One. Sheldon Tannen, the baby of the Kriendler and Berns families (he was fifty-two), greeted him with practised warmth. 'Downstairs for one, Mr Rusk? You know, I've meant to ask you. Every Wednesday night, 10.15 on the dot, you come in alone for dinner. Is that your night for working late?'

'No, Sheldon, it's my night for recovering from my mother's cooking.' Sheldon laughed uncertainly, and Henry ordered a Ballantine's and branch water: for once, Krug did not serve his need.

'And how's things, Mr Rusk?' asked Sig, the bartender.

'I don't know, Sig, I don't know. Tell me, what would you say if I told you I might go and live in Europe to avoid having dinner with my mother?'

'I'd say you'll feel differently in the morning, Mr Rusk, that's what I'd say.'

'Not a chance, Sig, not a chance. Tomorrow just brings me one day closer to next week's dinner.'

The cab hit another pothole, and Peter Acheson's head bounced off the roof, 'Goddammit, driver, why don't you steer round the holes?'

'Don't blame me, mack, blame the fucking mayor.'

At the apartment building on East 73rd Street, Peter went through the elaborate ritual designed to ensure he was not a teenage mugger in disguise. 'How was that name again, sir?'

'Acheson.'

'Got it. And is Miss Corley expecting you?'

'Yeah, and about four other people – she's giving a dinner party.'

The doorman, who was wearing a uniform like a Peruvian general's, whispered confidentially into the house telephone.

'Right, sir. Go straight up, 18B, the lady's expecting you.'

Peter shared the elevator with an unshaven teenager wearing a cashmere sweater and Patek Philippe watch, an elderly woman in silver lamé pants and a mink jacket, and her Pekingese dog, which kept wiping its nose on her sleeve. The teenager was smoking a very long, very thin cigar. 'Can't you read?' snapped the woman. 'It says no smoking.' The elevator stopped, the kid stepped out, and the woman said, as the doors started to close, 'And to think, he went to Yale.'

The boy turned and shouted, 'Yeah, and that's *why* I can't read.'

Marina Corley's apartment consisted of a huge living-room facing the East River, a single bedroom, and a kitchen in which it might be possible for two midgets to work simultaneously. Her apartment, like a thousand others in fashionable Manhattan, was made for show, and reminded Peter of a Yorkshire phrase he had heard from an Englishman: 'All lace curtains and no Sunday dinner.' Well, not much Sunday dinner.

A black maid in a crumpled uniform opened the door, and beckoned Peter inside. 'Miss Marina's having one of her moods again,' she said.

Marina, small and fair, kissed Peter's cheek absent-mindedly. 'Goddammit, Mary-Lou, I'm not in a mood. I'm just saying that when I come home from work I expect to find the apartment clean.'

'And I'm saying, Miss Marina, I don't do no heavy work, just the light work.'

'You call sponging the kitchen cabinets heavy work?'

'Sure do, Miss Marina. All that stretching and bending, that's heavy work.'

'Well, what do you do in your own apartment?'

'Don't have no kitchen cabinets, Miss Marina.'

Marina sighed heavily. 'Fix me a drink, Peter. That's what *I* call heavy work.'

Glasses clinking, they walked out to the terrace. In the dusk, with the lights glittering and the East River shimmering, New York looked like a travel agent's dream: mysterious, vibrant, romantic. But its skyscrapers were planted in dogshit and garbage, thought Peter, and the rich and successful frittered away their evenings arguing with maids over the difference between light and heavy work. Perhaps New Yorkers had once lived lives of quiet desperation. Now they had turned loud complaint into a minor art form, of which Marina was a skilled practitioner.

He had met her at a cocktail party three months before. It was one of those parties that induce claustrophobia in agoraphobes, and they had escaped, laughing with relief. A week later they had gone to bed together for the first time; it was satisfying, if unadventurous, but Peter was sure that neither would miss the other if the affair were to end as casually as it had started.

He had never discovered what Marina really did for a living. She had something to do, he knew, with a home-making magazine, and some vague connection with an early-morning television programme. Whatever her occupation, it paid enough for her to own a co-op apartment, dress well and ski in Europe. Marina was equally baffled by Peter's job.

'But what does a commodity dealer do?' she had asked that night they escaped from the cocktail party, and were recovering in the Italian Pavilion, on West 55th Street.

'Deal in commodities,' said Peter, who always tried to avoid explaining the complexities of the markets in wheat futures, soybeans, pork bellies, and other staples.

'No, I mean it. Just what do you do?'

'Well, there are companies that know they will need, say, 10,000 bushels of wheat come next September. So they buy them in the futures market for September delivery, and the price they pay now reflects what all the other people in the market think wheat will fetch then. If the guy who needs 10,000 bushels is right, then he will buy them today for a lower price than he would have paid in the market in September. If he's wrong, then he's lost; he could have bought the wheat cheaper in the spot market.

'Then there are the speculators, who play the markets the way the other people play craps. They'll speculate in anything – wheat, sorghum, pork bellies, silver, gold, anything in which there's a futures market.

'As for me, I sit in the middle doing what the clients tell me, and gambling on the side for myself.'

'And is there money in it?'

'Sure. On a big trade, you can make millions – or lose them.'

'Which do you do?'

'Oh, win a few, lose a few.'

In fact, Peter had just made a killing by betting right on winter wheat, and that morning had deposited a cheque for $75,000 in his savings account.

Since then, Marina had never asked another question about commodities; either they bored her, or she had mentally classified Peter as a kind of professional gambler, which was certainly not the kind of job about which she talked to her friends, who tended to be earnest lawyers and doctors involved – but not too deeply – in community action projects. Her lack of interest reassured him: it suggested she did not view him as a possible husband.

The doorbell rang, and the other four guests crowded through the narrow lobby. Two of them Peter had met before: Steve and Myrtle Cohen, both lawyers, both fat, and both loud-voiced. The other couple, whose last names Peter never did hear properly, were a Dr Richard something and his wife, Ellen. He was a psychiatrist; she, by the look of her, provided the kind of brisk, no-nonsense sanity he probably needed after a long day listening to other people's quirks and quiddities at a hundred dollars an hour. He was not a bad example of the breed, Peter noted: tweedy, relaxed, a sports fan (he was talking at the moment about *jai alai*, or *pelote Basque*, which he had seen on a trip to Florida: 'The fastest game in the world, and probably the most exciting. I'm astonished it hasn't spread more').

But New Yorkers, of course, can never resist discussing New York for less than twenty minutes or so, and soon the talk came round to the city's latest financial problems, and the plight of the middle classes. 'All I know is, it's costing us an arm and a leg to live here,' said Steve. 'Right, Myrtle?'

'Right, Steve.'

'And it's gonna get worse. We're gonna end up by paying more and more for less and less, until only the very poor and the very rich can afford to live here. You mark my words.' Steve seemed to take a gloomy satisfaction in his own regurgitation of what everyone in the room had been reading for years in the *New York Times* and *New York* magazine.

'Oh, I still love New York,' said Marina. 'It's still the most exciting place in the world. All those people who run away – well, I just think they're cowards.'

Peter flushed slightly; he had just been thinking that such a conversation was probably impossible in Paris, or Rome, or London; either those cities were not collapsing or they were not inhabited by people obsessed by visions of Doomsday.

'What do you think, Richard?' he asked.

The doctor looked at his empty martini glass, smiled, and said, 'I can probably answer better after another of these.' His wife, Peter noted, did not look disapproving or worried; perhaps the wife of a psychiatrist saw him as his patients did, all-wise and omnipotent, certainly in no danger of becoming a common drunk.

'Well,' said Richard, 'I don't want to give you a professional view. It would be too easy to say that most people take their problems with them. No, I'd say that there are good objective reasons for some people getting out of the city. I'd get out myself if I could make a living in a small town. Not that small-town people are all that well adjusted; they're just poorer and closer with their money than big-city people. But all that incest and bestiality in the boondocks! It's a potentially rich field.'

'Right, doctor, point taken; it's not necessarily escapism to leave the city. But what about leaving the country?'

'Why, are you thinking of emigrating?'

'Not exactly. Just getting away for a time.'

'Pity. If you'd said you were leaving permanently, I could have woven you a pretty little theory about that being a rejection of yourself.'

'But that wouldn't be very popular in America, would it?' said Marina. 'After all, we're a nation of immigrants.'

Dr Richard chuckled. 'Precisely. That's why I've never done more than think about the theory. Publication would ruin me; I'd be on the DAR blacklist, and American Legionnaires would demonstrate outside my window.'

Marina, Peter noticed, had not raised an eyebrow when he had said he might go away. If she had any emotions, she concealed them very well.

At that moment, there was a muffled explosion in the kitchen, and a keening cry from Mary-Lou. 'Shit,' said Marina, spilling half her Scotch over her pale grey pants suit.

'Miss Marina,' said Mary-Lou, 'that old broiler done played up again.'

Marina went into the kitchen, looked at the cooker, and said, half laughing, 'Why, Mary-Lou, I've told you a dozen times to keep it clean.'

'But Miss Marina, I done told you, I don't . . .'

'That's right, you don't do no heavy work.'

Surely, thought Peter, in Paris, or Rome, or London, or somewhere, anywhere but New York, there must be a maid who did do heavy work, and didn't talk like an extra from Central Casting?

'Bonjour, Lucien. Çà va?'
'Oui, çà va. Et vous, Michel?'
'Comme si, comme çà, mon vieux.'

Michel Jobert had been going to the Café des Sports for ten years. Like many of the little restaurants in the Fifties between Eighth and Ninth, it was run by a Breton family. There he could read *L'Equipe*, the French sporting paper, hear his own language, and eat food as authentically French as he could in any restaurant in France.

Lucien, the *patron*, was an old friend; so was the squat, bald Belgian who took bets on French races, on *le football* – on anything, in fact, happening in France or Belgium. Michel avoided the place at lunchtime; then it was filled with researchers from the Time and Life Building, trying out stumbling French acquired at Vassar or Smith. He also avoided taking colleagues to the Café des Sports; for them it would be the equivalent of chic slumming, although the food and wine were among the best in New York.

That night, he was meeting his *petite amie* for dinner, a French girl who worked for the United Nations as a tour guide. She was, in fact, almost as tall as he was, but slim instead of massive, dark instead of fair. She was diffident about her age, was Anne-Marie; he guessed she was in her late twenties, a comfortable decade younger than he was, and still in no hurry to marry. Theirs was a relaxed and easy affair. He was sure she had other lovers; she never questioned him about his ex-wives or girl-friends. When he asked her away for a weekend, she was usually available: when she was not, she merely said she was busy, without further explanation.

As he finished his *anisette* Anne-Marie came through the door, slightly breathless, her wide lips parted and long, dark hair falling over her eyes. With a characteristically impatient gesture she pushed it aside, slipped onto the bar stool next to him, and lifted her mouth for a kiss. The bartender automatically poured her a Beefeater martini with twist of lemon; martinis were her only concession to American culture.

The Café des Sports was quiet that night, its mood as peaceful as a restaurant in provincial France. Two waitresses gossiped in a corner; Michel heard just enough to know they were talking with shocked delight of some family scandal. At a table by himself, a middle-aged man with the ribbon of the *Légion d'Honneur* in his buttonhole read *L'Aurore* while he ate *tripes à la mode de Caen*. The French, thought Michel, were the hardest immigrants of all to assimilate; they even retained their regional characteristics. He, for example, drank *anisette* as an aperitif, which marked him as a *pied noir*. Lucien's cuisine was unmistakably Breton. Anne-Marie, who came from the South-West, was suspicious of all wines other than Bordeaux. They all read the *New York Times*, but they only believed what they saw in *Le Monde*, *Le Figaro*, or their regional paper.

Anne-Marie was talking about a film she had just seen, shredding its pretensions with quick French wit. 'Tell me, Anne-Marie, if you dislike America so much, why do you stay?'

She shrugged. 'It is amusing, for a while. Also, I must improve my English, is that not so?'

'Yes, you must, but you'll never do it if all your friends are French, you eat in French restaurants and read only French books and magazines.'

'There are sacrifices I will make for the sake of learning English, *chéri*, and there are sacrifices I will not make. It is enough that I live here, surrounded by Americans. Must I also pretend they are my friends? Besides, American men are hopeless lovers.'

'You speak from experience, of course?'

'No. But it is well known.'

Michel laughed, and took her right hand in his. '*Chérie*, you are adorable – adorably French. Me, I am not adorable, but I am French, and we do not transplant well. Wherever we go, we try to pretend we are still in France. Look round you here. What do you see? People who might just as well never have left Paris, or Lyons, or Nantes, or wherever it is they come from.

'So, I have made a decision. I am going back to Europe, though perhaps not to France – more likely Geneva, but that is almost France, and the frontier is a matter of minutes.'

'Your company is sending you?'

'No. I have had enough of making money for other people. Now, I start to make it for myself, and to have fun.'

'And this is the end of us?'

'No. You will not be in New York for ever, and I will be back from time to time.'

Anne-Marie shook back her hair, and speared the last of her *escargots*. '*Ça va*, Michel. But we might not be the same people back in France. Admit it, part of my attraction for you in New York is that I'm French, is it not so? But in Geneva or Paris –

there I would be just one French girl among many. Ah well, we shall see. Meanwhile, we must live, which reminds me: the wine is flowing like glue tonight...'

Dear Michel,

I am addressing this letter to you, with copies to Jacqueline, Henry and Peter, because I regard you as the instigator of this extraordinary 'Game' – indeed, ringleader is hardly too strong a word.

Over dinner the other night you all put to me very forcefully your belief that business is a game, and money a mere way of keeping score. You have also expressed, individually and collectively, your desire to see whether you can 'hack it' without the support of large institutions.

I want you to believe that I myself am not immune to the temptation of striking out on my own, of proving that I can prosper by the use of my own wits. And, of course, I share, in large measure, your discontent with life in this arduous city.

Against that admission, almost confession, will you weigh very carefully what I am about to say?

First, there is the large philosophical issue you have raised, and that is the purpose of the stock market, the commodity markets, banking, and foreign exchange. You have all been somewhat cynical, and that, too, I can understand. But these activities do have purposes other than the provision of profits for those taking part in them.

I can testify to those other purposes from my own recent experience. One client wished to raise additional capital, and could choose between an increase in indebtedness, or the sale of equity. The client chose to go public, and the stock market was the instrument that enabled him to raise an additional five million dollars. Is it not a good thing that the investor should be able to join the great adventure of building a large business out of a small one, an adventure that has helped to make this Republic of ours what it is today? Another example, again from my own experience. Another client, by making forward purchases of German marks in the market, was able to avoid the increase in the dollar price of imports that otherwise would have been inevitable. Is this, too, not beneficial? The result, as you will see clearly, is that either his profits are increased, or the price to the consumer is lower than it otherwise would have been, or both.

You will argue, I know, that the stock and foreign exchange markets are also the provinces of speculators, and that I cannot deny. But speculation is surely the froth on the surface, not the substance of these markets. There is much speculation, too, in the commodity markets; but surely their real function is to provide an exchange between buyers and sellers, each using their skills and knowledge to arrive at a market-determined price. To argue otherwise is to embrace socialism, and I cannot believe that any of you wish to do that.

Second, there is the whole question of your responsibility to yourselves. You have all made successful careers, which suggests that you are respected both for your skills and for your responsible attitudes towards the institutions for which you work. Do you not agree that to take a sabbatical and devote it to the making of money for its own sake, divorced from any other consideration, contradicts the whole course of your lives until now? And, if you wish to return to the institutions for which you now work, do you think they will regard you in the same light as they have done hitherto?

Third, and finally, you say that the sabbatical will give you a chance to know yourselves. If I may speak very frankly, and there is no other way, that search for identity smacks to me of self-indulgence. If, at your ages, you do not know who and what you are, then I do not think a few months in Europe or anywhere else will reveal much. Most of us 'find ourselves' in the daily routine of our work and the attitudes towards us displayed by our colleagues and by our families and loved ones (who may not always be the same people!). If you really are worried about your identities and personalities, then a good psychiatrist would probably help you more, at less cost, than the course you propose.

I ask you to ponder what I have said. This is not, I know, the letter you may expect from an accountant; but I have never interpreted my professional activities in the narrow sense that characterises the thinking of some of my contemporaries, and have always felt it my bounden duty to remonstrate with a client, whether corporate or personal, who is about to embark upon activities that I regard as unwise or injurious.

Please think carefully. I hope you will see the force of what I have said. But if you do not, then I shall, naturally, be pleased to monitor your activities in accordance with the rules you have all agreed.

Very sincerely yours,

Charles Kemble

Dear Charles,

About the only thing missing from your homily was a reference to God and Motherhood.

I, for my part, am determined to play the Game – and win.

Yours sincerely,

Henry Rusk

Dear Charles,

You must have thought deeply before writing your long and persuasive letter.

Unfortunately, it does not persuade me. I don't think I am fulfilled by what I'm doing, and even if I don't 'find myself' (why did you put that phrase in quotation marks?) in Europe, I'll have an interesting time there.

Best wishes,

Yours sincerely,

Jacqueline Eden

PS I *have* seen psychiatrists, and they left me more confused than I was before.

Dear Charles,

That was quite a letter! Seriously, I'm grateful for it. Gave me food for thought. But I'm really damned tired of sitting here in Manhattan, doing the same thing day in and day out, and making more money for other people than I'm making for myself.

You know the old phrase: 'He was working too hard to make any money.' Well, that's me.

See you in Brussels.

All the very best,

Peter Acheson

Dear Charles,

You forget that I am a foreigner in this country, and see it with different eyes from you. One thing that strikes me, and your letter confirms it, is the way Americans must moralise about everything. Even the permissive society is moralistic; it is a semi-conscious reversal of Puritan values, and if you don't get your share of fun and orgasms there is something wrong with you.

I know you mean it well, but why must Americans preach so much?

My answer is: if I see business as a casino, then that is how I see it. That is not a moral judgment. It is the result of observation, and is no more moral or amoral than concluding evolution is blind to beauty and ethics.

Michel Jobert

4

> Oh, London is a man's town, there's power in the air
> *Henry van Dyke*

Henry Rusk took another long look at the high-ceilinged dining-room, with its Georgian table, twenty matching chairs, and yellow silk curtains at the three windows facing Eaton Square.

'Right, I'll take it.'

The estate agent, a supercilious youth with an upper-class English accent that faltered occasionally on the vowels, said for about the fourth time, 'I really don't think you'll find anywhere better, Mr Rusk. Properties of this quality are extremely scarce.'

'And so are tenants, I should think, at the rent this place is.'

'You'd be surprised, sir, at how many rich Arabs there are in London now. But I know our client would much rather have an American. You'd be astonished if I told you of some things that Arabs get up to. Why, some of them hardly know what a lavatory is for.'

'Well, you don't have to worry about that with us Americans. We may be rough colonials, but we're learning fast.'

Henry had been in London two weeks. He found it much changed from his last visit, three years before. Eaton Square and the rest of Belgravia was still as immaculate as ever, to be sure, but years of economic decline had left much of London shabby and untidy, and many of the people simultaneously apathetic about their fate and resentful of the foreigners who crowded in to buy goods made cheap for them by the fall in the pound.

The Arabs were particularly resented. Almost every day the newspapers reported the sale of yet another stately home or London landmark to an Arab buyer. Fashionable London – Knightsbridge, Mayfair, Belgravia – was full of Rolls-Royces,

Bentleys, and Mercedes-Benzes carrying Arabs on a shopping spree. When Sheikh Ahmad Zaki Yamani, the Saudi Arabian oil minister, went to Harrods it stayed open late for him; reputedly, he spent over $100,000 in less than two hours.

At the Naval & Military Club, where Henry stayed while looking for a flat, an elderly member confided one day, 'These damned Arabs are buying our own country under our very noses. And for what? I'll tell you. So that we can import the oil to keep the working class gallivanting around in cars they can't afford. Bloody disgrace. I'll tell you, Rusk, this country's gone mad, completely mad.

'There's only one consolation. These Arabs are throwing the money around like drunken stokers after a year at sea, and one day they'll run out of the stuff.'

At lunch in the boardroom of a bank he got a somewhat different view, however. His host, Lord Boscastle, was tall, grave, and dressed in the sombre uniform of a merchant banker: superbly cut suit from Savile Row, gleaming starched white collar and striped shirt, a thin gold watch chain stretched across his neat waistcoat – as Henry had come to call a vest in his Oxford days.

The butler, who might have been a particularly distinguished bishop, poured vintage port reverently from a Waterford cut-glass decanter. A log fire crackled discreetly in an Adam fireplace. Boscastle looked appreciatively at the rich red port and said, 'Well, that's one British asset the Arabs won't get their hands on, I hope. Most of them are teetotallers, and those who drink are mostly at the stage of thinking Chivas Regal the ultimate sophistication.'

'How are they to deal with – financially, I mean? We just haven't come across many in New York.'

'Difficult, very difficult, I'm afraid. Remember, most of them were taken for what you Americans call a ride in the early days of their oil wealth. They're still suspicious, still very cautious. Oh, I know they throw their money around when they go shopping; but that's petty cash for most of them. When it comes to investing, they look at things from every angle four or five times, ask for opinions from half a dozen experts, and take their time.

'My God, do they take their time! I've had one young fellow out there in Riyadh for three months, at their request, and he hasn't even seen our client yet.

'Then, when they do make their minds up, they want everything done immediately, if not sooner. There are exceptions, of course. Take the United Arab Emirates ambassador in London, Mohammed Mahdi al Tajir. Bright as a new pin. But he was a banker and trader before that part of the world started producing any oil, and his business ideas are almost entirely Western. Young, too – can't be more than forty-three or so. But rich! He's worth billions now, and he'll be worth more before he dies. And they say the ruler of Dubai hangs on his every word. Yes, if Mahdi al Tajir gives a deal the nod, you can count on its coming off.'

'How do I meet him?'

'Ah, there's the rub. Everyone wants to meet him, so he's surrounded himself with more flunkeys than Howard Hughes did. Not that he's at all like Hughes. Far from it. Mahdi enjoys his money. Charming fellow, absolutely charming – or so I'm told.'

'You haven't met him?'

'Alas, no. Yet we've done business with his bank several times. Strange, isn't it? No, if I were you, I wouldn't waste time trying to meet Mahdi. Start with somebody more accessible. Ahmed Yussaini, for example. Went to Harvard Business School, and Winchester here. Fingers in a lot of pies. Just the chap for that LNG* tanker financing you're trying to do. Tell you what, if he comes in for a decent amount – fifty million dollars say – the bank will come in with the same. Then you'll be half-way there. But we don't want to be the first to commit ourselves. May sound a funny way of doing business to Americans, but you know how merchant banks are – very little money of their own, always a bit chary of committing their clients' money.'

A log blazed in the grate, then fell with a tiny thud. The clock on the mantelpiece whirred, paused, and struck the half hour. Boscastle sipped the last of his port, then dabbed his lips delicately with a heavy linen napkin. His pale blue eyes, bright

* Liquefied natural gas

under heavy lids, looked at Henry appraisingly. 'You're what, Rusk – forty-two, -three? Well, if you find that being a freelance doesn't really suit you, don't forget us here. I'm not too happy with our chap in New York. No question of getting rid of him, or anything drastic like that; but there'll be a discreet transfer in a few months' time, and if you'd like to step into his shoes, well, we'd all be very pleased.'

Henry smiled. 'It's kind of you. But there's something I have to work out of my system first. Let's keep in touch though.'

The butler with the sacerdotal air opened the tall double doors, and Henry almost expected a burst of ecclesiastical music. At the lift Boscastle shook hands and said, 'Now, don't forget: Yussaini is probably your man. Let me know.'

Down in the street the air was fresh but warm, the sombre architecture of the banks and insurance companies offset by the bright red double-decker buses that nudged through the narrow streets. A money-broker, wearing the glossy silk hat of his trade, stepped briskly along, and outside the Bank of England three men in virtually identical grey suits and bowler hats talked animatedly. Henry sighed with contentment, paused a moment to soak himself in the scene, then hailed a cruising taxi.

It was gleamingly clean, and the driver actually called him 'sir' – something Henry had not heard from a New York cabbie for years. As the taxi headed west, past the pink-grey *Financial Times* building and the huge bulk of St Paul's Cathedral, Henry reviewed his conversation with Boscastle. A cautious man, and a shrewd one; if he recommended this Yussaini, it was with reason. On impulse, Henry asked the taxi driver to stop, went into a phone kiosk, and called an old aquaintance, Jim Wrenn, a financial writer on *The Times*. Yes, Jim was free for a drink early that evening; yes, El Vino was handy; yes, he had met Yussaini, and could find out more from the newspaper's clippings library.

As he stepped back into the taxi cab, Henry thought how foolish people in the financial world were to regard journalists as mere recipients of information, much of it given grudgingly. The good financial writers knew a lot more than they could publish; properly handled, they could be superb sources of information.

Henry had met Jim Wrenn three years before, when Wrenn was doing a stint in New York. He liked the man on first meeting, appreciating the cool, analytical brain behind the disarmingly boyish countenance. They were not quite friends, but more than mere acquaintances, and Henry had both fed Jim with the occasional exclusive story, and invited him for weekends to his house in the Hamptons – since, unfortunately, occupied by his ex-wife and their two children. Henry knew that Jim felt faintly in his debt; now it was time for part of the debt to be repaid.

Two hours later Henry headed east again in another of London's ubiquitous black taxis, past Buckingham Palace, along The Mall, and through the rush-hour clutter of the Strand. The pedestrians' faces were pale and strained; at a corner, when the taxi stopped for a red light, Henry saw a newsvendor holding out a paper with the heading 'Pound in power dive'. Fine for him: he had his money in dollars, which would now go a little further. Lousy for the British, who had learned the hard way that every fall in the pound raised the cost of imports, but apparently did little or nothing to increase exports. Idly, he wondered whether Michel Jobert had bet on the pound's fall. Well, he wouldn't find out for months: the rules of the Game they had devised prevented any of the players revealing a move.

At two minutes before six the taxi pulled up outside El Vino, which despite its name was a British institution. As always, it was crowded with journalists and lawyers, all talking in that clipped way affected by Englishmen in the upper reaches of the professions. Jim was there already, sitting at a table, a bottle of Krug in front of him.

'You remembered the brand then?'

'How could I forget? Thanks to you and your Krug, the office got the idea I was becoming an alcoholic when they saw my expense account.'

'Well, if you are going to succumb to drink, it might as well be the best.'

'Try telling that to the bastard who signs my expense

account.'

For a few minutes they talked of mutual friends and acquaintances, of that day's fall in the pound, of Jimmy Carter's economic policies. Jim, like the good reporter he was, extracted more information than he gave, and Henry could see its being filed away for future use. There was a pause in their conversation, and while Henry ordered another bottle of Krug Jim fumbled in a capacious black leather documents case. The Krug arrived, Jim took a sip, and then said, 'Look, you don't have to tell me, but why are you so curious about Yussaini? A deal?'

'Right. But keep it under wraps for the moment.' Quickly, Henry sketched the outlines: an American shipping company, JZ International, was building three LNG carriers for charter to a consortium of oil companies. Total cost: $300 million. What it wanted was $250 million for fifteen years, at 8.5 per cent per annum, as a mortgage on the ships.

Jim pursed his lips. 'Difficult, very difficult, I'd say. I don't have to tell you – oil tankers are a drug on the market. And there isn't a merchant bank in London that hasn't been burnt by the collapse in the tanker market.'

'Yes, but LNG carriers aren't tankers.'

'Of course, of course. But you know how bankers are – if you don't mind my saying so: if it floats, it's a ship, and if it carries energy, it's a tanker.'

'That's where Yussaini comes in – or may do. These ships will carry LNG from the Gulf to Tokyo, they're fully chartered, and they're the one kind of ship that's actually in short supply. And the Gulf is his part of the world.'

'Yes and no. He comes from a little emirate that didn't join the United Arab Emirates. It has no oil worth mentioning, no natural gas, and is run by an emir who hates the others' guts.'

'Well, what kind of man is Yussaini?'

'Try to picture a man of thirty-five or so, extremely handsome in a way that's more Italian than Arab. Western-educated, but fiercely patriotic, very proud, a superb horseman, a top-class cricketer, plays tennis like a champion and – if he lives up to the legend – has women queuing up for him to bed them. On top of all that, completely fluent in

English, Italian, French and Spanish; and a poet in Arabic.'

'And as a businessman?'

'Oh, brilliant, no doubt about that. He inherited some money, a million or so, but now he's worth two or three hundred millions, and he heads a whole consortium of young Arabs with as much or more than he has. It's said – I can't vouch for it – that they can swing a billion-dollar deal without straining themselves.'

'So how do I meet this fabulous character, who sounds like a mixture of Rudolph Valentino, the Shah of Iran, David Rockefeller and Casanova. Have I left anyone out?'

'Yes. Baron von Richthofen. Yussaini is a superb pilot. Even collects old aircraft.'

'But how do I meet him?'

Instead of answering immediately, Jim handed Henry a thick envelope. 'Here you are, the distillation of *The Times* library, all Xeroxed for you. The one bit of advice I would give is don't try the direct approach. For all his Western education, he's still an Arab, and he trusts people who are introduced and vouched for, not institutions or people who write out of the blue.'

Jim looked at the big, old fashioned clock on the wall. 'Damn, I must go. If I don't get the next train to Orpington there won't be another for an hour.'

'Orpington?'

'London's Scarsdale.'

'Oh.'

Later that night, after a solitary dinner at his club, Henry settled down in Eaton Square with a 1945 Armagnac and the batch of clippings Jim had given him. Most simply filled in the picture Jim had drawn of an energetic, ambitious financier whose deals appeared to extend geographically from the Middle East to Australia (he had bought a coal mine there), and in scope from energy to publishing. But one clipping, dated the month before, held Henry's attention. Yussaini, it seemed, was building an entire collection of Second World War aircraft, and was still lacking a Messerschmitt 109. Henry pursed his lips in a silent whistle, opened an address book, and dialled a California number.

'Freddie? Henry Rusk here.'

'For Chrissake, where you been hiding?'

'I'm in London for a while.'

'Don't take any of those pounds, old buddy, I hear they're shrinking.' Freddie Kruger's hoarse laugh reverberated, and Henry could imagine his seamed, leathery face puckered in enjoyment of his own joke.

'Freddie, you've got a friend who deals in old aircraft, right?'

'Right, old buddy, Jack Westward, out in Vegas. Old autos and railroad locomotives, too, if you want any of them.'

'No, just an ME 109.'

Freddie whistled. 'They're kinda scarce, you know that? Shot down a few of 'em myself, come to that. Tell you what, call you back, right?'

Henry poured himself another Armagnac and thought it was highly likely Yussaini already knew of Westward; the world of vintage aircraft buffs was small. On the other hand, there was just a chance he did not, or had yet to ask Westward if he happened to have an ME 109 lying around. While he waited for Freddie's call, Henry looked again at the newspaper cuttings Jim had given him, and circled a name: Jonathan Hare, senior partner, Hare, Dowd and Christie. In the phone book he found their address, in a fashionable street in Mayfair. He put a portable typewriter on the table and roughed out a letter – his secretary could re-type it tomorrow.

Dear Mr Hare,

For the foreseeable future I shall be living and working in London as an investment counsellor, and from time to time will require legal services. Your name has been recommended to me by a client of the bank from which I am taking a sabbatical, Hunt, Grierson, and Company, of Pine Street, New York.

These services will be of a personal as well as business nature, and one matter that requires urgent attention is the temporary importation into Britain of a vintage aircraft, a Messerschmitt 109. I should be most grateful if you would suggest a day and time next week when we may meet to discuss that and other matters.

Henry laughed softly as he read the letter. That was a bait that should catch a very big fish. And if Westward didn't have a 109? Well, he could always explain that the deal fell through.

An hour later the phone rang.

'Henry, old buddy, you're in luck. Westward doesn't have a 109, but he knows where he can get one. Belongs to some real estate developer in Arizona who's fallen on hard times. Westward tells me it's a real beauty, flies like a dream, comes with spare engine, the works. Only trouble is, he wants a quarter of a million for it.'

'Tell you what, Freddie, you go look at it, and if it's as good as you say, get a thirty-day option on it, with ten per cent down, half of it returnable if I don't buy. I'll put a cheque in the mail tomorrow.'

'OK, call you back tomorrow. Roger and out.'

'Roger and out. And, say, thanks, Freddie.'

'Just pray I don't break my neck in the damn thing.'

Henry opened his pocket diary, and pencilled in 'Freddie' for Thursday. Suddenly, he smiled. Today was Wednesday; if he'd been in New York he would have just left his mother, and been on his way to Twenty-One for solace. Well, there was solace to be found in London, too.

In the square a fresh breeze was blowing. From the half-open windows of a house came the sound of laughter, and Henry looked in, to see a tall, elegant dining-room, rather like his own, full of people in evening dress. Outside the house, chauffeurs snoozed at the wheels of Rolls-Royces and Bentleys. But one chauffeur, a small, trim man in a grey suit with silver buttons, paced the sidewalk.

'Evening, sir.'

'Good evening,' said Henry.

'I see you came out of the Everleighs' flat.'

'The Everleighs?'

'Yes, sir, Lord and Lady Everleigh.'

'Well, I'm renting it.'

'They need the money from what I hear, sir.'

'Glad to be of help.'

'Can I drive you anywhere, sir? My people will be in there for another hour or so.'

'Sixty-Four too far?'

'Hop in, sir.'

The chauffeur opened the door of a Rolls-Royce limousine and Henry sank back into cushioned luxury. Silently, with hardly a vibration, the huge car moved off towards Mayfair, the chauffeur talking all the way.

'... and since I left the Duke, I've been working for this Armenian family. Sign of the times, sir. The Arabs have got all the money now.'

'But Armenians aren't Arabs.'

'They are to me, sir.'

As the Rolls stopped in Curzon Street a doorman rushed forward, followed by a receptionist in black tie. A Rolls still commanded a lot of respect in London, Henry thought as he handed the chauffeur two pounds.

'Good evening, Mr —?'

'Rusk, Henry Rusk.'

'Why, of course, Mr Rusk. Good to see you again.'

Bloody liar, thought Henry. He'd never been before to the Sixty-Four Club.

Inside, the former home of a noble family was crowded with remarkably glossy people. Most of the men, Henry noticed, were middle-aged to elderly; most of the women were in their twenties. In the bar the receptionist introduced Sid Wiese, one of the owners, a dark, smiling man with handlebar moustache and red carnation in the buttonhole of his dinner-jacket. Behind Sid's genial smile lay a very shrewd brain, Henry suspected; within five minutes he was neatly filed and classified as a wealthy banker on his own; likely to be a regular customer; and not to argue over the bill.

Sid smiled approvingly when Henry ordered a half bottle of Krug. 'Make it a bottle,' he told the bartender. 'The other half's on me.'

Neat, thought Henry, and not too ostentatious. A swirl of customers entered, and Wiese went off to greet them. A slim, pale hand picked up Henry's Dupont lighter, which was lying on the bar, and a low, husky voice asked, 'Do you mind?'

Henry turned to see a girl of twenty-two or -three, with pale blond hair reaching to her shoulders and a pair of green eyes set in a face dusted with freckles. He lit her cigarette; the girl steadied his hand with her own. It was cool and impeccably manicured, Henry noticed. Her glass was empty. She interpreted his look, and said, 'Yes, I would like one. What you're drinking will do, though I prefer Dom Pérignon.'

Henry laughed. 'One of the pleasures of life is trying to decide which is better, Krug or Dom Pérignon. I think Krug is; but every now and then I justify a bottle of the Dom as a bit of comparative tasting.'

The girl – her name was Anne – said she was an actress, and next month would start a new television series. Henry didn't believe a word of it. He had already docketed her as a girl who lived well but precariously by doing a bit of modelling here, a walk-on part there, and supplementing her income with 'gifts' from the men she met at the Sixty-Four Club and elsewhere. Not quite a prostitute; but not quite the girl she pretended to be, either.

'Do you want to go to Blenheim's?' she asked.

'Blenheim's?'

'It's a night club that Sid owns.'

'I don't think so. Do you know anywhere a little less noisy?'

'We could always try my place.'

'As long as the band's not too loud.'

'It won't be, I promise. Wait, I'll get my coat, and we can walk – it's just across the street.'

Her flat was what he expected: small, elegant in an impersonal way. The one surprise was a shelf of books. While Anne poured him a cognac – a John Exshaw, he noted with approval – he looked at the titles. History, historical biography, even a few volumes of the Cambridge Economic History of Europe. Strange choice for a – what? Tart? Whore? No, the words were too strong. He settled for trollop, which had a rumbustious, eighteenth-century flavour that he liked.

Anne laughed at his puzzled look. 'Oh, I do read, believe it or not.'

Henry settled back in the long, leather-covered chesterfield. 'I didn't imagine you were illiterate, but – well, the subjects are not what I expected.'

'For a girl on the game?'

'You said it, I didn't.'

'I wasn't always, you know. I even went to Oxford for a while. Dropped out, though. I decided that since I liked sex and money, the two might as well be combined. I have strict rules, though: only a man I like, a man who likes me, as well as wanting to fuck me, and no more than two men a week.'

'You must be expensive.'

'I am: £100 for all night. About $170 in your money. Tax free, too, which means I'd have to earn about seventy per cent more to net the same in any other job.'

Henry counted out $200 in twenty-dollar bills. 'The exchange rate's in your favour, tonight. Shall we?'

Anne opened the bedroom door, kicked off her high-heeled shoes, and unzipped her silk dress. Henry, still struggling with his shoes (why would the laces knot at this of all times?), saw with a surge of passion that her breasts were full for so small a girl, her legs slender but well-muscled. Naked, she lay on the bed, one leg slightly raised. With one hand she squeezed her right nipple. With the other, she rubbed her vulva slowly and gently. When he entered her, she was wet, and her breath rasped in his ear.

Anne gave a shuddering sigh, wrapped her legs round his waist, and moved urgently under him. Then, with a speed and violence that brought him quickly to climax, she came once, twice, three times. He looked at her face, wet with sweat, eyes closed under long lashes, and started to move out of her. 'No, no, not yet,' she whispered. 'Stay with me.'

Five minutes, ten minutes, later, Henry eased himself gently off her, and lay at her side, strangely at peace. Anne stirred and opened her eyes. 'Can you tell when a girl's pretending?'

'Usually. I don't think you were.'

'No. I told you I liked sex.'

'Maybe you should be paying me.'

'That's taking Women's Lib too far.'

'Is it taking male chauvinism too far to ask for a cognac and a cigarette?'

Anne swung her legs off the bed and walked silkily to the living-room. She returned with a bottle and two glasses, and a tiny apron hanging over her sex. Henry laughed. 'What's that for?'

'To stop the master getting any randy ideas about the maid.'

Henry looked at his watch. 'One drink, and I must be going.'

Anne pouted. 'You've paid for all night.'

'I've got to talk to a man about an aeroplane.'

'You're buying one?'

'No, but somebody I know might buy it. And if he does, he might just buy something I want to sell.'

'What's that?'

'A deal.'

5

> ... And Paris is a woman's town, with flowers
> in her hair
>
> *Henry van Dyke*

The long black Cadillac Fleetwood turned slowly into the narrow drive of La Grande Cascade, in the Bois de Boulogne. It was a fine, cloudless day, and the restaurant's terrace was crowded. the *maître d'hôtel* glanced at the car's diplomatic licence plates, and stepped forward, bowing slightly.

'*Bonjour, madame. Bonjour, monsieur.* You have a reservation?'

Jacqueline's host said, 'Sure do. Edgeworth.'

The *maître d'hôtel* ran his manicured index finger down the list, raised his eyebrows, and shrugged. 'I am sorry, *monsieur*. We have no record of it here. Are you certain?'

John Edgeworth said with acerbity, 'I heard my secretary make it. Table for two, one o'clock.'

'Perhaps she does not speak French too well, *monsieur*?'

'She *is* French, goddammit.'

The *maître d'hôtel* looked at his list again, then brightened. 'Of course, *monsieur*. I am sorry, it is down under Hedgeworth. This way, please, *monsieur, madame.*'

Edgeworth ordered a dry sherry for Jacqueline, and a rye with orange for himself, a concoction that put a sour look on the *sommelier*'s face. Edgeworth sighed. 'Goddammit, I love Paris but are there ruder restaurateurs anywhere in the world? Or do they specialise in insulting Americans?'

Jacqueline laughed. She was feeling far too happy with the day, the novelty of being in Paris, and the feeling of embarking on a grand adventure to be upset by a *maître d'hôtel* who might – just might – have made a genuine error.

'Don't worry, John. We're here, the sun is shining, we're going to have a delightful lunch, and you're going to tell me how to make a lot of money very quickly.'

Jacqueline had first met John when he was in the State

Department in Washington and wanted to set up a family trust fund with money just inherited from his grandfather. Her advice was good, and they had been friends ever since. Now he was commercial counsellor in the Paris Embassy, and one of the people she counted on for the kind of information she couldn't read in the papers.

John laughed, and took a sip of his drink. 'You're right. It's too good a day to let bad temper spoil it. Let's order, then we can talk business.' John, invincibly American, ordered a salad to start with, Jacqueline a *foie de canard frais*. Both took for their main course the speciality for which the Grande Cascade was famous; *cassolette de queues d'écrevisses* ('crawfish stew', as John described it, somewhat inaccurately).

For a few minutes they talked of mutual friends, of the cost of living in Paris ('formidable, horrifying'), and of the imperative need for a weekend cottage in the country. Then, as he finished the *écrevisses*, John turned serious. 'Right, Jacqueline, you want to find some clients in Europe, charge them for your advice and do a deal or two yourself, right?'

Jacqueline nodded. 'My idea was to find some rich French people who want to invest outside their own country. They're pretty scared by the prospect of a Socialist government, I hear.'

'They sure are. But you may have missed that boat. They've been scared ever since the municipal elections in 1977, and I'd guess most of them have got out of the country what they can. Don't forget, there are laws against investing abroad without permission, and most of the rich don't want to reveal how much they've made without paying taxes. No, I would say your best bet now would be the Spanish.'

'But the new government there is pretty middle of the road, isn't it?'

'Yeah, but the rich are still scared shitless, if you'll pardon the expression. The Left is very powerful, and all those demonstrations and strikes make the rich think a replay of the Civil War is about to start. If I were you, I'd invest in a trip to Spain and to Biarritz.'

'Why Biarritz? That's just a resort town, isn't it?'

'Yes, and for the Spanish it's what Geneva is for the French and Lugano for the Italians, a place just across the border to which you go with a case full of money.'

'But why would the Spanish put their money in France if the French are putting it somewhere else?'

'Search me. Maybe the Spanish have more faith in France than the French do. Or, more likely, they convert their pesetas into dollars, and just use Biarritz as a way-station. They can do that, because they're not French residents, and they're bringing foreign currency into the country.'

After the cheese, Jacqueline and John drank *Poire Williams*, the pear liqueur that is served in iced glasses from a bottle chilled to just above the freezing point for alcohol. It had been a pleasant lunch, Jacqueline thought, if bad for the figure, but though John had been illuminating about the French economy and political future none of his ideas sounded very practical to her. She could not see herself taking a case full of money from a client; it sounded too much like the Mafia skim. Still, once they had got the money across the border, she might be able to invest it.

'Tell me, John, the Spaniards who take cash to Biarritz – are they the sophisticated ones?'

'I wouldn't say so. I'd say that the really sophisticated Spaniard has a better way of doing it. But don't forget, a lot of people have made a lot of money very quickly in Spain in the past decade, and though they're pretty shrewd inside their own country, they're like babes in the wood outside it. Look, I'll give you some names in Madrid, Barcelona and Bilbao, people who can clue you in more than I can.'

John paid the bill with a five-hundred franc note; there wasn't much change left. Jacqueline did a quick calculation. Could lunch really have been ninety dollars? John saw her worried look, and laughed. 'The only thing to do in this city is close your eyes and spend, or pretend its funny-money. And this joint has got only one star in the *Guide Michelin*. Next time around, you can treat me to a three-star luncheon. You'll think you've made a down-payment on the business.'

Jacqueline eased out of the Cadillac at the corner of the Champs-Élysées and rue de Berri, where she was staying at the Hotel Lancaster. It was, she reflected, like staying in the home of a very rich, very discerning friend. Each room was different, furnished with antique furniture and rare oriental rugs, and the staff had the air of family retainers rather than hotel servants. As she walked into the lobby, the manager, John Iversen, was arranging flowers in one of the huge vases, a task he would never delegate. In the patio outside, a fountain played, and a white-coated waiter was serving afternoon tea to an elderly couple.

'Good afternoon, Miss Eden,' said Iversen, holding out a long-stemmed yellow rose to her. 'We have some good news for you, I think: a flat that sounds as though it's just what you want.' One of the many services that the Lancaster provided was advice to clients, and Iversen and the *concierge* had been trying for two weeks to find her a flat. As Iversen had explained: 'Try the agents, by all means; but very often the best places are rented privately.' This one, he said, was on the Île St Louis, overlooking the Seine, and a 'real snip' at 8,000 francs a month – 'about $1,650, Miss Eden.'

She smiled with difficulty. 'It had better be good, at that price.'

'Oh, it is, Miss Eden. It is.'

Twenty minutes later, Jacqueline was standing in the *salon* of the flat, a huge room opening onto a terrace high above the Seine. To her left was the massive bulk of Notre Dame, to her right the majestic sweep of the river, punctuated with bridges and lively with the *bateaux-mouche* tourist boats and heavily-laden barges. On one she could see washing strung on a line, and a car lashed to the deck.

She turned back into the *salon*, with its subtle blend of classic and modern decor and furniture. The *concierge,* a small, dark woman wearing a blue dress and apron, waited patiently. In clumsy French, Jacqueline said she would take it '*tout de suite*'. Yes, she would move in tomorrow, she decided, and to hell with the rent. In her mind's eye she could see herself giving smart little dinner parties. Did people still wear black ties in Paris? She supposed they did.

There was no need for her to do the cooking, Jacqueline had learned from Iversen. Any one of the great *traiteurs* would provide all the food, and waiters to serve it. As for ice cream, the best firm in Paris, Bertillon, was right there on the Île St Louis; Jacqueline remembered eating, years before, Bertillon's famous water ice, *fruits de la passion*. On the way back to the hotel she stopped the taxi, on impulse, at Hermès, and bought herself one of its classic leather handbags with gold fittings and a tiny gold padlock. Suddenly, she felt quite Parisian. All she had to do now was to start playing the Game. And perhaps John Edgeworth's ideas were worth investigating, after all. Still, she thought with a quick falling of her spirits, she had come to Paris almost unprepared, and all she had done so far was spend a great deal of money.

Back at the hotel, a postcard from Geneva was in her mail. 'Switzerland's where the money is,' it said. 'You have my permission to try to get some of it. Michel.' The bastard, she thought, seeing vividly his strong features and mocking smile. On the other side of the postcard was a photograph of an alp. By drawing vertical and horizontal lines, Michel had converted it into a graph, so that the peak showed two million dollars. Alongside, he had written his initials.

Jacqueline tore open an American Embassy envelope, and found a list of names, addresses and phone numbers from John Edgeworth. Alongside one name, el Conde Iribarne del Sepulcro y Torres, John had written: 'A good friend, Jaime. Have spoken to him – he's waiting for your call.' Jacqueline asked the hotel operator for the Barcelona number, and two minutes later heard a deep voice speaking almost flawless English.

'Ah yes, Miss Eden, our good friend John Edgeworth told me about you. I understand you can help us poor Spanish to salvage what remains of our fortunes, is that not so?'

'Well, I have a pretty good track record as an investment adviser.'

'Track record. That is a delightful Americanism. I collect them, you know; just one of my little hobbies. Yes, I know your firm, and it is of the best. There might be something you can do for me, perhaps not. When were you thinking of visiting Barcelona?'

Jacqueline replied instinctively: 'Next week. I have some clients to see.'

'Good. But why do you not fly by way of Mallorca? Then we could spend a weekend discussing matters. Just let me know when you will arrive and my man will meet you at the airport. My wife and I will be delighted to welcome you, and perhaps one or two of our friends as well.'

Quickly she asked the *concierge* to reserve her a flight to Palma de Mallorca, then called Edgeworth at the Embassy. 'John, this el Conde del Sepulcro, et cetera. What kind of man is he?'

'Quite a guy. Comes from an old family, as you'd guess from his name and title. Used to have thousands of acres of farmland, but sold most of it to his peasants, then went into business. He controls a kind of conglomerate: shipping, electronics, resort hotels, real estate development, anything that makes money. Age? About fifty, but doesn't look it. Doesn't look Spanish either; comes from Franco-Norman stock. What did he do in the Civil War? Nothing. His father fought on Franco's side, of course, but Jaime was only eleven or so when it ended. And he's always kept out of politics, as far as that's possible in Spain, which is not very far. But if the Left takes over, he's definitely on the wrong side.'

Two days later Jacqueline was on an Air France flight crowded with tourists. The mood was festive, the flight smooth. Looking out of the window, she saw on the horizon a sizeable land-mass. As it came closer, she could see steep cliffs and a barren landscape. Then, suddenly, the Boeing 727 was over the island of Mallorca, and started its descent to the airport, flying over farms, villages and the occasional small town. Jacqueline had expected a small primitive airport; instead it was huge, airconditioned and crowded with a dozen nationalities. Many of the British were already wearing straw hats, which contrasted oddly with their pale, suety faces; some were drunk, and two, trying to dance, fell over a suitcase. An airport policeman watched, his eyes impassive behind dark glasses. When the drunken British had tried twice to stand up again, he signalled to a colleague; wordlessly, they picked the men up and helped them through a door marked 'Botiquin'. A man standing next to Jacqueline at the baggage conveyor snorted and said to nobody in particular, 'Bloody disgraceful! Makes you ashamed to be British.' 'Hush, darling,' said the woman standing next to him. 'Remember your blood pressure.'

At last, Jacqueline's brown Vuitton suitcases arrived, and at the exit she saw a uniformed chauffeur scanning the crowds and carrying a neat sign marked: 'Miss Eden'. He took her case with a smile, and stowed it in the boot of a silver-grey Mercedes parked outside – illegally, she noticed, though it did not seem to worry the patrolling policeman, who smiled and saluted. The chauffeur spoke idiomatic but heavily accented English, learned, he said, when he worked in England for a Spanish banker.

The car moved rapidly and almost silently over well-made roads, lined on each side with windmills mounted on stone towers. 'For the irrigation,' said the chauffeur. 'In the earth, much water.'

'Have we far to go?'

'Yes, much, many kilometres. We go to Formentor, where all the rich live: el Conde, Douglas Fairbanks, Whitney Straight, and Mr Señor Fielding – you know, him who writes the travel books. I think he make much money telling people how to spend theirs, yes?'

'But where are all the tourists? All I see are farms and small towns.'

'Oh, the tourists, they go to the beaches at the other end of Mallorca. She is big, you know, this island. Most places, the *turistas* never go. All they want is lie on beach, get red, eat and drink.' He laughed a little scornfully. 'And for this they pay much, much money. I tell you a true story. In Mallorca, in the old days before the tourists, the eldest son of the family got the good farmland, and the youngest son the land by the sea. Is no good for farming, you understand? Then came the tourists, and the hotels. Then the oldest son find his land is worth maybe 25 pesetas a metre, and the youngest son's 200, 300, 500, more. But many of the youngest sons have gone to Argentina, Peru, Venezuela. Their families write: Come back, quick, you are rich. One man I know, he drive streetcar in Caracas. He come back, to find his 5,000 hectares are worth five million pesetas. He have heart attack, die!'

'Are you from Mallorca?'

'*Sí*, but I inherit farm. No good. *Mucho trabajo, poco dinero* – much work, no money, is correct English?'

The countryside had changed rapidly, from the flat farmland dotted with windmills to undulating uplands. Suddenly, as the car left a ravine, Jacqueline could see hills in the distance. 'Is Formentor there?'

'No, further, much further. But first we stop for a coffee, yes?' The car eased through a narrow gateway set in stone walls, and as the chauffeur opened the car door Jacqueline felt a draught of warm air. The restaurant was a long, low building with a terrace; inside, Jacqueline could see a dark, cool room with a tiled floor and a ceiling supported by massive beams.

The chauffeur went inside and returned with a plump, smiling girl. They were talking animatedly in a language Jacqueline could not recognise. Over the coffee and Spanish brandy, Jacqueline asked, 'What were you speaking just now? It wasn't Spanish, was it?'

The chauffeur laughed. 'No, I speak Mallorquín. It is like Catalan, but a little different. What you call it? When a language is the same but different?'

'A dialect?'

'*Sí*, a dialect. In Spain, most people do not speak at home what you call Spanish, and we call Castilian. Here, we speak Mallorquín; in Cataluña, Catalan. In Galicia, they speak Gallego, in the Basque provinces, Basque. Franco, he try to stop all that, make everyone speak Castilian. No work, though.'

Back in the car, Jacqueline dozed. Then she heard the chauffeur say, 'Now, we come to Formentor.' The car was moving up a series of hairpin bends cut out of the rock. Then it started moving down again, and she saw a hotel on the water's edge; in the bay, white yachts were anchored, and a speedboat was pulling a water-skier. The car started to climb again, turned through a pair of open iron gates, and stopped in front of a large two-storey house.

A tall, fair man wearing white trousers, white shoes and a pale blue shirt with turquoise scarf at the neck stepped forward, smiling. 'Ah, Miss Eden. So Emilio got you here safely. I am so glad. He is a good driver, but he talks too much.

First, you must see your room and freshen up, then we shall have cocktails on the terrace, yes?'

Jacqueline's room on the first floor of the house was large, light and airy; french windows opened onto a wide terrace on which there were *chaises-longues* and a parasol. The bathroom was almost as large as the bedroom and tiled from floor to ceiling; a door opened into a small sauna bath. Swiftly, Jacqueline showered and changed into a short-sleeved white linen dress; under it she wore a two-piece swimsuit.

The house bestrode a rocky spine. At the back was a terrace of marble tiles, an irregular oval swimming pool, and beyond it a low balustrade looking over the sea far below. Tables, chairs and umbrellas were spread around the pool, and in the sun's dazzling glint off the pool Jacqueline made out half a dozen people. El Conde rose from a *chaise-longue* to introduce her; the names sounded foreign and difficult. One of the women, teeth gleaming in an aquiline, tanned face, was el Conde's wife. She was much younger than he was – perhaps thirty to his fifty – and spoke with a strong American accent. 'Don't be fooled,' she said, laughing. 'My father was ambassador in Washington, and when he left I stayed behind to go to college. Very daring for a Spanish girl.'

A servant came up with a tray of drinks. Jacqueline chose a long gin and tonic, and sank into a low, cushioned chair. El Conde sat beside her. 'As we are all here for the weekend, don't you think we might be on first-name terms? Yours is Jacqueline, I know. My friends call me Jaime, and my wife is Inés. You are surprised by the informality, perhaps? Yes, it is true that not so long ago we Spanish were the most formal people in the world, but now we have learned to relax, to be more like the Anglo-Saxons. Would you like a swim, Jacqueline? The water is warm, I promise.'

Jacqueline unbuttoned her dress, stepped out of her low sandals, and walked to the diving board. Inés, climbing out of the pool, saw her husband looking at Jacqueline's long legs and narrow waist, and laughed. 'Oh, very much your type, Jaime. I shall have to watch you. She seems cool, but you wonder. Sometimes I think curiosity is stronger with you than sex.'

Jaime looked at her with a faint smile. 'Your analysis is

correct, my dear. But I have one unbreakable rule: never in our own house.'

Inés took off her bathing-cap and shook her black hair loose. 'You forget Dolores.'

'Ah, yes. Dolores. That was before I made my unbreakable rule, and she was unimportant – a mere matter of curiosity on my part.'

'She would not like to hear you say that.'

'Of course not. But she is, in her own estimation, much better in every way than she is in reality.'

In the pool, Jacqueline floated on her back, closing her eyes against the sun, still strong though it was starting to set. How should she start to talk business? Or should she leave it to Jaime? He seemed controlled, precise, determined, a man who did things in his own way and his own time. With a splash, she turned on her stomach and swam two lengths of the pool, puffing slightly. All that good food in Paris, she thought, was beginning to exact its price.

As she walked back to her chair she was unpleasantly conscious of the whiteness of her skin. Everyone else, she saw, had a deep tan, the fruit of many idle summers and of winter visits to the tropics. This whole place smelt of money; old, discreet money that gave off a perfume as subtle but distinct as the *pot pourri* her grandmother kept in the house outside Charleston.

'A good swim, Jacqueline?'

'I'm out of condition, I'm afraid.'

'Yes, in New York it must be difficult. A dreadful city, I think. It is bigger than the human scale. How wise you are to spend a year or two in Europe. You may never go back once you see what we have to offer. Strange, is it not? America was the New World, the land of promise. Now, more and more Americans see here, in the Old World, more of what they want. Somehow, we have learned to mix the modern economy with the past, and produce something new. Do you not feel so?'

'At the moment, I'm still so new here, I can't say. But, yes, the Europeans seem to take American products and ideas, and turn them into something which is more European than American. But I guess I'll get homesick for America before long. Most Americans do.'

'Or they go native, Jacqueline, and see no good in their own country. That is sad. A man or a woman should be a patriot before all else. Yet there are times when to be a simple, blind patriot is to be no patriot at all. You follow me?'

'Not quite.'

'Well, what I am about to say is complicated. You see, here in Spain we have a democratically elected government for the first time in more than forty years, and I am all in favour of that. Yes, my family supported General Franco, because he was the man for his times; but those times are over, were over, in fact, before he died. So now we have a democratic government. But we also have a very powerful, very militant left wing, running all the way from the official Communist Party to the Maoists, the Trotskyists and extremists whose labels I do not even know. The point they have in common is that, having lost the elections, they are determined to get power, or to wreck the economy. That is their way. Out of chaos will come the revolution, they believe. They are not happy to see the worker with his car and his own home; for them, that man has become a bourgeois, and there is no more terrible word of indictment in their vocabulary. Do not ask me why they think as they do; they are sick.'

'But I thought the Communists had committed themselves to democracy, to parliamentary government?'

'That is what they say. That is what some may believe. But it is not what I believe. Look at the history of Communist parties everywhere. What do you see? Lying and dishonesty as instruments of policy. In Communist countries what do you see? More lying and dishonesty, repression, violence, cruelty, inefficiency. Why do you think the East Germans had to build the Berlin Wall and the lethal fence along 1,800 kilometres of border with the West? To keep the West out? No, to keep their own people in. I sound like Senator Joseph McCarthy, perhaps.'

'I wasn't going to say it – but, yes, perhaps a little.'

Jaime smiled and lit a cigarette. 'I hope not. McCarthy was a drunken little politician whom I will never forgive. He turned anti-Communism into something of which all good liberals are still afraid. But your American Communists were not even serious. They were playing at politics. Can you see them getting shot, or working quietly and insidiously for years in factories to convert the workers, as ours have done? No. The American Communists were Americans first and Communists second: they believed in instant success. Here, they will wait, they will plot, they will plan, and then they will spring, and I think that any day now that is just what they will do. First in the two Regions that want autonomy, the Basque provinces and Cataluña, then in the rest of the country.'

'And you want to get some money out while you can?'

'You disappoint me, Jacqueline. Much of my money is already outside Spain. My money, and that of many, many friends of mine. That is where the patriotism comes in. I surprise you?'

'Frankly, yes. I don't see how it's patriotic to take capital out of the country when it needs all it can get.'

'I will explain. I, my family, my friends – we own land, hotels, mines, factories, ships. If the Communists take over, they will seize them all, together with any money we have in the bank. Then they will ruin the economy, as they have ruined the economies of other countries. Soon, there will be very little left. Then, if we are lucky, the people will rise, and get rid of the Communists, once and for all. Then Spain will have to be rebuilt. And how will it be done? With capital, some of which will be ours, money we have invested safely outside Spain. Most of it we have put in America. But there is much, much more to come. And why America? Because it is the least likely of all countries, except Switzerland, perhaps, to go Communist, or even Socialist. Now do you see why I wished to talk to you?'

Jaime leaned forward, and took off his dark glasses. His eyes were intent, his expression serious. Jacqueline suddenly realised that this pleasant, rather playboyish man, was obsessed by his theme, wild and fanciful though it struck her. Of course, it had a certain appeal. Few men could simultaneously protect their fortunes by hiding them away in another country, and convince themselves they were acting patriotically. Jaime must have a convoluted mind to weave so harmonious a pattern out of such unlikely threads. His voice broke in. 'Well, what do you think, Jacqueline?'

'I think,' she said slowly, 'that you've almost persuaded me it can be patriotic and ethical to get your money out of Spain, legally or illegally. What I don't see is where I fit into the picture.'

'That is simple. I have done my homework, you know. You have a very good reputation in New York. You were chief securities analyst for your firm's mutual fund, were you not? And am I right that the fund outperformed all others last year and the year before? Yes? Then you seem to be able to spot the phoney companies too. I am told you did what the Americans call 'pull the plug' on King Resources, yes? So. We need the best advice we can get.'

'Look, I'm talking myself out of a job, but you can get pretty good advice from stockbrokers and banks.'

'I do not think so. Brokerage houses are in the business of encouraging clients to buy or sell – which hardly matters, since the stockbroker gets his commission. As for bank trust departments – no. There are too many conflicts of interest. Do you think that a banker who is also a director of a major corporation goes to the trust department and says, "A word in your ear. Sell Mickey Mouse Corporation short, it's going to have a horrible year"? No, Mickey Mouse Corporation owes the bank money, and he will do nothing to damage it. Look at Penn Central! A board loaded with bankers, and they were either the last to know what was happening, or did not choose to tell their banks. Also, we want total secrecy. Only you and a handful of others know that all those companies in Bermuda, Liechtenstein, Luxembourg, Switzerland, the Bahamas come back eventually to my friends and to me.'

Jacqueline finished the last of her second drink and laughed. 'Well, you've talked me back into a job, thank goodness. But how do you see the relationship?'

'First, let me impress you we are not talking about small change. At the moment, our various companies have about $200 million in stocks and cash or near-cash. Soon that will be $300 million. What I propose is a basic fee of one sixteenth of one per cent of funds under management. That is about

$150,000 a year. Then, if the funds rise by more than an average of five per cent, you will be entitled to an additional one-eighth of each percentage point. Anything over ten per cent, and you will have one half of one per cent on the increase. I think those terms are fair, Jacqueline.'

She tried to stop the tremor in her hand as she lit a cigarette. The terms were not just fair; they were munificent, princely. Could Jaime be a confidence trickster of some kind? A fantasist? Clearing her throat, Jacqueline asked, 'And to whom would I report? Who would approve buys and sells?'

'You would report to me and to my friends. Most of them are here now – look.' And he swept his hand around the terrace at the four or five men to whom Jacqueline had been introduced earlier. 'As for buys and sells, you would have complete discretion up to, say, ten million dollars. Over that, my friends and I would have to approve. Now, time for a shower and a rest, do you think? In Spain we dine late. Let us say cocktails at nine.'

Upstairs, Jacqueline lay on her bed and thought about the conversation with Jaime. He was a strange man: charming but impatient, confident but in need of approval, cautious but headstrong, outwardly kind, but with a streak of cruelty. Reaching for her handbag, she took out a calculator and did some quick sums. Suppose, just suppose, she managed to make a fifteen per cent profit in six months. Basic fee on $300 million, $75,000; bonus $56,000; making a total of $131,000. Would Michel do as well? Peter? Henry? No, it wasn't enough. She'd better use some of her stake to play the market for herself.

Then she recollected, with a start, that Jaime hadn't actually given her the job yet. Indeed, he had implied that dinner tonight was not just a social occasion, but some kind of test. She rose from the bed, selected a blue-black silk chiffon dress from Balmain, and a few minutes after nine walked down the long staircase. Out on the terrace the lamps were lit, and a barman was serving a group of men in tuxedoes. A brisk little wind lifted her skirts as Jaime came forward.

'Ah, Jacqueline, you are more prompt than the other ladies. Now, let me introduce again my friends – I'm sure you didn't hear their names this afternoon. Gentlemen, this is Miss Eden, whom I hope will help us with our little problems...'

6

> There was a sound of revelry by night,
> And Belgium's capital had gather'd then
> Her beauty and her chivalry, and bright
> The lamps shone o'er fair women and brave men;
> *Byron*

When Peter Acheson told friends and colleagues he was going to Brussels, they commiserated. Dull, grey and provincial were the words that most of them used. As Peter rode from the airport to the city centre, he could see what they meant. The older buildings seemed dull and undistinguished, whereas the new ones were mere variations on Kellogg's cornflakes packets. Well, he thought, it's just a base, and I'm here to make some money.

His choice of Brussels was dictated by one simple fact: the commodities markets rise or fall with the interplay of supply and demand. The European Common Market's nine members are big buyers of American soybeans, thus influencing demand; they are big producers of grain, thereby influencing supply. Brussels, he reasoned, must be one of the best listening posts in the world, and the European Commission's headquarters the place in which to make friends.

The taxi turned into a square of high, small-windowed buildings, most of them with gilt decorations on their façades. 'The Grand' Place,' said the driver. 'Very touristic.' Peter's hotel, the Amigo, was in a narrow street just off the Grand' Place. It looked old, almost as old as the seventeenth-century buildings in the square; in fact, he soon learned, it was built just in time for the Brussels exhibition of 1958, and if some of the floors creaked, that was deliberate.

One message awaited him: 'Mr Rabinowitz says he will meet you in the bar at twenty hours.' It took Peter a moment to work out that twenty hours was eight o'clock. Just time to unpack and have a bath. A few minutes before eight, he walked into the small, low-ceilinged bar off the lobby. It looked as though Flemish burghers had been drinking in it since the fourteenth century. Now, it was crowded with Americans. Why so many, Peter asked the barman.

'ITT meetings week,' said the barman, as though that explained everything.

'What's that?'

'Once a month all the top ITT executives fly over from New York for a meeting in Brussels, their European headquarters.'

'And they all stay at the Amigo?'

'Oh no, sir, they stay at the Sheraton. ITT owns the Sheraton. But many of them drink here, to get away from each other.'

At that moment, Benny Rabinowitz walked in. He had always been well-padded, even at college, where Peter first met him. Now, he was gross, with a stomach that ballooned over his trouser-tops, and chins that melted into each other.

'Don't say it, don't say it! I'm fat. Right? Well, so will you be after a few months of Brussels food. My God, talk about calories; I don't know where these Belgians put it. And the sauces! You get the best food in Europe in Belgium, and don't let the French tell you anything different.'

Like Peter, Benny had started off in commodities brokerage. Then he had moved to a big grain exporting firm, and for the past five years had been its European vice president. 'I'll tell you, old chum, this beats Chicago any day. Brussels looks dull to you, I guess – it does to everyone the first time. But we've got some pretty good opera, one of the best experimental ballets in Europe, the Ballet Béjart, some fantastic art galleries, and a pretty active social life.'

'Yeah, but I don't speak a word of French.'

'Don't worry. There are thousands of Americans here, more thousands of Brits, and most of the Belgians you'll meet will speak English better than you do. What's more, they *like* Americans. Can you beat that? Their message isn't "Yanks Go Home". It's "Please send some more". Well, time to get moving. We're dining out of town, at the Château Ste Anne.'

Benny struggled behind the wheel of a Peugeot 504 and threaded the car through the narrow streets. 'Just one thing to watch in Belgium: the goddamn drivers. They're all maniacs. They didn't even need a driving licence until the Sixties, and most of them have never passed a test. They have priority from the right, and use it – look at that crazy bastard.' A tiny Citroën rushed out of a half-hidden alley, straight in front of the Peugeot. Benny sighed. 'You see that? He's got five kids in there, his wife, his grandmother, and the family cat, and he doesn't even bother to look.'

The car rushed over cobblestones, past the Royal Palace and a series of large parks, and ten minutes later turned into the driveway of the Château Ste Anne. In the gathering dusk, Peter saw what appeared to be a stately private home. Inside, in the high-ceilinged hall, half a dozen people were sitting on couches, talking quietly; to the right, there was a clink of glasses from the bar. As Peter and Benny sat over their drinks, the *maître d'hôtel*, Monsieur Roger, brought them menus. 'Not your week for a diet yet, Mr Rabinowitz?' he asked, his dark moustaches twitching with amusement.

'It's always my week for a diet, you scoundrel. It's just that every *maître d'hôtel* in the country has ganged up to keep me off it. Any of those *jets d'houblon* left?'

'Yes, sir. You're lucky. The season is a little late this year; they're not yet stringy. And may I suggest the roast baby lamb, sir? It's very fine.'

In the restaurant, a long, panelled room, Peter looked curiously at the *jets d'houblon*. 'What are these, Benny?'

'See if you can guess.'

'Not asparagus, though similar. Slight taste of mushrooms. No, they've got me beat.'

'Buds of hops, like the ones you get in beer. I don't think you can get them served like this in any other country. But you didn't come here to talk about food. Just what the hell *are* you doing in Belgium, anyway?'

Peter explained his idea – without mentioning the Game. Although the rules didn't say so, he felt the Game was a secret. Benny nodded. 'Well, you're right, of course. That goddamn European Commission has figures on everything, including the crops – in fact, particularly the crops. I don't mind telling you, I've made a dime or two in the futures market by keeping my ears close to the ground. This place isn't a bad listening post, by the way. It's a club – the Club International, but everyone calls it Château Ste Anne.

'Look over there: the man with the glasses and reddish face. That's Roy Jenkins, president of the European Commission. A Brit. Used to be in the British Labour Government Cabinet. Then he pulled out, or was pushed out. See that man over there? That's another Commissioner, Christopher Tugendhat. Another Brit. A Conservative this time. Half the people in this room work for the Commission.'

'But aren't they supposed to keep decisions to themselves until they're announced publicly?'

'Oh, sure. But the Commission's as leaky as a sieve. You know the difference between a confidential and a secret document at the Commission? Fifteen minutes. You still married by the way?'

'No. We got a divorce two years ago.'

'Well, that's another bit of luck. Eligible men are scarce as hen's teeth round here. There are thousands of girls working in the Commission, most of them busting a gut for a man. Find one working in the right department, and I'd say you'll know what's happening before her boss does.'

'Good idea. But I can't put an ad in the paper. Where do I find one of these girls who's willing to give all and tell all?'

'Simple. Just hang out in some of the pubs round the Commission. They're the Brussels version of East Side singles bars. You're not God's gift to women, Peter, but unmarried and with a few dollars to spend – why, you'll cut a swathe through 'em. Most of 'em are good-looking gals, too. If it wasn't for Ruth and about one hundred pounds of excess weight, I'd be right there with you.'

Over breakfast next morning Peter thought about Benny's idea. Somehow, he couldn't see himself hanging around pubs picking up young secretaries. He wasn't exactly shy. Diffident might be more the word. But, whatever it was, he could not easily start a conversation with a girl he didn't know. The last time he had tried it, soon after his divorce, he had stuttered, and his hand had shaken so much he spilled most of his drink into the girl's lap.

But perhaps he could advertise for a part-time secretary; there was just a chance that one of the girls at the Commission might apply. Even if she were in the wrong department, she might introduce him to the right girl eventually. And if she was pretty and willing as well, that would be a bonus. On his way out of the hotel, he stopped at the *concierge*'s desk. A part-time secretary, bilingual in English and French? Advertise in the two English-language weeklies, the *Bulletin* and the *Times*.

The advertisement came out the following week, a week that Peter spent looking for a flat and talking to businessmen and bankers to whom he had introductions. He found the flat within walking distance of the Commission, in a new building overlooking the Parc du Cinquantenaire. On the Monday, he moved in, and picked up the first of the replies to his advertisement. There were twenty to the ad in the *Bulletin*, eighteen to the ad in the *Times*. He scanned them. Only one of the applicants worked at the Commission; she did not say in which department. German, but fluent in French and English, aged twenty-seven, unmarried. He phoned her that night. '*Ja*, Fräulein Ertl speaking.' Her English sounded dreadful.

'Acheson speaking. About your reply to my advertisement...'

'Oh, Herr Acheson, I am sorry. I have my mind changed. But I hoff girl *freund*, also for the Commission *arbeitet*. She is good for you, I zink. *Moment, bitte*, she speak.'

There was a burst of German in the background, then a younger, less accented voice spoke. 'Yes, I am fluent in English and French, Mr Acheson. Four nights a week I could work. Yes, if you wish, I could meet you at the Amigo. Half an hour? Yes, that is possible. Please tell the barman you are awaiting me.'

Peter was expecting a young Brünhilde, but the girl who walked over to his table in the bar was small, slim and dark, with large grey eyes. No beauty, but neat, attractive, confident. 'I'm sorry about my friend, Mr Acheson, but she got cold feet – that is correct, yes? She always says she speaks fluent English but, as you can hear, it is less than perfect.'

Peter laughed. 'Well, my German doesn't exist, so she's nothing to be ashamed of.'

'Oh, but she has, Mr Acheson. Her parents have spent much money on courses for her; but Heidi is lazy. She will never study. Now, Mr Acheson, to business. Here is my *curriculum vitae*. Please read it.'

Ilse Winckler, he read, German citizen; born 1951. Education – he didn't understand what a Gymnasium was. Place where they taught physical training instructors?

Jobs: a bank in Stuttgart, another bank in Vienna, then the Commission. Current position: secretary, deputy director-general, Energy Secretariat. Languages: German, English, French. Shorthand in all three. Hobbies: skiing, photography, travel, opera, history. H'mm, serious girl.

'Well, that's pretty impressive, Miss Winckler. Look, let me tell you about myself. I'm in the commodities business – you know what that is. I've decided to operate out of Brussels because, well, frankly, I'm pretty tired of New York, and there's a lot of business to be done here.

'Because of the time change between here and the States, I'm going to be doing a lot of my business at night. I need a secretary to keep my files straight, send telexes, do some typing, maybe keep my accounts. I think you'll do. But first let me ask: Why would you want a part-time job? I hear they pay real well at the Commission.'

'And you hear rightly, Mr Acheson. But I like to ski in the winter, and there is no skiing in Belgium, whatever the travel posters say about the Ardennes. Then I like also to go to the opera, which is expensive. And I want to buy a Hasselblad camera. And to save.'

'But if you work in the evenings you can't go out with your friends.'

'That is not a problem, Mr Acheson. Brussels is a lonely place, I think.'

'But you know other girls at the Commission?'

'Yes, many, many of them. But I have not made many friends.'

'I know the feeling, Miss Winckler. Right, well as far as I'm concerned, it's a deal. Four nights a week, seven till ten – total of twelve hours. Say, we didn't discuss money. What do you charge?'

'Two hundred and fifty francs an hour.'

'Sounds fine to me.'

'Good night, Mr Acheson.'

'*Au revoir*, Miss Winckler, until tomorrow night: 19 avenue de la Renaissance.'

He watched her walk through the lobby, a small and lonely figure. Now why hadn't he asked her to have dinner? He returned to the bar for one more drink and pulled a calculator from his case. Let's see, 250 Belgian francs at 36.18 to the dollar: $6.90 an hour. At that price, thought Peter, she could afford to pay for her own dinner. He did another calculation. Assume that's what she was paid at the Commission for a forty-hour week... Christ, it was $13,248 a year, and most of it tax-free. She could pay for *his* dinner, too.

Promptly at seven the next evening, Ilse Winckler arrived at the flat. The weather was fine, and Peter was sitting on the terrace reading the *International Herald Tribune*, a Scotch on the low table beside his chair. From nine floors below came the voices of people in the park. To his left was the massive complex of exhibition buildings, and the triumphal arch erected in 1881 for the fiftieth anniversary of Belgium's independence. To his right was the Muslim mosque, for many years derelict, now refurbished; he hoped the *muezzin* would not call the faithful to prayer too loudly.

Ilse was wearing a lime-green linen dress, and her dark hair was gathered by a bow at the back. It made her look practical, almost severe, and she refused a drink: 'No, Mr Acheson, I am here to work.' She looked around the living-room disapprovingly. 'I don't see any filing cabinets, Mr Acheson. And where is the telex?'

'The telex waits upon the pleasure of the phone company, or whatever it's called here. The filing cabinets – well, I thought you might decide what we need. But there is a typewriter, and here are some letters I've roughed out.'

She took them from him, almost snatched them. 'These will take no more than one hour, Mr Acheson. Our agreement is for three hours.'

'True, Miss Winckler. But then we have to discuss the office equipment, don't we?'

'Yes, but that will take no more than one hour.'

'But I may have some cables for you to send by telephone. That could take several hours.'

'I doubt it, Mr Acheson. The Belgian telephone system is very efficient.'

Peter returned to his newspaper and Scotch. From the room next to the office he heard the clack of the typewriter. Ilse typed fast, perhaps too fast. Sighing, he sank into the chair, and sleep. When he awakened the terrace was dim, and for a moment he could not remember where he was. His mouth tasted foul. To his right he saw a vague shape waving something white at him. It was Ilse, with a sheaf of letters in her hand. 'Please, Mr Acheson, wake up.'

'Sorry, Miss Winckler. I had a bad night – calls from Chicago, Tokyo – they went on all night.'

'That is bad, Mr Acheson. A man must get his sleep. Mr Acheson, I have finished these letters. What shall I do now? Do you wish a cup of coffee?'

'No thanks, Miss Winckler. But you have one – or have a drink?'

'No, but I thank you, Mr Acheson. Did you hear the news on the radio, Mr Acheson, about the coffee in Brazil?'

Peter came wide awake. 'What news?'

'It is terrible. There have been cold winds and frost in Parana, and twenty per cent of the coffee crop is lost.'

'Why, that is dreadful, Miss Winckler. But not for me.'

'You don't drink coffee, Mr Acheson?'

'Sure I do. But I just bought some coffee futures. Did the radio say what happened in the markets?'

'Yes, the September futures price rose six cents in New York.'

Peter smiled, and did a quick calculation. He had an option on 50,000 pounds; his day's profit was $3,000.

'Tell you what, Miss Winckler, why don't we discuss that office equipment over dinner? Also, I made a lot of money today, so it's kind of a celebration.'

Ilse blushed. 'That is very kind of you, Mr Acheson. But do you think I'm dressed?'

'Hell, we're not going to a smart place. In any case, you look just fine. They won't throw you out.'

Le Charolais was two blocks from the apartment, a small, neighbourhood restaurant that served the best beef Peter had ever tasted. He had been there twice; already he felt an *habitué*. The *patron*, Willi Henderyckx, greeted him quietly, and suggested a round table in a corner. Only one other table was occupied, by an elderly couple who talked in low voices. Music played softly from hidden speakers; Bach, Peter thought.

Ilse looked round at the white walls, beams, and daffodil-yellow tablecloths and napkins. 'This is nice, *gemütlich*. I'm sorry, that is a German word. I cannot translate precisely. Cosy, perhaps?'

'Don't you think it's time we started using our first names, Ilse? It's an old American habit. We don't believe in formality.'

'Well, if you wish, but it is different in Germany. People can know each other for years and still be formal. My father is still *Herr Doktor Generaldirektor* to his assistant, after twenty years together.' She laughed, showing small, very white teeth.

'What is he director of?'

'A book publisher in Stuttgart, quite small. They publish poetry and *belles lettres* mostly, a few novels. But tell me about yourself, Peter: what you do, why you are here, and for how long.'

Peter was still talking when the coffee came, and found to his surprise that he had told the story of his life. He laughed with embarrassment. 'My God, I've been talking nonstop for an hour, all about myself, too. And we haven't even mentioned the office equipment.'

Ilse smiled and took a piece of paper from her handbag. 'Don't worry, Peter. Everyone must talk sometime. In any case, I had already made out a list.'

Peter glanced at it. 'Oh, just order the stuff, Ilse. And now, a brandy?'

Unexpectedly, she accepted, and both sat silent and thoughtful for a few moments, Ilse gazing at the tablecloth. Suddenly, she raised her head and smiled. 'You know, Peter, I have been wondering. The amount of soybeans Europe buys from America affects the price, you tell me. If you knew how much it intended to buy, you would be in a good position to make money?'

'Sure would. You got any ideas?'

'No, not at the moment. But I shall think about it.'

Willi shook hands with them at the door, his face dignified over his chef's white coat, and Peter walked Ilse to the subway station at Place Schuman, just by the Commission headquarters. She refused a taxi. 'No, no, Peter, it is only three stops. Besides, Brussels taxis are so expensive.' He watched her going down the escalator. At the bottom she turned, waved, and then walked on. Peter felt a pang of regret. He found her gravity and seriousness both appealing and a little sad. She should be having more fun than she did.

Back at the apartment, he dialled a Chicago number. The call went straight through.

'Ed? Peter Acheson. Hi. Yeah, I'm speaking from Brussels. How's the coffee market?'

'How's the coffee market? I tell ya, Pete, it's gone mad. Up six cents again today, it's gonna go up again tomorrow. Ya heard about Brazil? Yeah. Well, now there's a report from Guatemala – frost, a third of the crop gone.'

'OK, Ed. Tell you what we do. If it goes up another six tomorrow, sell.'

'Sell? Are you crazy? It'll keep going up.'

'Maybe, maybe not. But I want to be liquid. I may be doing something in soybeans. How're they moving?'

'Kinda flat. Crop reports are good.'

'OK. Buy me a three-month option of 50,000 tons of soybean meal. That'll do for a start. I'll be back to you.'

'You know something about soybeans I don't know?'

'That'd be telling, Ed.'

Peter put the phone down and laughed. If he knew Ed, he'd be telling everyone who would listen that Peter Acheson had an inside track on soybeans. He undressed quickly and settled happily into bed. If all went well, he'd have made $9,000 in three days on coffee. Could Jacqueline, Michel and Henry make as much so easily? He doubted it.

Within minutes, he was asleep.

7

> If individuals have no virtues, their
> vices may be of use to us
>
> *Junius*

Patches of morning mist still hung over Lac Léman, though the sun was close to its noon zenith. A mile away a white speedboat rushed towards the French side of the lake. 'Prince Sadruddin on his way home for lunch,' said Henk Vrijdel, eyes squinting against the bright light.

'I didn't know he worked,' said Michel Jobert.

'Oh, he does. He's the UN High Commissioner for Refugees. Turns all his salary back, and works like a maniac. He asked me to work for him once, as his publicity man, but the money wasn't good enough.'

Michel doubted Henk's story. Personable, knowledgeable and shrewd he certainly was; but nobody who had been in Geneva for more than a few months could have avoided hearing the legends that clustered round him, most of them unsavoury. He called himself a journalist, and wrote indeed for some Dutch papers and for an American news syndicate. But Michel was pretty sure he'd been employed by the CIA at one time, and knew for a fact he had been in the arms business – probably still was. Michel had helped to finance one arms deal, something Henk did not know, thank heavens: blackmail was not a word to put him off, provided the money was big and the risk small.

Yet, surprisingly, Henk was popular in Geneva; at least he was invited to all the right parties, and had the right people to his, when he played the piano with professional flair, and could give almost flawless impressions of any singer from Sinatra to Jacques Brel, and Georges Brassens to Elvis Presley. Henk's ear for languages was remarkable: he spoke French like a Frenchman, English like an Englishman, and was almost equally fluent in Italian, Spanish, Portuguese and German.

He always shrugged off this linguistic virtuosity as something inherent in the Dutch: 'Who can speak Dutch, apart from the Dutch and the Belgians? And who wants to speak to the Belgians?'

Now, on the terrace of the Hôtel du Lac, fifteen minutes' drive from Geneva, Henk was speaking French with a *pied noir* accent, knowing that it annoyed Michel, his long, narrow face laughing. 'Just what is it you're doing, Michel? It doesn't sound like you to take the summer off.'

'I keep telling you, I'm not taking the summer off. I'm taking some time to make money for myself, instead of the bank, and to have fun as well.'

'And you think I can help you to do both, is that it? Well, I may be able to help you have fun, particularly if you're paying. But making money – that's never been my strong point.'

Michel looked at Henk's well-cut suit, Sulka shirt and wafer-thin gold wristwatch. Outside, he knew, Henk had parked his BMW 3000, or perhaps his Jaguar V-12. 'Come off it,' said Michel, switching into English. 'I've never seen you wearing less than five thousand dollars' worth of clothes and jewellery, or driving less than fifteen thousand dollars' worth of car. And what about that house?'

'It belongs to my wife. That's one thing to be said for marrying a young widow: if you're lucky, she comes with a house.'

'This one came with a mansion.'

'Yes, but not much else,' said Henk. Oddly, thought Michel, that was probably true. When Henk did marry for the first time, at the age of forty-seven, it appeared to be for love; perhaps he kept one corner of his dishonest life pure, rather as Mafiosi did. Or perhaps the beauty and innocence of his Italian wife, Carlotta, had broken through the carapace of cynicism with which Henk had protected his heart for all those years.

They ordered another drink, and a waiter took their order for lunch: *Bündnerfleisch*, paper-thin beef cured in the mountains, and lake perch, to be washed down with a bottle of the local white wine. The last of the mist had gone now, and Michel could see clear across to the other side of the lake, which was empty apart from a white steamer moving silently in the distance. He felt calm, peaceful. No war had come to Switzerland since Napoleonic times, only the aftermath of war, in the form of discreet money, the United Nations, and peace conferences. Most other nations disliked the Swiss; Michel felt a perverse admiration for them and for their ability to make out of a country with four languages and few natural resources an oasis of orderly prosperity in a troubled world.

Henk finished the last of his *Bündnerfleisch* and moistened his lips with a sip of the wine. 'One thing I can help you with,' he said, 'and that's a house. A friend of mine is going away for a year or so, and wants to rent his place.' Michel smiled inwardly; the friend, he was sure, was offering Henk a commission.

'Thanks, but I've taken one, just along the shore at Nyon. I move in tomorrow. It used to belong to one of Bernie Cornfield's sidekicks.'

Henk laughed. 'If he was anything like his boss, the house probably comes with mirrors on the bedroom ceiling.'

'He never got around to it, poor guy. IOS collapsed before he moved in properly, and the mirrors are still stacked in crates in the garage. There's a double sunken bath, though.'

'Useful if you want your back scratched.'

'I don't think that's the idea.'

'May have been. Some of those IOS guys got their kicks in strange ways. One of them could only get it up if the girl was blindfolded. The joke was that she represented the ideal IOS investor – couldn't see what she was getting into.'

'Or was getting into her.'

They both laughed. Then Henk leaned back in his chair, lit a cigarette, and said, 'Well, I'm sure you didn't ask me to lunch just to tell dirty stories. What is it really?'

'Nothing in particular. Not yet, anyway. Look, do you remember when Crédit Suisse had all those problems in Chiasso?'

'Remember? How could anyone forget? It isn't every day that a major Swiss bank has to admit one of its branches was running a business on the side without telling anyone. How much did they commit the bank for? A billion Swiss francs wasn't it? About $500 million?'

'Well, Henk, something rather curious happened that you

may not have noticed. The Swiss franc dipped two days before the bank announced its losses. What's that suggest to you?'

'Somebody had inside knowledge, and unloaded a lot of Swiss francs.'

'Right. Now, what I want to know is – who sold? The bank, or somebody who just happened to hear?'

'It wasn't the bank, that I can tell you. There was an official investigation, and the bank had done no more than its normal trading.'

'So it was somebody on the outside, and he – or they – made a very nice little bundle indeed.'

'And you'd like to be in the same position next time there's going to be a bank scandal, right?'

'I couldn't have put it better myself.'

'That kind of information is worth a lot of money.'

'I'll give you ten per cent of whatever I make.'

'Better twenty per cent.'

'I'll go to fifteen.'

'It's a deal.'

They both smiled. Michel hadn't expected to get away with ten per cent. Henk, he was sure, hadn't expected to get twenty. As it was, they were both happy after scoring off each other.

Henk looked at his watch. 'I must run.'

Michel scribbled a number on his New York business card. 'Here. Keep in touch.' He walked Henk to the parking lot. Yes, as he'd thought, a BMW.

Upstairs in his room, Michel dialled the foreign exchange desk of an American bank in London. 'How's the pound?'

'Spot's pretty steady – $1.7230. Three months forward is weak – $1.7010.' Spot did not really interest Michel; that was the price being paid today. But the forward price – the price being quoted now for delivery of dollars against pounds three months ahead – gave him the feel of market sentiment.

'OK, I'll buy £200,000 forward at $1.7010.'

'Got you.'

Michel made a rapid calculation. The pound had been trading for months in the $1.71 to $1.72 range. At worst, it could fall to around $1.69, which would mean he had lost $2,000. More likely, though, it would rise to around $1.72, which would mean a profit of $4,000 give or take a few cents. He dialled another number, that of an American bank in Paris. 'How's the franc today?'

'Steady against the dollar, down against the mark and the Swiss franc.'

'What's the reason?'

'The Swiss and the Germans have just reported huge trade surpluses. The French franc could go either way – depends on the news.'

'And the Belgian franc?'

'Losing ground. But you know that market – so small, it's highly volatile.'

'OK, thanks.'

Nothing in the French or Belgian francs, Michel thought. He dialled Frankfurt. 'What's the news?'

'The mark's up again.' The dealer sounded bored: when was the mark not up again? 'In fact, it's bumping the top of the tunnel' – the mark was one of the European currencies tied together and known as the snake. It was supposed not to go below or above certain prices, known as the tunnel.

'Any more rumours about an official upward revaluation?'

'Oh, there are always rumours.'

'What's the spot rate?'

'At the moment, 2.4801 marks to the dollar, but that's up .0102 in the past hour. One month forward, 2.3609 to the dollar.'

'Right, I'll take a million marks at that rate.'

'Done. Roger and out.'

Michel made some more calculations, and noted them in his accounts book. Back at his desk in New York, he thought, he had known exactly what was happening in every major foreign exchange market in the world. Here in Switzerland, operating by himself, he was as handicapped as a man deaf in one ear trying to play bingo.

Currencies rose and fell not only with traders' and tourists' demand for them, but also with market rumours and hunches. An opinion poll showing that most Italians favoured a Socialist-Communist alliance could knock the lira; a blow-out in the North Sea oil fields could pare percentage points off the pound. Michel sat in the deep embrasure that formed the window of his room, and looked out thoughtfully at the lake. Wisps of mist were forming again, and as he watched a playful wind moved them over the water, as though it had a purpose. But the wind was as unpredictable as market rumours; and, like them, nobody really knew where it started.

Michel lit a Gauloise, went to the drinks cupboard, and poured a Calvados. Suppose, for a moment, he started the rumours? Or, better, suppose he could hear and act on a firm report before it became public knowledge? That was what he had suggested to Henk, and it sounded fine in theory. In practice, though, he would be lucky to catch one report a year before it was published. How much better, more certain, to put out the report himself – Michel's mind skirted round the word fabricate. It would need an imprimatur, however, some mark of authenticity, if it were to be believed without question, and have a measurable effect on the foreign exchange markets. Furthermore, it must never be traced back to him. He didn't know which Swiss law would catch him, but there must be one; and even a hint of his complicity would end his career as a foreign exchange dealer, as well as costing him the Game.

The phone rang, shrill in the afternoon calm, and Michel jumped, spilling some of the Calvados. He smiled wryly; if he was jittery already, perhaps he'd better drop the whole idea. The phone shrilled again. He answered impatiently, then lowered his voice as he heard: 'Yes, Michel, Freddie von Kastenberg. Yes, we're giving a little party tonight – you know the house, of course. How did I know you were in Geneva? It is a small town, my friend. Good. So we'll see you at 6.30? No, not black tie – just a simple buffet supper. *Wiedersehen.*'

Michel showered, shaved carefully, and chose a dark blue lightweight suit from the wardrobe. Freddie's idea of informality, he recalled, should not be taken too literally. Despite his cosmopolitan charm, and the ease with which he moved in Rome, London, New York, Paris and a dozen other capitals, he was still the German aristocrat, and had the money to maintain a little of the atmosphere of a minor German court at the three houses he owned, one near Munich, one on Long Island, and a third just outside Lausanne. He was a prince, of a royal family that had long ceased to rule, but was connected with most of the remaining sovereigns of Europe; it was part of his reverse snobbery to drop the title, while always ensuring, somehow, that people knew his rank.

What Freddie did for a living Michel had never really learned; perhaps he lived on inherited money, dabbling in property deals and publishing to amuse himself. Or perhaps the royal investments were wearing a little thin, like the royal blood; Freddie had been married twice, but still, in his midforties, had no children.

Michel drove his rented Mercedes up a narrow lane and stopped at tall gates of iron. A dark young man stepped out of the lodge, took his name, and spoke into a telephone. At the press of a button, the gates opened, and Michel drove under arching treetops until he reached the courtyard of a small château. A dozen cars were there already. Two of them, he noticed, were Rolls-Royces, and one was a Ferrari. His Mercedes 280 seemed workaday by comparison.

At the top of a flight of broad, shallow steps a butler waited in black jacket, striped trousers and wing collar. He inclined his head slightly at Michel's name, and led him wordlessly into a high-ceilinged hall. Freddie von Kastenberg left a group of guests and walked swiftly towards Michel, his blue eyes bright in a tanned face and fair hair thinning slightly on top. He greeted Michel in French.

'Ah, *mon cher*, how good to see you. First you must meet my wife – she was away, I think, when you were here last.' He took a small, pretty, dark woman by the arm: 'Michel Jobert, my dear. Michel, my wife, Ingrid.'

She put out a small, firm hand: 'I'm so glad you could be here, and on such short notice, too. Freddie is very bad about these things; he gives parties at the last moment, and then is surprised when nobody turns up.' Her accent was slight, so slight that Michel could not at first identify it. Swedish, perhaps; almost certainly Scandinavian.

Freddie was urging him away: 'There are some people I want you to meet, Michel. Then you and I must have a talk; I want to know why you are in Geneva, how long you will be here, whether I can be of any help.' He stopped before a group of five people, three women and two men. Michel recognised one of the men, head of a private bank in Zurich who had shocked his staider competitors by starting his own arts festival, thereby getting some useful but respectable publicity. He was slim, but athletic-looking; he did not resemble the typical foreigner's conception of a Swiss banker and, if the rumours were true, did not behave like one either. Not a man to be associated with too closely in public, thought Michel. But he might be useful some time. The other man was of medium height, dark, and in his late thirties. He shook hands with a strong grip and smiled, showing white, even teeth. Michel did not hear his name, and tried to place him. Probably Spanish or Italian, possibly Latin American. Then the butler came forward and said, 'Telephone call, Mr Yussaini.' Michel watched his narrow-hipped figure walking away, and thought that the handshake had fooled him; most Arabs shook hands limply.

Michel went on talking with the banker and his wife, who spoke no French, and German with a strong Swiss accent. The other two women, both young and dark, spoke together in Arabic, and Michel remembered enough to know they were planning a shopping trip to Paris. Yussaini returned, smiling. 'Ah, business, it pursues one everywhere, don't you find? I sometimes think my part of the world was better off before we had any telephones. That call was about something on which you may be able to advise me – if you will, that is. We are buying some shares in a German company, and must pay thirty days from now. Is it your view the mark will go up against the dollar?'

'I think so. The German economy's still gathering speed, and there's been another big trade surplus. America, on the other hand, has a big deficit, and people still don't quite trust Carter's economics.'

'And you, Mr Jobert, may I ask: have you put your money where your mouth is, as the Americans say?'

'Some of it. I put an order in today for marks.'

'I am so glad you have confirmed my judgment, Mr Jobert. I have just told my bank to make a forward purchase, too.' He laughed, and took a glass of champagne from a waiter's tray.

'Don't you feel it is usually ridiculously easy to make money? But let us not say it too loudly. People like to think it is very difficult, and perhaps for some it is.'

'Perhaps we don't all have your touch, Mr Yussaini.'

He would have liked to stay with Yussaini, but Freddie was moving him away to meet more guests. Few of the men, he noticed, were really elegant. A lifetime of making money seemed to have given most of them heavy jowls, or big bottoms, or both, and expensive tailoring could not entirely hide their sags and bulges. The forces of gravity had not yet triumphed over the women, however, and all were groomed in that way unique to the rich, as though they had been sprayed with a mist of money. Yussaini's two women – wife and her sister? wives? girl-friends? – were wearing identical diamond rings, made of white gold and so perilously thin that he was surprised they could get insurance; if, of course, they bothered.

At the buffet supper, served in a dining-room dominated by a table that could have seated fifty, Michel found himself sitting in an embrasure with Yussaini, who came strolling over with a plate of cold fish and caviare, the two Arab women walking behind him. 'Did you meet my wife and her sister? Jehann and Salma.' They shook hands, giving him only the barest glance, and went on talking in Arabic, this time about somebody's yacht. Yussaini wiped a morsel of caviare from his lips and looked at Michel with a smile.

'I am going to ask you a presumptuous question,' he said in his mid-Atlantic accent. 'Presumptuous, because it perhaps suggests I am better-known than I am. It is this: had you heard of me before we met?'

'No, I hadn't. Of course, your name is hardly unusual in the Arab world. But why do you ask?'

'Curiosity, though not entirely idle. Tell me, Mr Jobert, what do you think of the United States as a country in which to invest?'

'What can I tell you that you don't know already? Politically, extremely stable. I can't think of another country that could have gone through Vietnam and Watergate without any real challenge to the system. Economically – well, the world's biggest economy, though worryingly dependent on imported oil. I think that'll change, however, but not tomorrow. Management: just about the best. Labour unions: too aggressive for my liking, but essentially realistic, and not politicised, like they are in Europe. So if you want safety, stability, predictability, I can't think of anywhere better than the US.'

'And the dollar, Mr Jobert?'

'For the long term, the world's most stable currency, I'd say.'

'In the long run we'll all be dead, Mr Jobert, as John Maynard Keynes said. I mean for, say, ten or fifteen years ahead?'

'That is the long term, for me at least.'

'You mention imported energy, Mr Jobert. What do you think of oil tankers and LNG carriers?'

'I'd say forget about tankers for the next five years at least, until demand starts to catch up with supply. LNG carriers I don't know much about, but if they're trading out of the Middle East, I'd say be careful. They're floating bombs for a start. Second, even though they weren't affected by the last oil embargo, they might be by the next.'

'And if the LNG carriers are on fixed-term charters to major oil companies, would that affect your thinking?'

'Not really. It's a fixed rate of return, not very high, and if there were a war, the oil companies might be able to suspend the charter. Now let me ask you a question, Mr Yussaini. Why are you so interested in LNG carriers? Has someone tried to get you to finance one?'

'Mr Jobert, people are always asking me to finance projects: ships, hotels, banks, newspapers, magazines, real-estate development and even, if you will believe it, a computer to be manufactured in Egypt.' He laughed uproariously, and wiped his eyes with a fine lawn handkerchief. 'Don't think I am being unkind to the Egyptians, Mr Jobert. All Arabs are my brothers. But that plan was – well, a little premature, don't you think?'

'Just a little, But who would have said ten years ago that the South Koreans and Taiwanese would be making high-technology electronics?'

'Yes, you do right to remind me of that. Perhaps we shall see an Egyptian computer yet. Now, if you will excuse me, we must be going. But we shall meet again, of that I am sure.'

He rose, and the two women followed him, still talking, this time about a hairdresser in Geneva. Their speculations about his sexual activities would have brought a blush to a lorry driver's cheek.

8

> The rule is, jam to-morrow and jam yesterday –
> but never jam to-day.
>
> *Lewis Carroll*

Henry Rusk waited five days for a letter from Hare, Dowd and Christie. On the sixth day, Jonathan Hare's secretary telephoned. She was sorry, he had been in the Middle East. Could Mr Rusk see him tomorrow morning? Henry looked at a blank page in his diary; better not be too eager, though.

'Tomorrow morning is kind of difficult. How about the afternoon?'

'Well, Mr Hare's afternoon is very full, sir, but I know he does want to see you. Shall we say 4.30?'

Henry's impatience to meet Hare, and through him Yussaini, was not soothed by a story in that morning's *Financial Times*. A group of Arab investors, headed by Yussaini, had agreed to buy thirty per cent of the shares in a German engineering company, Eberhard, Bruder und Sohn. No price had been announced officially, said the paper, but it was believed to be about a hundred million marks – roughly forty million dollars at the current rate of exchange. All he had achieved, Henry reminded himself, was the purchase of an option on an ME 109 that he didn't want, and an appointment with a lawyer who might or might not lead him to Yussaini. Yet if he could pull off this financing deal, the waiting would be justified: he would get one per cent of the total, or $2·5 million. That would almost certainly win the Game for him.

The day dragged: more than twenty-four hours to wait until he saw Hare. For the first time in years, Henry felt lonely. He thought of going to the club, then rejected it. All those whining Brits would make him more depressed. Should he call Anne to see if she was free for lunch? Instinctively, he tried to put the thought from him. A whore, even one who was a nice trollop, was for the night, for bed, not for lunching in a public place.

Oh, to hell with it. She might be a whore, but she was amusing, good looking, discreet. He dialled her number. Her low, husky voice answered; yes, she was free for lunch, but had an audition in the afternoon. Yes, it was in the Soho area, and Wheeler's was a good idea. Henry phoned for a reservation, then went into the bedroom to find a tie, and looked at himself in the mirror. He saw, almost as though it were a stranger's, a fleshy, high-coloured face staring at him. 'All that good living is starting to show,' he muttered to himself, knotting a blue silk tie with white polka dots.

Outside, the day was sultry, and a few drops of rain fell on the parched lawns bordering Eaton Square. 'Heavy sort of day, innit, guv?' said the taxi driver.

'Yes,' said Henry. 'Bit depressing.'

'That's right, guv, depressing.'

By the time they reached Old Compton Street the rain was falling steadily, and there was an occasional blue-white sizzle of lightning. Henry went to the bar at the back of Wheeler's and grabbed the last table. In one corner he saw Francis Bacon, the painter, who had been pointed out to him during his last visit; in another Sir John Gielgud, the actor. The air was hot, the conversations loud, and Henry moved uneasily on the red plush banquette. Would anyone recognise him with Anne? It would be just his luck if Lord Boscastle walked in.

A few minutes after one, her hair shining with raindrops, Anne arrived, a slight colour in her pale cheeks. In his growing agitation, Henry had seen her as overdressed, flashy, instantly recognisable as a tart. Instead, she looked completely respectable, even prim, and he smiled both with pleasure and relief as she raised her cheek to be kissed. 'You know,' he said over the champagne, 'I've never heard your last name. How would I introduce you if one of my friends came in?'

Anne leaned close and whispered into his ear, 'As the best fuck in London?'

Henry felt himself blushing, and a tightness in his crotch. 'I'm not doing your advertising for you,' he whispered back.

They both laughed, and Anne said, 'Actually, it's one of the simplest and least appropriate of English names: Parsons.'

They both laughed immoderately at the joke, and Peter

Jones, the manager, looked at them benevolently as he handed them the menus. 'Let's hope you're still laughing when you see the bill,' he said, his round face crinkling with amusement.

Over lunch – they had Lobster Thermidor and the house Chablis – Henry found that Anne was both a good listener and a good talker. She said nothing profound or even original; but her summary of a play she had seen the night before, and of the homosexual leading man's difficulty in playing a lorry driver, was both perceptive and amusing. Over his Croft's vintage port (she refused any), he looked at her affectionately, remembering her as she had been the night they made love.

'What time's that audition of yours?'

'Half past three.'

'That's a pity.'

'It won't last long. I should be away by five at the latest. Are you thinking what I'm thinking?'

'Yes. Come to my place.'

'All right. Wait for me in bed.'

'Here's a key.'

Outside the restaurant he watched her slim back as she walked quickly through the dying rain. She seemed small and vulnerable, and he sighed. Then, catching sight of himself, tall and bulky, in a shop window, he gritted his teeth. 'You're a bloody fool,' he thought. 'Prostitutes with hearts of gold are schoolboy fantasies.' He bought an afternoon paper, with its predictable headlines telling of more violence in Northern Ireland, yet another threat to peace in the Middle East, and a bad day for the pound, then found a taxi and headed back to Eaton Square.

His secretary was typing in the study. Damn! He'd forgotten about her. He looked at her square, middle-aged face. 'Oh, Miss Jenkins, is that letter to Security Pacific National Bank ready yet?'

'Yes, Mr Rusk. It's just waiting for your signature.'

'Good, good. I hate to trouble you, but it's rather urgent; would you take it down to the bank by hand? Don't bother to come back, of course.'

'But I don't finish until five-thirty, Mr Rusk. It would be no trouble.'

'Please don't bother, Miss Jenkins. In this rain, you'll probably find it hard to get a taxi.'

'Well, that's very kind of you, Mr Rusk. I do appreciate it. And I have to do some shopping for my mother.'

Click. She'd gone. Henry looked at his watch: 4.30. Picking up a pile of documents, he went to the bedroom, undressed, put on a silk dressing-gown, and started to read. Five minutes later, he was asleep.

When he awakened the room was almost dark, and a hand was caressing his crotch. 'Hush,' said a voice. 'Lie still.' He lay back as a white body rose out of the bedclothes, then descended on him slowly and tantalisingly. In the half light he reached for Anne's breasts and squeezed her nipples. She moaned, started to move convulsively, then came to a rushed climax. For a few moments she relaxed, but then moved again, this time slowly and deliberately, until Henry spurted into her. Anne's low, husky voice startled him. 'Lovely, lovely, lovely,' it was saying. He drifted into sleep again. When he awakened, the last of the light had gone, and he switched on a bedside lamp. Anne was lying half-way down the bed, her left foot entangled in a sheet, her arms pulling a pillow round her head.

Gently, he slipped out of bed, put on his dressing-gown, and went to the bathroom. When he returned Anne was sitting up in bed smoking; light from the bathroom glinted in her right eye, turning it brilliant green. Henry sat on the edge of the bed and kissed her. Anne's lips were warm, her tongue teasing. He looked at the clock on the bedside table.

'Nine o'clock, Anne. Time to eat. Or are you going to Sixty-Four tonight?'

'No. Not after this. Can we eat here?'

'I guess not. A can of beans and a pot of yogurt is about all there is. Maybe some cheese. Plenty of wine.'

'No, I want to eat here. There's a late-night delicatessen not too far away. Let me go shopping.'

'I'll come with you.'

'No, you set the table.'

She dressed hurriedly, borrowed an umbrella and left. Henry heard a taxi stop, and from the living-room window watched her get in. He switched on the television. An unctuous voice was saying, '... and smart pets know the difference between Nutsies and the others. Remember, Nutsies are nibbly.' He walked back into the bedroom, sighed, straightened the twisted sheets, and went to the kitchen. No champagne in the fridge. He eased ice cubes out of the tray, and mixed a strong Scotch and water. In the living-room, a cowboy with an improbably red face was walking down a street of the Old West, his hands close to his pearl-handled revolvers in their holsters. Irritably, Henry switched channels. A voice said, 'Are you saying, then, that your committee will continue to occupy the college, even though the majority of students have condemned your actions?'

The camera switched to a hirsute person – Henry wasn't sure of the sex – dressed in a combat jacket. 'Yeah, that's just what we're saying. The rest of them have been brainwashed by the capitalist media.'

'And just what are your demands?'

'We're not saying until the authorities agree to meet us on a non-negotiable basis.'

'That doesn't sound very reasonable.'

'Reason is a bourgeois trick.'

As Henry switched off the television he heard the key in the front door, and Anne walked in with a big bag of groceries. A long French loaf stuck out.

'Any luck?'

'Pâté, steak, new potatoes, green peas, Camembert.'

'Sounds great. Let me help.'

'No, just pour me a Scotch. Like your steak medium or rare?'

'Rare.'

Henry finished setting the table, opened a bottle of Château Lynch Bages 1962, and sat in an armchair. The kitchen door opened, and Anne entered with a plate of pâté and hot toast. She was wearing only an apron and black stockings suspended from a garter-belt. Henry put his right arm round her waist, and with the other hand felt her left breast. The nipple was hard. She leaned down to kiss him, then freed herself gently.

'Don't you see the notice, sir? It says that customers are requested not to finger the help.'

When Henry awakened the next morning Anne had gone. His key weighed down a note to the bedside table. The note said: 'You paid for all night last time. So now we are all square. But be round again. Anne.'

He showered and shaved quickly, read the papers over coffee (most of them featured Yussaini: 'Arabia's mystery man', one called him), and by nine was on his way to the City for a desultory discussion about a small British conglomerate that was for sale. He lunched with a friend from university days who was now running the London branch of an American bank; for an hour they tried to recapture the old closeness, but failed. Henry was glad when he could decently get away.

Until his appointment with Hare, Henry killed time in the Naval & Military Club, known to its members as the In and Out, from the vast pillars on Piccadilly bearing those injunctions. Hare's office was just round the corner, in a high, red-brick building mellowed by age. The lift groaned slowly to the fourth floor, and Henry found himself in a tiny reception area dominated by a large switchboard.

Mr Hare was busy. Would he wait in the waiting-room? Henry was shown to a room so small that he wondered if Hare, Dowd and Christie specialised in dwarf customers. A girl brought him a cup of weak, lukewarm tea. At last, after he had read a 1968 copy of *Country Life* three times over, the receptionist took him to Hare. He sorted oddly with his miniscule offices, a tall, broad man with strong, prominent teeth and a hearty handshake. His phone rang constantly, and Hare waved apologies. Henry had the feeling he was just one glint in Hare's kaleidoscope. Suddenly, Hare hauled a gold watch out of his breast pocket, whistled, and said, 'We'll never get any peace here. Fancy a glass of champagne?' Without waiting for an answer, he opened the door, pushed Henry into the lift, and said to a man waiting by a car downstairs, 'Brown's.'

In the bar at Brown's, George the barman had a bottle of Dom Pérignon waiting. Hare tried a glass, grimaced, and said, 'Not bad, George, but not up to what His Excellency sends me.' George laughed; Henry didn't get the joke. Hare looked at him, his eyebrows twitching. Henry realised that the twitch was nervous. 'Very good,' said Hare, 'you're here for a while, you need some legal advice, and you've come to us. Very good. George, tell Jack to bring in those cigars, will you?'

'Yes, very good. Ah, there you are, Jack. Just pierce two, will you? Good fellow. Present from His Excellency. Now, what was I saying? Yes, legal advice. We'll do what we can, naturally. I can't promise to deal with everything myself – His Excellency takes up most of my time, but there are one or two bright young men in the firm.'

Henry could resist no longer. 'Who is His Excellency?'

Hare twitched again, and drew on his cigar. 'The Ambassador, of course. Now, where were we? Oh, yes, legal advice. No problem. Where's your letter? There was something else, wasn't there? Yes, you want to import a Messerschmitt 109. Yes. Have some more champagne? George! But you're not permanently resident here, are you? Shouldn't think you have to import it officially, but I'll get one of my chaps to find out.

'Strange hobby, collecting old aircraft. One of my clients does it. He's got dozens of them.' Hare lapsed into silence, and looked at his cigar, his face still twitching. 'How many have you got?

'Oh, just the one? Thinking of selling it? My client might be interested, might be. But it may be the 109E he wants – they're different, or so I'm told.'

'What's your client's name, Mr Hare?'

'Yussaini. You may have heard of him. Fingers in lots of pies. I'll tell him about this Messerschmitt of yours. Would you sell?'

'For the right price, Mr Hare.'

'And what would that be?'

'Not a penny less than $350,000.'

'Sounds a lot. Still, I'll tell Yussaini. Jack, Jack, where is that man? Ah, Jack, there you are. Pay George, will you.' Jack took a roll of bills from his pocket and peeled off two. Hare stood up, winked, and said, 'Well, I must be off to the opening of a new cocktail bar. Never pay for your own drinks, is my motto.' He strode away, Jack almost running to keep up with him.

Henry sat down with the remains of the champagne and saw

that he had chewed his cigar to a pulp. He was still baffled and bemused by Hare. All those obscure joking references, that twitch; his bantering but rather brutal treatment of Jack. Was Jack really a chauffeur? He went over to the bar, where George was polishing glasses. 'Tell me, George, is Jack Mr Hare's chauffeur?'

George looked up, amused. 'Well, he drives Mr Hare, but I wouldn't say he was a chauffeur, no.'

Henry shook his head and blinked several times. Were there subtle differences between British and American English that had escaped him all these years?

'Well, what would you say he was?'

'A gentleman who drives Mr Hare. That is, when Mr Hare isn't driving Sir John.'

'Sir John?'

'Yes, sir. Jack is a baronet.'

Henry left Brown's in a foul temper, feeling he had been the butt of a series of elaborate jokes perpetrated for obscure reasons. He had a lonely dinner at his club, and was in bed by 10.30. All night his sleep was disturbed by phantasmagoric dreams, in one of which Jack (or Sir John) was wearing eighteenth-century court dress while piloting the ME 109.

The next few days passed slowly and discouragingly. Convinced that Yussaini was a slender hope, and Hare a *poseur*, Henry did the rounds of London merchant banks with his LNG deal. At each he was met with exquisite politeness and a reluctant turndown. 'You see, Mr Rusk,' said one merchant banker, a cool young man with very large, very round blue eyes, 'the general view in the City is that tankers are likely to be a drug on the market for a long, long time.'

Patiently, Henry explained yet again that LNG carriers were not tankers, and that these were to be fully chartered to a consortium of major oil companies. The young man listened with a half-smile, then shook his head sadly. 'Of course, Mr Rusk. Of course. You and I know that LNG carriers are not oil tankers. But the board? They put them all in the same box. Silly, isn't it?'

Henry left feeling depressed and wondering how the British had ever managed to acquire and run an empire that once covered a quarter of the world's land surface. Perhaps the effort had been too much for them, and what he was seeing now was the burnt-out ember of a nation. His spirits lifted only slightly when he found a message at home asking him to call Hare. 'Very urgent,' Miss Jenkins had written, underlining the words three times.

He dialled Hare's number. 'He has somebody with him,' said the receptionist. 'But I'll see if he can take your call.'

There was a click, a long silence, and then Hare's voice. 'Can you pop round, old man? Yes, right away. Good, good.' Click. Cursing to himself, Henry picked out an envelope of photographs of the ME 109, which had arrived from California the week before, and took a taxi to Mayfair. A dark green Rolls-Royce limousine waited outside the office building, very conspicuous in a no-parking zone marked with double yellow lines. Upstairs, Hare was talking into the telephone while signing letters. His twitch, Henry noted, was worse than ever. He waved Henry to a chair, went on talking, finished signing the letters, slapped his secretary's rump, winked, then sprang to his feet. 'Right, Jean, we're just off. Come along.' He rushed out of the room, followed by Henry, who collided with Jack in the narrow corridor. Ignoring the lift, Hare plunged down the stairs, into the street, and towards the Rolls-Royce. He opened the rear door and threw himself down heavily on the cushioned seat. Henry followed, and Jack got behind the wheel. With hardly a sound the car moved off, and Henry glanced at Hare. His eyes were closed, and he seemed to be asleep. As the Rolls stopped at a light, Jack turned, put his finger to his lips, then pointed at Hare.

The Rolls wound through the rush-hour traffic at Hyde Park Corner, through Belgrave Square, and towards the river. Henry wondered where they were going, and to whom. Yussaini, probably; but with Hare anything was possible. He looked out at the streets. They were becoming dingy and mean. Still Hare slept. Now the car went over a bridge, turned right and followed the river upstream. Hare groaned, opened his eyes, rubbed them, blinked twice, and said, 'Still there? Good. Tell me, what do you think of the car? I'm thinking of buying it.'

'You can't go far wrong with a Rolls, I guess.'

Hare leaned forward, opened a door made of highly polished walnut, and took a bottle of champagne out of the tiny refrigerator. 'Imperial pints,' he said. 'I always find half bottles too small and full bottles too large at this time of day.' He laughed, opened the bottle with a practised twist of his wrist, and poured two glasses. 'Cheers.' Hare fiddled with a button, and the glass partition between the driver and the passengers' compartment descended. 'Jack, old man, how do you like the car?'

'It's one of their better ones.'

'Righty-ho, get His Excellency on the line, will you?'

Jack picked up a telephone, asked for a number, and a few seconds later said, 'H.E.? Jack here. Yes, we like the car. Yes, twenty-five thousand. Thank you, H.E.' He put the phone down and said, 'H.E. says that I can keep any change out of twenty-five.'

Hare laughed. 'I forgot to tell you. They phoned this afternoon to say they'd take twenty-two. Right, Jack, two for you and one for me.' He turned to Henry. 'That's what I like about buying cars for H.E. He never quibbles over the price and he very seldom uses a car. How many has he got now in England? Ten, fifteen? But I've steered him away from Cadillacs. Can't stand the things myself, and what I can't stand he's not allowed to like.'

Henry cleared his throat. 'Tell me, where are we going?'

'Good God, didn't I tell you? We're going to see Yussaini.'

'But where? And where are we now?'

'Jack, where are we?'

'Just getting into Roehampton.'

'Ah, almost there.'

A few minutes later, the car turned off the road into a drive, and Henry saw a small, gleaming white Georgian house surrounded by brilliant green lawns. Hare opened the door almost before the car stopped and jumped out, his heels crunching the gravel. A dark-skinned butler led them into a light and airy drawing-room looking across the lawn to the river. At the bottom of the lawn, a long, low pinnace was rocking gently in a private dock.

A smiling man of middle height stood in front of the Adam fireplace, both hands outstretched. 'Jonathan, it is good to see you. How is Emma?'

'Fighting fit, fighting fit. And Jehann?'

'I just spoke to her on the telephone. She is in Paris.'

Yussaini went over to Jack, shook his hand, then said to Henry, 'And you, of course, are Mr Rusk. Please, let us sit down.' He said something in Arabic, and the butler snapped his fingers. Another dark-skinned servant moved forward with a magnum of champagne in an ice bucket. A third servant handed round a tray of caviare. Yussaini raised his glass: 'Welcome to my house, Mr Rusk, and forgive me for bringing you out all this way from London. But I prefer to discuss business in my own home; it is a little idiosyncrasy in which my friends and associates indulge me. Tell me, you are now living in London?'

'For a while. My real base is New York.'

'That I know, Mr Rusk. Your name is not entirely strange to me, and I am not confusing you with the former Secretary of State, Mr Dean Rusk. You are related to him?'

'Not so far as I know.'

Yussaini raised his right index finger, and a servant poured more champagne. 'You know, Mr Rusk, I am often struck by this being a world of coincidences. Have you ever observed how certain numbers will repeat themselves in your life? I give you an example. By your calendar, I was born on the twenty-second of October. That is 22.10, if we use the British way of expressing the day and month. My telephone number here – and I did not request it – is also 2210. In Beirut, where I had an office until the war, my number was 1022. And if you look outside you will see the number plate of the excellent Rolls-Royce. It is 2044 – which is 1022 doubled, or 2210 doubled and reversed. Finally, you may be amused or even perplexed to know that my passport number is 7335 – which is 2210 multiplied by three and a half.

'I am reminded of all this by a coincidence of name. Just a little while ago, in Geneva, I met a man who, like you, bears the name of a former Foreign Secretary, Michel Jobert. Do you know him by any chance, Mr Rusk?'

Henry's heart bumped. 'Why, yes, I do, though not very well. How did you meet him?'

'We were guests at the same party, Mr Rusk. And it may amuse you to know that our host's telephone number is 37.57.00 – or 2210 multiplied by 170. Do you think such coincidences are random, Mr Rusk, or is there a pattern with a meaning we cannot perceive?'

'I guess I'd say random. But while you've been talking, I've just seen a set of numerical coincidences in my own life. I was divorced on the tenth September – which is 10.9 by the British method. And what is 10.9? Also 109 – which is the model number of the aircraft you want to discuss.'

Yussaini laughed and clapped his hands. 'Excellent, Mr Rusk. Excellent. What the pattern means, I do not know, but it makes me feel we are threads in a design that is being woven by a power greater than the human. But now let us talk about more immediate matters. You have photographs of the 109, certificate of airworthiness, and so on?'

He took the envelope from Henry, and looked approvingly at the photographs. 'Yes, the ME 109 is a beautiful aircraft. I have already, you know, a Spitfire and Hurricane, and even a Stuka, the German dive-bomber. Yes, she seems to be in very good order. Jonathan Hare tells me you want $350,000 for her. That seems high to me, frankly. What would you take? Give me your rock-bottom figure; although an Arab, I dislike haggling as though we were in a *souk*.'

'Well, I guess I'd take $300,000 for a quick cash sale.'

'So it shall be. My agent will inspect her, and if what he reports is satisfactory the sale will go through within two weeks. Jonathan, please draw up a fourteen-day option for me, with ten per cent deposit. Use the Number Three account, please.'

Yussaini rose, smiling, and put out his hand. 'We have done good business together, I think. Now, if you are not already committed elsewhere, may I suggest dinner here. When in England, I like to do as the English do, and I have had my chef trained to cook the English way. No, do not look alarmed. There is good English cooking as well as bad, and my chef is excellent. A Nubian, you know, like all the rest; a wild people, but they make superb servants, even though Idi Amin is one of them. Perhaps he needs a master. My family has had Nubian servants for centuries. Of course, not so long ago they were slaves. Indeed, the father of my butler was owned by my grandfather. Do not look shocked, Mr Rusk. Slavery ended in your country only three generations ago, or just a little more. And I am sure you have read your history. We Arabs sold you your slaves, but being a selfish people we kept the best for ourselves: the Nubians. Shall we dine?'

Yussaini led the way to a small but pretty dining-room, its *eau-de-nil* walls bright in the rays of the declining sun. A Sheraton table was set, and decanters of wine waited on the sideboard. Jack was dining with them, Henry saw. He had said little so far, but his voice was cultured and his manner now hardly that of a chauffeur. Hare had also been quiet, gazing into space, twitching occasionally, and apparently making a mental inventory of the furniture and paintings. These included, Henry saw, two indubitable Munnings and a Constable, as well as what might be a Turner. Making his own inventory, he estimated that the two rooms he had seen so far held furniture, *objets d'art* and paintings worth over a million dollars. The room was restful, and Henry felt he had been transported back into a Jane Austen novel. Even Yussaini, slim and handsome, could have been an Austen hero who had caught the sun, and Henry recalled that in the England of that period some fashionable houses had an African servant or two.

The food was superb, as Yussaini had promised: poached Scotch salmon with mousseline sauce, followed by roast rack of lamb accompanied by boiled new potatoes and green peas, with Stilton cheese to end. The white wine was dry and light, with an unusual tang, and Henry could not identify it. 'The first fruits of a little venture of mine,' said Yussaini. 'I have bought an English vineyard. Yes, England produced good wines in the Middle Ages, and now it is producing them again. No reds, I'm afraid; the soil and the climate are not right. So the red comes from another little venture of mine, in Bordeaux. I do not speak of it much. You know how the French are, very jealous of their land and of their vineyards. Jonathan Hare was kind enough to find the château for me, and make me almost a neighbour of the Baron Philippe de Rothschild. That amuses me, to think of the Arab and the Jew both producing fine wines in France.'

'I've often thought of buying into a vineyard myself, Mr Yussaini. But tell me, if it isn't a delicate subject, isn't it a little difficult for you, as a Muslim, to be in the drinks business?'

Yussaini threw back his head and laughed. 'We are not American Puritans, Mr Rusk. Have some port: it is rather rare. I have bought a stock from a Portuguese producer who is in much trouble because of the sad events in his poor country.'

Henry smelled the bouquet; it was rare indeed. For the first time that evening he felt relaxed, and was content to listen as Yussaini, Hare and Jack talked of mutual friends, of a race meeting to which they were all going, and of a yacht that an Arab businessman was buying. 'His taste is grotesque,' said Yussaini. 'If I didn't know who he was I would swear he was a self-made Jewish millionaire, probably in the textiles business.'

There was a silence, and Yussaini looked at Henry. 'You know, Mr Rusk, I have been thinking of our conversation about coincidence. It strikes me that it is a remarkable coincidence that you should be sitting in this room now.

'Consider. You come to London, you write to Jonathan Hare saying you need occasional legal services, and you mention that one of them is the importation of an ME 109. Just by coincidence, I happen to be another client of Mr Hare, and to be a collector of Second World War aircraft. Coincidence, Mr Rusk: the workings of an inscrutable fate? Or is it possible that human agency took a hand – nudged the machinery of fate, perhaps? And if that is so, what was the purpose?' He paused and took a sip of port after looking appreciatively at its rich colour.

'I am speculating, you understand,' he went on. 'But I doubt whether the sole purpose was to sell the aircraft for a profit. You are a rich man, Mr Rusk, and, in any case, I am not the only potential purchaser of the ME 109. No, I am inclined to think, Mr Rusk, that, in the English phrase, the aircraft was the sprat to catch the mackerel.'

Henry looked round the room. Hare was gazing intently at the ash on his cigar. Yussaini was pouring himself another port. Jack's head was turned away. Henry cleared his throat, but before he could speak heard Jack say, slowly and thoughtfully, 'Yes, Mr Rusk. A sprat to catch a mackerel. And it's as well to remember that the mackerel has similar feeding habits to the shark.'

For a few moments there was silence. Henry could hear the clock ticking on the mantelpiece, the crackle of an outboard motor on the river, a muted roaring in his own ears. When he spoke he was surprised by the steadiness of his voice.

'I'm not quite sure I take your point, Jack.'

There was another silence. Yussaini looked on the little scene with a slight smile, his eyes fixed on something behind Henry. Hare lit a cigar, his compulsive twitch temporarily absent. He spoke.

'I think you do, Mr Rusk. Mr Yussaini is fascinated by coincidence. You may not know, but he has endowed a chair at the American University in Beirut to take further Jung's theory of synchronicity. But, as he said, there are coincidences and coincidences.' It was the first time Henry had heard Hare speak three really coherent sentences. He looked at Yussaini, drew a deep breath, moistened his lips with his tongue.

'Very well, I'll level with you. I'm trying to finance an LNG carrier deal. I've got the documents with me. It's not easy: most banks think of LNG carriers as oil tankers, believe it or not, and because they've burnt their fingers on tankers won't hear one out. I know the problems: I'm a banker myself. OK, so I heard from a London merchant bank that you, Mr Yussaini, and some of your associates could easily finance this deal.

'But I also heard you were hard to reach, for which I don't blame you. So I did my homework. And what did I find? That you were looking for an ME 109. You know the rest. But at least we're talking.'

Yussaini laughed gently. 'I applaud your frankness, Mr Rusk. I really do. Your scheme was ingenious. Tell me more about the LNG carriers.'

Rusk outlined the deal swiftly, the figures clicking into place easily, the terms of the charter stated precisely. He felt powerful, back in control. For five minutes he held the floor, then judged his time was up. He summarised: 'So you can see, there's no risk. The charters have already been signed, the charterers are major corporations, and the ships will benefit your part of the world, the Gulf.'

Yussaini said nothing, but beckoned a waiting servant, who refilled glasses. Again, Henry was conscious of the silence and the tiny sounds that punctuated it. Then Yussaini spoke, patiently, as if to a child.

'A very good presentation, Mr Rusk. What you overlook, what you could not have known, is that this proposition came to me some time ago. I did not turn it down. I said I would think about it, and tonight you have given me fresh reason to think again.

'Frankly, I do not think the interest rate very generous. Nor am I very impressed by the fact that JZ International is offering its guarantee, in addition to the mortgage on the vessels themselves.

'As I turn the proposition around in my mind I come to a different idea. Why do my associates and I not contemplate buying JZ?'

'Do you know what its net worth is?'

'Very well. About $1·5 billion. What I suggest is that you go back to JZ and ask whether, in principle, the directors would be willing to recommend a bid to the shareholders. Do not mention my name, Mr Rusk. That would drive the price up immediately. Report back to me through Mr Hare: he always knows where I am.'

'And my fees, Mr Yussaini?'

'Shall we say one half of one per cent? That would be about $7·5 million – generous, I think.' Henry nodded. Yussaini added: 'There would be certain expenses, of course.'

'What expenses?'

'The main item would be one million dollars for Mr Hare.'

'A million? But is it legal for a British lawyer to take a commission?'

'Perhaps not in this country, Mr Rusk. But Mr Hare's firm has a branch in my country, and there such payment is not only legal: it is also a custom of the country.'

Jack drove Hare and Henry back to London. As Henry got out in Eaton Square Jack said, 'Don't forget, chum: a million off the top.' Hare said nothing. He was asleep again.

Henry slept badly that night, disturbed by vague dreams he could not remember afterwards, and awakened to find his sheets wrinkled and his pillow wet with sweat. He spent the morning on routine telephone calls and correspondence, lunched at home, and as he finished his cheese glanced irritably at his watch. Two o'clock in London: nine in the morning in New York. He dialled, was connected with JZ, was put through quickly to Frank Blaistow, the chairman, and explained the proposition. As he did so it sounded fantastic. Blaistow reacted as he had expected: dubiously.

'For Christ's sake, Henry, why should we sell out? We're doing fine. You seen our quarterly report? Per-share earnings up 8·2 per cent.'

'I know, Frank, I know. But this LNG deal is hard to swing. You know how the banks are: they're shit-scared of anything to do with ships at the moment, particularly ships that carry oil or gas.'

'They're crazy.'

'Maybe they are, Frank. But if the hands that sign the cheques are controlled by crazy people, where else do we go? And what happens if you don't get the financing? Cancellation fees to the shipbuilders, bad relations with the charterers. Frank, think about it at least.'

'OK, I will. But who are these Arabs? Are they for real?'

'I can't tell you who they are, not at the moment. But take it from me: they're smart, they're respectable, and they're for real.'

'OK, OK, so they're for real. But what will the regulatory agencies say?'

'You don't have to worry about a thing, Frank. JZ is incorporated in the Netherlands Antilles, right?'

'Right. But don't forget we're quoted on the New York Stock Exchange.'

'So what can Washington do? None of your ships is registered in the US, right?'

'Right.'

'So think about it and call me back, Frank?'

'Will do.'

Henry was sweating when he put the phone down. For the rest of the afternoon he killed time, waiting for Frank's call. Somehow, he was sure it would come through that day. At ten o'clock the phone rang.

'Henry? Frank here. OK, I'll tell you what we'll do. Our shares are selling for ten times earnings. We'll recommend a bid for fourteen times earnings. That comes to $1·6 billion, or thereabouts. And that's rock bottom.'

'Real rock bottom?'

Frank chuckled. 'Well, there's always a little scree on the rock, isn't there?'

Henry put the phone down with a smile. Yussaini and Frank were not too far apart. He dialled Hare's number. For once, Hare was free to talk, took down the figures, said he would speak to Yussaini.

9

> All men are ready to invest their money
> But most expect dividends.
>
> *T. S. Eliot*

Jacqueline looked at the men gathered on Jaime's terrace who were talking with her as though this were just a social evening. They ranged in age, she noted, from a stocky young man in his late twenties to a white-haired, elderly man whom she guessed to be pushing seventy, from one side or the other. For a few minutes they talked inconsequentially of the New York summer (appalling, they all agreed), of Formentor ('a jewel still pristine,' said the white-haired man), and of a summit meeting of world leaders the week before ('another exercise in polite futility,' said Jaime). Then there was a rustle of skirts behind her, and Jacqueline turned to see that Inés had arrived with four other women. All were elegant, shining; beside them, Jacqueline felt too tall, almost gawky.

There was a burst of conversation in Spanish, and Jacqueline felt a hand take her elbow gently. Jaime steered her out of the group to a lamp burning on the terrace's edge. 'Here,' he said, handing her an envelope, 'I know how confusing it is to meet so many people all at once. This is a list of our guests. It will give you some idea of them.' She opened the envelope. Inside was a sheet of paper, typed in double spacing.

'José-Antonio Aguila Ortrán,' she read, 'banker, industrialist. President, Grupos Industriales, Bilbao, Banco Aguila, Madrid. Born 1909.

'Francisco Antuñes Roca, president, Carrocerías Antuñes, S.A., Valencia; member of the board, Urbanización Santa María, Islas Canarias, and Urbanización Bahía Plácida, Islas Baleares. Born 1950.

'Emilio Alhorga y Martínez (Duke of Irún), chairman, Fuerzas Eléctricas de Vizcaya y del Norte; chairman, Cervezas Valldemosas, S.A.; board member, Cementos y

Cristalería de España. Born 1928.

'Roberto Sánchez Gómez, chairman, Compañía Bilbaína del Zinc, S.A.; board member, Inversiones Electronicas, S.A., and Construcciones Auxiliares del Norte, S.A. Born 1930.'

Jacqueline looked up from the paper to see Jaime's eyes shining down on her. 'Naturally, I should have given this to you before,' he said. 'The plain fact is, I forgot.' He laughed, his teeth shining in the lamplight and the rising moon. Jacqueline laughed, too, but did not believe him. When Jaime did something, or failed to do something, she had decided, it was for a reason. 'Now,' he said, 'let us return to the others. It is almost time for dinner, a little early by Spanish standards, but we defer to the habits of our North American visitor.'

As she sat down in the dining-room, Jacqueline saw that it was almost ten o'clock. She sat at Jaime's right, his wife at his left. At Jacqueline's right was the youngest man in the party – Francisco Antuñes Roca, if she remembered correctly. Looking around the table, she found it hard to realise that these men collectively commanded funds of close to half a billion dollars. They seemed small-time, almost provincial, with the exception of Jaime, who would have stood out anywhere as a cosmopolitan. Even so, his conversation that afternoon now seemed grotesque, fanciful, and she wondered again if he were merely talking big. For some minutes the conversation was dull, commonplace. Yes, the weather was marvellous; no, she had not been to Mallorca before; yes, she was living in Paris and liked it; no, she had never lived in France before, but spoke French – not well, but adequately.

Then Francisco Antuñes turned to her, his rather plump face anxious. 'Did Jaime explain our little plan to you this afternoon?'

'Some of it, yes. Sounds exciting.'

'You really think so, Miss Eden?'

'He made a lot of sense.'

'Oh, Jaime always does that. He is persuasive, don't you think?'

'I guess you could say that. But what do you think, Señor Antuñes?'

'Please, if we are to be colleagues, call me Francisco – or, even better, Frankie. All my friends do.'

'All right, Frankie. But I still want to know what you think.'

'I think he has conceived a great idea. It could be the salvation of Spain five, ten, fifteen years from now. You don't know our Communists. Like all Spaniards, they are people of strong passions; they do not understand compromise. They will ruin this country, of that I am certain. Then the people will be ready for democracy again. And my friends and I – we shall have the capital to provide the economic base.'

'And to be in charge,' said Jacqueline.

'Jacqueline, somebody must always be in charge of a democracy. That is not cynical. That is realistic. In America, you have your Supreme Court, which guards the Constitution like the Holy Grail. In England, they have a monarchy.'

'You have a monarchy here, too, Frankie.'

'Oh yes, and what a poor, uncertain thing it is! King Juan Carlos is on the throne because Franco put him there, and he is not – shall I say it? – the most intelligent of men. No, other guardians of democracy are needed, and we see ourselves in that role, unlikely though it may seem.'

Looking around the table, Jacqueline thought it was unlikely. Aguila Ortrán, the oldest of the group, had a strikingly strong face, but in his deep-set eyes and manner there was an autocratic impatience. The Duke of Irún, tall and fair, like so many Spanish grandees, looked a Bourbon, and probably was; Jacqueline recalled the old tag about the Bourbons, that they neither learned nor forgot anything. Roberto Sánchez, squat and short, had a ready smile, but a watchful look. As for Jaime – well, she still thought of him as a playboy who had found a cause, a dangerous combination of frivolity and seriousness. A servant refilled her glass – the wine was Marqués de Riscal, she noted automatically – and she heard a rhythmic ringing from her left. Jaime was rapping his glass with a fork to gain attention. The conversation died, and Jaime said, 'Gentlemen, you have all met Miss Eden – whom you may call Jacqueline if you wish. You have all read her dossier.' He turned to Jacqueline: 'Yes, I must apologise. My man in New York provided a very full and interesting dossier on you. Most of it was very complimentary, I must say.

'So, gentlemen, you know who she is and why she is here, apart from providing us with the pleasure of her beauty and her company. You know my views; but if we are to ensure democracy in Spain we might as well be democratic ourselves. Jacqueline, these gentlemen will have some questions to ask you. Please answer them frankly. Gentlemen, the floor is yours.'

Jacqueline noticed that Jaime had not mentioned the other women at the table. They sat there, decorative and silent, apparently accustomed to being ignored during serious discussions.

The first question came: 'What are your views on IBM?'

'A little bearish over the next few years.'

'Why is that? Surely IBM has a technological and marketing lead over every other competitor?'

'Yes, but it's been very slow off the mark with mini-computers, and I think the market is splitting into one for very large computers, in which IBM is relatively weak, and mini-computers, where it is weak. The mini-computers have some built-in computing capability, but they can also be hooked up to larger computers. I don't see IBM in trouble, but I do see it losing market share.'

'Miss Eden, what do you think of the prospects for the big American automobile companies – General Motors, Ford, Chrysler?'

'They're having problems, and they'll get worse. I don't see the market for cars declining much in numbers, but Detroit's profits have traditionally come from big cars with lots of options. I don't think they're geared up, technically or psychologically, to selling smaller, basic cars. And they're at a disadvantage when compared with their European and Japanese competitors. Of the three, I'd say Ford was the best bet: it's strongest in small cars outside America, and could import them. Look at the Fiesta. What has GM to match that? And Chrysler? It has the 180 in Europe, but not the productive capacity to supply America.'

'But what about Mr Henry Ford? He drinks, doesn't he?'

'Maybe. But so do most Detroit executives. He just gets more publicity.' Laughter. 'In any case, Henry Ford isn't Ford.'

'Miss Eden, Jacqueline, are you hopeful about the construction industry?'

'Yes, but not just yet. I'll tell you why I'm optimistic. There's a huge pent-up demand for new housing. Furthermore, there's a continuing flight from the city in many parts of the States. Add the two together, and you have the recipe for a boom. But not just yet, and not nationwide. I'm not too bullish on real-estate developers. I'd go for the big companies that make kitchen units, toilets. They have both the replacement market and the new equipment market.'

'Jacqueline' – this from the Duke – 'what are your ideas about the conglomerates? Gulf and Western, ITT, and so on?'

'I think they're an idea that had its time, which was the Sixties. ITT I'd deny is a conglomerate. It describes itself as a multi-market company. In fact, most of its profits come from telecommunications and electronics, which are related organically. Yes, I know what you're going to say: without the chairman, Harold Geneen, the company may lose its drive. But I don't believe it. He has a very good management team there, and ITT is bigger than he is. I'm moderately bullish on ITT over the long run – say, five to ten years.'

'The big American banks, Jacqueline. Citibank, Chase, Bank of America? Do you see them doing well?'

'Banking is not my subject, Señor Aguila. But, for what it's worth, here's my view. The big banks, particularly the New York banks, took some bad knocks in the early Seventies. Too many of their loans are soft or suspect – loans to their own real estate associates, to Third World countries. I'm particularly down on Chase; I don't think David Rockefeller is so much a banker as a front man for his family. The next generation of management, which is coming up fast, will take a harder look at loan policies. Growth will be slower, but it will be sounder. I wouldn't buy bank stocks now, except to go short; I would wait until the next big dip in the market, and try to pick up some bargains.'

Jacqueline felt sweat under her arms and between her breasts and legs. A lock of hair fell in her eyes; she swept it back impatiently. Jaime rapped his glass again for attention. 'Gentlemen, it's getting late, and we have asked our charming guest enough questions. Jacqueline, my dear, our thanks to you. Now, let us move to the terrace for coffee and, perhaps, a brandy.'

Outside, the air was still warm, and the moon shone brightly. Jacqueline walked to the edge of the terrace and looked down. A hundred feet below, the sea broke against jagged rocks, the surf phosphorescent in the moonlight. She felt a hand on her bare elbow, and shivered. 'You did very well, my dear. I think everyone was impressed. Now, may I suggest, a word or two with the ladies? They feel a little neglected, I fear.'

After the interrogation in the dining-room, the women were relaxing: glittering birds of paradise who chattered only about hairdressers, couturiers, children. They were dull, no doubt about that; but for a moment Jacqueline envied their cosseted, protected, vapid lives. She sighed, and leaned against the balustrade. Inés rushed to her side. 'Oh, my dear, these men are so thoughtless. You are tired! No, I insist; it is time for bed.'

The long day, the wine and the questions combined to make Jacqueline's limbs heavy. She reached her bedroom in a daze, threw off her dress, and collapsed on the bed. Within minutes she was asleep, her sleep disturbed by vague dreams. Early in the morning, as the dawn slanted through her bedroom window, she awakened. For a moment, she could not remember where she was. Then she remembered, sighed, and reached for a cigarette. The air was cool, and she pulled a blanket over herself. Slowly, her body warmed, and her right hand moved slowly towards the fork of her legs.

Slowly, slowly. Her fingers gripped her pubic hair, pulled; she felt herself moistening. With her middle finger she parted the hair, felt her clitoris, rubbed slowly. 'Coming, coming,' she breathed to herself. Her legs opened involuntarily, she inserted her index finger, and started to jerk convulsively. Within seconds, she had an orgasm, then another. A delicious languor crept up her legs, and she continued to massage her vulva, breathing deeply. Again! Again! Jacqueline's legs jerked convulsively once more, and her eyes stared glassily. After a few moments, she reached for her cigarette, which had burned low, took one puff, and walked towards the dressing-table. Legs splayed, she watched herself as her right hand moved in her vagina and her left hand pinched and squeezed first one nipple, then the other. Her legs jerked out straight, and she came again. For a few moments she sat slumped, her hair falling over her face, then went to the bathroom for her morning shower. She felt calm, rested; but afterwards, as she combed her hair at the dressing-table, and saw her face in the mirror, she wondered, guiltily, would I get the job if Jaime and the rest knew what I'd just done? Jacqueline knew little about Spanish men. She had always heard that they expected their wives to be virgins, and found their real pleasures with mistresses or prostitutes. No, she thought, I am not Spanish wife material – far from a virgin, and too keen on sexual enjoyment.

She rang the bell, ordered breakfast, and was downstairs by 8.30. The house was deserted, apart from maids dusting and polishing. Outside on the terrace a brisk wind blew the awnings; the air was cool, though with a hint of heat to come. Jacqueline leaned on the balustrade and looked down at the tiny private bay, with its boatdock and beach. She heard a light footfall behind her, and turned to see Jaime.

'Good morning, Jacqueline. You slept well, I trust? Yes, you look rested. What do you say to a little trip in the boat? The others will not be down for hours, I fear. Let me say, Jacqueline, you gave a very good impression. The assignment is yours, I am sure.'

He opened a gate in the balustrade, and moved quickly and certainly down steps cut in the rock. The boat, when Jacqueline reached it, was bigger than she had thought it the night before. Jaime pressed a button and the engine fired, sounding throaty and protesting in the early-morning air. He cast off a rope, and the prow turned towards the open sea. Soon the engine settled down to a purr that was almost drowned by the slap of waves against the hull. Spray started to break over the bow. 'Go into the cabin,' Jaime suggested. Jacqueline shook her head. She was enjoying the fresh air and salt water.

Jaime turned the wheel, and the boat started to ship water over the bow. Jacqueline's cotton shirt was soon soaked. Jaime looked concerned. 'My dear, you are wet through. Unfortunately, we have no oilskins aboard. But there might be a sweater below.' Jacqueline ducked into the cabin, opened a locker, and found a white sweater inside. Shivering, she unbuttoned her shirt and pulled the sweater over her head. As she did so, the engine slowed, and she found Jaime beside her. Without a word, he pulled her towards him, his tongue trying to find a way into her closed mouth. His hand moved under the sweater, up to her breast. Jacqueline felt herself being pushed firmly but gently to the daybed. A hand moved up her leg, under her skirt, into her panties. She moaned, tried to push Jaime away. His hand gripped the waist of her panties and, without thinking, she raised her hips. The panties slid off easily.

Phrases formed in her mind, formulas of rejection. She tried to say them, but Jaime's mouth covered hers. Suddenly, she felt him, hard and warm, moving gently but insistently against her. She opened her legs. He was inside her. For the next few minutes Jacqueline thought nothing, as Jaime moved with slow deliberation. Suddenly, with a shivering, shuddering cry, she came, clinging hard to his shoulders. Her eyes closed, and she passed into a satiated peace. When she opened her eyes, Jaime was looking at her intently. 'You know, Jacqueline, for a moment I was worried? You lost consciousness for a few seconds.'

Jacqueline lay back on the cushions, still dazed. Her mind formed a sentence, 'That was all wrong.' Her lips quivered; she could not say it. The boat's engine was still purring quietly, and a breeze blew through the cabin door. She shivered; she was naked, she realised, apart from her bra. She couldn't remember undressing, or being undressed. Jaime kissed her lips, moved his mouth down her neck, undid her bra, and sucked her nipples. His mouth moved downwards again, and she felt it sucking her clitoris. She moaned, moved her hips, moaned again, and screamed as Jaime's tongue sucked her. She opened her eyes, and for a moment could not tell where she was. Then she saw Jaime looking down at her. 'You know, my Jacqueline, you are a very passionate lover?' Jacqueline shook her head slowly. 'No, I mean it, Jacqueline. There is nothing to be ashamed about.' She rolled on her side, and buried her head in a pillow, feeling the tears start in her eyes. Jaime stroked her hair. 'Do not cry, my Jacqueline. You are wondering about my wife, are you not?' Jacqueline nodded. 'Well, there is no need to worry. Only last night, she said to me, "That Miss Eden is your type." She was right. She knows me well. We have a comfortable arrangement: I do not ask about her lovers, and she does not ask about mine. Is that not sensible?'

Jacqueline raised her head. 'Yes, sensible and horrible. Why marry if you are going to be unfaithful to each other?'

Jaime looked at her with a smile, laughed, and kissed her on the cheek. 'My little American, you are so wise about the stock market, so rational about everything. But you do not understand how we order things in Spain. In your country, a night at a motel is reason for a divorce. Here, we do not believe in divorce. The family is everything, everything. So we maintain the outward appearances. And who is to say that your system is superior to ours? Which is better, a system of morals that compels people to divorce for a passing passion, or one that recognises man and woman will err?'

'So I'm a passing passion?'

'Yes, my Jacqueline, a passion that will pass in three months, six months, a year. I do not wish to marry you, you do not wish to marry me. Is that not right?'

'I wouldn't marry you if you were the last man in the world.'

'But you will come to my bed, won't you? No, don't cry, don't look outraged. Try to face the truth for once.'

Jacqueline nodded slowly.

'So there, you see,' said Jaime, 'we have broken through your puritanical conventions to reach a kind of honesty. The honesty of the flesh.'

Jacqueline sat up, brushed her hair out of her face, and lit a cigarette. She looked at Jaime, liking but resenting what she saw. 'Just tell me one thing,' she said. 'This job. Do I get it because we made love? Or do I lose it because we did?'

Jaime laughed, took her cigarette, puffed it, and returned it. 'Let me answer obliquely. There is a certain maid in our house in Madrid. I deflowered her – that is the word, I think – when she was fifteen. She still works for us, even though she is married to a worthy young husband, a television repair man with his own shop. Do you think I would promote her because our flesh met? No. I would not. Nor would I fire her. Yes, the job is yours. And if our business discussions are continued in rather more intimate circumstances – well, that is an added pleasure, a bonus.'

'You're a bastard, Jaime. Lovable, but a bastard. Let me ask you another question. That worthy young TV repair man: did you set him up in his shop?'

'You are getting to know me, Jacqueline.'

10

> The Government are very fond of statistics. They add them and they multiply them and they subtract the square root and they make beautiful charts about them. But you must always remember that in the first instance they are dependent on the village watchman who just puts down what he damn well pleases.
>
> *Josiah Stamp*

As the days passed, Peter found himself warming to Brussels, which had seemed so drab and characterless when he first arrived. Each morning he would breakfast on the terrace of his flat, then walk for fifteen minutes in the Parc du Cinquantenaire; usually cadets from the military academy would be out for a run, watched curiously by elderly men and women who sat, gossiping, on benches. Peter would then pick up the day's papers at the neighbourhood news stand, go home, and browse through them over a cup of coffee.

By ten o'clock, he was on the phone to European commodities dealers, picking up information, sensing the trend in the markets, and making a few cautious deals, mostly in agricultural commodities – soybeans, grain, coffee, cocoa. On balance, he was guessing right, and winning steadily but modestly. Only once had he gone short, offering cocoa he did not have in the belief the market would drop. His losses could have been enormous if the market had risen strongly, and he had been forced to buy so as to honour his commitment. In fact, he guessed right, and cocoa fell, leaving him with a clear $35,000. But it had been a nail-biting time, and Peter vowed not to gamble so heavily again – unless he had inside information.

Presentación, the Spanish maid who had come with the flat, offered to cook lunch each day, but Peter preferred to explore. The tram that ran alongside the Parc du Cinquantenaire, then dipped into a tunnel to become a subway train, took him to the city centre within minutes, and he would wander round the market area before settling on a restaurant in one of the narrow streets. Alone but content, he would savour both the rich food and the conversation all around him; he still could not understand more than a few words of French, but usually could get the mood of what was being said.

In the afternoon, when it was morning in America, he would phone and telex the Chicago commodities market; sometimes a broker would phone him with a tip, and he would make a cautious play. In Europe and in the US he was making money, but not at a rate to give him any confidence he would win the Game. He had replied to Michel's taunting postcard with one of his own, showing a Brussels skyscraper: 'The sky's my limit,' he wrote. From Jacqueline he had a friendly but non-committal note, and from Henry a postcard showing the Changing of the Guard at Buckingham Palace.

After the electric bustle of New York, Brussels was mellow, relaxing, and Peter felt himself becoming lazy, less ambitious. He saw few people. Once, Benny Rabinowitz asked him to dinner, and Peter dutifully asked him back a week or two later, together with an ITT executive and his wife. Twice, he went to American Club luncheons at the Hilton, but found them curiously provincial, as though Brussels were merely an illusion, and he was attending a Rotary meeting in a Mid-West manufacturing town.

Four nights a week Ilse came to type, file, and keep his personal accounts in order. After that first night at the Charolais, when she had been friendly, almost affectionate, she had reverted to being polite but distant. She still used his first name, though as seldom as possible, and refused anything stronger than coffee. Twice, he had reminded her of her suggestion that a contact in the Commission would be useful; both times, she said merely that she was still looking.

One hot evening, when lightning scribbled across the sky and rain splatted on the terrace roof, he heard her key in the lock, and she came in shaking an umbrella. To his surprise, she was smiling widely. 'Peter, I think I have done it!'

'Done what?'

'You know – found somebody in the agriculture department.'

'Great, just great. Tell me more.'

'She is another German girl, and she has just been transferred there. She is the director-general's secretary. And, best of all, I know her very well; we come from the same part of Stuttgart.'

'How do I meet her?'

'I think you must give a party. Then I can ask her, saying you needed another girl to make up the numbers. Is that a good idea?'

'Couldn't I just meet her for lunch, or something?'

'No, Peter. I do not think that a good idea. We must be subtle.'

'Yeah, but there's one problem: I don't know anyone.'

'Well, there is your friend Mr Rabinowitz, and Mr Bradley from ITT. Then there is the vice-president of the Chase Manhattan Bank. Oh, if you think, Peter, you know enough people. And perhaps I could ask my boss and his wife. We can easily have a party for twenty people.'

Peter looked at her. She was glowing, her hair glistening from the rain. He laughed. 'Tell me something, Ilse. All these weeks you have been kinda distant – not like that night at the restaurant. What went wrong?'

'I was worried, Peter, that I was not keeping my promise. I thought you were annoyed with me.'

'For Christ's sake, Ilse, you didn't promise anything. You just said you'd help if you could. And now you have.'

'And now you can give me a drink to celebrate – a Scotch, please.'

Drinks in hand, they went out to the terrace. The rain had died away and the lightning had retreated to the distant horizon. Ilse leaned against the railing, her face a pale blur in the dusk. Suddenly, Peter leaned down and kissed her on the cheek. She turned her head and he kissed her on the lips, which parted slightly. He took her glass and put it on a table alongside his, then took her chin in his hand, raised her mouth, and kissed her again. Her arms went round his neck, and he felt her pressing against him, her legs trembling. Without a word, they went inside, and sat on the couch. He kissed her again, caressed her breast, moved his hand down, touched her knee, and started the slow, slow climb to her groin. Ilse stiffened, then relaxed, her breath rasping in his ear.

He felt her panties, hesitated, slipped his hand inside, touched her pubic hair. She was wet. Suddenly, she pushed his hand away. 'No, Peter, no. Please. You see – I am a virgin. Please don't be cross, please do not laugh.'

Peter sat up and looked at her. 'I'm not cross, Ilse. Disappointed, perhaps, but not cross. And why should I laugh?'

'Because I am twenty-seven, and what girl today is a virgin at twenty-seven?'

'Perhaps you have religious objections?'

'No, it is not that. I don't know what it is. I cannot talk about it, not yet.'

'But you wanted to make love just now, didn't you?'

'With my body, yes, but there was something in my mind stopping me, and I do not understand it.'

'Do you know what I suggest? Dinner. Le Charolais again?'

She nodded, smiled, and kissed him on the cheek. 'You are such a kind man, Peter. So many men would have said: "*Fort mit Schaden!*"'

'And what does that mean when it's at home?'

'Let it go; good riddance.'

'I would never say that, Ilse, believe me.'

'I do.'

The restaurant was quiet once again, and over dinner they planned their cocktail party for the following week. Ilse was warm, gay, confident, and over liqueurs Peter reached for her hand. 'Tell me, how do I say, "You're a darling", in German?'

'*Du bist meine Liebling.*'

'*Du bist meine Liebling.*'

She smiled. 'You're laughing at my pronunciation?' asked Peter.

'No. It is only that I did not give you the German for "a darling". I gave it for "my darling".'

'I'm glad you did.'

'And I am glad you are glad.'

One warm, sunny night a week later Ilse arrived half an

hour earlier than usual, and started to supervise the maid and her husband, who was to act as waiter. Cocktail snacks were laid on a table on the terrace, ice buckets waited for champagne. By calling on all the friends he had in Brussels, and on friends of friends, Peter had managed to invite thirty people; enough, he thought, to make a respectable showing.

The doorbell rang, and Peter heard Ilse speaking in German. She ushered in a tall girl with short, light brown hair. 'This is Traudl Knopf,' she said, with the air of a magician who has just performed a difficult trick.

'Good evening, Mr Acheson,' said Traudl. 'It is good of you to ask me.' Her English was even better than Ilse's, almost without accent, her eyes prominent and bold. No virgin, thought Peter, then was instantly ashamed.

'Come Traudl,' said Ilse, 'you must help me.' Traudl smiled at Peter, held his eyes briefly, then followed Ilse. Her walk reminded him of a phrase from Zola: 'She balanced her haunches.' He sighed, picked up a newspaper, put it down, and fidgeted while he waited for the next guest to arrive.

Everyone was late; but the first arrival was followed quickly by another, and within an hour all but two of the guests were there. Peter, who had dreaded the party, soon found himself enjoying it. Presentación, smart in black dress and starched apron, handed round the snacks; her husband, equally smart in white jacket and bow tie, turned out to be a proficient barman. Peter thought back to Marina Corley's maid, who didn't do any heavy work. Presentación, whether washing floors or acting as waitress at the end of a long day, seemed to enjoy heavy work, to thrive on it.

The talk was light, inconsequential. Nobody talked of money, sex and imminent municipal disaster, as they would have done in New York. Down in the park, voices still sounded in the gathering dusk, and Peter smiled wryly. Dick Bradley, the ITT executive, said, 'I guess I know what you're thinking. Those kids wouldn't be playing at this time of night in Central Park, or any park in any big American city. Right?'

'Right. How long you been here, Dick?'

'Three years in Brussels, two years in London before that. One of these days they'll order me back, and I dread the thought. I love America, but not the parts of America I'm likely to go to, and that's for sure.'

Ilse beckoned, and Peter excused himself. 'Peter, when are you going to talk to Traudl?'

'Well, it's kind of hard here. She seems to have quite a crowd round her.'

'Do you know what I thought, Peter? Why don't we ask her to have dinner at the Charolais after the others have gone?'

'Good idea.'

A few minutes later, Benny Rabinowitz and his wife apologised: babysitting problems, they said. Soon, the party started to break up, until only Peter, Ilse and Traudl remained. Presentación was working happily in the kitchen, clearing up the debris while her husband stacked the dishes. They waved cheerfully as Peter and the girls left.

During the short walk to the restaurant, Peter realised that Traudl had drunk enough to make her a potential problem. She stumbled several times, and her English was less fluent than it had been. Her laugh seemed louder, too. Fortunately, the restaurant was almost empty, and Willi sat them at a table far away from the other diners. Firmly, Peter ordered a bottle of dry white wine; another Scotch, he thought, and Traudl would either make a scene, or pass out. Strangely, the wine seemed to sober her, and after she had finished her first course, a hare pâté, she was in control of herself again.

For a few minutes they talked of the party, of Brussels, of Maurice Béjart's experimental ballet. Then Peter said, cautiously, 'I hear you've just changed your job.'

'Yes, now I am working for the director-general of the agricultural department. Such a boring man! He is the typical French *fonctionnaire*. But it is the most important department in the Commission.'

'How come?'

'Well, you know, the Common Market is supposed to be like your United States – no tariffs between the states, complete freedom of movement of goods, labour and capital. But it has not worked out that way, and about all it has achieved, if that is the word, is the agricultural policy. But I am sure you know all this; it is famous – no, it is notorious.'

'I guess I don't know too much. Please go on.'

Traudl swallowed some wine, lit a cigarette, and said, 'Well, it is very complicated. But, essentially, the agricultural policy is designed to ensure that the least efficient farmers do not suffer competition from the most efficient. And that means all farmers are protected from foreign competition.'

'So how come Europe imports American soybeans?'

'Because they cannot grow enough for themselves. You see, the agricultural policy produces shortages of some crops, and surpluses of others. You have heard of our butter mountain, our beef mountain, our lakes of milk and wine, surely?'

'Sure have.'

'Did you know we have sold butter to the Russians for less than it costs to produce, only to find the Russians have sold enough of it on the world market to make a profit – and keep hundreds of thousands of tons for themselves?'

'Sounds crazy.'

'It *is* crazy.'

'But what about soybeans?'

'Oh yes, soybeans. We have to import those from America to feed the cows and the bulls to create the milk lake, the butter mountain, the beef mountain.'

'You must be kidding.'

'No. I am telling you the literal truth.'

'But who pays for all this?'

'You should not have to ask: the taxpayer and consumer.'

'Any chance of a change in the policy?'

'There are always rows, always rumours. Why, we are preparing a recommendation now – but I should not talk of it.' Traudl smiled tipsily. 'But I will. We are recommending what you Americans call a crash programme to increase soybean production, and substitutes for soybeans.'

'So you can continue to produce surplus butter, milk and beef?'

'Exactly so.'

'And is the recommendation likely to be accepted by the governments?'

'I expect so. But please do not tell anyone – it is a secret.'

'Believe me, I shan't say a word.' That was one promise he could keep, Peter thought. If the word got out that European demand for soybeans would fall, the price would slip; before it did he would already have sold soybeans short, meaning he could make a profit by honouring his contract with a purchase below the price at which he had promised to deliver.

'What I wonder,' he said, 'is why the European Community doesn't reduce its dairy product and beef surpluses by cutting soybean imports. That makes sense, doesn't it?'

'Of course, it does,' said Traudl, drinking more wine. 'And until we increase our own soybean production, that is exactly what the Commission recommends.'

'Immediately?'

'Yes, at the next Agriculture Ministers' meeting.'

Peter was tense with frustration; he would have liked to know when the meeting was, but reflected it was probably a matter of public record.

Ilse cut in. 'Peter, all this is very dull. Who cares about soybeans, milk, butter. Let's have a liqueur!' She was, he thought, either fairly drunk, or moving the conversation skilfully past the point where his questions would arouse Traudl's suspicions.

Traudl nudged his knee under the table. 'Ilse wants to keep you for herself,' she said. 'But not just yet. I want a cognac.' She nudged Peter's knee again. 'You like German girls, don't you, Peter?'

He answered, as steadily as he could, 'I know only two German girls, you and Ilse. And I like you both.'

Traudl took a hearty swallow of her cognac. 'That is not an answer to my question.'

'What was your question?'

'I forget.'

There was a long silence. Ilse broke it. 'I am very tired, and it is very late. Can we go?'

Peter signalled for the bill, and said in stumbling French, '*Je voudrais un taxi, s'il vous plaît.*' Willi nodded gravely, and went to the telephone. Traudl was staring, glassy-eyed, at the daffodil-yellow tablecloth. Ilse reached for Peter's hand under the table, found it, squeezed, and smiled.

Traudl raised her head: 'I know, you are afraid I will be the raspberry.'

'Gooseberry,' said Peter, automatically.

'Gooseberry, gooseberry? What is that?'

'*Die Stachelbeere,*' said Ilse.

'A horrid fruit,' said Traudl, starting to cry. 'It is bitter, sour. You have insulted me.' Peter started to speak, but Ilse interrupted. She spoke in German, and slowly Traudl's face started to clear. Traudl leaned towards Peter, took his hand, looked into his eyes and said, 'I am sorry. You are a nice man. What Ilse has told me has changed my mind.' Peter, feeling his drinks, could only smile. At that moment, Willi announced that the taxi was waiting. Traudl suddenly regained sobriety, stood up steadily, and walked to the street with only a hint of a stagger. She got in the taxi first, and Peter kissed Ilse as she stood on the sidewalk.

'Tell me, what did you tell Traudl to change her mind?'

'That you are always good to me. Good night, dear Peter.'

He walked back to the flat, weaving slightly, and headed straight for his bedroom, but not before noticing that Presentación and her husband had erased all traces of the party. His last words before he went to sleep were slurred and muttered. But they had something to do with heavy work.

11

> To dear-bought wisdom give the credit due,
> And think for once a woman tells you true
> *Alexander Pope*

Michel drove out of the gates of his rented house and turned his new Citroën-Maserati's long nose towards Divonne. Thirteen kilometres to go. Could he better his own record of ten minutes? The low, powerful car rode the narrow, winding roads as though it were on rails, and within six minutes Michel was at the frontier. As usual, the guard just waved him through. Three minutes later Michel parked the car outside the casino, showed his passport to the receptionist, and after a barely noticeable nod from another man was allowed through. How many people knew, Michel wondered, that every casino in France had its staff of *physionomistes* – men with photographic memories whose job was to recognise an undesirable who had been banned and was trying to slip in under another name?

In the *grand salon*, with its predictable cast of discreetly rich men, superbly coiffed women, and envious hangers-on, the night's play had barely started. Michel was a gambler by nature, but this form of gambling he despised; the odds were firmly on the house's side, and he remembered a conversation years before with old François André, who ran the casinos at Deauville, Le Touquet, and elsewhere. André must have been eighty at the time, and seemed frail as he leaned on a stick. But his voice was firm, and his mind alert. 'Do you play?' he asked Michel. 'No, *monsieur*, but I have a mind to try.' The old man laughed harshly. 'Take my advice, and do not. You see this casino, you see my hotels, you see the staff. Do you know how we all live? From the gambler's eternal hope that he can beat the system. Once or twice he can, perhaps; but the odds are on our side. You have the look of a gambler. I think you could not play for small stakes, for fun. Either buy a casino; or find a form of gambling which allows you to even the odds, or perhaps get them on your side. I owe your father a favour or two. Tell him what I have said.'

Michel did not, but soon afterwards asked to be transferred to the foreign exchange department of Crédit Lyonnais. Now, as he looked at the faces in Divonne, some anxious, some desperate, a few masked in imperturbability, he thought of François André again, recalling vividly the parchment-thin skin, the alert eyes, the slight tremor in his blue-veined, mottled hands. Soon afterwards, André had died, and Michel sent a wreath to his funeral. The card read: 'From one who received and used good advice.'

At one table a tall, dark man was playing roulette. To everyone, he was simply 'the Iranian', and whenever he entered the casino a small crowd gathered round him, attracted by the legend of a man who won or lost millions of francs in an evening. Tonight, he was winning, and the chips stacked in front of him were worth 200,000 French francs – about $41,000, Michel calculated automatically. The Iranian placed a stack of thousand-franc chips on a square, the wheel turned, the croupier's metallic voice rang out, and his rake pushed another pile of chips at the Iranian, who threw one back. '*Merci infiniment, monsieur,*' said the croupier, dropping it into a slot in the table. Was it really true, Michel wondered, that croupiers had no pockets in their tuxedoes, to ensure they were not tempted to take a few illicit chips for themselves? Probably, he thought; France was still a Catholic country, by habit if not faith, and the injunction that one should avoid the occasions of sin retained its appeal.

He walked to the bar and looked around. Henk, chronically late for appointments, was still not there. Michel ordered a Scotch with Perrier and lit a Gauloise. Suddenly, unnervingly, he felt someone kiss his right cheek, turned and saw Anne-Marie. His heart skipped. 'Good God! What are you doing here?'

She laughed, and swept back her obtrusive hair with that characteristic gesture. 'That is simple. I telephoned your housekeeper, and she told me where to find you.'

'Yes, but what are you doing in Geneva, in Divonne?'

'That, too, is simple. I transferred from the UN in New York to the UN here. No, no, not because of you, *chéri*. You are just an additional attraction. I was tired of New York, tired of pretending I was in France.'

'But Geneva is not France.'

'Michel, you are contradicting yourself. Remember what you said in the Café des Sports that last night before you left? "Geneva is almost France – the frontier is a matter of minutes."'

Michel kissed her. 'Your memory is almost too good. What will you drink? A martini?'

Anne-Marie pouted. 'Martinis are for New York, for Americans. No, a whisky-soda.'

'That is not French.'

'No, but it is *très snob, n'est-ce pas?*'

The bartender, whose hearing seemed preternaturally good, was already placing a Scotch and soda in front of her. She clinked glasses with Michel. As she did so, Henk bustled up with his wife. Michel felt a twinge of irritation; this was supposed to be a business dinner. Then he relaxed. Perhaps he could persuade Anne-Marie and Carlotta to spend an hour at the tables, while he talked with Henk.

Anne-Marie and Carlotta made a striking contrast, he saw, one tall, the other short and tending towards plumpness. As for Henk, he was immaculate in a dark grey silk suit, dazzlingly white shirt and Gucci shoes. As he reached for his drink, his coat sleeve rose, to show Hermès cufflinks and a thin gold watch held to his wrist by a gold strap. The impression was sombre, but rich. Carlotta, beside him, was another study in how to display wealth without ostentation, her green chiffon dress obviously made for her, and complemented by an emerald necklace, earrings and ring.

Over dinner they talked lightly, inconsequentially, Henk switching easily from French to English, and English to Italian. Like the chameleon he was, he spoke to Anne-Marie in Bordeaux-accented French, to Michel in the rapid, clipped accents of a *pied noir*. Was Henk conscious of what he was doing? Michel thought not. Henk had prospered by being all things to all men. Probably, he thought, Henk would speak Italian with a Sicilian accent if he were with a Mafioso, and verbally at least become an Old Etonian if he were talking to an English aristocrat.

Dinner was over at last, the liqueurs were low in their glasses, and the mood was mellow. Michel roused himself. 'Anne-Marie, why don't you take Carlotta to the tables? Here, buy some chips and see if you are lucky.'

Anne-Marie looked, for a moment, as though she were about to argue, then smiled. 'I can take a hint,' she said in English. 'In any case, I need to go to the pipi-room.'

Michel watched them go, ordered another Calvados, and looked round. The nearby tables were deserted. In a corner, two waiters gossiped. Henk looked at him expectantly. 'A nice dinner, Michel. But it wasn't the purpose of the evening, was it?'

'No. I've been thinking about our last conversation, the one about getting inside information and acting on it quickly. We could wait a long time for that to work.'

'And you're in a hurry? Running out of money, Michel?'

'Thank God, no. But I've a reason for wanting to make a certain amount by a certain date. Let's say it might be better if we took a more active role. Tell me this: how do the foreign exchange markets get their information – the information that suggests the mark will rise, the pound fall, and so on?'

'You should know the answer better than I do, Michel. But I would say it's a mixture of market rumours, official statements, newspaper reports, the way currencies move.'

'You've left out one source, Henk: wire service reports.'

'Sure. But what's this all about? If you're all that interested in a wire service, you can always subscribe to AP-Dow Jones, UPI, Reuters, Agence France-Presse, even Tass, I guess.'

'I'm not so interested in what comes out of a wire service. I'm more interested in what goes in, and how.'

Henk leaned back in his chair and looked sombrely at Michel, his face laughing no longer. 'I think I can see what you're driving at, but – hell, you'd better tell me.'

Michel signalled for the bill, paid it, and said, 'How about a breath of fresh air?' Henk nodded, and they walked through the casino, where the Iranian was still playing, the stack of chips in front of him even bigger than it had been two hours earlier. Anne-Marie and Carlotta were at his table. Michel noticed that their piles of chips were in big denominations, and totalled far more than he had given Anne-Marie.

Outside, the air was still warm, and a half moon shone on the formal gardens. Two chauffeurs talked quietly, one leaning against a Rolls-Royce limousine with diplomatic plates; the Iranian's probably. Michel took a deep breath, lit another Gauloise, found himself hesitating. Henk, for once, was silent. Michel cleared his throat.

'Let me ask you something, Henk. Have you ever done anything dishonest – really dishonest, that is, something you could go to jail for?'

Henk laughed shortly. 'That's quite a question. I guess the answer has to be yes, once or twice.'

'Right, so we can take it that moral scruples don't worry you too much. If the odds are good, and the payoff is big enough, you'll take the risk?'

Henk stopped pacing and turned to look at Michel. His face was pale in the moonlight. He spoke slowly. 'You seem to have me taped, Michel. But there are things I'll draw the line at: violence and drugs, to name two.'

'But not violence by proxy, Henk?'

'What the fuck do you mean?'

'Well, Henk, you don't imagine those M-16 carbines you helped to ship to the Provisional IRA were going to be hung on the wall as souvenirs, did you?'

'I had no idea – wait. How the hell do you know about that?'

'You needed some money, and it came to you from a numbered account at Crédit Suisse in Lugano. I could quote you the number; it's my account.'

Henk swore in Dutch. It was the first time Michel had ever heard him use his own language. Then he was silent, and Michel looked at him coldly. 'Even if you didn't know the IRA were buying, you still didn't think the M-16s were just for show, did you? That's what I mean by violence by proxy.'

'OK, OK. You've made your point. Are you planning to rob a bank, is that it?'

'Yes, but in the nicest possible way. By telex. By using the banks' greed and *naïveté* against them. Do you want to know more?'

'I can guess the half of it, but go on. But remember that I'm just a listener. I'm not committed to anything.'

Swiftly, Michel unfolded his plans. Foreign exchange traders were, to a man, born gamblers, and forever dreamed of the hot, inside tip. If one could know half an hour before anyone else that a certain country's balance of payments was in heavy deficit, that the rate of inflation had risen or fallen, that its government was about to fall, he could clean up by placing buy or sell orders, according to whether the news was good or bad. Even if the news were public and official, announced either by a wire service or over the radio, traders could still hope to get an edge by being quicker off the mark than their fellows. Only seldom would they bother to check a report; if it came over a reputable wire service, particularly if the report was attributed to an official source, they accepted it without question.

Henk laughed, nodding his head. 'I thought that was it. You want me to get a buddy in Reuters, or some other agency, to tip me off before a story goes out, isn't that right?'

Michel took him by the elbow, leaned down, and said quietly into his ear, 'No, my Flying Dutchman. I want you to put the report on the wire at a prearranged time. Well before, I'll have either bought heavily, or gone short: it depends which story we put out.'

Henk snatched his arm away. 'You're crazy, Michel, quite crazy. You can't just walk up to a wire service editor and say, "Hi, old buddy, the French Communists have pulled a *coup d'état*. Put it on the wire." He'll check and re-check.'

'Yes, but what if *you* were the editor?'

'But I'm not, and not likely to be. Look, Michel, I'll tell you the truth. I've done pretty well in this town, but there are stories about me. I have enemies. If there's one thing the wire services pride themselves on, it's accuracy and impartiality. They don't think I'm that kind of journalist. Perhaps I'm not. No, that wouldn't work. Have you got any more half-baked ideas, or can we go back inside?'

'Henk, you're sweating up the wrong tree.'

'You mean barking.'

'Sweating and barking. My idea is quite different: you would be the writer and the editor, but the wire service wouldn't know it. Ever. You know what a wire-tap does: it extracts electrical impulses. We are going to be wire-tappers in reverse: we shall feed impulses into the wire service telex line. Listen...'

For several minutes the two men walked up and down the gardens. At last, Henk laughed, and grasped Michel's hand: 'I give it to you, partner. You may be a crazy genius, but you're still a genius. Robbery by electricity! Whoever heard of such a thing?'

'Don't be too euphoric, Henk. You still have to find an electronics expert who's good at his job and will keep his mouth shut. Your CIA contacts should help you.'

Henk leaned against a wall and laughed helplessly, his shoulders heaving and eyes watering. 'Oh, Michel, you don't say you believe that story, do you? I put it around myself: makes me into a man of mystery, acts like an aphrodisiac on the women. Talking of which, shouldn't we see what Anne-Marie and Carlotta are doing?'

Inside, the gambling was at its height, and the crowd at the Iranian's table was bigger than ever. His pile of chips seemed neither larger nor smaller, and his face was still impassive. He looked bored, perhaps was bored, moving as automatically as a worker on a production line. Anne-Marie and Carlotta were no longer there. The men found them in the bar, a half-empty bottle of Dom Pérignon on the table between them, their eyes feverish. '*Caro*,' said Carlotta, jumping up and hugging Henk. 'I won 10,000 francs, *ten thousand!* Look!' She waved a sheaf of bills at them, laughing happily and a little hysterically. 'Look! I took it in hundred-franc bills – it seems more.'

Anne-Marie pulled a packet of bills from her handbag. 'And I, *chéri*, made your thousand francs into 9,000. Is that not good?'

Henk and Michel looked at each and laughed. 'It's everyone's lucky night tonight,' said Henk, still laughing.

'Why, have you been winning too?' asked Anne-Marie.

'No,' said Michel. 'But we're going to, very soon.'

'How can you be so sure?'

'Because of something an old man named François André told me many years ago. It was very simple, very good advice: get the odds on your side.'

Later that night, Anne-Marie sat in Michel's bedroom,

looking out over the lake. She was wearing one of his pyjama tops, leaving her long legs bare, one of them tucked under her on the window-seat. Suddenly, she shivered.

'Cold, *chérie*?'

'Yes, perhaps. Michel, that man Henk: is he a friend of yours?'

'Not really. More of a business acquaintance.'

'I do not trust him, Michel. He is like quicksilver. You cannot pin him down. And have you noticed how he mimics everyone? He is like that little animal – what is it called? Chameleon?'

'I know what you mean. I, too, do not much care for him. But he can be useful.'

'I think he does not know what he is, or who he is.'

'*Der Mann ohne Eigenschaften?*'

'Michel, don't speak German. You know how I hate that barbaric language.'

'It's the name of a novel by Musil: the man without qualities. I think that's our friend Henk; a man with so many qualities, he has none.'

'Oh, let us stop talking about him. Let us make love instead.'

They came to an exploding, clashing climax that Michel felt sure could be heard by half the village. Afterwards, as they lay smoking, Anne-Marie kissed him gently on the cheek and whispered, 'I love you, Michel. No' – and she put a finger over his lips – 'do not answer. Just because I love you, you do not have to love me.'

Early in the morning, as the dawn touched the lake with rose and the mist swirled, Michel sat in an armchair smoking. He looked at Anne-Marie, her long hair spread over both pillows, her left breast above the sheet. Did he love her? When she had startled him at Divonne, his feelings had been mixed, a blend of pleasure and annoyance, tinged with fear that she had followed him blindly and possessively. Now, seeing her so peacefully asleep, he felt close to her, grateful, at ease. He looked at the clock: time to be moving soon. Then he remembered: it was Saturday. He crushed out his cigarette and went back to bed. Anne-Marie murmured in her sleep, and pressed against him, a half-smile on her full lips. Michel turned out the bedside light, kissed her forehead gently, and whispered, 'I love you, too.' Soon, he was asleep, and did not wake until the sun streamed through the window.

That day, he thought little about business, or his plans with Henk. For forty-eight hours at least, he was happy to relax with Anne-Marie, to show her the little towns along the lake shore, and to laze. For lunch, they went to the Auberge de Dully, seven kilometres north-east of Nyon, and sat full of food, sun and wine on the terrace overlooking the vineyards, sipping ice-cold *Poire Williams* and content to say little. Anne-Marie was quiet, reflective, withdrawn. Michel knew she had something on her mind, yet hesitated to ask her what it was. Afterwards, they walked, hand in hand, along the village street and out into the country, then back by a different route to the car, hot to the touch in the late afternoon sun.

As Michel started to turn the ignition key, Anne-Marie put her hand over his and leaned against him. 'Darling, do not drive away just yet. I have been thinking all day about what I said last night. It was weak of me, wrong of me. You have never pretended to love me. I think you like me, are fond of me; but love – no. Now, by coming to Geneva, by what I said last night, I may be spoiling everything.'

There was a question mark at the end of her sentence, and when Michel looked at her, the half-parted lips were trembling. He kissed them gently. 'You have spoiled nothing,' he said. 'You have improved things by being here. As for love – well, perhaps I am not ready yet. But if you came to live with me, then we would find out, wouldn't we?' He heard himself say it with surprise; he had not meant to, had not even thought of it. Anne-Marie said nothing, but kissed him. The answer was in her tear-wet eyes.

He drove slowly back to the house, and felt a pang of pleasure as he saw it, white and mellow in the sun, shaded by ancient trees and set in bright lawns. Perhaps, he thought, a home is what I want. His housekeeper handed him a message: please telephone Monsieur Vrijdel. He crumpled it savagely; the message was an intrusion from a world that had no place here. 'Please tell Monsieur Vrijdel, if he calls again, that I've gone away for the weekend, and won't be back before Monday morning.'

12

> The cruellest lies are often told in silence.
> *Robert Louis Stevenson*

Pressures of business have for many years prevented me from travelling as much as I would like, but Nancy and I seldom miss an annual visit to London. It is, beyond doubt, a city where a gentleman can still live in something approaching the elegance that my great-grandfather, William Kemble, must have enjoyed in Victorian times. To be sure, many of the old landmarks have disappeared, and parts of London are infested by the blue-jeaned, long-haired young people who have become an international tribe. Even so, it is possible to forget their existence in a fine old establishment like Brown's, my home-from-home since I was a boy.

Unfortunately, Nancy has strong ideas about hotels, and when we stayed there on our honeymoon complained the rooms were poky and the beds creaky. I had not noticed these defects myself, and said so; but now we stay at the Connaught, just off Grosvenor Square, another fine old establishment that still upholds the best of English traditions. Even Nancy cannot complain, particularly since the Connaught is much favoured by one of the Mellons with whom she has become friendly.

That did not prevent her from being somewhat excessively curious about the reasons for our trip, half way through 'the Game' that Miss Eden, and Messrs Jobert, Rusk and Acheson were playing – unwisely and against my advice, I must stress. 'Who are these people?' she demanded once more as we settled into our suite. 'Why are we jetting all over Europe to see them? And why are you so mysterious about the whole thing?'

I replied, as patiently as possible: 'Nancy, my dear, I have explained, not once, but several times, that they are clients who are, more or less, in business together. I am personally auditing their accounts. And they are, I may say, paying for part of this trip. I cannot quite understand your apparent objections. What could be more pleasant than visiting London, Paris, Geneva and Brussels?'

'It would be a damned sight more pleasant in the spring,' said Nancy. 'London is over-run with tourists. Paris is dead, except for Americans. Brussels and Geneva I know nothing about, and care less.'

She was still suffering from jet lag, of course, despite a one-day stop-over in Dublin, and I saw unaccustomed lines on her face. 'Let us go down to the bar and have a libation,' I said.

'If you mean a drink, you've made yourself a deal,' said Nancy. 'I'm damned if I know why you have to use fancy words like libation. Next thing, you'll be calling a cocktail shaker an alembic.' It takes a lot to destroy Nancy's sense of humour.

The wood-panelled bar was quiet and welcoming, and an extra-dry Bombay martini soon restored Nancy to her usual spirits. 'Where would you like to dine, my dear?' I asked. 'The food is excellent in the restaurant here.'

'How often do I have to tell you I can't stand hotel food? In any case, it's like a morgue. Think of somewhere better, for God's sake.'

'Rules, in Maiden Lane?'

'Another of your stuffy English places. Try again.'

Eventually, we settled on the Empress in Berkeley Street, comfortably close and far from stuffy. At first Nancy looked round dubiously, but then sat at the piano bar, where an excellent pianist and singer, Mike McKenzie, played several of her favourites. I should, perhaps, have realised that a combination of fatigue and several large drinks were having their effect on her. But I did not, and it was a very tired and somewhat helpless woman who returned to the Connaught later that night.

Next morning she opened one eye when breakfast arrived, then went back to sleep. I thought it prudent not to wake her, and left for my appointment with Rusk. His place in Eaton Square was quite splendid, and he himself looked trimmer and less flushed than when I had seen him last. 'Well, Henry,' I said as we shook hands, 'London seems to be agreeing with you.'

To my surprise, he looked downcast. 'Socially and personally it does,' he said, 'but business is damned slow. I've been working on this LNG financing night and day, but I just haven't pulled it off yet. When I do, of course, it's two and a half million for me. But if I don't – well, see for yourself.'

Under the rules of the Game, players' personal expenses were not deductible; but the direct cost of doing a deal was – for example, the cost of purchasing shares. Henry's accounts were simple, and I read them quickly:

Profit on sale of ME 109, less agent's commission	$45,000
Profit on forward purchase of sterling, net	18,000
Profit on sale of Rolls-Royce, net	3,800
Commission on placing of debentures for Woodcat Investments Inc, net	27,000
	$93,800
Add: interest on $250,000	10,670
	$104,470
Less: Loss on British Petroleum shares	6,298
Net profit	$98,172

I raised my eyebrows. 'There's nothing to be depressed about here, surely? You've got the supporting documents, I assume?'

Henry nodded, and passed over a folder. I put it in my document case, then looked at his accounting again. 'Forgive me, but I'm mildly curious. Have you gone into the aircraft and auto businesses?'

He flushed. 'Good God, no. The ME 109 was a sprat to catch a mackerel.'

'An extremely large sprat, I'd say. And the Rolls?'

Henry looked embarrassed. 'Well, you know there's a long waiting-list for the new Rolls Camargue? I just happened to hear that the people who own this place had one on order, then found they couldn't afford it. So I took it off them, and sold it on to a man who just had to have one.'

'Who was this impatient man?'

Henry avoided my eye, and mumbled, 'Well, that's the strange thing. I don't know his name. Everyone calls him H.E., and I guess he's an ambassador – probably an Arab one. I sold it to him through my lawyer's chauffeur – if he is a chauffeur.'

'Either he's a chauffeur or he isn't.'

'Well, it's kind of hard to explain.'

'I think you'd better, Henry. You know the rules: we must be certain that every deal is genuine, and though I'm casting no aspersions on you, the rules must apply to all players. What would I say if one of the others asked if this was merely a paper deal?'

Although it was far too early, Henry went to the liquor cabinet, in which was concealed a small refrigerator, and took out a bottle of Krug. After pouring two glasses, he told a confused, somewhat rambling story about a lawyer who was accompanied everywhere by a man who may or may not have been a chauffeur, was almost certainly a baronet, and was sometimes driven by his boss.

Either he was telling lies very badly, or I was hearing the phantasmagoric recollections of a drunken night on the town. I know, of course, that the class relations in Britain have become rather mixed and chaotic, this being the result of the politics of envy encouraged by the country's Socialists. After allowing for that, though, I still found Henry's story difficult to follow, and made a mental note to examine very carefully indeed the documents relating to the purported sale of the Rolls.

Henry sighed. 'I know it's hard to believe, but I'm telling the truth. And what about the others? You'll probably find they have some improbable stories to tell. How are they doing, by the way?'

He was elaborately casual as he asked the question, pouring me a glass of champagne I did not really want, and keeping his voice low. I looked at him severely.

'Henry, let me remind you of the rules. Until the final accounting, no player may know another's score. But the answer is that I haven't visited them yet, so I couldn't tell you if

I wanted to, or were empowered to. And, to put your mind at rest, I shall certainly give none of them the slightest clue, hint or inkling of your score.'

Henry nodded sadly, looked at his watch, and stood up. 'Time for lunch, I think, or at least to make a move.'

Eaton Square was gleaming in the sun, the long colonnades of pillars in front of the houses as straight and regular as a Guards regiment on ceremonial parade. Henry hailed a taxi, and we moved through the formal architecture of Belgravia to his club in Piccadilly. I have always liked London clubs; they are real, not the somewhat self-conscious imitations to be found in New York. In the bar, overlooking Green Park, Henry ordered a champagne for himself, and a Bombay martini for me – made very well, I must say, even though martinis are not an indigenous English drink.

I felt relaxed, happy to be in London again, which I often feel is more my natural home than New York is. Henry talked well and amusingly of London social life. He had been to Royal Ascot, even gone to the Royal Enclosure, thanks to a banking friend, and on August 12th – 'The Glorious Twelfth', as the British call it – had celebrated the start of the open season on grouse by shooting a hundred or so on a friend's Scottish estate. He had also seen a remarkable number of plays, although he had told me in New York that the theatre bored him. 'Perhaps a woman is changing your ways?' I said lightly. Henry's face reddened.

'I'm not leading a celibate life, if that's what you mean, Charles. But a lot of women have tried to change me, and a lot have failed. Come, let's have a glass of port in the smoking-room.'

Afterwards, walking back to the Connaught, I thought that Henry had been curiously devious. He had hedged when I asked him to explain how the ME 109 was, in his phrase, 'a sprat to catch a mackerel'; been unconvincing in his explanation of the Rolls-Royce sale; and as bashful as a schoolboy when I hinted, delicately, that there was a woman in his life. I hoped that Jacqueline Eden would be more forthcoming. In a curious way, though not much older than any of them, I felt *in loco parentis*.

Rain was sweeping over the flat countryside and suburban industrial buildings as our taxi took us from Charles de Gaulle airport to the centre of Paris. Nancy was quietly furious; like so many Paris taxi-drivers, this one had a notice in three languages forbidding smoking. I, too, was quiet. After the theatre last night, we had gone to the Savoy restaurant for dinner, stayed to watch the cabaret, and run into old J. J. Chetwynd and a lady who was certainly not his wife. My head throbbed slightly, and I was glad my appointment with Jacqueline was not until the evening. Prudently, I had not hinted that my Paris client was a woman, and a young and pretty one at that, but had arranged for Nancy to dine with old friends.

The rain had almost stopped when we reached the Place de la Concorde. A watery sun shone on the wet sidewalk, almost blinding us, as we stepped into the cavernous lobby of the Crillon. In our suite was a bouquet of flowers from the head of the Paris accounting firm with whom we maintain correspondent relations, a bowl of fruit from the hotel management, and a note confirming Nancy's dinner that evening. Nancy was still quiet, but unpacked with her usual swift efficiency, before vanishing into the bathroom. After she returned, and sat before the dressing-table in her panties, bra and slip, I thought again how young she looked, fresh from the bath and without make-up. Nancy does not like compliments, however; in fact, turns them away with what other people might think was ill grace.

At last, she stood up, put on a dark blue cocktail dress, and smiled. 'How about a drink, Charles? Oh, I forgot: a libation.'

'You took the very words out of my mouth, my dear.'

The Crillon bar has been modernised recently, and I myself do not find it an improvement on the past. Still, it remains quiet and comfortable, the roar of traffic on the Place muted to a dull hum, and the barmen are as grave, calm and skilled as ever. Perhaps because of the hotel's proximity to the American Embassy, they serve good, large martinis, though at a price that not even a New York clip-joint would charge. After a second drink I kissed Nancy lightly on the cheek, and said, 'Well, my love, work calls. Have a good evening, and if you can't be good, do be careful.' Nancy usually likes these wry little jokes, and her slight response that evening was, no doubt, the result of the previous night's long session at the Savoy.

The streets were drying rapidly as a taxi whirled me along the right bank of the Seine, over a bridge, and to the Île St Louis. I have never liked Paris as much as London, sharing a *Time* writer's feeling that 'much of the architecture consists of arid arabesques'. That evening, though, in the evening sun, it looked particularly beautiful, and when I saw Jacqueline's apartment I understood why, in her few letters to me, she had described her life with apparent pleasure.

She looked more beautiful than ever: tanned, lithe and confident, her huge eyes glowing, her shoulders left bare by a wispy cocktail dress. After the usual pleasantries exchanged by people who do not know each other well – questions about London, the flight, and the hotel – Jacqueline said, 'I thought we'd talk business here over a drink, then go on for dinner. Does that suit you?'

'Perfectly, perfectly. Where are we going?'

'I'll leave the choice to you, Charles.'

I was surprised, and said so: 'You've changed, Jacqueline. As I recall, you were a very determined young lady, a bit of a women's libber.'

She blushed slightly, delightfully. 'That was New York. The men are different here. They don't make decisions into a demonstration of male chauvinism – or not as much.'

'Would the Taillevent suit you?'

'Of course.'

I dialled the number and reserved a table for two hours later.

When I put the phone down, Jacqueline had the accounting ready for me, neatly tabulated, and bound into a folder containing supporting documents. She gave me another surprise: her profit already stood at $217,850, about a third of it in fees and bonuses from people described as 'Spanish clients', and the rest from stock market dealings on her own account.

'You've done very well, young lady. Shall we go through it item by item?'

Jacqueline nodded, and sat beside me as I ran through the records. She had been dealing, it soon became clear, not only on the New York and American Stock Exchanges, but also in London, Brussels and Zurich, though mostly in American stocks and bonds quoted in those cities.

'Who are these Spanish clients?'

Jacqueline drained the last of her Campari and soda, 'Do you mind if I answer that over dinner? We should be going – a taxi may be hard to find at this time of night.' She went to the telephone, dialled, and spoke in what, to my ear, sounded like fluent, idiomatic French.

'It'll be here in three minutes. I'll just get a wrap.'

We went down in the elevator, one of those typically French elevators with a tiny cage and double, glass-panelled doors. This taxi-driver was not a non-smoker; acrid fumes were belching from a cigarette covered in yellow paper, which he kept in his mouth while talking to Jacqueline, simultaneously forcing his way through the traffic as though he were at the wheel of a Mack truck. After the Champs-Elysées, with its strolling crowds and aggressive drivers, the Taillevent was a peaceful oasis with smiling *maître d'hôtel* and attentive waiters. The place was just over half full, and at a nearby table I recognised Baron Guy de Rothschild and Sir James Goldsmith, the Anglo-French financier, with a slim short-haired man who was, Jacqueline said, Jean-Jacques Servan-Schreiber, politician and publisher. 'They're all in business together,' she explained. 'Goldsmith is a major shareholder in one of the Rothschild companies, as the Rothschilds are in his; and Goldsmith is backing some of J.J.-S.S.'s publishing ventures.'

'You seem to know all the gossip.'

'It's part of my business.'

Swiftly but discreetly Jacqueline identified other celebrities: Prince Michel Poniatowski, President Giscard d'Estaing's former Interior Minister ('They're still friends, but Ponia was too tough with the Left for Giscard's liking'); a movie producer whose name I didn't catch; and a youngish, blond man with a peculiarly impassive face, Baron Edouard-Jean Empain, a billionaire Belgian industrialist, according to Jacqueline.

I calculated swiftly. If Jacqueline were right – and she seemed confidently knowledgeable – the men in this room controlled assets of some $20 billion. In the light of that thought, the prices on the menu dwindled into insignificance, and I took the lead by ordering *foie gras* to start with, followed by one of the house specialities, *Canetons de Challans au citron*. We were already drinking a Chablis, as aperitif, and for the red I chose a 1959 Château Mouton Rothschild – partly, I suppose, because Baron Philippe de Rothschild's brother, Guy, was sitting nearby, his bald head gleaming.

As the first course arrived, I asked Jacqueline, 'Now can you tell me about these mysterious Spaniards?' I glanced at her; she was gazing at her plate, and was slow to answer.

Finally, after swallowing a sliver of smoked salmon, she said, 'It's a long and complicated story. I have a friend in the American Embassy here, and he gave me a list of potential investors in Spain. One of them is a count, an extraordinary man, and...'

But my attention had been distracted. At the far side of the room, waiters were pulling out a table set for eight, and the *maître d'hôtel* was ushering in a party of four women and four men. I recognised one of the men first, Jacques Lefèbvre, with whom Nancy was supposed to be dining that night. Then I saw Nancy herself, resplendent in cocktail dress, her face a little flushed.

'My God,' I said involuntarily, 'it's my wife.'

Jacqueline looked more amused than alarmed. 'So? You're merely having dinner with a client, right?'

'Yes, but... well, to tell the truth, Jacqueline, I somehow let her think that... well...'

'That I'm a man?'

I nodded, speechless, and wondered how I could have been so careless, so foolish, not to find out whether the Lefèbvres were dining at home. Vivid, unpleasant memories of a scene with my previous wife flashed through my mind. To be sure, the circumstances were a little different – not to put too fine a point on it, my wife had returned home unexpectedly to find me in bed with Nancy.

I moistened my lips with the wine, and at that moment

Nancy looked in our direction, her lips moving inaudibly. On legs surprisingly shaky, I rose, and walked over. 'My dear! What a surprise!'

'And not a pleasant one, eh, old boy, old chap?'

'But, Nancy, I can explain everything.'

'You always can. Meanwhile, give my regards to *Mister* Eden – and my congratulations. He's the best female impersonator I've ever seen.'

There have been many times when, to put it frankly, I have wished that Nancy would talk less. Even her silences can be eloquent, however, and during our trip to Brussels on the Trans Europ Express she sat tight-lipped and wordless, her eyes shielded by dark glasses. Intermittently, she read a novel, *The Philanderer*, by Stanley Kauffmann. At other times, she gazed through the window at the flat, featureless plains of northern France. I tried to read the *International Herald Tribune*, which, under the influence of its parent publications, the *Washington Post* and *New York Times*, was continuing its unrelenting attack on business, and that day featured a particularly unpleasant, inaccurate criticism of the accounting profession.

Nancy was still silent after we had reached our room at the Amigo. I cleared my throat. 'My dear, don't you think we should forget that foolish misunderstanding of last night? Surely you don't think that I ... ?'

'No, I don't. A girl as beautiful as *Mister* Eden wouldn't look at a fat, pompous old man like you. And she can probably tell at a glance that you're about as good in bed as a one-armed monkey is at playing Beethoven. What pisses me off is that you are a coward and a liar. *And* you made me look a fool. But no, I don't think you're screwing her, and I don't think you would if you could. You'd probably worry about the sanctity of the client relationship, or some other crap. All it would mean, though, is that you were finding an excuse, because you doubt your own manhood. Rightly. That's all I have to say.'

'Well, it's not all I have to say.' I felt my temper rising. 'May I remind you that you had plenty of chance to test my manhood for yourself before we got married?'

'Yes, and that was some time and several thousand drinks ago. Furthermore, your wife found us screwing in her bed, which didn't leave me any choice except marrying you if I wasn't to look a heartless tramp.'

'Nancy, when you're in this mood, I think I know the cure.'

'Yes, a drink, a fucking libation. Well, that's one thing you're right about. Dulls the synapses, old boy, clouds the memories, deadens the pains, lover of mine, book-keeper extraordinary, my Casanova of accrual accounting.'

Nancy did cheer up as we sat in the bar, or at least talked in tones approximating her usual ones, and thawed further when I telephoned Peter Acheson to postpone our meeting until the next morning. For once, she did not even protest when I suggested eating in the hotel, saying she was too tired to go out and, in any case, didn't care what she ate. But I knew, of course, that this was her oblique way of being conciliatory, even though it did not extend to her allowing me into her bed that night; instead, she sat up late over a book. I was glad she had finished *The Philanderer*. She was now reading Eric Berne's *Games People Play*.

Brussels was grey and rainy next morning as a taxi took me to Peter Acheson's apartment, skittering over cobbled streets and manoeuvring round cream-coloured streetcars. Peter was just as I remembered, plump and twinkling. He had always been cheerful; now he seemed additionally so, and I expected his accounts to show a substantial profit. To my surprise, they did not. His dozens of commodity deals had netted him only $68,900 after deducting several big losses. I could not, of course, even hint that he was well behind Henry and Jacqueline, but merely said, 'Well, you seem to have been busy. Are you satisfied?'

He laughed. 'Hell, Charlie, it's only a game.' I dislike being called Charlie, but said nothing. He went on: 'But at least I'm ahead of it. Brussels is a great little city. I'm enjoying life. And you know what? I don't even think of how the others are doing. Maybe that's the way to win, huh?'

I didn't think so. However, he might yet be the tortoise who beat the hare. For some time we went over his accounts, which were in impeccable order, each deal and its results recorded, and buy and sell orders neatly filed. I noted the handwriting on some of the items, a foreign, spiky writing. 'You have a secretary?' I asked. Peter nodded, smiling. 'Belgian?'

'No, German. She works at the European Commission down the street, comes to me in the evenings. Very efficient, very pleasant.' He said no more, but I thought that in his manner there was a warmth suggesting she was not only a secretary. Why not? A lonely, divorced man in a strange city needed company, particularly a woman.

Peter was looking out from the terrace when I returned to the living-room. The rain had stopped, but the sky was still grey, with only a patch of blue here and there. Peter looked at his watch. 'Have we finished here, Charlie? OK, let's head for lunch. We're going to the Château Ste Anne. Great place. You'll love it.'

On the way, while Peter drove his dark blue Peugeot 504 skilfully and fast, we made plans for the evening: a cocktail party given by an American diplomat, dinner at Comme Chez Soi ('one of the best restaurants in Europe'). Peter seemed to be popular at the Château Ste Anne, and to have acquired a few words of French, though heavily accented, even to my ear.

Over the brandy, he leaned forward confidentially. 'You know something, Charlie? Europe is my continent. Sure, I'm a long way from Bosnia, or wherever it was the grandparents came from. But I'm closer here than I am in the States. Just look around. Europe has a style, a set of traditions, an elegance we simply lack in the States. These waiters: they're not ashamed of their jobs, they're proud of being good waiters. Take my maid. Spanish, bright as a button, dignified. She prides herself on being a good maid. And her husband: he's a mason, but when I need him he serves at table, and somehow he can be polite and helpful without losing dignity – what the Spanish would call, I guess, *el honor*.'

I nodded, torn between my own feelings for England and my love for the United States. Love? No, more like respect.

Peter went on: 'America's supposed to be the New World, right? Well, I don't think it is, any more. It's become rigid, stratified. You know what that British writer, Aldous Huxley, said? America went from adolescence to senility without ever experiencing maturity.'

That was too much. 'I don't think he did say that, Peter. Even if he did, he was wrong. I'm not a flagwaver, but America is a great country. And while we're taking quotes from books we don't quite remember, do you recall what happened to the young Englishman in Evelyn Waugh's *The Loved One*? He fell so much in love with the American way of life that the English community in Hollywood got up a subscription to send him home. They accused him of having gone native. That's what will happen to you – in reverse.'

Peter laughed, called for the bill, and drove me back to the Amigo. Nancy was at the hairdresser. The *concierge* gave me a telegram from Michel Jobert: 'Sorry, but have gone Middle East. Accounts airmailed you New York. But if you want to use villa Nyon you're welcome. Regards.'

Upstairs, I checked on the rules. No, Jobert had not broken them by postponing – or cancelling, in reality – our appointment. He was sailing close to the wind, however. And why could he not have telephoned instead of sending a telegram? I guessed he did not want to be questioned about the reasons for his trip.

13

> Suddenly through the power of gold
> Everything that seemed so hard to bear
> In a gleaming golden glow is cloaked.
> Sun is melting what was frozen
> Every man fulfils his hopes.
>
> *Bertholt Brecht*

Charles Kemble's visit left Henry Rusk confused and uncertain. Kemble's probing questions about the ME 109, the Rolls, H.E., and Hare's quasi-chauffeur, had focused fears until then vague. Now he felt he was slipping, that the others in the Game were getting ahead of him; that he had played good cards badly. He recalled too vividly every detail of that extraordinary evening with Yussaini, Hare and Jack. At one moment he had thought that his chances with Yussaini were dead; at the next, Yussaini had proposed an even bigger deal than the LNG financing, and even Hare, attracted by the prospect of a million tax free, seemed eager and co-operative.

But since that brief phone conversation with Hare almost a month ago nothing had happened. He had called Hare, of course. The man was always either out, or in conference or, when he was available, evasive. Henry sighed and looked out at Eaton Square, sere in the late-afternoon sunshine. Without much hope he dialled Hare's number again. To his surprise, he was put through immediately. 'Ah, yes, Henry Rusk,' said Hare's clipped voice. 'Where have you been keeping yourself?'

Henry felt his chest and temples surge with anger. 'What do you mean, where have I been keeping myself? I've been sitting here by the goddamn phone waiting for you to call back!'

'Strange, very strange. I'm sure we tried to call you. Well, perhaps we didn't – small firm, you know, everyone overworked. Now, what was the point, the point? Yes, I've got it. Could you fly to the Gulf tomorrow?'

'Tomorrow?'

'Yes, tomorrow. Yussaini wants to see you.'

'Well, sure, yes, if I can get a flight.'

Hare laughed. 'Don't worry about that. You'll go in his personal 707, with just one other passenger: Jack.'

'Why Jack? And what's his real name?'

'Surely you know, good God? Sir John Horton. Good God, *everyone* knows that. I think.'

'Well, I didn't know. And is he really your chauffeur?'

'You could say that, yes. On the other hand, perhaps you couldn't. But you're wasting time, old fellow. Jack will pick you up at nine o'clock sharp tomorrow morning. Got your jabs?'

'Got my *what*?'

'Jabs, old fellow. You know, all those inoculations and thingummybobs against yellow fever, blackwater fever, the pox.'

'No.'

'Ah well, not to worry, Mr Tusk. Jack's a medical doctor. He'll give them to you, backdate the certificate. Sound fellow, Jack, very sound.'

'Yes, but . . .'

'Happy hunting, Mr Dusk.'

There was a click, and Henry looked at the phone, his head buzzing. Once again he felt out-manoeuvred, manipulated, the possible victim of an elaborate practical joke. He sighed. Was it worth going? He supposed so. Whatever Hare's eccentricities, Yussaini seemed sound enough, if a little arrogant.

But it would be bloody hot in the Gulf. He went to the wardrobe in his bedroom and checked his lightweight suits. All neatly pressed; thank heavens for a good, conscientious housekeeper. Henry picked up the bedside telephone and called Anne's number. He got her answering service, left a message for her to meet him for dinner at the Mirabelle, then took down a suitcase from a shelf in the wardrobe and packed methodically.

He was a few minutes late at the Mirabelle. Anne was already sitting in the bar, her pale hair gleaming, a Cartier watch on her wrist, his most recent gift. She looked elegant, almost aristocratic, and Henry felt a wave of affection for her.

He had almost forgotten how they met, and stifled his speculations about her spare-time activities. He knew he was half in love with her, and castigated himself. He was almost twice her age, at a time in life when most men were susceptible to extreme youth; yet when he contrasted her with his ex-wife, with most of the women he had known, Anne was more desirable, more intelligent, a better companion.

They ate their dinner side by side on a banquette, Henry very conscious of her slim limbs and faint, elusive perfume. She ate delicately, neatly, as she did most things. Only her love-making was earthy, robust, a contrast that Henry found exciting.

Briefly, he told her about this trip to the Middle East. Her questions were intelligent, but circumspect, her comments sensible. 'I think you're right to go,' she said. 'But I just wish it were by a scheduled flight. Private aircraft have a much worse accident record.' Henry wondered again at the odd bits of information, always correct, that Anne collected.

Henry cleared his throat. 'That play you thought I should back, Anne. I've been thinking about it, and I'll come in for £20,000.'

'Not just for my sake, Henry, not just because I've been promised a bit part?'

'No, no, not because of that, Anne. I've read the script, heard a reading, looked at the producer's track record. I think it's got a much better than even chance. Tell him to call my secretary tomorrow. I'll sign the cheque tonight.'

Anne took his hand, kissed him gently on the cheek, and said, 'Darling, you're a good man, do you know that? Your wife must have been mad to let you go.'

'She was mad, that's for sure. Mad at me, mostly.'

Their love-making was tender that night and afterwards, as he looked at Anne, her face buried in a pillow, her fair hair spread over it, Henry felt another wave of gratitude and affection. He awakened early, to find her side of the bed empty. He put on a robe and went to the kitchen. She was drinking coffee and reading the *Financial Times*, her long hair gathered by a bow at the back. Henry poured himself a coffee and picked up *The Times*. Neither spoke, and Henry was grateful. He was always silent until after his third or fourth coffee. The news was bad, as usual: more political violence in Argentina, another skyjacking by Black Septembrists, earth tremors in Northern Italy, a governmental crisis in France. Henry turned with a sigh to the financial pages, where the news was comparably sombre. He finished his third coffee.

'Goddammit, Anne, is there no good news in the world? Or is it just that the papers don't report it?'

She looked up, smiling. 'Don't you know the old saying? Good news is no news?' She went back to her paper, and Henry went to shower, shave and dress.

Promptly at nine, the doorbell rang. Henry kissed Anne and went outside. Jack was sitting in the back of a Bentley. A chauffeur took Henry's bags, and he climbed into the car. Jack was looking trim in a pale grey lightweight suit – a very expensive suit, Henry noticed.

Quickly, Jack outlined the schedule: takeoff at 10.30, a stopover at Geneva to pick up some packages for Yussaini, arrival in the Gulf at 11.45 in the evening, local time. They would both stay at Yussaini's house.

'And when do we return?'

'That depends,' said Jack.

'Depends on what?'

'A lot of things.' He lapsed into silence, picking up a newspaper and clearly discouraging further questions.

At Heathrow airport they got VIP treatment, being whisked through Customs and Immigration and out to the apron where the 707 was waiting. A steward and two hostesses welcomed them, and the pilot came aft to shake their hands. From his accent, he was almost certainly a Scot, Henry thought.

The plane's interior was discreetly luxurious. Forward, just behind the cockpit, was a lounge with six easy chairs, low tables, a bookcase, and thick carpeting. Behind that was a conference area with radio telephones and even a radio telex. Then came a small dining area, and finally four bedrooms and a shower.

Henry and Jack were the only passengers, as Hare had promised, and Henry found the experience somewhat eerie.

Never before had he travelled in so large an aircraft so empty. A stewardess strapped him into his chair, the jet taxied to the runway, and within minutes they were airborne. As the 707 levelled off from its steep climb, the note of the engines dropping to a soft purr, Jack said, 'We'd better see about those jabs, hadn't we?'

'Are you really a doctor?'

'You'll find me in the directory.'

Henry took off his jacket and rolled up his sleeve. Jack swabbed the skin with surgical alcohol, selected an ampoule from his medical bag, and pressed the plunger. Within minutes he had finished, and handed Henry an international health certificate. It was already made out, Henry noted, and backdated ten days.

'Now for your visa,' said Jack. 'Give me your passport.' He took a rubber stamp from another bag, pressed it on an ink pad, and stamped Henry's passport, finally signing it. 'There, that's done.'

'Are you a Gulf immigration official as well?'

'Something of that sort.'

Henry looked at Jack's clear, rather harsh features and clipped moustache, tapering but powerful fingers, and elegant suit and shoes.

'Look, Jack, we're going to be together for a few days, and we might as well get to know each other. First of all, I'm Henry, not Mr Rusk. Right?'

'Right, Mr Rusk.'

'Second, you appear to be a medical doctor, to be empowered to issue visas, to be a baronet, and to be Hare's chauffeur. It just doesn't add up, it really doesn't.'

'Oh, but it does, Henry, it does.'

'Well, you convince me.'

'Let's answer the last question first. Am I Hare's chauffeur? The answer is: yes, I drive him. But what rhymes with chauffeur? Gopher. You know, I go for coffee, I go for drinks – I'm a gopher. That's what I am, and if some people think I'm merely the chauffeur – well, you'd be surprised what they'll say in front of a servant, as though he were deaf, or too stupid to understand. Very useful. Next: yes, I am a doctor, but don't practise. Yes, I am a baronet, and I am empowered by the Government of Aqtar to issue visas. Have I answered your questions?'

'Not entirely. Why do you work for Hare? Surely you could do better?'

For the first time since Henry had known him, Jack laughed heartily and unguardedly, his pale blue eyes twinkling. 'Henry, do you know how much a doctor makes in England these days? If he's lucky, very lucky, about £15,000 a year gross – say £8,000 a year net after taxes, again if he's lucky. Do you know how much I make with Hare? Seven, eight times that amount, and most of it outside England, where the tax people can't get at me.'

'But if you make so much, what does Hare make?'

Jack shrugged. 'Who knows? Enough to run a huge country house in Suffolk, a château in France, a London house, a yacht. Let's say £300,000 a year.'

Henry did a quick calculation: about half a million dollars. He raised his eyebrows and whistled. 'And he pays taxes on that lot?'

'Don't be silly. Everything he owns is in the name of a company – even the cars. His taxable income is probably £20,000, no more.' Jack beckoned and a stewardess came over with a bottle of Krug '59 in an ice bucket. Jack pointed: 'You see, Henry, we've done our research into you. That's why I'm telling you all this: you're on probation as a member of the family.'

'The family?'

'No, not the Mafia. Our family. We don't let everyone get close to our clients. We screen very carefully, both to protect them, and ourselves.'

After the 707 left Geneva, the stewardesses served lunch, and in the afternoon Jack and Henry went to separate bedrooms for a sleep. When Henry woke the sky was dark, and he took a shower. It was hard to believe he was aboard an aircraft; most of the private jets he had flown in had been eight-seaters, twenty-seaters; none had this princely magnificence.

Dinner was superb: caviare followed by roast baby lamb,

then a tray of cheeses, some French, some from the Middle East, made either of goat or ewe's milk. Jack seemed relaxed, almost genial, as he lounged in his chair with a glass of 1928 Armagnac at his elbow, a Romeo y Julieta cigar in his mouth.

Henry was conscious of not having done something he should. Yes! He had forgotten to tell JZ International he was going to the Middle East. He mentioned it to Jack, who raised a languid hand. The younger of the two stewardesses, a small, dark girl, moved to his side. 'Henrietta, Mr Rusk wants to send a telex.' She returned with a notepad and pen. Henry dictated a brief message; five minutes later, she came back with a copy of the radio-telex. When Henry saw the notation 'in-flight telex', he smiled: that should impress Frank Blaistow. All *he* could muster was a Grumman Gulfstream.

Even at midnight Aqtar was stiflingly hot, and Henry found himself sweating on the short walk from the jet to the arrivals building. A crowd of Arabs, most in traditional dress, waited by the barrier, but Jack led Henry through a door marked 'Private', was saluted by an official in smart uniform, and walked out to a Cadillac Fleetwood waiting at the kerbside. After a half-hour drive over bad, poorly-lit roads, they arrived at a pair of high iron gates let into a wall that stretched into the distance, then drove along a smooth hardtop. The house, floodlit and with lights blazing from a dozen windows, was huge, built in modified Arabian style. From somewhere came the roar of the sea.

A Nubian butler opened the door, and Henry found himself in a covered courtyard. A fountain splashed in the middle and luxuriant trees stretched up towards the glass roof. The air was pure and cool; Henry wondered about the airconditioning bill, then remembered that in Aqtar oil and gas were almost as cheap as fresh water. Yussaini was sitting beside the fountain, immaculate in white tuxedo. He rose, smiling. 'So good of you to come, Mr Rusk. I hope you found the flight comfortable. It is too late to talk now, you agree? Shall we meet for breakfast at, let us say, eight o'clock? Good. One of my boys will show you your room.'

Henry's room was a suite decorated in a style that only hinted at its Arabian location. A servant was already unpacking his bags, his pyjamas were laid out on the huge bed, and he could hear a bath filling. Henry sighed. The Rockefellers, the Mellons and the DuPonts could afford such luxury, he supposed, but somehow did not indulge themselves in it.

He was wakened next morning by a servant, who shook him gently. A tray of coffee and croissants was waiting on his bedside table. French croissants in Arabia were a bit much, Henry thought, and bit one dubiously. It was hot and surprisingly good. There were also copies of the previous day's *New York Times*, *Wall Street Journal* and *Washington Post*. Henry wondered how they had arrived so quickly, then reflected they had probably been flown by Concorde to London, in another Concorde to Bahrein, and from there to Aqtar. He skimmed the news, shaved quickly, and was just ready to meet Yussaini when Jack tapped at the door. 'I thought you'd need a guide,' he said. 'This place is a bloody maze.'

They met Yussaini in what probably passed for a simple, informal room in that part of the world: 40 feet long, 30 feet wide, and at least 20 feet high. Yussaini was in jellabah and kaffiah; the traditional dress made him look sterner, less the playboy that he often seemed, a man who would be powerful and of consequence even if he were not immensely wealthy. His manner, too, had changed; it was more businesslike, less elaborately courteous.

'I had meant to talk business this morning,' he said, 'but the Emir wishes to see me. Jack, you know Aqtar well. Please show him such sights as we have, and explain our history. I shall be back by lunchtime. Shall we say one o'clock?'

He stood up, and with a swirl of his jellabah was gone. Jack laughed. 'You're getting the treatment, Henry. Yussaini is better than most, but he insists on showing people like you and me that we're in his country now, and don't forget it.'

'Do you think he'll be back by one?'

Jack shook his head decisively. 'I doubt it. We may not see him again today. In fact, don't be surprised if you're still here a week from now. Come on, let's see those sights.' He led the way along a corridor, through a door, and into a huge garage. There must have been twenty cars in there, ranging from Rolls-Royces, Cadillacs and Mercedes-Benzes to station wagons and a Range-Rover. Jack waved at the glittering assortment: 'Take your pick.'

'Doesn't he care if we use a Rolls?'

'Not Yussaini. He buys a Rolls as casually as you would buy a Timex watch. I've a fancy for the Mercedes 450. Right?'

He drove the car fast along the winding roads, leaving a cloud of dust behind him. Along the way they passed camels and donkeys, poorly dressed men riding bicycles and motor-scooters, and a double-decker bus, still marked London Transport, lurching along, wildly overcrowded.

The town was small, grimy and poor. As they walked through the *souk*, where merchants called shrilly to them, Henry felt as though he were an extra in a Hollywood movie, and almost expected to bump into Sydney Greenstreet and Humphrey Bogart. Jack was a poor guide; he had seen it all before, found it boring, and communicated his boredom. 'Come on,' he said after half an hour, 'let's go for a ride in the chopper.' They recovered their car, which was surrounded by a crowd of urchins, and headed for the airport. Yussaini's helicopter pilot was American, a veteran of Vietnam, where he had commanded a Cobra gunship. Yeah, the Gulf sure was boring, but the pay was good and the work light, he said.

As they moved along the coast, Henry saw the offshore oil production platforms, smoke and flame billowing from the blow-off stacks, and the wake of an occasional small boat on the green, almost transparent sea. 'Sir,' said the pilot over the inter-com system, 'that's Dubai.' He pronounced it Doo-bhay, his Southern accent thickened by the microphone. 'Aqtar don't have no awl yayt.'

An hour later, they were back in the car. 'Not very interesting, was it?' said Jack.

'Oh, I don't know. Tell me, who does all the work on those platforms?'

'Mainly Europeans and Americans. Onshore, of course, all the dirty work is done by Pakistanis, Arabs from poorer parts of the Middle East, Iranians.'

'They got their families with them?'

'You must be joking. Apart from the Europeans and Americans, most of the rest are illegal immigrants.'

'So what do they do about sex?'

'If that's a tactful way of asking if there are any brothels, the answer is yes. Strict colour bar, too. One lot of brothels for rich Arabs or anyone with a white skin, another lot for the lower-class Arabs, Paks, and so on.'

Henry looked thoughtful. 'And how long do the Europeans stay on the platforms? At a stretch, I mean?'

'Oh, I don't know. A month, maybe two. Why?'

'They must get pretty randy. Anyone ever thought of floating brothels?'

Jack stopped the car and stared at Henry. 'Now *that* is what I call a bloody good idea. Bloody good. You mean a neat little craft with a dozen girls aboard, booze, perhaps a piano-player?'

'Yes, I guess so.'

'A bloody good idea. Do you know, I think we can sell that one? There's a lot of fighting aboard those platforms – big, tough Germans trying to bugger somebody else's fancy-boy for lack of anything better, and a lot of sheer frustration. Yes, you may have hit the jackpot there. We can sell it to the oil companies: improved efficiency, and all that rot. The Emir may be a bit sticky, but it's amazing what a bit of *baksheesh* will do. Would you put up the money, Henry?'

'Well, I guess so. How much, do you think?'

'Oh, let's be modest: two fifty-footers to start with, that's about a hundred thou, I suppose. Working capital another fifty. Let's say a hundred and fifty. Dollars, of course.'

'Couldn't we rent the boats?'

'That's another corking good idea, Henry. You're firing on all four today. I know just the fellow to rent them, too. Comes from New Orleans, runs an offshore servicing business down the Gulf.'

'Where do we get the girls, though?'

'That's the least of our worries. I'll call Madame Claudine.'

'Who's she?'

'You haven't heard of Madame Claudine? Used to run the best house in Paris, then wrote her memoirs. Now she's in the agency business. You want a dozen girls, assorted shapes, sizes and colours, and she'll have them on the plane to you in a jiffy.

Old pal of mine, too: when one of our Arab clients gets an itch, I soothe it – with her help. Why, there was one fellow, no more than five feet tall, insisted on six Swedish blondes, all over six feet. Cost him a packet, but he got them.'

Jack started the car and accelerated fast towards Yussaini's villa, scattering pedestrians and cyclists. They arrived just before one o'clock. The butler handed them a note. It said: 'Sorry, Mr Rusk, but have had to fly to Cairo. Back tomorrow or next day. My house is your house. Yussaini.'

Henry's face turned red, and he smothered an oath. Jack laughed. 'You'll never survive out here if you take that sort of thing seriously. In any case, we've got plenty of work to do. Got to launch our brothels – literally.'

'But I wasn't serious, Jack. I was kidding. I don't want to go into the white slave business.'

'White slaves? What on earth are you talking about? Half of them won't be white, and all of them will work willingly. Why, it's a whore's paradise: plenty of work, armed guards to make sure they're not murdered, healthy sea air, proper contracts, all expenses paid. They'll be queueing up, old man, you mark my words.'

Henry thought for a moment. It probably wouldn't come to anything. Even if it did, he could always back out. He nodded: 'OK, but don't commit me until I've got the whole scheme on paper. And keep my name out of it.'

'Pity. I'd thought of branding their rumps with our corporate slogan: "Rusk and Horton. Every girl personally tested."'

14

> I heard, down the long valley of my bones,
> The cry of home run like a calling hound...
> Belly and brain, I lived America
> *Paul Engle*

Jacqueline found it hard not to laugh when Charles Kemble returned to their table that night after what was, clearly, an embarrassing scene with his wife. His lips and hands were trembling, his face was flushed. Nancy, in contrast, appeared to behave as though nothing had happened, smiling at her host's jokes, and contributing to the conversation. Kemble tried to talk lightly, but his heart was not in it. He soon lapsed into a gloomy silence, picking at his expensive food, but drinking his wine as if it were water.

They left early, Kemble dropping off at the Crillon, and Jacqueline taking the taxi on to the Île St Louis. The night was warm, though with a cooling breeze, and she sat on her terrace, looking at the lights of Paris and the few barges on the Seine. On the whole, she thought, Nancy's intervention had been fortunate. Jacqueline had not wanted to talk about her Spanish clients. She could not do so without remembering that morning on the boat, when she had surrendered to Jaime like an eager whore, and all the times since, in Barcelona, in Paris, and once, good God, on the sleeper from Barcelona.

She did not like Jaime, she thought; he was cruel and arrogant, too sure of himself, too certain that everyone would do his bidding. The trouble was that most people did it, as she was doing. She did not like his politics, either, or the thought that by investing their money so well she was helping him and his friends to achieve aims with which she disagreed. So why did she make love so eagerly with Jaime? Why did she make money so enthusiastically for him and his fellow conspirators? – for that's what they were, she realised.

The second question was easier to answer than the first: by

making money for them, she made money for herself, and enjoyed the satisfaction of using her professional skills. The two were linked, though, the affair with Jaime and the making of money for his political purposes. Perhaps, she thought, both had the lure of the forbidden, the attraction of the immoral.

The breeze had freshened, and Jacqueline shivered. To her left, the twin spires of Notre Dame reared into the sky, outlined against the glare of Paris. They reminded her, suddenly, of a girl she had met years before, a devoutly Catholic girl who had confided that the greatest sexual thrill she could imagine, one that recurred in her dreams, was to make love on the altar of a church. Jacqueline had thought at the time the girl was slightly crazed; now she understood, remotely, how she felt.

She shivered again as a cloud crossed the moon and the breeze fluttered her wrap. Time to go indoors, she thought. For once, the magnificence of the apartment did nothing to lift her depression. On the contrary, it reminded her that money could come at too high a price: the sacrifice of her few principles, the shattering of her peace of mind. She poured herself a large brandy, something she seldom did when alone, and sat on the couch trying to read a translation of Simone de Beauvoir's *The Mandarins*. After a few minutes, she threw it down impatiently. Simone de Beauvoir and her lover, Jean-Paul Sartre, talked and wrote incessantly about morality; but Sartre, at least, had never spoken out against Communist duplicity, against violence and repression, unless it were in a bourgeois, capitalist nation. She thought his ethics flexible, his standards double, and tonight was in no mood to be reminded of her own willingness, even eagerness, to compromise, dissemble, excuse herself. She was in no mood for solitary drinking, either, she realised, and poured the contents of her glass back into the bottle, corking it firmly.

As she did so, the telephone rang. She looked at it apprehensively. At this hour, who could it be? She lifted the receiver.

'Miss Eden? You don't know me: Nancy Kemble.'

'No, but I saw you tonight, and I want to apologise.'

'You don't have to. It wasn't your fault.'

'No, I guess it wasn't.'

'Miss Eden, I'm sorry if I spoilt your evening. But I also want to ask you something. May I?'

Nancy sounded emotional, slightly drunk. Jacqueline's stomach tightened; she was too tired, too overwrought, to cope with a drunken, jealous wife.

'Are you still there, Miss Eden? Look, I know it's late, and I've had a few drinks, but I've got to talk to you. Please, please, Miss Eden, don't take Charles away. Oh, I know you wouldn't do it deliberately. But he's such a romantic, such a fool. If you gave him any encouragement, even without meaning it, he would fall in love with you.

'I love him, Miss Eden, I really do. I know I don't show it in the right ways. I'm acid with him, and I insult him. But he's all I've got, God help me. He's a lousy lay, he's pompous and insensitive, and there are times when he bores the pants off me. But you can love a man in spite of his faults, can't you?'

'Nancy. Can I call you Nancy? Listen. Charles really isn't my type, and I hardly know him. He's just my accountant, that's all. I don't expect to see him again for months, and then it will be in his office. So don't worry, please don't worry.'

'I'll try not to. I won't. But I would if you saw him regularly. You're the kind of nice girl I was once, Jacqueline, and that's the kind he falls for.'

Sitting up in bed afterwards, Jacqueline found herself strangely affected by the conversation. Nancy sounded a highly-strung woman, and she had been drunk, no doubt of that. Yet there had been real fear in her voice, and Jacqueline wondered why a woman who so obviously loved her husband could say such harsh, uncharitable things about him to a stranger. Suddenly, Jacqueline put her head on the pillow and wept. Through her sobs, she wondered why she was crying. The answer came to her in a flash of clarity: I am crying for myself, and all the other people who make such a mess of their lives because they are torn by conflicting impulses, who know where happiness lies, but are blown off course by storms they brew themselves.

Jacqueline had often read in novels, usually bad ones, that time passed in a blur. She had regarded this as a transitional device, akin to the leaves that fluttered off calendars in old

Hollywood movies, or the second act of a play: 'Edgcumbe Castle, some days later.' Now she knew that time could pass in a blur. To be sure, she went punctually each day to the office she had rented near the Bourse, studied securities analysts' reports punctiliously, placed her buy and sell orders accurately, attended diplomatic cocktail parties. But between her and the events of her daily life there seemed to be a gauze curtain, softening outlines, running one day into another. The one thing not softened, not blurred, was a pain in her chest, a pain associated with the tears that sprang readily to her eyes.

The gauze curtain fell and the pain mysteriously went with a call from Jaime two days later. He was in Geneva; he would be in Paris the next day. Suddenly, Jacqueline was clear-headed, cool. Yes, she could meet him for dinner; yes, drinks at her apartment first would be fine. Seven o'clock? Done. She buzzed for her secretary-bookkeeper, a sombre woman who worked four afternoons a week. 'Madame Leclerc, please make up the accounts to date. El Conde will want to see them tomorrow. Here are the slips.'

'*Oui, madame, certainement.*'

The phone rang; a broker in New York asking whether she still wanted to sell those AT&T shares, even though they were rising. Yes, she said: they'll probably fall tomorrow. We've got a profit; let's take it. She made a notation: $102,409 for Jaime, $7,850 on her own account.

She looked at her watch. Ten minutes before her usual quitting time; but to hell with it. Outside, she saw the streets clearly for the first time in days, felt a sudden need to be anonymous, and told a taxi driver to take her to the Boulevard St Germain. She got out at the Deux Magots, its sidewalk tables still crowded despite the chill, found an empty one, and ordered an *anisette*. It reminded her of Jobert, of Rusk, of Acheson. How were they doing, what were their scores, what had they learned about themselves on this sabbatical from reality? She wouldn't know until January; on the other hand, after tomorrow she wouldn't really care. At a table behind her, four people were arguing furiously, their tones so jagged and words so biting that physical mayhem seemed imminent. But it was, Jacqueline reflected, just the French getting excited. On the boulevard drivers hooted furiously at each other, and across the street riot policemen sat in their bus smoking and playing cards, while two of their colleagues stood on the sidewalk, looking suspiciously at every passing youth with long hair.

Countless American writers, she thought, from Hemingway and Fitzgerald to those whose names were remembered only by literary historians, had sat at the cafés along this boulevard, rhapsodising about France, romanticising its workers, its peasants. But most had gone home again, unless the booze got them first, because a person torn from native roots was as doomed to wither as a plant torn from the earth, and they all realised it, even if most would not admit it. So that was one thing she had learned about herself: America was her land, her native earth.

A light rain started to fall, whipped by a brisk wind that had sprung up suddenly. Jacqueline looked at her watch and decided to go. Taxis whirled by, all busy, and she stood indecisively on the pavement, thinking with a shock that she had no idea which bus, if any, would take her to the Île St Louis. Furthermore, she did not know whether a passenger had to give exact change on a Paris bus, as in New York. She laughed grimly, thinking that when the rich and pampered were without the cocoon that sheltered them from life they were as helpless as children. Well, the only thing to do was to find out.

She crossed the boulevard, boarded the first bus that stopped, and after two transfers found herself close to home. She walked through the rain, coatless and without an umbrella, but curiously confident, almost happy. Back home, she stripped off her wet clothes, showered, and put on a negligee. For once she would eat at home, listen to some music, read, and have a really early night, perhaps even call her mother in Charleston, something she had not done for months.

When she awakened next morning, she felt rested, confident. She had almost eleven hours, she thought, to prepare for Jaime. As she dressed, and over coffee, fragments of speeches went through her mind. She rejected them. It would probably be better to tell Jaime of her decision without too much preparation; she knew from experience that once deflected from a prepared statement she floundered, and never recovered her poise or pace.

She came home early from the office that day and changed into her severest dress: black, cut to conceal her figure rather than accentuate it, long sleeves. She looked at herself in the full-length mirror in her bedroom. She still seemed too young, too informal, in her own eyes. A pity she didn't wear glasses. She tried on a pair of sunglasses, and laughed: too much, too phoney. Hair? She gathered it at the nape of her neck and tied it with a black velvet bow. Slightly better.

The doorbell rang, and her maid answered it. Jacqueline had asked her to stay on; she felt less vulnerable with another person in the apartment. Jaime was smiling, his teeth white in his tanned face, as he walked into the living-room, stretching his arms wide. 'Ah, my Jacqueline, how are you?' He tried to kiss her on the mouth; she moved slightly, so that his lips touched her cheek. He did not appear to notice and that, she thought, was one of his faults: he could never imagine her turning him down. If a woman was less receptive than usual, he probably put it down to pre- or post-menstrual nerves.

He asked for a Scotch on the rocks. Jacqueline drank a light whisky and soda, determined to keep her head clear that evening. For several minutes they talked of mutual acquaintances, of the New York stock markets (they were rising), of impersonal things. Then Jaime leaned forward, put down his glass, took Jacqueline's hand, and said, 'My friends and I are very impressed by what you have achieved, Jacqueline. Very, very impressed. They want you to sign a long-term contract. So do I.'

The moment had arrived. Jacqueline took a sip of her Scotch. 'No, Jaime. I am sorry. I am going back to the States.'

Jaime laughed. 'Why so serious, Jacqueline? Why the tragic look, the black dress? Frankly, I think you will do even better there. You will be more in touch with the markets, is that not so?'

'Right, Jaime. But I still don't want to sign a contract. The fact is ...'

'... that you want to be free to serve other clients? I see no problem.'

'No, you've got it all wrong. I've been thinking about the objectives of you and your associates, and I just don't agree with them.'

Jaime frowned. 'Jacqueline, we explained those objectives to you that very first weekend in Mallorca. What has changed your mind? Who has been talking to you?'

'Nobody, Jaime, nobody at all. This is something I have decided for myself.'

'No, Jacqueline, that cannot be. Who has been in touch with you? It must have been the Communists.'

'Jaime, that is preposterous, ridiculous. I had my doubts from the beginning, but, what with one thing and another, I smothered them. Now I can't smother them any longer. For God's sake, Jaime, try to understand. Here I was in Europe, all alone, trying to make it. I visit you in Mallorca. It's a strange, exotic place to me. Then there was – well, the boat. And all that money, and ...'

'And what, Jacqueline, and what?'

She realised he would never understand the Game. 'And my ignorance of Spanish politics, and the persuasiveness of your friends.'

'Jacqueline, it is not possible you should leave us.'

'Not possible? I've just done it.'

'I repeat, Jacqueline. It is not possible. You know too much. You know the names of all my associates, of every company in Liechtenstein, Switzerland, Luxembourg, that we control. You know our political programme. No, Jacqueline, what you suggest is not possible, is not practical. I must forbid it.'

'Forbid it? You can't forbid me to do anything, Jaime.'

She looked at his face, now hard, the eyes very blue and unwavering, and felt an inward shudder.

'Jacqueline, I don't think you understand. We are not going to risk our political future, the future of Spain, on the whims of a foolish little girl.'

'You don't seem to think I'm so foolish when it comes to investing.'

Jaime laughed harshly. 'You are a technician, my dear, and

that is all. A narrow specialist. A very good one, but a narrow specialist. What do you know of wider matters, of larger issues? Nothing. *Nada!* No. You are not leaving us. That is final. The last word.'

Jacqueline felt panic rising in her. 'Well, you tell me something, then. You say I can't resign. I say I have done. Where do we go from here? How do you intend to stop me from getting on a flight to New York? Have some of your bully-boys rough me up, drop me in the Seine?'

Jaime did not answer, but pulled a large envelope gently from his soft leather documents case. 'I regret the unpleasantness, Jacqueline, but there are bigger issues at stake than my feelings or your American prudishness. In here are some photographs, just a small selection. I'm sure you don't want to see them. But let me assure you they exist, they are real. For example, you have some very interesting habits when you are alone and feeling in need of a man. I should add, by the way, that these are only stills from a videotape; the whole sequence is really most interesting, almost artistic.'

Jacqueline felt faint and sick. Jaime looked at her intently, almost tenderly, and put the envelope back in his case. 'You are convinced?'

Jacqueline nodded, her mind chaotic with half-formed thoughts. At last she raised her head. 'Yes, I'm convinced the photographs exist, if that's what you mean. Tell me, how did you get them? And if you're in them, how can you blackmail me?'

'Rather naïve questions, Jacqueline,' said Jaime, drinking his Scotch cheerfully. 'By the way, may I have another? Thank you. Yes, rather naïve questions, my dear. The sequence showing you pleasuring yourself was, of course, taken by a concealed camera in your bedroom. As for the footage in which I appear, I doubt whether anyone could identify me from my back view or, in some sequences, from an intimate part of my anatomy receiving extremely intimate attentions from you. Very pleasurable attentions, too, I should add.

'Now, it is time for dinner, don't you think? I know we eat late in Spain, but we are in Paris, and I refused that plastic junk on the flight that they offer as an apology for lunch.'

'Jaime, I can't believe it. First blackmail. Now you calmly suggest dinner. How do you think I can eat after that? I feel sick, sick. Sick and degraded.'

'What you did, you did of your own free will, Jacqueline. If it didn't degrade you then, how can it degrade you now?'

'Because you planned the whole thing from the start. It was a set-up. Why else should you have photographs taken?'

'Would you believe me if I told you that such photographs are a hobby of mine?'

'Not for a moment. You're not the type. And I remember what you told me once: "The best aphrodisiac is a beautiful, willing woman, not her image."'

Jaime smiled, seemingly at ease in a discussion of unemotional academic theory. 'You're right, of course. Pornography has always bored me. But I must ask you to believe me that I would never bring this kind of pressure to bear – blackmail is an ugly word – for personal gain. Unfortunately, in the practice of politics a man must often do things to which he would not stoop in his private life. Now, may I suggest we leave for dinner? I really am hungry, and I'm sure you will find that you are, too.'

Surprisingly, when Jaime's chauffeured Mercedes reached the Grand Vefour, Jacqueline found she was indeed ready to eat. Jaime seemed determined to make the evening pleasant, telling malicious but friendly anecdotes about his friends, and exaggerating absurdly but amusingly the hypocritical rectitude of Swiss bankers. His charm, thought Jacqueline, was both a weapon and a shield. Over coffee and liqueurs, he became serious again, though the note of menace had gone from his voice.

'So it is agreed, then, is it not, that you continue to work for us, on the same terms as before? If you wish to return to New York, then we have no objection. Indeed, you may be placed more advantageously there than here.'

'I guess I have no choice. But answer me one question. Do you always carry those photographs around with you, or did you have a special reason tonight?'

Jaime laughed. 'May I answer that in the car, Jacqueline? I can be much more explicit there.'

He paid the bill and led Jacqueline outside, where the Mercedes waited. At the touch of a button a glass divider shut them off from the chauffeur. Jaime switched on a tiny, focused overhead reading lamp, opened his documents case, and handed Jacqueline the brown envelope. 'Please open it.'

'I'd rather not.'

'No. I insist.'

Hesitantly, she lifted the self-seal flap, and pulled out the papers inside. They consisted of a long report in English on a Swiss private bank.

'I don't understand! There are no photographs.'

'Oh yes, there are, and from my description of one sequence you must know there are. To convince you further, I can tell you exactly what you said when you brought yourself to climax.' He leaned close and whispered in Jacqueline's ear. She felt herself blushing in the dim light.

'Jaime, you're a shit.'

He laughed again, apparently genuinely amused. 'Many women have said much the same, though most with more eloquence and elegance. But I am coming to like American directness. Now, here is my hotel. Felipe will take you back to your apartment. Good night, Jacqueline. I am glad to think we are still together in this great adventure.'

How strange, she thought, that Jaime had not tried to emphasise his mastery by taking her to bed. Or was he trying to keep her off-balance? Probably. He was a strange, complex, terrible man, beyond the imagining of the most ardent American women's liberationist, determined to maintain his supremacy by any means, and contemptuous of concession. She hated him, loathed him; yet, strangely, she did not despise him. He was amoral rather than immoral, a natural force the cursing of which would hurt him as much as cursing hurt the wind or the rain. But could he be outwitted, as the wind and the rain were by a roof and walls? By midnight, she had an idea. By two in the morning, when she was sodden with fatigue, the idea had become a plan. She set her alarm for seven, and dropped off to sleep within seconds.

Usually, after only five hours' sleep, Jacqueline was lethargic. That morning she felt vibrant; not even the grey skies could dampen her mood.

At nine, she unlocked the door of her office, took out the statement of accounts prepared by her secretary book-keeper, and smiled. Now for the *Herald Tribune* and its stock market reports. She worked quickly, noting those stocks that had risen the day before, those that had fallen, those on which her portfolios were showing paper losses.

By noon, she had punched the tape for a dozen telexes to brokers in New York, London, Paris, Brussels, Zurich. She read them over, made a few corrections, smiled. Then something that had been nagging her all morning turned to certainty. How could she protect herself against violence?

She called John Edgeworth at the American Embassy. They had met a few nights before at a diplomatic cocktail party; he had been as friendly as ever, as ready to help.

'What kind of trouble, Jacqueline?'

'Kind of hard to explain. Let's put it this way: I need somebody for forty-eight hours or so to make sure I'm not roughed-up. Trust me. I've done nothing criminal – just annoyed some pretty ruthless people.'

'Have you thought of the police?'

'I don't want to make it official.'

'Well, there's an outfit called the Section Action Civique, le Sac, set up under de Gaulle as union-busters, red-baiters. It's still around. I guess you could hire a couple of their guys. Nasty types, but effective. I'll call you back.'

He didn't. Instead, Jacqueline heard a harsh, heavily-accented voice speaking English. 'I understand you need some help, yes?'

'Yes, I need two men to act as bodyguards for two days, perhaps three. Armed, if possible.'

'All my men are armed. Is this anything to do with the police, with the government?'

'No. It's entirely private. Let's say it's trouble with a man.'

'I would need to meet you to discuss it. Be at the Gai Moulin, Boulevard Clichy, at two. Ask for Monsieur Gaston.'

The Gai Moulin was a large, bustling *brasserie* full of off-duty taxi drivers and hard-faced men. There were few women; those few also had hard faces, and looked at Jacqueline suspiciously. She sat at a plastic-topped table, the only one vacant, and wished that somebody would turn down the jukebox. Near the entrance, two youths in leather jackets were playing a pinball machine, punching it just hard enough to bump up the score, but not to set off the tilt light. A waiter came, an elderly man with grey hair, a disillusioned face, and a long, dirty apron. Jacqueline ordered a coffee and asked, as casually as possible, if Monsieur Gaston were there. The waiter muttered incomprehensibly. Suddenly, a trim man of medium height sat down opposite her. He looked tough and intelligent, and for a few moments said nothing, studying her face.

'Well, *mademoiselle*, what is the problem?'

'I'm an investment adviser working in Paris, and a client, who used to be a boy-friend, has been threatening me. It is a business quarrel, also a personal one.'

'Can we know the name of this man?'

'No. But he is not French, and he has nothing to do with the police or government here. All I want is protection, nothing else. I just think he may send somebody to attack me.'

'And you need two men?'

'Two on guard all the time for the next forty-eight hours, possibly seventy-two.'

'Very well. Ten thousand francs, in cash or two thousand of your American dollars, also in cash. Half in advance. Half when we complete the job. We keep no records. We issue no receipts. My name is not Monsieur Gaston. The Section Action Civique is not involved. Do you understand?'

'Perfectly.'

'When do you need the men?'

'Five o'clock tonight at my office, then at my apartment, and right round the clock until we finish. Seventy-two hours from now I shall leave Paris. That will be the end of the job.'

'Good. Give me your addresses, your telephone numbers, and have five thousand francs waiting.'

He left, and mingled with the crowd. Jacqueline shivered, paid for her coffee and took a taxi to her bank. Back at her office she telephoned Jaime at his hotel. He was out. She telephoned a company of which he was a director, got him out of a board meeting, and said: 'Now listen very carefully, because I shan't repeat it. I have sent telexes to brokers in the US and Europe. They are instructions to sell rising stocks short, to sell everything that is currently showing a paper loss, and to buy the stocks I know will fall over the next few days.

'Those telexes say that the orders are to be executed unless I countermand them by noon tomorrow, Paris time. But I won't unless you have those photographs here, together with the videotapes, the negatives – everything.'

'Jacqueline, you have gone mad. How much is this crazy gesture likely to cost us?'

'At least $50 million. I can't tell about the short sales, of course: it depends how much the stock rises above the price at which we've promised to deliver. But it could easily be another $20 million.'

'Jacqueline, you are bluffing. You have authority to commit us only for $10 million.'

'You know that, Jaime, and I know that. But nobody has ever told the brokers. They'll do what I tell them.'

'Jacqueline, what you want is not even in Paris. I am not sure I can get it by twelve noon tomorrow.'

'You'd better damn well try, Jaime. Rent a jet.'

'I'll have to call you back.'

Jacqueline put down the phone and looked at it grimly. There was a knock at the door, a heavy, aggressive knock. A burly man in a black leather jacket opened it; he looked like a lorry driver or off-duty cop. 'Mam'selle Eden? Monsieur Gaston sent me, Jacques. This is Raoul.' His companion was slimmer, but just as tough-looking, a stubble of beard at his chin. He did not smile, but leaned against a filing cabinet, watching Jacqueline from behind dark glasses.

'The money,' he said.

Jacqueline handed him an envelope. Raoul counted the bills, returned them to the envelope, and stuffed it inside his windbreaker.

'*Çà va, c'est juste.* Now what?'

'You stay with me round the clock. Are you armed?'

Jacques smiled at her contemptuously and patted his leather jacket. Raoul did not even smile, but said, 'What do these men look like?'

'I've no idea. Their boss is a tall man, slim, fair, about fifty, a Spaniard. He probably won't do the job himself.'

'Name?'

'Jaime. I don't know the rest of it.'

'*Et ta sœur*. Where next?'

'I'm going home by taxi. You'd better follow. Have you got a car?'

Neither answered, but walked out of the door, leaving Jacqueline to lock it, and carry a bag heavy with files and copies of the telexes she had sent that day. Without the proper coding, Jaime would not be able to cancel the instructions, even if he broke into the office.

In the street, Jacques mounted a motor-bike, and Raoul got behind the wheel of a battered Renault. Jacqueline thought, but wasn't sure, that a strolling cop nodded to them. She hailed a cab, got in, and looked behind her. A tall, slim man, fair-haired, was entering her office building; he looked like Jaime. She leaned forward and told the cab driver she had changed her mind; go to the Gare du Nord instead. In that sleazy area around the railroad terminal to the north, she thought, she could pass as a passenger killing time, and her bodyguards as workers having a drink before going home.

She chose a big, anonymous café, noisy with waiters' shouted orders, crowded with a bizarre mixture of people: workers in coveralls, Algerians, a few bourgeois couples with suitcases. It would do nicely.

Jacques and Raoul, she saw, were standing at the bar drinking beer. Neither took any notice of her, until she went to the toilets at the back of the café. When she came out of the women's lavatory, Jacques was standing in the narrow corridor.

'What's the idea?'

'I thought I saw Jaime.'

'You should have let us bash him.'

'No. But he'll probably go to my apartment next. We may catch him waiting there.'

'Good idea.'

15

Private information is practically the source of every large modern fortune.

Oscar Wilde

Peter wakened with a hangover the morning after the cocktail party. A lukewarm shower left him able to focus his eyes. He was still shaky, though, and several cups of strong black coffee made him worse. After the fourth one, he felt sick, went to the bathroom, and vomited. He looked in the mirror, and saw a pallid, slack face staring back at him from bloodshot eyes. He shuddered as he turned away, was attacked by a wave of dizziness, and shuffled to his bed. For an hour he lay there, his stomach churning and temples pounding.

At last he felt able to start breakfast all over again, this time with toast and butter. He wondered how Traudl was; suffering from the grand shakes, no doubt, and trying to remember how much she had told him about the Commission's plans for a soybean self-sufficiency programme. How accurate was she? Despite her drunkenness, she had been lucid, if loud-voiced, and seemed to know more about the Common Agricultural Policy than any pretty girl of her age should do.

He poured himself coffee, feeling distinctly better, buttered another slice of toast, and wandered out to the terrace. The morning was bright, with a brisk wind chasing small clouds across the sun; cadets from the military school were already running round the park, and Peter envied their youth and fitness.

Could he risk going short on Traudl's tip? He doubted it. It had been only a draft proposal, she said; and he wasn't even sure how the European Community made decisions. In a bookshelf in his office he found a primer issued by a British bank. 'Policy decisions are made by the Council of Ministers,' he read. 'Any group of ministers from the member-countries may be deemed the Council. For example, agriculture, foreign, and finance ministers regularly sit as the Council. In theory, a decision may be taken by a simple majority; in practice, the Council of Ministers insists on unanimity, which means that many proposals before it are watered down so as to make them acceptable to all members.

'The Commission is the executive of the Community, charged with the task of implementing decisions made by the Council of Ministers.

'The Commission may also recommend policies to the Council of Ministers, and does so regularly on a wide range of topics. In principle, the Commission need consult nobody before recommending a new policy or a change in an existing one. In practice, so as to give its recommendations a good chance of being accepted, it consults with the member-countries, usually through their permanent representatives in Brussels, who hold ambassadorial rank.'

That didn't take him much further, Peter thought: it only confirmed that the Community was a hive of competing groups. Did he know anybody likely to have inside knowledge? Vaguely, he recollected meeting an American diplomat, on the staff of the US Mission to the Community. Sonnenfeldt? Sonnenberg? That was it! He thumbed through his address book and found the entry, remembering the man better now, a tall Mid-Westerner with craggy features he had met at Benny Rabinowitz's. It had been a fairly drunken evening; probably Sonnenberg wouldn't remember it too clearly. Certainly, he was worth a try. He dialled the Mission's number.

'Sure I remember,' said Sonnenberg in a deep, rasping voice. 'Quite a party, huh?'

'That's the understatement of the century,' said Peter. 'I said I'd call you for lunch. It's been on my mind. When are you free?'

They compared calendars. Sonnenberg's was full for weeks ahead. 'Sorry, Peter, you know how it is: visiting firemen all the time. There's only one possibility: today.'

Peter tried to keep the elation out of his voice, hesitated, then said, 'Well, sure, Jim, I guess I can make it. How about the Carlton, one o'clock?'

'Fine, see you there.'

Peter thought the Carlton too consciously glossy, too studied; he had chosen it because the US Mission was within walking distance. Sonnenberg was already in the bar when he arrived, a tomato juice on the table in front of him. Peter ordered a Bloody Mary, and Sonnenberg said, 'I'll join you in that.' Peter was relieved: Sonnenberg on the wagon might not be as forthcoming as Sonnenberg off it. The *maître d'hôtel* brought two huge menus, but Sonnenberg waved his aside: 'I know what I'm having. Half a dozen oysters and a pepper steak, rare.'

Peter chose the same; he didn't want to waste time stumbling through menu French, only to find himself surprised by what arrived on his plate. He cut the wine waiter short, too: 'Half a bottle of Chablis, then a bottle of Bordeaux. I'll leave the choice to you.'

At first they talked of Brussels (Sonnenberg didn't like it), of a Belgian political-financial scandal ('Typically Belgian,' said Sonnenberg. 'This country invented Watergate'), of mutual friends. Then, as they finished the oysters and the last of the Chablis, Sonnenberg said, 'You're a commodity broker, right?'

'Was, Jim. I'm taking a sabbatical and dealing for myself.'

Sonnenberg raised his bushy eyebrows. 'Kind of risky, isn't it? A make or break business?'

'It can be. The biggest risk is when you go short.'

'You know, Peter, I'm pretty ignorant about these things. Tell me how going short works.'

'OK, say you think that pork bellies are gonna fall. You contract to sell pork bellies you haven't got at a price above the one you think they'll reach on the day you have to deliver. If you're right, you can buy in the spot market to cover your contract, and pocket the difference.'

'And if you're wrong?'

'Then you're in trouble. Say your contract is for $50,000, but the price doubles. Then you're fifty thousand bucks out. I've known rich guys, savvy guys, busted flat in the commodities markets. They hear some inside tip, think they're gonna make a killing, and get killed instead.'

'So you don't believe in hot tips?'

'Yes and no. You've got to check them out. What usually passes for a hot tip is just a market rumour, here today and gone tomorrow, if not sooner.'

'Yeah, but it can affect the price, Peter?'

'Oh, sure, for a few hours, and if you get in and out fast enough you might make a few bucks. No, what I call a hot tip is knowing for sure of something real before anyone else does. For example, if you could know before the market that frost had damaged half the Brazilian coffee crop, you could really clean up.'

'So why are you sitting in Brussels instead of São Paulo? You'd be closer to the scene, and the weather's a damn sight better there.'

'Oh, Brussels isn't too bad a listening-post. I heard a rumour a few days ago that could be interesting, that the European Community's going to put a ceiling on soybean purchases and start a crash programme to reduce dependence on American imports.'

Sonnenberg looked up from his steak and laughed. 'They've been saying that every year since the Nixon Administration threatened to put a lid on soybean exports. When was it? Seventy-two, seventy-three? It never comes to anything.'

'Well, I heard it's gonna be different this year. The Commission is ready to endorse it, and they've sounded out the members.'

'OK, Peter, so a ceiling on imports is possible: if it were low enough, it would hit the price quite heavily. But self-sufficiency? Who's kidding whom? Do you know anything about growing soybeans?'

Peter laughed, embarrassed. 'Not too much, Jim, just what I've read. And I don't think I've actually seen a pork belly, either.'

'Well, I was raised on a farm, and you can take it from me: there's no way the Europeans could grow themselves enough soybeans to replace imports from the US, particularly at our price. They don't have the climate, they don't have the right soil, they don't have the volume. They'd be crazy to try.'

'I thought the Common Agricultural Policy was crazy already?'

'That's for sure, Peter. Any policy that can simultaneously produce a glut of butter and sugar, and a famine of meat and potatoes, has to be crazy.'

'So a crazy soybean policy isn't impossible?'

'With that bunch, nothing is impossible. Let's just say it's improbable. Probably depends how they're feeling about us that day.'

'Us?'

'Yes, us – the Americans.'

Peter was depressed as he rode home in a taxi. What had seemed a good idea, to use Brussels as a listening-post, was turning out to be more difficult and hazardous than he had thought. That the Commission would recommend a cut in soybean imports seemed likely; but if Jim were right, the Agriculture Ministers might reject it, or keep it on the back burner until their next meeting. As things stood, not even a modest gamble was justified. What he needed was to know before the rest of the world did that the Ministers had decided on a cut. But how could he do that? All afternoon, as he made phone calls and sent telexes, Peter pondered that problem. It seemed insuperable. Wild ideas coursed through his mind: bugging the Ministers' meeting with a radio transmitter, smuggling himself in disguised as a security guard.

Perhaps it would be better to forget about the whole thing, and count himself lucky that he had spent a pleasant few months in Brussels, met Ilse, and made some money, even if he lost the Game. He found his feelings about the Game changing from day to day, sometimes from hour to hour.

He didn't mind losing it, he was sure; what he did mind was the thought of Michel or Henry taking part of his winnings. He hadn't disliked Michel as much as Jacqueline had, but still found him arrogant and patronising. As for Henry, he was all that Peter despised in the Eastern banking establishment: smug, hypocritical and, almost certainly, not very good at his job, in it more because of family and education than native ability and drive. In one mood Peter thought the whole idea of the Game foolish and juvenile, and wondered at himself for agreeing to play it – indeed, at the outset being enthusiastic. In another mood, usually brought on by his having made money on a deal, he thought the Game expressed a truth about business life: that it really was a game, and half the fun came from playing against others, with no holds barred.

His mood today, Peter thought, was probably the result of a hangover, and too much to drink at lunch. Pouring himself a Scotch, he thought he was drinking altogether too heavily. He must cut it out – but not just yet. When Ilse arrived, she found him sitting on the terrace, as he usually was at that time of the evening. The wind had died, and the sky was serene, the few clouds tinged with pink by the setting sun. She kissed him. 'You seem depressed, Peter.'

He roused himself. 'Not really. Just tired, a little hung-over, that's all.'

'Did you think Traudl was helpful?'

'Yes, very. But what she told me won't be conclusive until the Agriculture Ministers decide; and if I don't know that until the rest of the world does, I shan't be much further forward. I need at least a one-hour beat – better two hours.'

Ilse looked thoughtful. 'Traudl could help you with that, Peter.'

'I don't see how. And I don't see why. I mean, why should she help me to make money?'

'In return for money.'

He looked at her, astonished. Her face was young, innocent; he didn't know what the German was for bribery, but was sure it was a word she abhorred.

'Do you know what you're saying, Ilse? You're saying I should bribe a civil servant to give me advance information. You don't let me make love to you because of some obscure scruples; yet you suggest bribery as though it were nothing. I don't get it, I really don't.'

Ilse smiled. 'You are so American, Peter. My emotions, my body, are one thing; paying for information that does you good, but nobody else any harm, is quite different. Can you not see the difference?'

'Well, sure, there's a difference. I'm just surprised that a girl who can be so moral in one way can be – well, amoral in others.'

He held up his empty glass. Ilse took it, and returned with a fresh drink for him and one for herself. He looked at her intently, her face pale in the setting sun.

'In any case, Ilse, what makes you so damn sure Traudl would take a bribe?'

Ilse raised her glass: 'Cheers, darling. Because I have talked to her. She is a girl with expensive tastes, Peter. Her family were rich, until she was eighteen or so. Then her father died, and her mother found that instead of leaving a fortune he had left debts. He had been taking money out of the company, and he had gambled – oh, millions of marks. Poor Traudl cannot forget the days when she had everything; she spends far more than she earns.'

Peter sighed, feeling simultaneously relieved and shocked. 'So how much does she want?'

'One thousand dollars.'

'Seems reasonable, provided she delivers. Tell me how it would work.'

Ilse leaned forward, her face eager. The Agriculture Ministers, she said, were the most disputatious and quarrelsome of all the Community ministers. Their meetings started at ten in the morning; often, they went on all night, and sometimes lasted for two or three days. Security was tight at the start; later, it became lax. Traudl would not be in the conference room itself, but in a room nearby. Even so, she would know what was decided. Peter would wait in the press bar downstairs. When the soybean policy had been decided, she would join him for a drink, and give him a slip of paper. It would simply say 'yes' if the Commission recommendation had gone through. If it had not, the paper would be blank.

Getting Peter in would be no problem: Traudl had a lover who was a correspondent for a German paper. He would ask the press department for a pass for a friend, saying Peter was a visiting American journalist who had not had time to be accredited. In fact, Ilse said, if he arrived carrying a camera nobody would even ask for his pass. The camera should be plausible, though: something professional, like a Nikon or a Hasselblad with flash.

Peter laughed. 'You're a wonder, Ilse, you really are. When did you dope all this out?'

'Oh, over lunch. She is quite enthusiastic. It is not just the money, Peter. It is also the adventure: she is bored. And she does not like her boss, because he takes everything so seriously.'

'Let me think, Ilse. It's tempting, but it's dangerous. I don't know what the penalty is for bribing a Eurocrat's secretary, but it's gotta be horrible.'

He got up, and walked to the balustrade of the terrace, his half-finished Scotch in one hand. There wasn't all that much chance of being caught, he thought: only Ilse, Traudl and he knew of the plan, and each had good reason to be discreet. No, what was worrying him was ethical rather than legal – a scruple that almost amused him. What, after all, was the real difference, he wondered, between lavishing hospitality on a contact, in hope of learning something useful, and paying Traudl? A difference of degree or of kind? He recalled, years before, when he was in his twenties, dating the secretary of a partner in a commodities brokerage, hoping she would let slip some nugget of information that would help him to make his fortune. To this day, he could not say with certainty whether he was attracted more by her body, which she gave to him, or by potential information, which she did not.

Looking at the tranquil Brussels skyline, Peter sighed. In New York he seldom thought of ethics, because there simply wasn't time. Here, with plenty of time, he had become introspective. Did Michel, Henry and Jacqueline suffer from similar scruples? He doubted it, somehow, despite the Game's rule against illegal activity. He drank the last of his Scotch, and walked to the office, where Ilse was typing. She did not hear him; he stood looking at her for a moment, wondering at the complex mind inside that tidy head. Suddenly, she looked up, stopped typing, and smiled. 'Well, Peter. Have you thought?'

He leaned down and kissed the top of her head. 'Sure have. Here's a blank cheque – go buy a Hasselblad tomorrow.'

'A Hasselblad?'

'Yeah. If I'm gonna be a photo-journalist, I might as well have a serious camera, right?'

Once he'd made his decision, Peter felt calm, confident. The captain of an airliner probably felt the same, he thought, when he had switched on the auto-pilot, and could relax before the next test of his skills came. He made his preparations precisely. Ilse taught him how to handle the Hasselblad, which he found both complex and curiously comforting, a piece of machinery so skilfully wrought that it communicated reliability.

One evening he met Traudl for a drink, at a café far from where either lived: he did not want to be seen with her by mutual friends, or by any of her colleagues from the Commission. Her stare was still bold, and she held his fingers while he lit her cigarette; but Peter realised these were simple reflexes, almost as meaningless as a nervous laugh in anyone else. Otherwise she was cool and businesslike.

'Soybeans are the third item on the agenda. But fishing limits and butter subsidies come first, so I don't think the Ministers will reach soybeans until the evening, at the earliest.'

'OK, but I'd still better be there, right?'

'Yes, you should be. These meetings are not predictable. There is no difficulty over your press pass: my friend has fixed it.'

'Does he know I'm not a journalist?'

'Yes, but I have told him you are writing an article for an American magazine.'

'How about *Soybean Digest*?'

'There is such a magazine?'

'Sure. Published in Iowa.'

They both laughed. Then Peter turned serious. 'Look, there's only one thing that bothers me slightly. I don't like the idea of a written message. Can't you just tell me what happened?'

'No, that is dangerous: I am not supposed to say anything. People might hear.'

'OK, I tell you what we do. Now remember this. If you ask for a Scotch on the rocks, that means a ten per cent cut in soybean imports, right? If you ask for a Scotch and water, you say 'fifty-fifty' when I ask how much water you want, and that means a five per cent cut. If you ask for a coffee, that means no cut. Got it?'

'Yes, it is not difficult. But what happens if there is a bigger cut than ten per cent?'

'Could there be?'

'Oh yes, it is quite possible.'

'OK, this is what we do. You ask for a Scotch, and I'll say: "How much water?" You'll answer with the percentage cut, like this: "Oh, fifteen per cent, please." Simple, huh?'

Traudl laughed again, this time heartily. 'You know, it is all very funny, more like a game than real life, don't you feel so?'

'A game? That's just what it is, baby, a big game played for high stakes.'

'How much could you win or lose?'

'I guess I could make fifty thousand bucks. But I could lose the same, or more. I don't think I will, though. The soybean futures market is pretty weak: stagnant demand, a very good crop. Yeah, I calculate a ten per cent cut in European imports could depress the market enough to make me fifty thousand or so. But until I've unwound the whole damned deal I'll be biting my fingernails right down to the knuckles.'

He looked at his watch, and drained his glass. 'OK, so we're both clear. Any changes, and we communicate through Ilse, right?'

The Ministers' meeting was five days away. Peter passed them quietly, doing small, routine deals: a few thousand dollars risked on silver going up, another few thousand on corn, cotton and wheat, this time on the assumption they would fall. Agricultural commodities had been weak all summer; some of his earlier 'shorts' were paying off nicely. His only misjudgment was cocoa, which had fallen when he thought it would rise. Even so, he was well ahead of his own game, if not of the Game: $91,415 clear.

He should have been happy, but wasn't. He'd hardly been out of Brussels since he arrived, he realised: one weekend in the Ardennes, that wooded range of hills in which the Allies had nearly come unstuck when the Germans counter-attacked towards the end of World War II; another weekend at Knokke-Le Zoute, a crowded coastal resort, both with Ilse, and both in separate bedrooms. As Benny Rabinowitz had warned, he had put on weight, and his only other trip out of Brussels had been to London where he had seen a tailor ('I recommend this pattern for the fuller figure, sir' – bastard!) and two plays, one so densely English that it baffled him, the other so intense as to depress him.

His spirits lifted on the morning of the Agriculture Ministers' meeting. Here was action at last, a game to be played, money to be made. The day was crisply autumnal, and leaves crunched underfoot as he walked down the Avenue de la Renaissance to the building where the Ministers were meeting. With his press pass in his pocket and the Hasselblad strung from his neck, he felt professional, and the cop at the door let him in with a friendly nod. Photographers were crowding eagerly round a small man with a self-important manner; Peter hoisted the Hasselblad, and took a few shots. Who the man was he would find out later. Then there was a confused cry, and the photographers headed for the entrance, where a man with a grim face was talking French into a microphone. Peter took a few shots of him, too, handling the Hasselblad with sensuous pleasure.

The crowd of journalists and photographers broke up into small groups, the television lights faded and went out, and there was a slow, general move to the bar. Peter ordered a coffee, took it to a table, and sat reading the *Herald Tribune*. A man with a battered, broken-veined face sat down opposite, sighing and breathing heavily. 'Haven't seen you before, old boy,' he said. 'Don't tell me you're the latest arrival in this bloody awful town.' He took a hearty swallow of his Scotch, and gazed challengingly at Peter from blue, bloodshot eyes.

'No, I'm not here permanently.'

'What's your paper, old man?'

'I'm a freelance. At the moment I'm doing a feature for an agricultural magazine.'

'American, eh?'

'That's right.'

'I'm a Brit, myself. You can probably tell. Been stuck here for bloody years. Gets more boring all the time. And these Agriculture Ministers are the worst of the lot. Go on and on, usually till the wee hours. Thank God, the bar stays open. Here, let me buy you a drink – all on the expenses, old boy.'

He lurched off to the bar, spoke briskly in bad French, and returned with two Scotches. 'Cheers. My name's Dick Benyon, by the way – *Daily World*.'

'Peter Acheson – *Soybean Digest*.'

Benyon looked at the Hasselblad and raised his eyebrows. 'And on what they pay you can afford a Hasselblad?'

'Well, no. I write for other magazines, too.'

'I should have gone to America years ago. That's where the money is, old man.'

Benyon looked meaningfully at his glass. Peter sighed, went to the bar, and came back with two more Scotches.

'Cheers.'

'Cheers.'

Benyon was silent for a moment while he lit a cigarette with a kitchen match. 'Are you going to sit here all day, old boy?'

'Not if I can help it.'

'Well, if you don't have to file, you might as well piss off. There's no chance of these buggers deciding anything before dark.'

'Are you staying?'

'Got to, old boy. Early deadline.'

'But what will you write if nothing has happened?'

'Don't let that worry you, old man. I'll find something. For instance: "After an all-day meeting in Brussels, Common Market Agriculture Ministers were still deadlocked tonight over the size of next year's butter subsidy to consumers." Once you've got the intro, old man, you can carry on for ever.'

'When will they get to soybeans?'

'Don't know, old man, and don't care. The British reader doesn't know what a soybean is. Don't think I do, either. Are they the whatsits in soy sauce? Now, there's an idea, old man. Chinese food is a craze in Britain. Yes, we might do a little piece on that: "Europe threatens British Chinese restaurants." Yes, I like that. Time for another little drinkie on the strength of it.'

'Not for me, thanks.'

'Oh, come on, old man, they're only thimblefuls. Bloody Belgians don't know how to serve a proper Scotch. Probably water the stuff, too – anything for a franc, those buggers.'

'Cheers.'

'Cheers.'

They sat in silence for a few moments, Peter feeling a faint buzzing in his ears and a tightness at his temples.

'Tell me, Dick. How long does it take for the press people here to issue a communiqué after the meeting has finished?'

'Oh, it could be hours. But there are always leaks, old boy. The official communiqué, though – two hours at least. Of course, they've got the bloody things written before the meeting starts. Just a matter of choosing the right one, or doing a scissors and paste job. The way they carry on, though, you'd think they were writing deathless prose. Bunch of little Flauberts, that's what they are. Then they've got to translate the bloody thing into every language you can think of, except Serbo-Croat. Oh, words are a flourishing industry in this barracks, believe me.'

'And you really think I don't need to come back until tonight?'

'Certain, old man. They'll just pick their noses up there until after lunch.'

'Well, I'll see you later. Thanks.'

'One for the road, old boy?'

'No thanks. I'll take a raincheck on it, though.'

Peter walked back to the apartment, cooked himself a hamburger, and then went to bed, setting the alarm for five. He wakened refreshed, showered, and went out to the terrace. A gusty wind had blown up and was tossing the branches of trees in the park; on the horizon, dark clouds were massing. He recalled the old joke about Brussels: 'If you don't like the weather, wait a minute.'

As Traudl had forecast, security at the Ministers' meeting, never very strict, had virtually vanished, and he walked into the building unchallenged. There was a bigger crowd of journalists than before, some looking distinctly the worse for wear. Benyon was slumped in a chair and snoring. He looked old and vulnerable, and Peter felt a pang of pity for him. In a corner, four photographers were playing poker. Suddenly, one threw his cards on the table, stood up, and walked away. The other players looked round. One beckoned to Peter; he shook his head. He didn't feel like becoming entangled in a game that could end in a drunken quarrel.

The next few hours reminded him of waiting for a train that

never came. He had brought a paperback novel with him, but it soon palled, and he alternately dozed and sat looking round the press bar. The journalists were in three categories, he decided: those who remained alert, awake and sober; those who drank steadily, with no visible effects; and those who had fallen into drunken stupors. Yet, oddly enough, the behavioural category into which they fell did not always correspond with their abilities. He recognised an American journalist who wrote perceptive, analytical stories for the *New York Times*; he was sunk in drunken sleep. Another journalist, whom he had met at a cocktail party and written off as a lightweight, was as fresh and alert as though he had just arrived.

Towards midnight, Peter was dozing when he felt a hand shake his shoulder: Traudl. 'Hullo there,' she said. 'Buy me a drink?'

'With pleasure. What'll it be?'

'Scotch and water.'

The bartender pushed the Scotch towards Peter. 'How much water, Traudl?'

'Oh, make it fifteen per cent, please.'

They raised their glasses, and Traudl gave him the suspicion of a wink. She downed her drink in three swallows, and walked away. Peter finished his more slowly, trying to still a rising clamour of excitement, then picked up his camera, and walked towards the exit. Outside, rain was falling heavily, lashed by a strong wind. He jogged towards home, the camera banging heavily against his chest, the rain spraying his face. He felt exultant. A *fifteen* per cent cut in soybean imports! That could make him sixty thousand bucks, or more.

16

> Prognostics do not always prove prophecies – at least
> the wisest prophets make sure of the event first.
>
> *Horace Walpole*

Michel Jobert had gone no further east than Vaduz, the village capital of Liechtenstein, where cows outnumber people, and tax-haven companies outnumber cows. He had been there once before, to sign the papers for setting up an *Anstalt*, the Liechtenstein form of company that offers a secrecy more impregnable than a numbered Swiss bank account does, its true ownership and activities known only to the shareholders and the lawyer who created it. Michel had more than $200,000 to the credit of his *Anstalt*, money that no tax authority in the world knew about, money that was safe from everything except global cataclysm, or a rush of morality to the heads of Liechtenstein's legislators – a happening as unlikely as the Second Coming.

Even so, he did not like Vaduz, its people or its cows, which were as obtrusive as the *Anstalten* were reclusive. To be sure, he was glad not to meet Kemble, who was both a bore and likely to ask probing questions; but if Henk had to arrange a meeting with an electronics expert, why could it not be in St Tropez or anywhere more attractive and interesting than Vaduz – which gave Henk a wide choice?

But Henk had insisted on Vaduz, and on their travelling separately. This electronics expert, he had said, was a Liechtensteiner who had worked for the Swiss telephone department, was now retired, was much in demand for his skills, and saw potential clients at his home, or not at all. That explained why Michel was sitting in his hotel, in the shadow of the ruling prince's castle, listening to the clang of out-of-tune cowbells, and drinking a particularly bad white wine, pressed on him by the hotel proprietor with the compliments of the house. Michel was sure it would find its way to his bill; he didn't think that Liechtensteiners gave anything away.

On the other side of the lounge a black African was talking in guarded tones to a man who looked like a lawyer, and Michel recalled the old, unproven story that the assassination of Patrice Lumumba had been ordered and paid for through an *Anstalt* owned by Belgian industrialists who wanted to install a more tractable leader in his part of the former Belgian Congo. Liechtenstein was an annexe of Switzerland, thought Michel. In Switzerland, hostile leaders met to resolve their differences; in Liechtenstein, their emissaries met, ignoring each other studiously, to arrange assassinations, stash away rival dictators' money, and in myriad ways contradict all that their governments proclaimed publicly.

Michel looked at his watch; Henk was twenty minutes late. He pushed the wine to one side and walked out to the village street, bucolic and bland in the autumn sunlight. That Vaduz was a capital of a kind was demonstrated by a newspaper rack displaying papers from all over the world. A headline in the London *Financial Times* caught his eye: 'Dollar falls on mark revaluation rumours.' He smiled; his judgment was confirmed, and he would be several thousand dollars to the good.

There was a glimmer of metal in the distance, then the purr of a powerful motor, and he saw Henk driving up in his V-12 Jaguar. Michel raised his right arm, looked at his watch, and tapped it. Henk got out of the car gracefully, a smile on his thin lips. 'OK, I'm late. Sorry. Got stuck behind a truck. Let's have a drink, and I'll fill you in.'

They went into the hotel; Michel's wine had been cleared away. He ordered an *anisette*, Henk a Scotch, and they looked at each other warily. No, thought Michel, Henk's was not a face to trust; he would sell to the highest bidder, and then not stay bought. Only fear of exposure, of punishment, would keep him loyal. Michel sighed, suddenly sickened by his reliance on so venal an ally.

'OK, Henk, now brief me for this meeting with this genius of yours.'

'Hey now, I didn't say he was a genius. I said he was the best in the business – or the best available to us, which comes to much the same thing.

'Name: Anton Schwarzenbach. Age: sixty-something. Thirty years with the Swiss Post Office. Now retired. Describes himself as a consultant. Specialises in electronic surveillance. Completely trustworthy.'

'Oh? Who says so?'

'Friends of mine. People who've used him.'

'So we'll let that pass. But I've never known a crook yet who could be trusted.'

'Wait a moment, Michel. He is not a crook. He is a highly skilled professional.'

'Yes, who sells his services to the highest bidder without asking too many questions. What does he know about us?'

'About you, nothing. About me, that I'm a friend of a client. About our plans, nothing. You can tell him or not, as you wish. Make up your own mind after you've met him.'

'I shall. Does he speak French, English?'

'Both. Not fluently, but enough.'

'One more thing, the name. Isn't there a Swiss politician named Schwarzenbach who wants to send all the immigrant workers home?'

'There certainly is. He wants to maintain the purity of the Swiss culture, such as it is. Most people think he's a racist.'

'Sounds like my kind of man. And your Schwarzenbach: is he related?'

'He says not. But he thinks like the other Schwarzenbach.'

'Let's go.'

Anton Schwarzenbach lived in a chalet in the hills above Vaduz. It was built in traditional style, surrounded by a garden, and looked over a valley dotted with Liechtenstein's ubiquitous cows, their bells sounding plaintively in the crisp fall air. Michel and Henk found him in the garden, tying up a rose bush, a big man with a massive bald head that gleamed in the sun. He greeted them austerely, and led the way indoors to a living-room cluttered with kitsch: ornately carved furniture, a collection of Dresden-type shepherds and shepherdesses, a cupboard full of fluted and decorated glassware, gleaming in the sunlight that streamed through the window. Over the tiled fireplace was a motto burned into a wooden plaque. Michel could not read all the spiky, *fraktur* German script, but saw it said a lot about God, the home and children.

Schwarzenbach settled himself heavily in an overstuffed armchair. 'So, gentlemen, what is it that I can for you do?'

Henk started an explanation in fluent German; for the occasion, Michel noted, Henk was using the sing-song intonation and soft consonants of Austria. Presumably, the Liechtenstein dialect was beyond even him.

Schwarzenbach grunted and asked Michel in English, 'And you, Herr Jobert. What do you say?'

'Very simple. I want to put a message out on a wire service without their knowing. I'm not expert in electronics; but it seems to me that if you can tap a telephone or telex message, you can feed one in.'

'Technically, you are correct, Herr Jobert. But it is more complicated than that. Where would this be done?'

'In Geneva, I think.'

'That is good: I have worked there. But one thing I must ask. Why is it Geneva? Herr Vrijdel tells me you live near there. Is it good that you should be close? Also, is the message you are sending about Switzerland? If not, then would the bureau in Geneva be sending the story?'

Michel looked at the big man, impressed. He turned to Henk. 'You know, Herr Schwarzenbach has something there. Geneva is a bit close to home, and it does restrict us to a story about Switzerland.'

Henk nodded. 'Yes, that had been bothering me. Paris would be better. Most of the wire services use Paris as a relay centre for their European bureaux. We could have a much wider range of choice there. Would you do the job in Paris, Herr Schwarzenbach?'

'*Ja, natürlich*. I have good friends in Paris who would help. Very good friends, Herr Jobert, who would say nothing afterwards. We have done business together before.'

'And what would you and your very good friends in Paris ask for the job?'

'If it took no more than one week to do, then my money would be ten thousand American dollars. My friends would want two thousand dollars.'

'What would they do for that?'

188

'They would identify the cable out of the office you choose. That is essential. Do you know what is under the streets of every city, Herr Jobert? Sewers, yes, but also millions of cables and wires – telephones, telex, electricity. It is like spaghetti. But there is a key to them. My friends have the key.'

'Are they in the telephone and telegraph department?'

'No, Herr Jobert. But I shall not say what they do or who they are. There is no need for you to know. They will not know of you.'

'Technically, how will you do the job?'

Schwarzenbach smiled icily. 'There is no need for you to know that, Herr Jobert. It is enough for you that it can be done. But I will tell you a little. On the day you choose I shall tap all outgoing telex messages. Then, at exactly the time you say, I shall delay the real messages, storing the information, and insert your message, with the correct code number. Then it will go out, followed by the messages I have stored. The delay will be no more than two, three minutes – not long enough to be noticed by those who are receiving the messages. Then I shall pack up the equipment, and go. There will be no trace.'

'Will you want me with you while you are doing this?'

'No, Herr Jobert. There will not be room – I shall be under the street. I shall telephone you when the message has gone.'

'You have phones down there?'

Schwarzenbach looked at him pityingly. 'Herr Jobert, if I can tap a telex line and send a message, I can tap a telephone line and send another, is it not so?'

'I guess so, yes. Look, Herr Schwarzenbach, we are putting ourselves in your hands. I think it's fair we should know a little more about you, don't you?'

'Very well. For many years I was in the technical department of the Swiss Post Office. Also, I worked with the security forces very often. Yes, we do tap telephones in Switzerland, Herr Jobert. Now, I am retired. So I do two or three special jobs a year. Yours is a little one. Some are big, very big.'

'I'm going to ask a very indiscreet question: Why?'

Schwarzenbach laughed, became almost genial. 'First, I am bored doing nothing. Second, I enjoy the money. Here, look.'

He walked ponderously to a desk, took out a photograph album, and handed it, already open, to Michel. He saw a Schwarzenbach transformed, almost elegant in white trousers and striped blue sweater, leaning on the rail of a yacht, his arm round a young and pretty girl. Both were laughing. In the background was a harbour, probably in the South of France. Schwarzenbach reached over Michel's shoulder and turned the album to another page. In this photograph he was at the wheel of an open MG sports car, a different girl beside him.

Schwarzenbach took the album back and replaced it in the desk. Michel nodded, amused. 'Yes, Herr Schwarzenbach, I can see you couldn't afford that kind of life on a pension. OK, we're on. The job will be three weeks from now. Does that give you time?'

A nod of the bald head.

'Herr Vrijdel here will be your contact. We want to send the message out on the wires of European Financial News Service. It will be a very short message. I haven't decided yet exactly what it will say; but it will have something to do with a rise or a fall in a particular currency. We'll meet in Paris; Herr Vrijdel will give you the exact dates. Money: do you want some in advance?'

'Fifty per cent is customary.'

'OK, you'll get it in any way you want. Just tell Herr Vrijdel.'

Schwarzenbach took them to the door, shook hands, and returned to the rose bush. Michel looked back from the road. The big man was tying up the bush with neat, precise movements, apparently the complete householder, concerned with nothing more than the state of his garden next spring. Michel laughed and shook his head. 'My God, what a character! The typical bourgeois, you'd think. Instead, the playboy of the western world. Thank God for human weakness and folly. It makes life easier for people like you and me, Henk.'

They returned to Switzerland as they had come, separately, but not before Michel had sent postcards to Henry, Jacqueline and Peter. Each bore an identical message: 'The coup is coming.' He grinned as he posted them. That would worry his rivals, particularly now that the Game was within six weeks of ending.

As he drove towards Geneva, enjoying the smooth power of his Citroën-Maserati, Michel thought about the Game. He was ahead, he was sure of that; but what mattered was not so much the money, pleasant though it was to see his winnings rising, but the thought of beating the other players. Peter was a pleasant, innocuous fellow, without much character; there would be little satisfaction in beating him. His real targets were Henry and Jacqueline. Henry annoyed him, caught him on a raw edge, with his assumption of superiority, his superciliousness; Jacqueline typified what he disliked in women, a keen competitive sense coupled with a prickly assertion of women's rights, and a bleeding heart for what she called minority groups – as though everyone didn't belong to a minority group of one kind or another.

Yet he was grateful to his rivals in the Game. They had given it a spice, a tang, that he would have missed without them. Most people were combative, Michel thought; he more than most. But they needed a clear, identifiable rival against whom to compete, whether in sport, business or politics. That was what was wrong with monopolies, whether private or state-owned: with little or no competition, they became fat, slothful, complacent. Then, when competition did come along, they were ripe to be knocked off their perches and plundered. The only exceptions were the few monopolies and oligopolies, like General Motors, which deliberately created internal rivalry, pitting division against division, executive against executive.

He was cheerful as he turned into the gates of his villa, saw the lights in the windows, and imagined the dinner Anne-Marie would be cooking. She had turned out to be a competent cook, willing to take risks with unfamiliar dishes that usually paid off. Altogether, she was easy to live with, asking few questions, making few demands. Alerted by the scrunching of his tyres on the gravel, she ran down the steps and into his arms, her long hair flying, her eyes glowing. 'Just in time, *chéri*. We have a surprise for dinner tonight.' Michel sighed contentedly.

His good mood continued while he and Henk prepared for the Paris coup. Untrustworthy Henk might be, but he was meticulous in his preparations, careful of every detail, and more cautious than Michel would have been. He vetoed, for example, their staying respectively at the George V and Plaza-Athénée: 'Too many people know us, Michel. There is no need to advertise our being in Paris. We should stay at modest hotels in different parts of Paris.

'You speak enough German to manage, don't you? Good. When we speak by telephone – and that should be as little as possible – it must be in German. Fewer French people speak German than English. When we meet, let it be in an obscure café somewhere – not a place where we are likely to encounter people we know.

'I will tell Carlotta I have gone to Frankfurt. You tell Anne-Marie you have gone to Brussels. In fact, we shall go there; but then we shall take the train to Paris. Why a train? Because there is no record of your name, that is why.'

Michel felt a pulse of apprehension. 'Don't you think all these precautions are a bit elaborate? Or do you think somebody is on our trail?'

'I'm thinking of afterwards, Michel. You can't put a fake story out on a wire service without questions being asked. There'll be a hell of a stink. Another thing: in whose name will you be dealing in the foreign exchange markets?'

'I'd thought of using a Liechtenstein *Anstalt*.'

'OK, good. But don't use it to deal in the Zurich market. The Swiss can break an *Anstalt*'s secrecy if a crime has been committed in Switzerland.'

'Anything else?'

'Yes. Money. I'll need some walking-around money – say, a thousand. Also, I want to change our arrangement. Instead of taking fifteen per cent of your winnings, I'd prefer twenty-five thousand, win or lose.'

'You're throwing money away.'

'Maybe. But I'd rather have ten per cent of something than fifteen per cent of nothing.'

'OK, but not until Schwarzenbach has sent the message.'

'Done.'

Five days later, Michel flew from Geneva to Brussels and checked into the Sheraton. It was large and impersonal enough not to notice if he didn't spend the night there. He unpacked one suitcase, hung his clothes in the cupboard, left a shaving kit in the bathroom, then took a taxi to the station. Two and a half hours later he was in Paris, and checked into the Hôtel Blanche, in the ninth arrondissement. Nobody, he was sure, would recognise him there. Henk had arrived in Paris two days earlier; he was staying at the Hôtel Lenox, in the seventh.

D-Day was the next day, and H-Hour 10.30. He phoned Henk, speaking in German. 'All going well?'

'Yes. Our friend arrived the day before yesterday. He reports he has found the location, and will be there first thing tomorrow morning.'

'He has the message?'

'No. I thought we'd better go over it again. Let's meet at the Café de la Gare, St Denis.'

'For Christ's sake, do we have to go so far?'

'It's better. Eight o'clock?'

'Right.'

For once, Henk was early, and Michel saw him sitting at a corner table. He was wearing a windbreaker, and could have passed for a worker; he even had a copy of *L'Équipe*, and instead of Scotch was drinking a beer. He greeted Michel in French, and handed him the draft story they had gone over so many times in Geneva.

'Bulletin. Paris, Thursday (EFNS) – French President Valéry Giscard d'Estaing has decided to dissolve the National Assembly and call new elections, sources close to the Elysée Palace said today.

'One aide said the President had made his decision because the conservative majority in the Assembly had blocked several important pieces of legislation, and was preventing the government from "carrying out the policies that the government knows are desired by the majority of French people".

'The President's move took most observers by surprise, since the latest opinion polls show that the Socialist–Communist alliance would take sixty per cent of the seats if an election were held immediately. However, the President has said in the past that if the left alliance won he would serve out his term "and work with the new majority as constructively as possible".

'The left alliance's manifesto includes promises of higher social security payments, nationalisation of all banks not yet state-controlled, and of key industrial companies.

'Official spokesmen at the Élysée Palace refused to confirm or deny the President's reported decision. One said: "An announcement will be made in due course."'

Michel chuckled. 'Reads perfectly. But don't you think it might be stronger? Couldn't we make the announcement official?'

'No, Michel. The way we've worded it, everyone will believe it, and nobody will believe the official spokesmen when they deny it – which they will do. I guess Giscard will have to appear on television himself to stop that one.'

'But what will happen when the news service denies ever sending the message?'

'Nobody will believe them, either. They'll just think somebody got at the editors. No, leave it the way it is. What's your strategy?'

'I've already gone short on the franc. Tomorrow, when it drops below the rate I've offered – 4.78 to the dollar – I'll pick up enough to cover my contracts, and show a nice big profit. I reckon it'll go to 4.30 or even lower. Then, knowing this report will be denied, I'll also buy francs in the spot market, and sell them next week or next month when the franc comes back again. If I'm right on both trades, I stand to make a quarter of a million, maybe more.'

'And if you're wrong?'

Michel shrugged. 'I could lose the same amount, or more. But it won't wipe me out, believe me. Look, we've been over this so often there's no point in talking about it again. Let's have some dinner.'

Henk brightened. 'There's a good little restaurant around the corner. Not in the Guide Michelin, not in the Guide Kléber, but still damned good.' It was, and surprisingly cheap: just under $20 for a three-course meal, wine, service and taxes.

Michel looked round the little restaurant, saw the quiet families dining together, an old man in a corner by himself reading a newspaper, and felt a twinge of conscience. What he was planning to do would knock the franc, make imports more expensive, perhaps even boost inflation by a trifle. Then he put the scruple aside. Bigger speculators than he did the same thing every day of the week; the difference was they used their financial muscle to buy or sell currencies so heavily that they rose or fell according to plan.

Absurdly, Michel and Henk argued over who would pay the bill, then laughed. 'Good God,' said Henk, wiping tears from his eyes, 'here we are planning a financial coup, and we quarrel like kids over who should pay less than a hundred francs. Ridiculous!'

Back at the hotel, Michel phoned Anne-Marie; if she called him in Brussels and found him out all night, his alibi might be shot. She was sleepy and loving, and Michel went to bed content with the day. He awakened next morning at eight, enjoyed his coffee and croissants, and whistled cheerfully while he showered. The day, he saw, was bright and sunny. He had nothing to do until 10.30 or a few minutes after, when Schwarzenbach was due to call him. He pulled a sweater over his head, went downstairs, and out into the bright sunlight, still whistling, still cheerful.

At a corner news stand, he bought an armful of papers – *Le Monde, Le Figaro, France-Soir* – and sat down at a café table. He turned to *Le Monde* first, even though it had been printed the previous afternoon, knowing that its liberal attitudes would get his adrenalin flowing. As he could have predicted, the front page featured stories about suffering Africans, a political crisis in Morocco. Then he picked up *Le Figaro* and felt himself shivering. A banner headline proclaimed that the President had decided to dissolve the National Assembly and call for new elections. For a wild moment, he thought that Schwarzenbach had sent the fake story on the wrong day, at the wrong time. Then, reading *Le Figaro*'s story, he saw that the announcement was official.

Michel threw money down on the café table, and sprinted back to the hotel, up to his room, and to the telephone.

'Henk? For Christ's sake, can we get hold of Schwarzenbach? We can't? Well, look at today's papers. Yes, we're a bloody sight better political forecasters than we are conspirators.'

17

> Wavering between the profit and the loss
> In this brief transit where the dreams cross
> *T. S. Eliot*

'Relax, for Allah's sake,' said Jack. He and Henry were sitting on the terrace of Yussaini's house in the late evening, their faces cooled by a breeze from the sea. Henry wriggled in his *chaise-longue*; after a long, hot day he still felt sticky, despite a swim in the pool and a cold shower. 'I think I'm getting prickly heat,' he muttered.

'Nonsense, Henry. You're just suffering from Arabian twitch. Symptoms: extreme nervousness, pathological dislike of all things Arab, and a desperate desire to go home. Cause: immersion in an alien culture. Cure: as your doctor, I prescribe a visit to the local night club. Herds of crumpet on the hoof there.'

'I don't get you.'

Jack took off his dark glasses and looked at Henry indulgently. 'My dear fellow, crumpet is what you Americans call quail or quim, or so I believe. Our interest is purely commercial, of course: we shall be inspecting and possibly testing potential members of the crew of the good ships *Venus* and *Aphrodite*.'

Henry groaned. 'I wish I'd never mentioned the idea. I'm still not sure I'm serious.'

'I am. I take seriously anything that will make a lot of money for a minimum of risk and effort. If the Emir is willing to grant us a licence and take ten per cent of our company, and Madame Claudine is delighted to be our recruiting agent, why should you develop twinges of conscience and distaste?'

'Because I'm a banker, not a pimp, that's why.'

'A fine distinction, if you ask me. Come along now – we'll be late.'

'Why, is there a floor-show?'

'Not that you'd notice. No, we're meeting Chuck Royston.'
'Chuck *who*?'
'Royston. Your memory's going, Henry. He's the man who's going to charter the *Venus* and *Aphrodite* to us.'

'For Christ's sake, Jack, I came here to meet Yussaini, not to prance about in some dingy nightspot talking about floating brothels.'

'You came here to make money, Henry, and Yussaini or no Yussaini, you're going to make it – or I am, at least.'

Henry followed Jack to the garage. Jack looked over the selection of cars, whistling tunelessly under his breath, then walked over to a Range-Rover. 'No point in leaving a Rolls outside to be scratched by some drunken idiot,' he said.

'I thought Yussaini didn't care about his cars?'

'He doesn't. But I do.'

The Range-Rover bounced over the bad road on hard springs, turned into a maze of narrow streets, and stopped in front of a long, low building with a neon sign that read 'C... Hump.' Jack laughed: 'It's really called the Camel's Hump, but I like that name better. Anyone who enters these doors is a chump – unless he's on business.'

A blast of airconditioning hit Henry as he walked into a small, dark room that was vibrating to a pop group on the tiny stage. The head waiter, surprisingly smart in a white tuxedo, led Henry and Jack to a table well away from the dance floor. An ice-bucket and bottle of champagne appeared out of the darkness, and a disembodied hand shone a tiny flashlight on the label: Dom Pérignon. Henry felt slightly better.

The pop group crashed into its finale, there was scattered applause and, for a moment, comparative silence. Then a spotlight shone on a piano, and an elderly man started to sing 'Manhattan'. Henry noted that he was not at all bad; in fact, very good. He turned to Jack. 'Who owns this joint?'

'An American, name of Dick Winters. The word is that he can't go back – some trouble over a shoot-out in New York. He says the Mafia are after him; more likely to be the police. Or perhaps he's just trying to make himself more interesting, and for that I don't blame him: he's a dull sort of chap. Ah, there's Royston.'

A tall man of about fifty, with a bland, expressionless face, sat down at their table. Henry, now accustomed to the gloom, saw that Royston was wearing a silk suit, heavy gold watch and diamond ring. He spoke in a drawling Louisiana accent, and his eyes were hooded and lazy. Henry suspected that Royston didn't miss a thing, and was not a man to meet alone in a dark boardroom at night.

He ordered a rye and orange juice on the rocks, shook some Tabasco sauce into it, stirred, and took a long swallow. 'Now then,' he said, looking at Henry, 'you're the party who wants to take a little joy and female companionship to the boys out on the platforms, am I right?'

Henry nodded. 'Yes. But not as my philanthropic contribution to the mental health of this area.'

Royston laughed loudly and slapped the table with a huge hand. 'I like that, I like that. Hear that, Jack? Your friend's got a real sense of humour, yessir. Right. Now let's get down to the nitty-gritty. You want two fifty-footers, cabins, salon, mebbe a little dance floor on the aft deck. Airconditioned, of course. Right. I can fix those up in no time. Just convert two of my old work-boats in my own yards – say a month.

'OK. So I provide the boats, crew, fuel, maintenance. For a one-year charter, the price'll be seventy thousand dollars per boat, plus ten per cent of the gross. That's a fair offer; take it or leave it.'

Henry sipped his champagne and thought. 'Could I have a private word with my partner?'

'No need, Henry,' said Jack. 'That's a very fair offer. Do you know what the crew alone will cost for two boats? About fifty thousand. No, I say take it.'

'It still seems steep to me.'

Royston leaned forward. 'Henry – you don't mind if I call you Henry, do you? Henry, I know what your gross will be. Five girls to each boat, total of fifty customers at least per day at fifty bucks each. That's two and a half thousand bucks a day, seven days a week: that's about nine hundred thousand a year gross. Then there are the drinks: let's say each customer has two at five bucks each. That's another ninety thousand bucks a year, give or take a dime or two. So your gross is around one million.

'OK. So I'm taking ten per cent, or a hundred thousand, plus another hundred and forty thousand for the boats – let's say a quarter of a million. You're gonna be paying the girls five hundred bucks a week each – that's two-sixty thousand a year. So your net is around half a million, less ten per cent to the Emir, leaving you with around four hundred and fifty thousand net, net net after taxes. Except there ain't no taxes in this part of the world. Am I right, gentlemen?'

Henry nodded. 'Put it like that, and I suppose you are.'

'No other way to put it, Henry. When I came out here six years ago, I had exactly twenty thousand bucks. Do you know what I'm worth now? Around fifteen million, net. Know how I did it? Always looked at the facts and figures. That's one thing I learned from my old daddy. He never looked at a fact if it didn't suit him, and died as poor as the day he was born, mebbe poorer, since he owed a sight.'

The pianist had stopped singing, the pop group was back, and conversation became impossible. Royston leaned towards Henry and shouted in his ear: 'See you tomorrow, around noon, at Hare's office. We'll get the deal signed up right then and there. Enjoy yourselves.'

He vanished into the gloom, and Henry drank the last of his champagne. Jack nodded, and led the way to a tiny bar at the back of the room that was shielded from the pop group by a screen. They sat in low, comfortable chairs, and a waiter put another bottle of Dom Pérignon on the table. Two girls sat down, wordlessly, and smiled. One was small and very dark; probably Iranian, thought Henry. The other was equally small, but fair. Both had hard, predatory faces, and wore ball gowns about ten years out of date. 'You like me?' said the fair one in a strong but unidentifiable accent.

'Not very much,' said Henry.

To his surprise, she smiled, and he realised that she could not understand English. She turned to the dark girl and said something. The dark girl smiled, too, and said to Henry, 'My friend say she like you, too, very much.'

Jack laughed. 'You can probably have both of them for the price of one, Henry. You've made a hit.'

Henry shuddered. 'No thank you, Jack. They're not my style.'

'You're too fastidious, old man. This is just the kind of girl we're going to have on our boats.'

'What kind of man would want them at fifty bucks each?'

'The kind of man out on the production platforms. You haven't seen them. They'll fuck anything that's hot and hollow. As for the Arabs, you know what they say: "A woman for children, a boy for variety, a goat for pleasure." Come on, let's go.'

Back at the villa there was a message from Yussaini: he would definitely return the next day. Henry went to his room, took out a pocket calculator, and checked the *Venus* and *Aphrodite* figures again. If anything, he thought, Royston had underestimated the gross; in an eight-hour day, surely, a girl could service more than ten men? A million-dollar operation; that raised it from the level of pimping to – well, a business returning him more than two hundred per cent net on his investment. He recalled that a German firm running brothels and sex shops had gone public. The issue had been oversubscribed, too, if he remembered correctly. Why stop at two boats? He pressed the buttons on his calculator and whistled, astonished at the total: fifty boats would bring a net of $10 million a year. Put that on a price-earnings ratio of, say, twelve, and the company's market value would be $120 million. Say that he and Jack sold forty per cent of their shares: each would receive $24 million in cash, and retain shares worth $36 million. This, he thought, was an idea worth discussing, even at two in the morning. He pressed a button on the house phone. 'Jack? You weren't asleep? Good. Listen. Can we have a conference? Yes, it's urgent.'

Jack arrived in a silk dressing-gown; he looked, thought Henry, like an actor in a Thirties play, probably the villain, but a witty, urbane one. Quickly, Henry went through the figures, finishing with the idea of going public. Jack was sceptical.

'Oh, I'm sure we could work out a deal with the rulers along the Gulf. But going public? Who would buy the shares?'

'I've thought of that. What business are we in? Offshore

services, right? So we describe it as that. If we go public in Europe instead of the United States, we shan't have to bother with an SEC registration; in Frankfurt, for instance, the authorities are a damn sight less fussy than they are in Washington. Jack, we're onto a winner – no doubt about that.'

'And no qualms now about being a pimp – your own word?'

'This puts a different dimension on it, Jack. A well-managed, well-financed company offering R & R to offshore production workers; that's something different. There's only one thing that worries me: the Mafia.'

Jack laughed heartily. 'If that's all, stop worrying. They've got their own Mafia on this coast. They're called sheikhs. Square them, and you can do what you want. Actually, come to think of it, they'd probably buy shares. So would some of the girls, believe it or not. And Madame Claudine and her rich clients – why, they'd probably jump at it. Yes, Henry, you've convinced me. But now, for Christ's sake, let's get some shut-eye. You want to be fresh for Yussaini tomorrow.'

'Oh, screw Yussaini. This deal is bigger than anything he's got to offer.'

'True, true. But even if you are worth sixty million bucks in your dreams, a real six million is a nice piece of loose change. Now, goodnight – definitely.'

Henry slept well and dreamlessly, and was up before the servant arrived with coffee. He showered and shaved briskly, listened to the news on short-wave radio, and was relaxing by the fountain when Jack found him soon after eight o'clock.

'Yussaini's just phoned,' said Jack. 'He wants a meeting at six tonight.'

'I'll believe it when I see him.'

'This time, he's serious – I think.'

'If he isn't, I'll move into a hotel and work on *Venus* and *Aphrodite*.'

'I shouldn't even try, if I were you. There's only one hotel in town, and it's always full. And if you moved out of here, Yussaini would take it as a deadly insult. When he says his house is your house, he means it.'

'Where's Hare's office, by the way?'

'In Dubai. We'll take the chopper – it's about an hour's run.'

The helicopter headed out to sea, and looking down Henry saw, set in the clear green water, dozens of platforms stretching to the horizon. Jack tapped his shoulder and said through the intercom system, 'I know what you're thinking, Henry: customers.'

'Yes, and then we've got Kuwait and Bahrein and Saudi Arabia. It's a big market, Jack, a very big market.'

The chopper put down on a pad close to the harbour. 'Royston's yard,' said Jack. 'Nice and close to the office.' Hare's office was, in fact, a bungalow, and his man in Dubai a gangling youth of twenty-eight or so, a shock of reddish-yellow hair hanging over one eye. He was so unmistakably English that Henry asked, 'Get much cricket out here?'

The young man's manner changed from lethargy to enthusiasm. 'Rather! We've got a pretty good English side. Beat the Pakistanis last Sunday. Next Sunday we play the Indians. Do come along.'

Jack coughed meaningly. 'Jolly good show, and all that, Freddie, but we're here on business.'

'Oh, terribly sorry. Yes. Now where's the file? Ah, here we are. Yes. We've incorporated a company in Luxembourg – no local taxes if you don't trade there. What did we call it? Oh, yes: Offshore Personal Services. All shares in the name of bearer. That was right, wasn't it? Good. The directors are a Luxembourg lawyer and accountant. We've also opened two bank accounts for the company, Mr Rusk. One is with International Westminster Bank in Luxembourg, the other with the Arab Bank here. Both denominated in dollars.'

Henry nodded approvingly. Juvenile and lethargic he might appear to be, but Freddie had obviously worked fast and well – indeed, had set the whole thing up in less than a week. 'Very fast work. Many thanks.'

Freddie blushed. 'Oh, do you think so? I must confess I spent a few hours at the telex.'

'You know that Royston is coming in?'

'Yes, Mr Rusk. He's already sent me a copy of the proposed time charter. I think it's all in order, but I've made one or two suggestions – here, and again here, and also on the fourth page. The main point is that he should offer the company an indemnity if either of the boats is out of action for any other reason except an act of God. Of course, he can insure to cover himself; but I think he should bear the insurance premium, not the company.'

Royston arrived a few moments later, elegant in a pale grey silk suit, white-on-white shirt, and Gucci shoes. In the daylight, Henry saw what he had not seen the night before: under their heavy lids, Royston's eyes were brilliant blue, as brilliant as precious stones. He listened quietly to Freddie's amendments to the charter contracts, and agreed to them all.

Henry and Jack signed, as agents of Offshore Personal Services, and Royston leaned back in his chair. 'Well, gentlemen, that's what I call a good morning's work. Want to see photographs of the boats I'm gonna convert?' Henry saw a long, low boat, painted black; in the background was an oil rig. 'Ex-French Navy,' said Royston. 'Can do thirty knots if you push her. 'Course, she'll be white when she goes on charter. The other one's ex-British Navy: twin diesels, sixty feet. I'm throwing in the extra ten feet for nothing. Here are the drawings. See, we'll have seven cabins, each with a bidet – essential equipment on a ship like this. There's the galley. I'm putting the bar up on deck, under a plexiglass bubble. That way, you have extra space below, but still get the airconditioning. No crew quarters; reckon she should be back in port every night – or early morning, more like.'

Freddie said, 'If you want, gentlemen, you can sign right now. Please initial the amendments.' Henry hesitated, and looked covertly at Royston, who in the daylight seemed even tougher and more formidable than he had the night before. Then, with an eagerness still tinged by reluctance, he initialled the changes in the contract, and signed at the end. Jack did the same, followed by Royston. For a moment there was silence, broken by Royston.

'I reckon this calls for a little celebration, gentlemen. I'd thought of a little luncheon at my place, Louisiana-style. But first, mebbe you gentlemen would like to take a peek at my yard.'

They went out into the sun, which was brazen and relentless in the noon sky, and climbed into Chuck's car – a white

Cadillac Fleetwood – for the short journey. Henry was surprised by the yard. Unlike most of the Gulf businesses he had seen so far, it was tidy and well equipped, its workers neat in off-white coveralls emblazoned with the corporate logo, and hard-hats in bold orange. A long, black-painted boat was up on a slip: a crane was lifting an engine out. 'That's your first,' said Royston. 'The *Venus*. Just giving the engines a thorough overhaul – they've only done five hundred hours since new, should be no problems. Over here now, this is where we service the electronic equipment.' He walked into a low building in which a dozen men and fifty women were working. The women, Henry noticed, were Oriental. Royston saw him looking, and laughed. 'Yeah, all the girls are slant-eyes – Korean, mostly. The fuckin' Japanese taught them how to assemble TV sets and radios, so I picked up the best of 'em, brought 'em here on contract.'

'Any problem about work permits?'

Royston laughed as though at a good joke. 'They don't *have* no work permits, Henry. I like it better that way. Keeps 'em in order, gives me a gun at their heads, just in case they get any strange ideas about more money or shorter hours.'

'But if they're here without work permits, doesn't that mean you're in trouble?'

'Pardon me saying so, Henry, but you don't know much about this part of the world. I've got permission, semi-official, to employ them without work permits. But they don't know that; any of 'em gets bothersome, and I can just ship her out at a moment's notice, no questions asked. Know why you find so many Americans like me out in this part of the world? It's just like America was, sixty, seventy years ago. Your old American robber barons would have felt at home here. Everything's up for grabs, everything's got a price. Only one difference: no democracy here, no trouble with interferin', smart-ass lawyers and newspapermen. Can't last, though; good things never can. I give it five more years, mebbe seven; but by then I'll be back home in Lafayette Parish, ready for some of that home cookin'. Which reminds me, we're due for lunch.'

Royston's home, a half-hour drive away, was set on a low bluff overlooking the sea, a huge, rambling bungalow surrounded by green lawns and shaded by a species of tree Henry could not identify.

'Eucalyptus,' said Royston. 'Cost a goddamn fortune to import from Australia. Now I've a fuckin' tree surgeon who costs me thirty thousand bucks a year – or did, till I sold the local sheikhs on trees. Now he's running a business, and making me a hundred thousand a year. I'll tell you, these sheikhs are just goddamn suckers for prestige. One of them saw my trees, nothing would content him until he'd got his own. Now, they all got trees. Would you believe it, one of the fuckers came to me last week, said he had to have a California Redwood – had heard it was the world's largest. Well, I'm getting him one, but it's gonna cost him a hundred thousand bucks by the time he's finished. Know why this emirate has four football stadiums? Because the ruler's got three sons and a nephew, and each has his own team. 'Course, they don't play American football; that would be too tough. No, they play soccer.'

Henry had expected Royston's house to resemble the man; to be opulent, ornate and tasteless. Instead, it was a contrast with its owner, a suave blend of contemporary and Arabian decor, the walls of the living-room hung with nineteenth-century European paintings of Arab scenes. He complimented Royston, who shrugged. 'Don't blame me, blame my wife. There's only one room she didn't touch – mine. That's where we'll have a drink.'

Royston's room was huge – at least forty feet by thirty – and was a mixture of library, office and museum. One wall, from floor to ceiling, was lined with books. Henry looked at some of the titles and was reminded of the surprise he had felt in Anne's apartment in London. Royston, or somebody living in the house, read history, biography, economics, psychology and sociology; one whole section of about five hundred books was given over to Middle Eastern history. Another wall was lined with marine models, from tiny Gulf fishing boats and dhows, to nineteenth- and early twentieth-century sailing- and steam-ships, all of them detailed and professional.

'You seem to have a lot of interests, Chuck.'

'You talkin' about the books? Well, I told you I go for facts.

What I do is, I have a young man – Oxford graduate – who makes me a summary of the best books in every field. Then, when I've read the summary, I either say, "Shit, that's all I need to know," or I read the book itself. Take the Middle East. You'd be surprised how many people come out here without knowing a damn thing about the place, and leave knowing very little more. That way, a man can make some damnfool mistakes, like calling Muslims Mohammedans, or talking about the Arab nations. Fact is, they don't worship Mohammed; they worship God or Allah, and they think there's just one Arab nation – which is a lot of hogwash, in my view, but there it is. Oh, there's a whole lot of boobytraps out here.'

They sat in comfortable leather armchairs with their drinks; Chuck, Henry noticed, was still drinking rye with orange juice and Tabasco. The door opened, and a huge black woman entered. 'Mr Chuck, yo' dinner is a-spoilin'. I ain't gonna sweat masel' in that kitchen of yaw's if you don't come to table when I call you.' Her round face quivered indignantly, and she wiped her hands on her apron. She was, thought Henry, straight out of a Thirties movie: the Aunt Jemima of yesteryear now banned from screens large and small by black pride and white guilt.

Royston obeyed her indulgently, and slapped her spreading rump as he passed her. 'Don't you get uppity with me, Dolores, or I'll send you back to pickin' cotton.' Dolores laughed uproariously and waddled to the kitchen. Her lunch was excellent: chicken gumbo, crawfish in a rich sauce, and apple pie with fresh cream. A little heavy for the climate, thought Henry; but then, Lafayette Parish in summer was probably not much cooler than Dubai in the fall. They drank California wines: an Almaden Chablis to start, followed by Zinfandel.

'Did you bring Dolores out with you?' Henry asked.

'Sure did. She was my auntie's cook, then my auntie died, and she's worked for me ever since.'

'She's got a work permit, I assume?'

'Yessir. And I pay her US Social Security for her. I treat her right, don't you worry.'

Henry looked at Royston, who was sitting relaxed over his

wine. What a curious man he was, a mass of contradictions. He treated his Korean workers as little better than slaves; but prided himself on treating a black American as though she were an important executive. He came on strong, as a ruthless, brutal and narrow entrepreneur; but apparently paid an Oxford graduate to tutor him – for that's what his system amounted to, essentially. He could be caustic about the Arabs; yet showed a deep knowledge of their culture, and sensitivity to their feelings.

Jack roused himself, looked at his watch, and said, 'We'd better be moving, Henry. Yussaini can be days late for us, but heaven help us if we're half an hour late for him.'

Back at Yussaini's villa, Henry found a note. Yes, Yussaini had returned, and looked forward to a conference at six-thirty, followed by dinner. Henry bathed, shaved for the second time that day, and before dressing called Jack on the house phone. Yes, said Jack, a tuxedo was a good idea; Yussaini liked his guests to be formal.

Henry found Yussaini in the central courtyard, sitting in a chair under a tree, and apparently absorbed in the sight and sound of the fountain. He was wearing a white tuxedo, and his manner was once more European rather than Arab. 'My dear Henry,' he said, springing up and putting out his hand. 'I really am most dreadfully sorry for this delay. I hope you spent your time usefully and enjoyably? Indeed, I even hear rumours that your time was not utterly wasted. Now, can we discuss JZ? Good. Let us go to the library.'

A servant waited with a bottle of Krug and a plate of caviare spread on toast. Yussaini raised his glass: 'Your very good health, Henry. You don't mind if I call you that, do you? I, of course, am Ahmed. Now, about JZ: I have not wasted your time. I have discussed this with my associates, and we are ready to make a bid.

'Yes, we are prepared to offer $31 per share. That comes to $1·4 billion, or about 12·5 times earnings. You think they will accept that?'

'No. They say $1·6 billion is their rock-bottom figure.'

'Ah. As you know, Henry, I do not believe in bargaining. Unfortunately, the Americans do – while all the time saying, of course, that they bargain to keep us Arabs happy, because they think we have a bazaar mentality. Such is the irony of life. So I suggest you offer $1·4 billion. They will come back and say – no, $1·6. Then we shall say: Let us compromise. How about $1·5? And they will be happy. And so shall we, since we think the company's real worth is closer to $2·3 billion.'

'How do you figure that out? Its net book is only $1·5.'

'I will tell you. First, after the long depression in shipping rates, caused by the worldwide recession, there is a real prospect of a recovery. Eight of JZ's tankers are on charters due for revision next year. Next, on six ships they have made the mistake of taking out mortgages. They have a net equity in those ships of $350 million. Yet their return on that equity is only 6·5 per cent net after taxes. We shall refinance those ships so as to release the $350 million, and re-invest it to show us at least ten per cent, almost certainly more. Finally, they have their operating headquarters in Manhattan, in a building in which they have a fifty per cent equity. We value that equity at $100 million. Furthermore, it is a bad investment: they are getting a net return of only seven per cent. We shall sell that equity, and move the operating headquarters to London.'

'Excuse me, Ahmed, but are you sure that's wise? After all, JZ is an old-established company with...'

'Old-fashioned ideas, Henry. Let me explain. We would ask the key managers to move with us; and I am sure most would agree. Then there are two hundred other employees in headquarters. In New York, JZ pays them an average of $22,000 a year, including social security and fringe benefits. In London, we could employ two hundred people at an average of $12,000 a year. What is the saving? About $2 million a year. More, in fact, because JZ really does not need two hundred people.'

'You certainly have done your homework, Ahmed. I guess I should have looked at JZ differently.'

'Perhaps yes, perhaps no, Henry. You are a banker. You look at collateral, at cash flow. You are not a management consultant, a company doctor, or an entrepreneur. I am a little of each. I look at a company and ask: "Ah, what do the figures *really* say?" You know where I usually find the answers? In the footnotes. They are all there, for everyone to read; but most people cannot be bothered with the fine print. Then, when I have decided on the company's real worth, as distinct from what the figures apparently say, I ask: "And how can this company be improved?" If it cannot be, and that is rare, then I leave it alone. I am not interested in passive investments.

'Now, why do you not send JZ a telex with my offer? Put it in the name of Woodcat Investments, S.A., Luxembourg.'

Henry stared. 'But I just...'

'Yes, I know. You have just raised long-term capital in the market for Woodcat Investments, Inc. That is a subsidiary of the Luxembourg company. We did not need the money; we did want to see how you would perform, and you passed your test very well.'

Henry felt manipulated again, and Yussaini must have seen his frown, for he said, gently, 'Please understand, Henry, many people with excellent reputations come to us, but we like to decide for ourselves. And, you must agree, you made some money out of our little test.'

Henry nodded, and smiled. 'Yes, I guess that's right. Now, just one thing. JZ will want to know that this Luxembourg company has the funds. How do we assure them?'

Yussaini walked to a desk, opened it, and returned with a letter. It was from Crédit Suisse, Zurich, certifying that Woodcat had on deposit 'with this and with other banks known to us' funds 'ample to proceed with a purchase in excess of $1·5 billion'. Henry tapped the letter. 'This will do. OK, how do I send the telex?' Yussaini pressed a button on the telephone, and within seconds a tall, graceful girl in her mid-twenties opened the door. 'This is Miss Grierson, Henry. Please dictate any message you wish to attend to. I'll see you for dinner in about half an hour.'

The girl closed her book after Henry had dictated, and said, 'That will go within twenty minutes, Mr Rusk. Is there anything else?' Her accent was English, he noted.

'Yes. I've been here the best part of two weeks, and never seen you. Do you work here, or somewhere else?'

'I'm usually in Mr Yussaini's London office. This time I've been travelling with him. Now I'll be staying for a week.'

'Will you be dining with us tonight?'

She shook her short hair, which sparkled red-blond in the dying rays of the sun. 'I'm afraid not. Mr Yussaini has strict ideas about – well, keeping employees and guests separate.'

'Well, perhaps you and I could have dinner one night.'

She shook her head. 'Not a good idea on his home ground, Mr Rusk. But in London – well, perhaps.'

'OK, it's a date.'

She left the room with a graceful swirl of her skirts, and Henry poured himself the last of the champagne. The door opened, and Jack looked round its edge. 'You look relaxed, Henry. All well?'

'Yes. He's making a bid for JZ. I think they'll take it.'

'So that's six million for you, a million for Hare and me, give or take a few thousand either way. When will you know?'

'I guess we should get an answer tomorrow.'

'But you think they'll accept?'

'They'd be crazy not to.'

'Then let's just hope they're sane.'

18

> Revenge is a kind of wild justice, which the more man's nature runs to, the more ought law to weed it out.
>
> *Francis Bacon*

Jacqueline's taxi turned onto the Île St Louis, its diesel engine growling, and stopped outside her building. She was about to open the door when Jacques shouldered her out of the way. 'I'll go first. Give me your key.' He entered the tiny lift, leaving Jacqueline waiting in the lobby; when she looked towards the street, she saw Raoul leaning against his car, reading a newspaper and smoking. He could have passed as a plumber waiting for a client.

The lift came down, empty, and Jacqueline pressed the button for her floor. Jacques was waiting on the landing, a cigarette in the corner of his mouth. For a moment, the whole enterprise seemed so melodramatic that she was tempted to laugh, to ask Jacques whether his style came from the French movies, or their style from him. He jerked his head. '*Ça va, madame*. OK, I'll wait in the kitchen. Raoul will wait downstairs. Then we'll change places. When it gets dark, we'll both wait up here. Two hours on, two hours off. Where can we sleep?'

Jacqueline showed him the spare room. He looked at the white walls, the long curtains over the double windows, the bathroom. 'Not bad, *madame*. Anything to eat?'

She showed him the kitchen, the refrigerator, the freezer. 'Can you cook, *madame*?'

'Sure. What do you want?'

'Some of that pâté. A steak. Red wine. Perhaps some cheese.'

'OK, I'll get it for you.'

'No. Wait half an hour. I don't like to eat too early. How about a drink – whisky, perhaps?'

She poured him a large one, a smaller one for herself. Jacques sat at the kitchen table, his leather jacket unzipped, and looked at her with a smile. 'Now tell me, *madame*, this Jaime – he is your boy-friend?'

'He was. I also work for him.'

'He's rich, yes?'

'Very. He's also a bastard.'

'In this life, *madame*, one cannot have everything. He keeps you in this apartment?'

'Certainly not, Jacques. I keep myself.'

'So you are rich, too.'

'I guess so. Let's change the subject. What is your plan if Jaime comes, or sends somebody?'

'Raoul will follow them upstairs. When the bell rings, you keep out of sight. We'll deal with them.'

'No guns, please.'

'That depends, *madame*. If they use guns, so do we – silenced. We're professionals. Probably they will be, too. But I'd rather use this.' Jacques took a flick-knife from his hip pocket; the blade gleamed.

Jacqueline looked away. How many men had that blade killed, wounded? She dared not ask. 'Another drink, Jacques?'

'No, thank you, *madame*. Something to eat, perhaps.'

Jacqueline took pâté out of the refrigerator, a fillet steak, French beans. Jacques watched her, his look amused. He ate, she saw, with surprising delicacy, and drank sparingly of the wine. He refused a coffee: 'No, I must send Raoul upstairs.'

Raoul said nothing as he seated himself at the kitchen table. 'Pâté and steak?' Jacqueline asked. He nodded, lit a cigarette, and looked out of the window. 'A drink, Raoul?' He shook his head, and poured himself a glass of wine. In France, Jacqueline remembered with amusement, a drink is something hard, like whisky; wine is as innocuous as water. Feeling defiant, she poured herself another Scotch, larger than the last one, and set the table for Raoul. He ate slowly. Determined to make him speak, Jacqueline asked: 'Do you like your steak medium or rare?'

'Rare.'

'Do you never talk, Raoul?'

'Only if there is something to talk about.'

She looked at him as he ate. His face was intelligent, no doubt about that; and despite his stubbled chin and rough clothes there was something almost elegant about him. She tried to imagine him well shaved, wearing a suit. Yes, he would be elegant, and the ruthlessness in his face would make him attractive. She felt a tremor along her backbone, and wondered if Jaime had given her a taste for tough, ruthless men. Possibly: they were, in so many ways, preferable to the kind, weak men she had known in the past, the men who achieved cruelty by promising too much to too many people, stretching themselves, their time, and their capacity for love. With a Jaime, or perhaps a Raoul, illusion was difficult; they promised little, but delivered it.

Jacqueline started to pour herself a third Scotch. Raoul rose and took the bottle from her. 'You don't need that. You should eat. Let me cook. You don't know how.'

'That's ridiculous. I – '

'Sit down.'

He looked in the refrigerator, took out a carton of cream; looked on the shelves, found a packet of green peppercorns, and put them on the table. Fifteen minutes later, he served her a steak with pepper sauce, a salad with piquant dressing, and beans cooked to the point where they were still crisp.

'That was delicious, Raoul. Where did you learn to cook?'

'Where I learned to fight. In the Foreign Legion.'

'But somebody must have taught you?'

'Yes. A German. Trained as a chef in France, then joined the SS. Like many, he took refuge in the Legion.'

'Where is he now?'

'Dead.'

'And he was your friend?'

'Yes.'

'But a German, and an SS man?'

'He was a man. That's all I know.'

'Not many French people think like you.'

'I'm not French.'

'Not French? Then what are you?'

'Australian.'

'But your name? And the way you speak French?'

'My name is not Raoul. My French is not perfect. It just seems so to you, because yours is terrible.'

She thought of arguing, then realised that her French was poor: heavily accented, ungrammatical. 'Tell me, Raoul...'

'I'll tell you nothing more. I'm here for a job. Now I'll go to the street; Jacques will wait up here.'

He removed his dark glasses, showing prominent, pale blue eyes. 'One thing I will say, for your own good. Forget any ideas about me as a man who wants to expiate his past. I have a way of life. I chose it. I like it.' He walked to the front door, closing it gently behind him. Not until he had gone did Jacqueline realise he had spoken in English, a clear, upper-class English.

She returned to the kitchen, and started to wash up. Jacques knocked on the door, almost timidly: 'I'll take that coffee now, *madame*.'

She took her own coffee into the living-room, and sat on a couch, half reading a copy of *Newsweek*. She looked at her watch: 9.30. Jacques cleared his throat behind her. '*Madame*, it may be a long night. It is best that you get some sleep. We'll wake you if we need you.'

Jacqueline was about to protest, then found she could hardly contain a yawn. 'What will you do, Jacques?'

'Oh, wait in the kitchen, perhaps here. Don't worry: I shan't go to sleep.'

Jacqueline showered swiftly and went to bed. She was asleep within minutes. When she awakened the window was dark, and by the digital clock at her bedside she saw it was almost one-thirty in the morning. What had wakened her? She listened. The apartment was quiet. Then she heard a slight noise at her window. Her heart pounded, and for a second she had to bite back a scream. Then her common sense returned, and she walked noiselessly to her bedroom door, opened it, and saw Jacques on the couch, reading a magazine. His eyes widened when he saw her. Jacqueline put a finger to her lips, and said softly, 'In my room. A man or men.' Jacques grinned, pulled a slim black box from his leather jacket, and pressed a button. 'That will alert Raoul,' he said. 'Wait in the kitchen, *madame*. We can take care of this.' He switched off the lights.

From the kitchen door she saw Jacques move behind the couch, kneel, and pull a gun from his pocket. There was a faint click from the front door, and Raoul came in; a gun was in his hand. He melted into the shadows by the bookcase. The bedroom door opened silently. In the dim light from the living-room a man's figure was framed, his face unrecognisable under a stocking mask that squashed and distorted his features. He held something in his right hand, but Jacqueline could not identify it. From the shadowy corner where Raoul was standing came a slight noise, a plop, and the man at the bedroom door gasped. Something fell from his hand, hissing on the carpet. Suddenly, Jacques rushed forward and kicked the man expertly in the face, then in the ribs. Raoul moved forward, gun in hand, switched on the lights, and kicked the intruder again.

Jacqueline saw that a small bottle had fallen from his hand, spilling a pool on the carpet. It was sizzling, and a patch of the fawn carpet had turned black.

'Acid,' said Jacques. 'It was meant for you. Back in the kitchen, please. There is probably more than one of these animals.' He turned the lights off again, and kneeled behind the couch, where he was hidden from the front door. Raoul gagged the raider, tied his arms behind him, and pulled him into the bedroom, closing the door softly. There was a long silence. Jacqueline felt herself shivering uncontrollably.

The front door clicked and opened. Suddenly, the lights blazed, and at the same time the gun in Jacques' hand gave that apologetic little plop. The man framed by the front door fell forward, groaning. Jacques rushed forward, kicked the man's head, scooped up a gun, and kicked again. From the bedroom came a cry, a gurgle, and a low, whining voice. Raoul opened the door. 'Two. That's all. What do we do with them?'

'Do they admit who sent them?'

'The first one said he didn't know – a man in a café. The second one will have to wake up before we question him. Jacques, get the water.' Jacques came back from the kitchen with a plastic bucket full to the brim. Raoul threw it at the man in the lobby, who groaned, opened his eyes, then closed them again. Raoul kicked him on the side of the neck. 'Wake up, *salaud*, or the next bucket will be acid.' The man opened his eyes again. He was young, perhaps twenty-three, and had long, untidy hair. Raoul laughed. 'He's easy. Yours, Jacques.'

Jacques dragged the man to the couch, laid him out, and showed him the vial of acid. 'You see this? You know what it is? Here, try a little.' The man screamed as a drop fell on his hand. 'OK, the next goes on your pretty face. Now, who sent you?'

'I don't know.'

'You don't know? You just broke in here? Try some more acid.'

The man pitched and turned, then screamed. 'No, no. It was a man in a café, a man I don't know. He gave us five thousand francs to take the lady downstairs.'

'Downstairs here?'

'Yes.'

Raoul looked at Jacques and nodded. Jacques hit the prostrate man on the temple with his gun, once, twice, three times. He handed the gun to Jacqueline. 'Here, *madame*. Just in case this one wakes up. But he won't. We'll be back.'

'What about the man in the bedroom?'

'He's dead.'

The gun was heavy in her hand. She looked at it curiously. It was just a lump of metal, blue-black in the half light; yet it was also strangely comforting, so efficient, so quiet, so lethal. The man on the couch stirred, muttered. Jacqueline aimed the gun at his head. He opened his eyes slowly, muttered again, then tried to sit up. He saw the gun and fell back, with one hand held in front of him. 'No, please, no. It's not my fault.'

Jacqueline sighted the gun, this time about three inches to the left of his head. Again there was that soft, almost obscene plop, and she saw a hole appear in the cushion. The man on the couch screamed and sobbed, his limbs thrashing. Jacqueline watched him with detached amusement and fired again. The bullet clipped his left ear and he fainted. Jacqueline stood over him. 'Why, you poor little man, you're nothing when you're on the wrong end of a gun, are you?'

There was a noise from the lobby, and Jacques and Raoul

walked in behind Jaime and his Paris chauffeur, Felipe. Raoul had a gun in his hand, Jacques a knife. Jaime's left cheek was smeared with blood, and his hair was ruffled, but he was cheerful. 'I am proud of you, Jacqueline. You have learnt so much in the past few months that you anticipated this move. I have underestimated you. However, the game is still mine, I think.' He turned to Raoul.

'How much is Miss Eden paying you? Ten thousand francs, fifteen thousand? Whatever it is, I shall double it, treble it. Name your price.'

Raoul looked at Jacques, and nodded. Jacques raised his knife, and pushed it slowly towards Jaime's throat. Jaime stepped back until he touched the wall. He opened his mouth, started to speak, stopped. Raoul turned to Jacqueline. 'Shall we kill him now or later?'

'Later. First I want to tell him something. Jaime, do you know why you can't buy these two? You don't, do you? Raoul, please tell him.'

'I didn't like the way you offered the money.'

'Oh, should I have said please, gone down on my knees, perhaps? I know what kind of scum you are: you sell to the highest bidder. Here is my final offer: one million francs.'

'*Merci, monsieur.* We have a client already.'

'Jacqueline, reason with these madmen.'

'I don't think they're as mad as you are, Jaime. They didn't plan to drop acid on *your* face.'

'I knew nothing about the acid.'

'Then you should have been more careful, Jaime.'

Raoul broke in impatiently. 'What shall we do with him? Kill him?'

'No. Just disgrace him. I leave it to your imagination.'

'Thank you. I suggest you go out, *madame*. Find an all-night café, or a cabaret. We'll clear this place up. You'll hear no more.'

'What about the dead man?'

'I said: you will hear no more.'

'Raoul, please come here. I want to speak to you.' She led him into the kitchen. 'Raoul, Jaime has something I want — something of mine. Tell him that he will be killed unless I have it back.'

'Very well. Now go. Telephone before you return.'

Jacqueline pulled on a shirt and slacks, combed her hair, and ran downstairs. The night was cool and windy, and she walked for five minutes before finding a taxi. For a moment she could not think of where to go, then asked for the Calavados bar on the avenue Pierre Premier de Serbie, just off the Champs-Elysées. A black pianist was playing songs from the Thirties, and a middle-aged couple, decidedly drunken, were holding hands at the bar. Jacqueline ordered a coffee and cognac. She looked at her watch: only 2.15. The violence seemed to have lasted for hours; in fact, it had all been over in thirty or forty minutes. She went to the phone and dialled her own number: no answer. The barman, white-haired and benevolent, beckoned to her. 'I think you would be happier at the bar, *madame*. The gentleman who has sat down at the next table to yours is looking for company. You are not in the mood, perhaps?'

Jacqueline nodded, grateful for his tact, and ordered another coffee. The pianist was still playing softly. 'When love congeals,' he sang, 'it leaves behind the faint aroma of performing seals.' Jacqueline smiled. She had always thought that a mere ingenious rhyme; now it seemed to contain a cosmic truth. She looked at her watch again: 2.35. She dialled her own number again. This time Raoul answered. 'Your apartment is ready for you.'

'Raoul, I feel like a celebration. Do you know the Calavados? OK, join me here. Yes, with Jacques, of course.' While she waited for them she listened, fascinated, as the pianist went through his repertoire of Rodgers and Hart, Cole Porter, Ira and George Gershwin, Irving Berlin. When Raoul and Jacques entered, they were like denizens from another world, menacing in their thick leather jackets. The barman looked at them challengingly. 'It's all right,' said Jacqueline. 'I know them.'

They ordered beers. Drinking, she thought, was not their weakness. She took an envelope from her handbag. 'There, that's the other half of the bargain, with a bonus.'

'We don't deserve the bonus,' Raoul said. 'We should have

thought of the bedroom window. That type got into another building, and crawled along the roof.'

'What did you do with Jaime?'

'You'll find out.'

'No, tell me now. You didn't kill him, did you?'

'Not physically, no. Socially and politically, almost certainly. We left him and Felipe naked outside the Spanish Embassy, trussed up like chickens. We wrote a word on his back, too: *Maricón.*'

'What's that mean?'

'Homosexual.'

'What a pity it won't get into the newspapers.'

'But it will. A photographer, a friend of ours, will deliver pictures and the story to all the papers and agencies this morning. With Jaime's name, too: we took it from his passport.'

Jacqueline laughed shakily. 'You know, I wonder if we have been too cruel. There was a moment, back there, when I wanted to kill him. But...'

'You forget he sent two men after you, one with acid. And it may not be over. You'd better go to a hotel. Otherwise, we'll have to guard the apartment.'

'I think I'd like to go home. Jaime may try to phone me; he still has something of mine.'

'OK, let's go.'

Raoul's battered car was parked across the street. She climbed in, and nodded off to sleep as he drove through the deserted streets. Back at the apartment Raoul and Jacques stretched out on couches in the living-room; she fell into her bed, and was asleep instantly. When she wakened, the sun was streaming through the windows and the telephone was ringing. She lifted the receiver: 'Hullo?'

'Miss Eden? A mutual friend has asked me to deliver a package. Would it be convenient now?'

'Make it half an hour from now.'

'Very well.'

She put on a negligee and walked to the living-room. Raoul was asleep. From the kitchen came small noises; Jacques was making coffee. His face was stubbled with beard and tired, but he smiled cheerfully and poured a cup of coffee for Jacqueline as she sat at the table.

'Jaime's sending a man with the package I want.'

'We'll be waiting.'

'I don't think he's going to try any rough stuff this time.'

'He'd better not.'

'I forgot to ask last night: what did you do with the dead man?'

'Dumped him in the Seine.'

He said it so nonchalantly that Jacqueline shuddered. Raoul and Jacques were likable in a way, but she had to remember that they were killers, out for hire, though not without a certain rough morality of their own. Or was it that any enemy of a client became their enemy, and automatically offended some obscure ethical code? And what sort of family life could such men have?

'Are you married, Jacques?'

'Of course. Look, here is my wife and son.' He handed over a blurred colour photograph. A pretty woman peered out, her eyes squinting into the sun. A boy of about four was laughing and pointing. Jacques handed over another picture. In this one, he was sitting on the sand, his son beside him, his wife in the background.

'A very handsome boy,' said Jacqueline, handing the photos back.

'He is smart, too,' said Jacques. 'Now my wife is expecting another. We want a girl this time.'

'And Raoul. Is he married?'

Jacques laughed. 'Not that one. He likes women too much to marry one.'

There was a ring at the doorbell. Jacques motioned to Jacqueline to stay in the kitchen and went out, closing the door behind him. A few seconds later there was a tap at the door and Raoul opened it. He carried a large package wrapped in brown paper and tied with cord. 'Is this what you want?'

'Give me a moment, please. In private.' Raoul closed the door and Jacqueline cut the cord with trembling fingers, ripped the paper, and saw reels of tape, a dozen or more negatives, and a bulky envelope. She opened it, her face flaming as she saw herself alone, with Jaime. She looked round the kitchen. How could she hide the photographs? She saw a plastic garbage bag, stuffed the whole package inside, and took it to her bedroom. On the way, she saw Raoul sitting relaxed but watchful, and Jacques standing over a nondescript man in a grey suit who was sitting uneasily on the edge of a chair. Jacqueline closed the bedroom door behind her, hid the package at the bottom of her wardrobe, and returned to the living-room. 'All right, Raoul, he can go. The package is what I wanted.'

Raoul walked to the front door, opened it, and said to the man: 'Now get out. If you want to know what happens to people like your boss, look at the afternoon papers.'

'Now I must keep my end of the bargain,' said Jacqueline. 'Can you come with me to the office?'

'Let Jacques stay here. You never know.'

'I don't think there's any danger. Jaime wants me to do something now, and only I can do it.'

'Yes, but when you've done it, who knows?'

'I'll be on a flight out of Paris this afternoon.'

'That's not a good idea. Your destination can be traced. Where are you going?'

'London.'

'Take the train, then the ferry.'

'Thanks for the idea, Raoul. And thanks for everything.'

'A job is a job.'

At the station Jacqueline bought a copy of *France-Soir*. On the front page was a headline: 'Spanish aristocrat in mystery kidnapping.' There was a photo of Jaime, taken from the back. It had been cropped to cut out his bottom, and the word *maricón* airbrushed into invisibility. Jacqueline smiled. That was as much as one could expect from a newspaper owned by an extreme right-winger who probably thought Jaime was one of the future saviours of Europe.

19

> The breath of her false mouth was like faint flowers,
> Her touch was an electric poison
> *Percy Bysshe Shelley*

Peter was wet to the skin by the time he got home from the Ministerial meeting, his shoes squelching and his glasses blurred. He felt elated, though, and when lightning flickered and there was a growl of thunder thought the natural drama of a stormy night peculiarly appropriate to the occasion. He looked at the bar, decided against a drink, and put the kettle on for coffee while he changed into dry clothes.

He whistled cheerfully but tunelessly as he wrote a telex message – the same one would go to four brokerages where he maintained accounts. All instructed the broker to sell his soybean contracts, which were already showing a profit, and to go short. Peter hesitated as he came to the figures. How much should he risk? At last, he decided on two hundred and fifty thousand dollars in all, calculating that about forty of that would come from the forward contracts he was now selling. What price should he gamble on? March soybeans were standing at $7·80. The European Community's decision should clip that price heavily: perhaps to $6·50, but more likely $6·60–$6·70. He'd stick with that, not gamble on too big a fall, and if he was right would make a dollar a bushel, perhaps more – a total of over $70,000.

Peter tapped out the overseas code on the telex keys, waited for the automatic response, then tapped the number of a Chicago broker. There was a few seconds' delay, then he saw the broker's answer-back code, pressed the tape button, and watched the first of his messages going. Half an hour later he had finished, and leaned back in his chair with a sigh, watching the first, faint fingers of dawn through the window. Suddenly, he was hungry. He went to the kitchen, looked in the refrigerator, and decided to have bacon and eggs. The smell and sizzle of the bacon roused him. He looked at the kitchen clock: 5.30. Was it too early to call Ilse? Probably. Better to wait until after breakfast. He turned the eggs, poured a cup of coffee from the percolator, and set the table. The kitchen was warm and cosy, and as he ate breakfast Peter felt pleasantly tired and relaxed. He poured another coffee, took it to the living-room, and dialled Ilse's number. It rang twelve times, then he heard her voice.

'Just thought I'd let you know it all went to plan, honey.'

'What was the cut?'

'Fifteen per cent, would you believe.'

'And have you sent your telexes?'

'Sure have. Those brokers will think I've flipped my lid until they hear the news.'

He put the phone down gently, went to his bedroom, collapsed into bed, suddenly tired beyond endurance, and slept dreamlessly. When he wakened he saw by the bedside clock that it was close to noon. He showered and shaved, whistling happily, and in his dressing-gown went to the living-room. Presentación had already cleaned up, and left the morning papers on the table. He looked through them quickly: not a word about the soybean decision. Peter made coffee, switched on the radio, and turned to the American Forces Network for the news. Another row in Congress over energy policy. A skyjacking in Florida. Inflation rate down half a percentage point in the last quarter. Nothing about soybeans. He grinned, then started to worry. Could Traudl have been wrong? Or could the Ministers have changed their minds? He put the thought from him. Once made, a decision was irrevocable, at least for that meeting; or he hoped it was.

Restless and nervous, he paced out to the terrace to watch the storm from under the roof. Lightning darted, and appeared to hit the skyscraper that housed ITT's European headquarters. Peter chuckled. That sign of heavenly wrath should please all the critics of multinationals. He went back inside and drank another coffee, his mood improving. What he needed, he thought, was a relaxing weekend away from Brussels, perhaps more than a weekend, somewhere he could hear English spoken and feel less of a stranger than he did with French in his ears most of the time. London perhaps? An unenterprising choice, but a relaxing town where he knew a few people.

And this time, he thought, he would not take Ilse. The strain of her being so near, yet so unattainable, would make him tense. He dialled Sabena. Yes, they could let him have a seat that evening, returning on Monday. He wondered where to stay in London, then recalled that a friend had recommended the Ritz-Carlton. Belgian telephone operators spoke English, thank heavens. A very English and, to Peter's ears, very supercilious voice answered. Yes, the voice admitted languidly, they could just manage to let him have a room, although London was full, very full. He put down the phone with a smile, half annoyed, half amused by the hotel receptionist. Could any nation in the world be as snooty as the English, he wondered, and at a time when they needed every overseas visitor they could scrape up?

He walked down the street to Le Charolais, enjoying the rain, which had dwindled to a few light drops. A pale sun had emerged, and the streets shone, their gutters still gurgling with water. Le Charolais was almost full, but Willi found him a table, served a Scotch without being asked, and nodded approvingly at Peter's choice of *blinis aux caviar*, followed by roast saddle of hare. Peter looked round, seeing that young, pretty girls graced most of the tables. Not for the first time, he half reproached himself for his obsessive interest in Ilse, an interest that had dulled his eye for other women.

When he left the restaurant the rain had stopped and the air was warm, almost summery, despite the trees' bare branches and the hint of cold in the pale blue sky visible between fleeing storm clouds. He packed, called a taxi, scribbled a hasty note for Ilse ('called away on business'), and checked his telex. No response from the brokers, but that was not surprising: it was still early in Chicago. And what could they say, except to question his judgment, perhaps his sanity?

The flight was crowded, and as he waited in the departure lounge Peter nodded to some half-familiar faces, meanwhile talking desultorily to an American executive he had met at several parties. After the no-smoking sign went off he lit a cigarette, noting with surprise it was only his third or fourth that day, and ordered a Scotch, justifying it with his habitual nervousness over flying. His neighbour in the next seat was reading a Brussels afternoon paper, *Le Soir*. Peter glanced at the headlines; they still didn't mean much to him. He took a chance: 'Pardon me, but is there anything in the paper about the Agriculture Ministers' meeting?'

The man looked at him, smiled, and replied in good but careful English: 'They are still meeting, *monsieur*. But last night they apparently decided to put – what do you call it, a ceiling, a limit? – yes, a ceiling, on soybean imports.'

Peter breathed a sigh of relief and ordered a second, celebratory Scotch, thankful that the Belgian next to him had gone back to the paper, apparently fascinated by what seemed to be a story dealing with bicycle racing. A curious people, the Belgians, Peter thought, divided by language, and united chiefly by a common love of bicycle racing, tax evasion and food, with the monarchy coming a poor fourth. He smiled, closed his eyes and dozed until the plane touched down at London.

Less than an hour later he was unpacking in his room at the Ritz-Carlton, a hotel that he found luxurious but faintly intimidating, a process that started when the reception manager turned out to be a very tall, very slim and very elegant young man wearing black jacket and striped trousers – the embodiment of English starch and style. Beside him, as they walked a long corridor to the room, Peter felt short, squat, undistinguished, the archetypal ugly American. Should he tip such a dignified creature? Obviously not.

'Where's the bar?'

'The bar, sir? We don't have a bar. You can either call room service or order a drink in the lounge. Enjoy your stay, sir.'

Peter tried to decide whether it was more seemly to have a drink in his room, or to sit alone in a lounge doubtless filled with people who would make him feel even more out of place than the reception manager had done. Well, at least he wouldn't be visible in his room. He pressed the button for room service, and a waiter appeared within seconds; so promptly, indeed, that for one wild moment Peter wondered whether the reception manager had whispered discreetly, 'Better wait outside Number 107: the fellow's obviously desperate for a drink.'

While he sipped his Scotch and admitted that the Ritz-Carlton at least served a large one, with plenty of ice, he wondered what to do that evening. There was nothing in the rules, he recollected, to prevent his seeing Henry Rusk. He called the number; no reply. He checked his address book, and suddenly felt reluctant to see mere acquaintances with whom he would make meaningless conversation. He picked up the phone.

'Give me the hall porter.'

'Hall porter, here.'

'Hi, Acheson here, Room 107. I don't feel like eating in the hotel tonight. Can you recommend a good restaurant? Maybe Italian. Somewhere fairly lively.'

'Well, sir, some people do like Tiberio.'

'Sounds fine. Do I need to reserve?'

'I'll do it for you, sir. Eight-thirty?'

'Sounds fine. What's the address?'

'I'll have it waiting for you downstairs, sir, with the taxi.'

Peter felt better, and poured into his glass a little of the bottle of the duty-free Scotch he had bought at Brussels airport and had meant to keep for Ilse. There was a television set in the corner of the room, and he switched it on. As the picture cleared, a voice said: '... leaving little prospect of an early settlement of the strike. Meanwhile, at British Leyland in Longbridge, a further 3,000 workers came out today in support of a welder who claimed the job hurt his wrists. The company has offered him suspension on full pay pending arbitration, or transfer to a different job at a lower rate of pay. The union concerned has refused both offers, claiming the man is being victimised. Our industrial correspondent reports that if the strike is not settled soon 55,000 Leyland workers will be laid off for lack of components.'

Peter raised his glass and toasted the picture of militant workers carrying placards saying: 'No victimisation!' Some British workers, he thought, had found in the labour unions a substitute for religion, and practised it with all the bloody-minded enthusiasm that their forebears had expended on narrow, puritanical sects. A strike over one man's hurt wrists, thought Peter, was not all that different in spirit from the message of the Bible's promise that not one sparrow should fall without God's knowing about it – an admirable statement of principle, but hardly a foundation for a functioning industrial society.

At the Tiberio, in Mayfair, there was no sign that anyone had anything more important in mind than an evening of good food and good wine, and Peter felt, as he had at lunchtime, a twinge of envy at the sight of so many men sitting with pretty girls, none of whom looked as though she would withhold her body from a man she liked. These were obviously rich people, or they at least had good expense accounts: the menu prices were high, and even in the low, discreet lighting Peter could see the glitter of jewellery, the sheen on the women's skin that came from beauty treatment. He sighed over his lasagne. A weekend in London was not turning out to be a good idea, after all. He hurried through the rest of his meal, refused a brandy, and on his way out asked the head waiter where he could get a late-night drink, remembering British liquor laws that closed all the pubs at eleven in the evening.

The head waiter looked at him appraisingly. 'The Sixty-Four Club is just up the street, sir. It's a members' club, but you shouldn't have any trouble.' The night was cold; Peter shivered as he walked up Curzon Street, looking with mild surprise at the array of Rolls-Royces, Bentleys, Daimlers, Mercedes-Benzes, Jaguars and Aston-Martins parked bumper-to-bumper. No sign of recession here, he thought; or perhaps it was the last fling of the British, the waltz before a Waterloo they were going to lose.

The club receptionist, elegantly bearded and wearing a tuxedo, greeted him as though he were an old acquaintance half forgotten. 'Ah yes, Mr Acheson. Now, sir, are you a member? You're not? No problem, sir. Just sign here. I'll introduce you to Mr Wiese. Mr Sid Wiese.'

Peter found himself shaking hands with Sid, whose handlebar moustache was bristling. Sid murmured the names of people standing around him. Peter shook hands with them, and asked for a Scotch. Swiftly but unobtrusively, Sid discovered Peter's nationality, occupation and low spirits. Somehow – he was feeling a little dazed – Peter came to sit on a stool at the bar. On his right a middle-aged man with a huge belly was talking earnestly to a girl who might have been his daughter but wasn't. The stool on Peter's left was vacant. Then, as he put down his drink and looked in the mirror over the bar, he saw a girl with short, dark hair and a huge expanse of *decolleté* sit down next to him. He turned, and saw a face with pale, regular features and a mouth so vividly red that it was like a scar. She moved her lips in a smile, showing white, even teeth.

'Buy you a drink?' said Peter, conscious that he was starting to slur his words.

'I'll take a glass of champagne. I haven't seen you here before. Just visiting London?'

'Yeah. Over for the weekend.'

'Staying with friends?'

'No. I'm alone.'

The girl raised her glass. 'Cheers. My name's Pat, by the way.'

'I'm Peter.'

Half an hour later, without quite knowing how he got there, Peter was in Pat's apartment. Through a fog, he saw her undressing, until she was wearing only black panties and brassiere. He noted, with mere theoretical interest, that her breasts were small but high, and her hips narrow. Pat raised her arms. 'Come along, darling. I'm waiting for you.'

Peter lurched to his feet, feeling a wave of both nausea and distaste. 'Gee, I'm sorry, Pat, but I guess I just don't feel like it.'

Her face changed, and she put her hands on her hips. 'I knew I shouldn't have brought you here, but you kept begging me. Pissed out of your mind, that's your trouble. Well, you still owe me fifty pounds.'

'Fifty pounds?'

'That's right, and not a penny less.'

Peter summed up the last of his will and sobriety. 'I'll give you twenty-five, and that's it. Otherwise, I'll vomit all over your carpet.' He started to laugh weakly, and Pat started forward in alarm.

'OK, you shit, give me the twenty-five. I never want to see you again.'

'I feel the same, baby.'

He felt his way carefully down a steep flight of stairs, and out to the street. It was unfamiliar to him, narrow and winding. Where was he, for Christ's sake? He saw a policeman walking slowly and purposefully along the sidewalk on the opposite side of the street. Peter crossed, weaving slightly. The policeman looked at him coolly. 'Yes, sir, and how can I help you?'

'Where am I?'

'Shepherd's Market, Mayfair. Had a fair drop to drink, have you, sir?'

'Just a little.'

'Well, I ought to run you in for being drunk and incapable, but I suppose you can get home. Where do you live?'

'Brussels.'

'You won't get there tonight, sir. Are you staying in a hotel in London?'

'Yes, the Ritz-Carlton.'

'The best thing you can do, sir, is find a taxi, while I pretend I never saw you.'

The policeman moved on. Peter leaned against a lamp-post, his nausea diminishing in the cold air, until he saw a taxi. The driver stopped, surveying him doubtfully. 'Not going to be sick, are you? Sure? OK, hop in.' Back at the hotel, Peter lurched along the corridor, and found the keyhole in his bedroom door curiously elusive. At last, the door clicked open, and he saw with relief his bed, turned down ready for him, the bedside lamp glowing cosily. He collapsed on the bed fully clothed, and only wakened when the telephone rang later that morning. It was Ilse. Her voice was cool, formal; his was hoarse, roughened by drink and too many cigarettes. He cut into her recital of telephone and telex messages.

'For Christ's sake, darling, get over here. I need you.'

'What's wrong, Peter? You sound dreadful.'

'I feel it. Please, get the flight tonight. I've got to see you.'

She agreed, and he put the phone down shakily. He rang for breakfast and telephoned the hall porter for the morning papers. After two coffees, he was well enough to look at the headlines, then to turn to the commodity market reports in the *International Herald Tribune*. Yes, soybeans were down, and a story on the financial page predicted further falls. Peter smiled, closed his eyes, and went back to sleep. When he awakened, it was noon, the sun was slanting through the half-drawn curtains, and his breakfast tray had vanished. He moved cautiously, looked with distaste at his rumpled trousers, and walked hesitantly to the bathroom. His face looked back at him from the shaving mirror, and he winced at the boiled gooseberry eyes, the slack jowls, the stubble of beard, remembering his last monumental hangover, after the cocktail party in Brussels. 'You idiot,' he whispered to that unhappy face in the mirror. 'You idiot, you're turning yourself into a crock of shit.'

20

> Well, fancy giving money to the Government!
> Might as well have put it down the drain.
> Fancy giving money to the Government!
> Nobody will see the stuff again.
>
> *A. P. Herbert*

Late in the day on which President Valéry Giscard d'Estaing had wrecked at least half his plans to make a foreign exchange killing, Michel was back in the villa at Nyon. Anne-Marie was not there; the housekeeper said she had gone out to dinner with friends. Michel frowned and ran a hand through his fair hair. He went to the liquor cabinet, poured a large Scotch, and downed half of it at a gulp. The phone rang; it was Henk.

'Yes, I'm back in Geneva. Look, what the hell do we do now?'

'Well, things aren't so bad, Henk. The franc took a big plunge today. In fact, bigger than I'd expected, so I'm doing fine with the short selling. The trouble is, I'd expected the franc to recover when the markets discovered the story was a hoax. Now it's for real, so there's no point on gambling on a big rise.'

'You'll still have to pay Schwarzenbach. He wasn't to blame.'

'Naturally. Nobody was to blame, unless it's you.'

'Why me?'

'You're the journalist. You're the one who should have known that Giscard might really dissolve the Assembly.'

'Is this your way of saying you're going back on our deal? Because, if it is, I don't like it.'

'You're not getting twenty-five thousand, that's definite.'

'That was the deal, Michel.'

'Yes, and you, my political adviser, let me down. I'll give you half.'

'No chance, Michel. It's twenty-five thousand, or else.'

'Or else what? A spot of blackmail?'

'Oh, come on, Michel, that's not my style. But we had a deal, we're partners, and now you're trying to renege.'

'Originally you were going to get a percentage. I'll still pay it.'

'No, Michel. We changed the deal: twenty-five thousand.'

'Screw you, Henk. I'm paying Schwarzenbach in full because he delivered. I'm not paying you in full, because you didn't deliver in full. As simple as that.'

'Well, screw you, too, Michel. I'll take the half, but it's the last deal I'll ever go into with you. I don't like chisellers.'

Michel grinned as he put the phone down. As he'd expected, Henk had buckled eventually; he wasn't a fighter, particularly when he had no weapons. Michel poured another Scotch – tonight, somehow, *anisette* didn't meet his need – and wandered into the kitchen to cook bacon and eggs. He was finishing the last of them when Anne-Marie returned, vivacious and flushed from an evening of conversation, food and wine.

'How was business, Michel?'

'Oh, *comme çi, comme çà*. It's good to be back.'

'But why are you sitting in the kitchen eating bacon and eggs? There are better things in the fridge.'

'I had something on the flight.'

'Michel, was that Henk involved in this business?'

'Why do you ask?'

'Because he left when you did, and returned tonight: I was with Carlotta. He seemed unhappy.'

'Well, we had a little argument. Nothing serious.'

'I tell you, Michel, I don't trust him.'

'Well, don't worry. I shan't be doing business with him in future.'

Anne-Marie was passionate in bed that night and afterwards, as he lay smoking and looking at the window, silvery with moonlight from the lake, Michel felt deep contentment. In her, he thought, he had found a spirited companion, one who was generous, good-humoured, warm – all the things his wife had not been. Yet, he recalled, before their marriage she had seemed the most glowing of girls, and the only hint of the character she was to become was one he ignored, a discontented droop of her lips when her face was in repose and she was off guard Perhaps marriage would change Anne-Marie, too. But then he looked at her sleeping face, and saw that the lips were still full, half smiling, generous.

The next few days were busy as the franc tumbled, enabling Michel to buy back in the market what he had promised to deliver, and to show a substantial profit. Timing was everything, he thought, as he saw the franc fall to 4·40 to the dollar, then 4·39, recover slightly, and then slide again inexorably. If he had been too greedy, he would have waited for it to fall even further, and perhaps been too late; too timid, and he would have taken any profit, rather than steel his nerve and seize the right price and moment. The franc touched 4·36, and hovered there, moving up and down by fractions of a cent. Was it the time to go long – to assume a rise? He thought so, and bought the equivalent of $100,000. For a day or two, the franc's movements were inconclusive. Then it rose half a US cent above the price at which Michel had bought, and he unloaded – another $4,500 to the good. The next day, the franc rose a further eighth of a cent, and Michel reflected with satisfaction that an amateur would have been plunged into gloom at the thought of a lost profit. He was happy to have got in and out for a real profit, rather than to have held on, gloating over paper gains.

The short days were bright with winter sunshine, the mountains on the other side of the lake clear in a whipping wind that brushed the air clean. Michel took long walks beside the lake, lunching in little *auberges* and, once, at a lorry drivers' café on the lakeside road. The food was good, hearty and cheap, the conversation vigorous in a half dozen languages. Michel walked home along the lakeside path, his cheeks stinging in the wind, his trouser waistband slack around his middle, a welcome sign that daily exercise was shedding the flab he had accumulated in New York.

His good mood was broken by a letter waiting for him at the villa. It was from the Swiss immigration authorities, and said they had reason to believe he had been working in Switzerland, which was contrary to the terms of his temporary residence permit. Would he please present himself at the office the following Monday? Michel called his lawyer, a large, fat man of Italian descent. 'My dear Monsieur Jobert,' said Maître Scipioni, 'you have absolutely nothing to worry about. You have not been working, have you?'

'No. I've been protecting my investments, and that is surely an activity that will appeal to every Swiss.'

'Very droll, *cher* Monsieur Jobert. But in what manner have you been protecting them?'

'Oh, selling those investments that show a profit, and buying investments that seem likely to rise.'

'Very sensible. No, I think you have nothing to worry about. Even so, I think I should accompany you to this meeting. A Monsieur Huber, you say? Well, I will call him to say I will be there.'

Huber was a trim, greying man in a grey suit, of the type of *fonctionnaire* Michel had encountered in a thousand meetings in France, Switzerland and Belgium – wherever, indeed, the civil servant was imbued by the belief that he was there to protect the state rather than the citizen. He was, like all his indistinguishable fellows, both polite and inflexible. He outlined the regulations in a dry, clear voice, his metal-framed glasses glinting. Maître Scipioni showed some impatience. 'My dear Monsieur Huber,' he said, 'we are familiar with the provisions.'

'Naturally, *cher maître*. Nevertheless, it is my duty to ensure that your client understands their precise meaning. The accusation is serious.'

Scipioni pounced on the word. 'Accusation? So we are dealing with a denunciation?'

'I did not use that word, *cher maître*, because there is no denunciation, in the formal sense. Let us say that we have cause to believe, from a third party, that your client has engaged in activities that are contrary to the regulations, inasmuch as they relate to the practice of his profession rather than the protection of his investments, as he claims.'

Huber looked at Michel. 'I must ask you to answer this, Monsieur Jobert, and not your *avocat*. Am I to understand that you have not been acting as a foreign exchange dealer?'

'Absolutely. I have no clients. I am a private investor.'

'Can you prove that?'

'How can I prove a negative?'

'Nevertheless, our information is to the contrary. It is that, on behalf of others, including a Liechtenstein *Anstalt*, ownership unknown, you have been engaging in large foreign exchange movements.'

'May I know the name of the Liechtenstein *Anstalt*?'

'Certainly, *monsieur*. It is Junius A.G.'

Michel stifled a smile. Junius was his own *Anstalt*; but the shares were, of course, in the name of bearer, and only his Liechtenstein lawyer knew the real ownership. Michel decided to take a gamble. 'I've never heard of the company. Are you sure you have the right name?'

'Completely sure, *monsieur*. Junius was the name of an anonymous writer in eighteenth-century England, who criticised in a newspaper of the time the British government's policies towards many issues, particularly towards the American colonies – as they were then. His identity has never been discovered, though there are various suggestions. The name is appropriate, do you not agree, for a Liechtenstein *Anstalt*, doubtless owned by a person, or by persons, hoping for a similarly immortal anonymity?'

Michel realised that this particular *fonctionnaire*, though outwardly identical to the rest of the breed, was dangerously alert. 'I'm surprised, Monsieur Huber, that you should be so well informed about eighteenth-century English history.'

'I took a degree in history, Monsieur Jobert, and eighteenth-century England was my speciality. That is why this case has particularly interested me – the coincidence, if you understand.'

Scipioni broke in. 'Are you calling this a case?'

'Why, yes. What would you call it?'

'I would call it an unsubstantiated accusation, probably a confusion of identities, and almost certainly the result of malice on somebody's part.'

Huber shrugged. 'Unfortunately, much of the information that comes our way is the result of malice. I regret it, but cannot ignore the information because of personal distaste. This has been a preliminary discussion, however. We may have to discuss the matter again. On the other hand, we may not.'

Scipioni rose, effusively polite again, and thanked Huber for his courtesy. They all shook hands, and Scipioni held open the door for Michel. Outside the drab, anonymous building, he asked: 'So what do you think, *maître*?'

'I think you have an enemy. Now tell me, between lawyer and client, what is this Junius A.G.?'

'My own company.'

Scipioni gaped. 'But why did you not say so? That would have settled the matter immediately.'

'Because it is where I have put away a lot of tax-free profits over the years: more than $200,000, if you must know. I don't trust the Swiss any longer. They're co-operating more and more with the tax authorities of other countries, particularly the United States. OK, so I may not return to the US to live. But I have a lot of investments there. You see my point? If the Internal Revenue Service could prove I should have paid taxes on the money in Liechtenstein, then they could seize my US assets. So what's the worst that the Swiss can do? Fine me? Deport me? Cancel my residence permit?'

'Yes, I see your reasoning. But who could have known about Junius?'

'So far as I know, just my lawyer and me. I don't think I've mentioned it to anyone else.'

'Well, *cher monsieur*, somebody knows, and somebody is out to damage you. I assume you are not willing to make a deal with the American IRS? They would be lenient if you volunteered the information.'

'No. Never. Do you know how I regard governments and taxes? I think they're like alcoholics – the more they have, the more they want. Put a bottle of Scotch in front of a drunk, and he drinks it. Give a government a dollar, and it's spent.'

'So it is a principle with you?'

'Yes. One of my few. Perhaps my only one.'

Scipioni laughed, his cascade of chins shaking. 'It is not a bad principle. But it must be difficult to observe in practice, surely?'

'Not with a good lawyer and a good accountant.'

Michel drove home in a relaxed mood, though still puzzled. Clearly he had an enemy; and one who knew more about his affairs than he should. Michel searched his list of acquaintances. Several, he saw, had good reason to be annoyed with him; but only one so recently that he stood out as a suspect, and that was Henk. Michel shrugged, and lifted the phone: the best strategy was certainly to have it out with the man.

Henk's voice was cool, distant. 'A drink, Michel? I don't see why. I told you I would never do business with you again. As for friendship – well, that is all in the past, surely?'

'I still think we should meet. There may be somebody on our trail.'

'That's different. Where?'

They arranged to meet at the Casino in Divonne; perversely, perhaps sentimentally, Michel thought the story should end where it had started. Henk's manner was cool when they started to talk – he was, characteristically, half an hour late – but it thawed within minutes. Henk was, thought Michel, a man who could nourish and embellish a grudge in the absence of its object, but was incapable of maintaining a frosty manner. That quirk made him no less dangerous. However friendly he might seem now – and Michel could not convict him of insincerity – he would almost certainly cherish his grudge once he was alone.

'So who is on our trail, and why?' said Henk.

'I don't know. But I had a curious conversation today, and it suggests that somebody knows more about me than he should. If he knows so much about me, then it's likely he knows a good deal about you.'

'You're being mysterious. Tell me.'

Michel recounted his meeting with Huber, leaving out only the name of his Liechtenstein *Anstalt*.

Henk shrugged one shoulder. 'It sounds as though you should worry, not me.'

'Was there any reaction to the fake story we sent?'

'Not that I've heard. Why should there be? It was journalistically incompetent, I grant you; but announcing hours after it happened – and then as an inspired guess – that

Giscard had dissolved the Assembly isn't likely to set the Seine on fire.'

'Let me ask you a question, Henk. Are you still sore about the deal?'

'Yeah, a little. I'd thought we were partners. Then you reneged. But so what? It's water under the bridge. There'll be other days, other deals.'

'I thought you said there wouldn't be any more deals between you and me.'

Henk smiled, his lank hair falling over his brow. 'Well, you know me, Michel, I'm always open to suggestions.'

'And you have no idea who could have informed on me?'

'Not the slightest. Believe me.'

'Oh, I do, I do.'

'I'm not sure I like the way you said that.'

'I don't like what's been happening.'

Michel paid the bill, and they walked slowly towards the *salon des jeux*. The table at which the Iranian played was almost deserted, its star attraction absent. What had happened to him, Michel asked. Henk grinned: he'd gone bankrupt. Not through gambling, though: his winnings had been keeping him afloat for years. No, the Iranian had plunged in business as well, and most of his investments had gone sour. Remembering the Iranian's strong, impassive face, and the casual flick of his wrist as he staked a fortune, Michel had to repress a shudder. He could imagine that urbane, imperturbable man living in dingy, middle-class respectability – a pensioner, a man broken by his failure, too old, too shattered, to recover the confidence that had sustained him in the past. He put the thought to Henk, who laughed. 'You're being romantic, Michel. Men like that don't crumple. They either break completely, kill themselves, or they bounce right back.'

Outside, in the moonlight, Henk looked at Michel, his expression mocking. 'I wonder which you would do, Michel? I don't think you'd take adversity well.'

'You forget that I've known it. What do you think it's like to lose your country, your home, your patrimony?'

'You exaggerate, Michel. Algeria was never your country. You just thought it was.'

'It was real for me. There's hardly a day when I don't think about our home, our land, our life. But I survived, I bounced back.'

'So you did. But that was twenty years ago. Perhaps the elastic has become brittle. Just a little strain, and it might snap.'

Michel was about to accuse Henk of pulling on the elastic, then bit back the sentence, and summoned his will to smile, put out his hand, go through the social ritual.

For more than a week Michel heard nothing from Huber. Then Scipioni called him. Yes, he said, the matter was serious; they should meet, not discuss it on the telephone. Michel drove into Geneva, parked his car half a block from Scipioni's office, and walked up the hill, sweating slightly despite the chill of winter air. The lift was tiny, rickety; and Michel wondered how a man so large as Scipioni could tolerate it. Inside the office a receptionist looked at Michel out of large, exophthalmic blue eyes. Maître Scipioni was waiting, she said, and stood up with a flash of thigh. Michel felt a surge of lust, then shrugged mentally; he was sure the girl would offer a sensational night, but wondered what they could talk about over breakfast.

Scipioni's private office was strangely out of keeping with the man. Whereas Scipioni was fat, self-indulgent, the room was austere, and its nearest concession to sybaritism was a vase of opulent roses on the window-sill. The lawyer himself was, as always, elaborately polite; his manner suggested that Michel's journey from Nyon, thirteen kilometres away, had been a feat comparable to a dangerous safari.

Michel cut short Scipioni's effulgence. The lawyer cleared his throat, and could not resist a final flicker of complaisance: 'I would not, of course, have troubled you, *cher monsieur,* unless I had regarded it as absolutely necessary. You understand that, I am sure?'

'Of course,' said Michel, unable to resist irony. 'You know that my hours are full – that my time is at a premium.'

Scipioni beamed. 'How well you put it, *cher monsieur*! Clearly, you understand my regret at the necessity.'

'Naturally. And you yourself, of course, are a very busy

man. That is understood.'

Scipioni touched his forehead with a handkerchief. 'Not as busy as yourself, Monsieur Jobert – but, yes, there are certain calls on my time.'

Suddenly, Scipioni was businesslike. 'The fact is, and I regret to say it, that the immigration authorities appear to have obtained, or to have received, certain documents showing that you have dealt in foreign exchange on behalf of Junius A.G.

'Very well. You know, and I know, that this is your company. But you have certain objections to explaining that fact to the Swiss authorities. So you appear to be faced with a choice. Either you admit to your ownership of Junius, and thereby satisfy the immigration authorities; or you continue to deny it, and almost certainly face an order to leave Switzerland. Take the first course, and you run the risk of being asked to pay American taxes; take the second, and you face the certainty of finding it difficult, if not impossible, to return to this country.'

Michel lit a Gauloise, inhaled deeply, and blew out the smoke in a long breath. 'Tell me, *cher maître*, what is this so-called evidence – these documents?'

'Ah, that is difficult to say with any precision. But Monsieur Huber hints – no, more than hints – that they are copies of telex messages between you and foreign exchange brokers on behalf of Junius.'

Michel frowned. 'And how did Monsieur Huber obtain these?'

Scipioni shrugged his huge shoulders. 'Frankly, I do not know, and Huber will never tell us. In any case, that is surely less important than the fact that he has them. You agree?'

Michel paused for a moment, thinking hard. 'Yes and no, *maître*. If somebody has copies of telexes, it suggests he obtained them for a purpose. And that he knows a great deal more about my affairs than I would like. As for his purpose – well, it is obvious that he intends to punish me, and I doubt if he'll be content with making me *persona non grata* in Switzerland.

'So I think there are two things we should do. First, I will immediately sell all my holdings in the United States. That way, the IRS won't be able to touch me. Second, we'll tell Huber that I own Junius. That should stop the inquiry stone dead.'

Scipioni nodded gravely. 'Yes, I can see the wisdom of what you propose. But surely you are now paying a high price to remain *persona grata* to the Swiss but, possibly, to prevent yourself ever from going to the United States again?'

Michel gave a slight shrug. 'If the IRS ever found out about Junius, I'd probably be assessed for all the taxes I owe, plus a fine: say $175,000. So I have to decide whether it's worth paying that much to be free to return to New York. Do you know the city? Well, I can tell you it's a place that some people would pay good money to avoid. Not me: I can stand it. But I guess I have to regard America as another country from which I'm exiled.'

21

> ... it is always a good idea to close your books each year, especially if you are in partnership. As the proverb says: 'Frequent accounting makes for lasting friendship'.
>
> *Luca Paciola, 1494*

New York was bitterly cold on the January day that Kemble had chosen for the final accounting. Dirty snow lay in hard-packed drifts, and pedestrians slid on icy sidewalks, their coats whipped by a sadistic wind out of Canada. Inside Kemble's offices, those converted brownstones on Murray Hill, radiators hissed, and in the conference room a log fire sputtered in a wide fireplace. The room was warm, cosy, and its furnishings and decor suggested that a mid-Victorian family had just stepped out of their sitting-room for an hour or two.

From a gilt, ornate frame a portrait stared out, the face fleshy, the eyes challenging. It was the firm's founder, William Kemble, and his great-grandson, Charles, sat beneath the portrait, stressing the resemblance by wearing a high-lapelled, dark tweed suit, a brown tie knotted into a stiff collar, a gold watch-chain spread across his waistcoat. He cleared his throat, and smiled at Henry, Peter and Jacqueline, who were sitting with him at the heavy Victorian dining-table. 'First, Michel sends his apologies,' said Kemble. 'He phoned to say he has the flu. So he'll accept the outcome of this meeting, whatever that may be.'

Rusk took a Romeo y Julieta cigar out of his mouth, exhaled a cloud of smoke, and said, 'That's damned unsatisfactory, Charles. It may not be in the rules, but surely there's a presumption that all players will be present for the final accounting? What happens if we want to question him about certain transactions?'

Peter laughed. 'You're being pessimistic, Henry. If you're the winner, then you know as well as I do that you won't give a damn. And if you're one of the losers – well, we can always phone him, I guess.'

Rusk frowned. 'That's not the point, Peter. The point is that he should be here, and I want to put that on record. Jacqueline, what do you think?'

She shrugged, looking pale and drawn. 'Oh, technically you're right, Henry, but let's get on with it, shall we? I want to know who won.'

There was a moment's silence. Kemble cleared his throat. 'Well, the winner is Jobert, in fact. His total profits were \$291,517·45. The next is...'

'Nonsense, Charles,' said Rusk, half rising from his chair. 'My winnings are more than six million dollars, and you've got the documents to prove it. What kind of idiocy is this?'

Kemble raised a warning hand. 'Henry, I'm afraid you're wrong. The rules quite clearly state that profits must have been received before midnight on December the thirty-first. What you have are documents showing that JZ International has agreed with Woodcat, and Woodcat has agreed with JZ, that there should be a merger. I agree, your fees are \$6·3 million; but the merger hasn't gone through.'

'Nonsense, Kemble. The agreement is legally binding on both sides. You're quibbling over a technicality, and I won't have it.' He stubbed out his cigar angrily, and looked round the table. 'But suppose – just suppose – I accept your point: what are my profits without the JZ fees? Tell me that.'

Kemble looked down at his papers, shuffling them rapidly. 'I'm afraid you still lose, Henry. You're about \$12,000 behind; \$12,113·82, to be precise.'

'And how do we know that Jobert's figures are accurate? I think it's very suspicious his not being here – I told you so at the outset.'

'We know,' said Kemble, 'because I've audited his figures, and checked all the supporting documents, that's why. Remember another rule: I am the umpire or referee.'

'And let me remind you of another rule, Charles, the one that says a player will be disqualified if he or she breaks the law of the country in whose jurisdiction he was at the time of doing a deal. How do we know what Jobert got up to? That's probably why he isn't here – he doesn't want to be questioned.'

Jacqueline broke in. 'Henry, we could say the same of you, couldn't we – of all of us?'

Rusk turned towards her, his face red and angry. 'I deny it, I deny it absolutely. But the argument is quite pointless. I have won, even without JZ. Charles, there's one deal I didn't mention, because I regarded it as private, and that's the sale of shares in a company operating in the Middle East, Offshore Personal Services.'

Kemble blinked. 'I'm not sure we can count profits unless they were in your original accounting, Henry.'

'Why not? The rules say nothing about that.'

'They do by inference. They say that each player will provide me with an interim and final profit and loss statement, the final one to be ready by January 15th.'

'Another of your damned technicalities, Kemble. I've got all the supporting documentation. I can prove that I sold my shares for $200,000 in cash.'

Acheson blew on his glasses and replaced them firmly on his nose. 'That's all very well, Henry, but why didn't you say so before? You think Jobert is behaving suspiciously, and perhaps he is. But your behaviour is kind of odd, too, don't you think? Jacqueline, what do you say?'

She paused: 'I think Henry here didn't disclose the Middle East deal because it was either illegal or shady, or something of the kind. Certainly, it's something that Henry didn't want to disclose unless he had to. So the question is, Henry, what does Offshore Personal Services do?'

'That, young woman, is no concern of yours. I'm willing to discuss it privately with Charles here, but not with anyone else. Middle Eastern politics are involved.'

Kemble raised his hand: 'Do you agree, Jacqueline, Peter, that I should have a private conference with Henry?'

They looked at each other, then nodded. Kemble and Rusk left the room, and Jacqueline and Peter relaxed. 'I could do with some more coffee,' said Peter. 'Let me find the secretary.' He put his head out of the door, returned to the table, and sat down, his glasses glinting.

'Tell me, Jacqueline, what do you make of all this?'

'I don't feel like giving up any of my winnings to either Jobert or Rusk.'

'Neither do I. Would you join me if we said we'd fight it in a court of law?'

'Yes, I sure would.'

'Shake, partner.'

They shook hands, smiling tensely.

'Peter, tell me something. Did the Game do anything for you?'

He took off his glasses, rubbed his eyes, smiled. 'Oh, I guess so. Showed me I could prosper outside the corporate womb, which is something. Also, I met a girl, and we're getting married: she's my consolation prize. And you?'

'It was kind of traumatic. Oh, sure, I proved I didn't need to work for a company – I could make it on my own. But how, and with whom? I got tied up with some real shits, Peter. And the trouble was: I knew they were when they offered me the contract, but I sat on my conscience, saying "Hush now, hush". In the long run, though, my good old American puritanism triumphed. You got a wife out of it. I certainly didn't get a husband.'

'What do you think of European men?'

'Big question, big continent. But if it's time for generalisations: well, they have a style that most Americans don't, and they're so goddamn dominant it's almost a pleasure to be submissive.'

'I don't think European women are submissive. I think they're pretty goddamn shrewd and tough, if you want the truth, and so subtle that men don't know they're being manipulated.'

'That's horrible. Why can't there be an honest relationship?'

Peter shrugged, and smiled wryly. 'Since when were human beings honest with each other? Perhaps they should be, but they sure as hell ain't.'

They were silent for a moment, and then the door opened. Rusk's face was still angry, Kemble's flushed but bland. He sat down at the head of the table.

'Henry has behaved very decently, as one could expect. I've

persuaded him that because he didn't include Offshore Personal Services in his original accounting, it cannot now be included. On the other hand, he insists on a special audit of Jobert's figures. What do you feel about that? Jacqueline?'

'What I feel is that we should call the whole Game off. If we're all going to start auditing each other, who knows what will come out?'

Rusk pounced. 'That suggests you have something to hide, Jacqueline.'

'Don't we all? You can't convince me that you're passing up several hundred thousands of dollars of winnings – our money, by the way – just because you've had a cosy little talk with Charles. You've got something to hide. Well, so have I, and maybe Peter and Michel have. So if you're going to wash Michel's dirty linen in public, you might insist on washing ours – and we might insist on washing yours. It's up to you.'

'I'm with Jacqueline,' said Peter. 'I vote to call the whole Game off. Let's each keep what we've made, and forget the prize for the winner.'

Jacqueline nodded: 'I agree.'

Henry snorted. 'You can afford that view, Jacqueline. You've no chance of winning.'

'That isn't quite correct, Henry,' said Kemble. 'To repeat the figures: Jobert $291,517; you made $279,404; Jacqueline $268,550; and Peter $198,827. So Peter is definitely out of the running; but Jacqueline is still in it if she challenges either you or Jobert successfully. You see my point?'

Henry looked furious, but said nothing, obviously waiting to choose his next words with care. Jacqueline leaned across the table towards Kemble. 'Listen, we're all forgetting that somebody else is involved: Jobert. At the moment, Henry's talking as though he has won, or could win. But on the figures, Michel already has. So why don't we phone him?'

Kemble drummed the fingers of his right hand on the table, pursing his lips and looking judicious; or, perhaps, playing for time. 'Yes, yes, Jacqueline, you're right; indeed, I'd thought of that myself. Clearly, we can't take a decision without him. Yes, I'll get my secretary to call him.' He pressed a button on his telephone, and a few moments later his secretary walked in, a tall capable woman with greying hair and a sturdy, corseted figure. No challenge there for Nancy, thought Jacqueline.

'Why, of course, Mr Kemble,' she said. 'I've got the number in my book.' She smiled round the room, as impersonally as an air hostess announcing that the flight was about to land, or even to crash.

Rusk's voice rumbled again as the door closed behind her. 'I don't like any of this. How do I know that the three of you aren't in a plot against me?'

He looked challengingly into each of their faces, while Kemble waved a minatory finger. But before he could speak, Peter broke in. 'You're just being paranoid, Henry, because you can't stand being a loser. Now shut up.'

Rusk started to stand up, then sank down again, turned to Kemble and said loudly and harshly, 'When you speak to Jobert, tell him I'm not a party to this – this loose interpretation of the rules. I reserve my position, do you understand?'

Jacqueline sighed, becoming bored by the whole argument. 'Oh, for God's sake, Henry, you can't have it both ways. First you try to sneak in JZ, even though the deal hasn't gone through. When that doesn't work, you try to bring in Offshore Personal Services, against all the rules. Now you're waving the rules at us as though they're holy writ. What the hell are you worrying about? If the JZ deal goes through, as you say it will, you'll have made more than six million dollars. Are you so hungry you need to take a quarter of everyone else's money as well?' She stared at him, her eyes passionate, her lips a firm line, ready to attack again.

Rusk shifted in his chair. 'It's a matter of principle. I've accepted that JZ is ruled out. I've voluntarily chosen not to argue over Offshore's eligibility. So I *am* obeying the rules. You're the ones who are using blackmail.'

'Blackmail? I only said...'

'That if I didn't fall in with your ideas, you'd insist on everybody's being re-audited, and you implied – no, you damn well said – that you'd be looking for dirt. In my book, that's blackmail.'

Jacqueline's lips trembled, and her hand shook as she lit a

cigarette. 'Henry, if you think that's blackmail, you have a lot to learn, believe me. I ...'

At that moment the phone rang, and Jacqueline cut off her sentence. Kemble lifted the receiver gently, almost ceremoniously, and switched on the telephone loudspeaker.

Michel's voice boomed into the room, his accent thickened electronically. 'Yes, thank you, the *grippe* – how do you call it, influenza? – is much better now. So who is the winner?'

'Well, there's a little problem about that,' said Kemble, his voice smooth and unctuous. 'Henry seems to feel – he's with me, by the way, and he can hear this conversation – Henry seems to feel that your profits are not quite, well, quite what they purport to be.'

Across 3,500 miles of wires and circuitry Michel's laugh came loudly. 'I thought we'd have trouble with that one. So what does he want to do?'

'The fact is,' said Kemble, 'he wants a special re-audit of your books – wants to go behind the papers to the people. But Jacqueline and Peter won't agree. They say that either we agree that everyone keeps his profits, without paying a quarter to the one who made the most – who is you, Michel – or they'll insist on a special audit of Henry's profits. The question is: where do you stand, Michel?'

'With Jacqueline and Peter. Can you hear me, Henry? If you want to dig for dirt, then I'll do the same for you. There's plenty to be found, too. I'll just mention two names: Royston and Madame Claudine. You see, I have my friends in the Middle East, too. I can tell you all about Offshore Personal Services.'

For a few seconds there was silence, apart from the magnified hum of the telephone background static, and Henry's heavy breathing. Then he said, quietly and almost tonelessly, 'Tell Jobert I don't truckle to blackmailers.'

Jobert's laugh reverberated through the room. 'I can hear you, Henry – wonders of modern technology. Call it blackmail if you want: the French word is *chantage*, much prettier. But I'll let you down lightly. We'll call the Game off, and each keep our winnings, and I'll say no more about your little adventure in the Middle East. *Au revoir, mes enfants.* I trust you to make

Henry see reason.'

Rusk picked up his papers from the table and stood, massive and angry, moving his lips silently. Then his words came: 'I'm not the man to take this lying down. You'll be hearing from my lawyer. That's all I have to say.' He turned on his heel, and walked briskly to the door, his broad back straight and rigid.

As the door closed behind him, Kemble expelled his pent-up breath, puffing out his cheeks. 'That really surprises me,' he said. 'Rusk – of all people. I never expected him to behave like that.'

Peter laughed. 'Charles, you're a damned good accountant, but you're no judge of people, believe me. I spotted him for a phoney the moment I met him. All that veddy-veddy British act, him and his goddamn Krug champagne ... He's a hypocrite all the way through. What I want to know is why he backed away from any mention of Offshore Personal Services once we'd challenged him?'

'I think I can answer that,' said Jacqueline, smiling. 'Everyone in France knows who Madame Claudine is. The French have a word for it, as usual: she's a *proxénete*, or pimp to you and me. So I'd guess that Offshore Personal Services has something to do with prostitution.'

'Oh, surely not?' said Kemble, looking shocked, his heavy jowls sagging. 'That isn't what he told me. Don't let's forget who the man is: respectable banker, Harvard and Oxford, member of some of the best clubs, old, wealthy family.'

'Oh, Charles, you really are a bit – well, trusting,' said Jacqueline, laughing. 'My God, there was one man I met in Spain, a client in fact, with a pedigree as long as your arm, and he was one of the worst shits you could imagine. I won't tell you what he was up to – but if you want shittiness in a highly refined, sophisticated form, then look for it in those good, respectable old families you so much revere.'

There was a hurried knock at the door and Kemble's secretary came in, with no smile on her face now, only a worried, urgent look. 'Mr Kemble, I'm sorry to interrupt, but Mr Rusk – he's fallen on the steps, and I think he's broken his leg. I've called an ambulance, but I thought you should know. He's in great pain.'

Peter started laughing, and for a moment Jacqueline looked at him in astonishment. Then she laughed, too, while Kemble and his secretary hurried out of the room, as though fleeing from lunatics.

'Oh, God, I shouldn't laugh,' said Peter, taking off his glasses and wiping his eyes with a handkerchief. 'But if anyone had it coming to him, Henry did. What's the old saying: "Pride goeth before a great fall"?'

'A cliché, Peter. But I'll forgive you this time.'

22

> The only thing that men learn from history, is that men don't learn from history
>
> *Poincaré*

In a long professional career I have come to rely very little on people's honesty or loyalty. No accountant who has been on the inside of merger negotiations, and seen the chiselling and cheating, or who has had to audit the books of corporations trying to raise their reported earnings, can afford to take anything except a somewhat sceptical view of human behaviour. Even within our own profession, I regret to say, there are people whose honour and integrity are less than they should be – and though I name no names, we can all think of certain accounting firms associated with corporate crashes and scandals.

Even so, Henry Rusk's behaviour disappointed me very much, for I still hold to the belief that our fine old families uphold standards that are, alas, either challenged or scorned in the modern world. Since that day when he walked out of our offices, I have heard nothing from him directly. But I have heard from his lawyers – and again am disappointed, since the firm is old, its senior partners are stalwarts of the American Bar Association, and they should know better than to pursue totally meretricious claims.

Hardly had I sent Rusk a bottle of champagne and a bouquet of flowers to his hospital room, than this law firm wrote to claim damages from Kemble, McKenzie and Horton alleging that his fall was caused by ice on our steps. Now I am the first to admit – though not to Rusk's lawyers, of course – that a very small amount of ice had remained at the sides of the steps. But no prudent person would have trodden on it, since the middle of the steps was clear and dry. In my view – and it is a view our lawyers have expressed forcibly – Rusk's fall was caused entirely by his own negligence, the result, no doubt, of his having left our offices in angry, impetuous mood. I have good reason, too, to fear that his fall was also the result of his having imbibed too much at lunch time – a habit of his, I regret to say, and one that appears to be growing on him with the passing years. Well, we shall defend the claim, since I see no reason why our firm – or, more accurately, our insurers – should pay out for an accident that was entirely the man's own fault. As for the size of the claim – it is obviously ridiculous, since there is no way in which a broken leg could be worth $190,000. But that sum is, I note, within a percentage point or two of one quarter of the total profits shown by Jacqueline, Michel and Peter. In short, Rusk hasn't given up on that front, either, and still thinks he won.

Of the other three 'Foreign Secretaries' I have mixed news. To my surprise, Nancy and Jacqueline have become firm friends, not that they see much of each other: Jacqueline is working for a charitable foundation based in Atlanta, Georgia, the home state of a president I am viewing with increasing dismay, since his policies towards business appear equivocal, and those towards the Soviet Union curiously ineffective. But let us leave that aside; one day, this nation's voters will come to their senses, and put a Republican back in the White House. But to return to Jacqueline: Nancy tells me she is handling the foundation's investments, and doing a very good job.

'That's fine, my dear,' I said. 'How is her personal life, though? She has always struck me as a somewhat lonely girl.' Nancy snorted – we were in our apartment, and she could afford to be her usual, vivid self. 'You mean her sex life, don't you, Charles? Why you can't say so, God alone knows. Oh well, I'm married to a man with a gift for euphemism, and I should just thank the Lord it hasn't turned to periphrasis yet. Right, to answer your question: yes, there is a man in her life, and if I know her, and if I know men, and I can speak as an authority on both, a certain amount of fleshly intercourse will be taking place occasionally.'

Nancy's conversation usually amuses me, but this time I was slightly annoyed: she had missed the point, I thought. 'My dear, there's a world of difference between "fleshly intercourse", as you put it, and a happy, secure, loving relationship. Does she have that as well?'

I watched Nancy as she rose from her chair, and walked impatiently to the window of our living-room: her figure was still young, lithe, but I'd noticed an increasing tension in her manner, although I forbore to mention it. She turned towards me, and I was surprised by the passion in her face. 'Charles, one of the most infuriating things about you, and one of the nicest, goddammit, is your innocence. Jacqueline is thirty-three years old, damned attractive, but still thirty-three. Also, she's bright – bloody bright. So what kind of man is she likely to find? Most men of her own age are scared of her: she's too intelligent, too forceful. So she has to look for an older man. OK, so she finds one. The likelihood is that he's married, or rebounding from his former wife. Her chances of finding a – what did you call it? – "a happy, secure, loving relationship" are extremely small. But if you want specifics, and I guess you do, she's having an affair with a man married to a crippled woman. He can't divorce her, because he's too nice to do that. But he does love Jacqueline. So, if that's a happy, secure and loving relationship – well, she's got it, for what it's worth.'

Nancy sat down again, her face flushed, and handed me her empty glass. 'Give me another libation – your word, not mine, but one that's growing on me. Like a fungus.'

The next morning, I had a letter from Peter, inviting me to his wedding in Stuttgart. It is unlikely that Nancy and I will be there; it is a city I avoid as often as possible. Peter sent me a photograph of his fiancée who looks pretty enough, in a conventional way. Let us hope she makes Peter a good, stable wife; he needs one. As I detected almost at our first meeting, he is capable of emotional decisions, such as his one to stay in Brussels. Paris or London, perhaps; but Brussels, that grey little capital without even a river to call its own? Peter is, to be frank, one of those people to whom the passing years bring age, not maturity.

Looking back on that whole episode with 'the Foreign Secretaries', I blame myself for not having been stronger – not having stopped the Game before it started. It did none of them any good. Peter has expatriated himself. Jacqueline is wasting her talents and her life in Atlanta, and Nancy hints at some disastrous personal relationship in Europe. As for Michel: well, I had a most disturbing telephone call from the IRS. What did I know, they demanded, of a Liechtenstein *Anstalt* named Junius? Nothing, I replied, but they hammered away. Surely, as Mr Jobert's accountant, I knew it was his personal investment company; that he had used it to salt away profits on which he should have paid US taxes? That is a most serious matter – appalling, indeed, since there is a world of difference between tax avoidance and tax evasion, the one usually accomplished with the assistance of a skilled accountant, the other usually done on the sly.

Michel took a characteristically frivolous attitude when I phoned him in Switzerland, laughing as he said, 'It's all true, you know. But you need not worry; I have sold all my investments in the US, and the proceeds are where the IRS can never touch them. Tell them to go and get screwed.'

'Michel, I must remonstrate. They will probably try to extradite you.'

'That I doubt, *cher* Charles. Switzerland does not extradite anyone for tax evasion.'

'But you can never return to this country.'

'Not under my own name, certainly. But I can live with that prospect. Charles, do not sound so gloomy, so downcast. I have excellent bad news for you.'

'How can bad news be excellent?'

'Wait. You know our friend Henry? Well, that deal between Woodcat and JZ is not going through; the Arabs are going to pull out. So it is goodbye to that six million dollars, is it not?' He laughed heartily before going on.

'Also, I have solved the mystery of Offshore Personal Services. It is, as we all suspected, a matter of operating floating brothels. So, when the Emir realised how huge the profits would be, he revoked the licence and took over himself. But, being an Arab gentleman, he paid Henry $200,000 for his shares. It amuses me, to think of our pompous friend being a pimp.'

'But he is not a pimp, Michel. He has sold out.'

'So he is an ex-pimp, or a failed pimp. Yes, a failed pimp: that is even worse, don't you think?'

ACKNOWLEDGEMENTS

Thanks are due to Faber and Faber Ltd for permission to quote extracts from T. S. Eliot's 'Choruses from "The Rock"' on page 105 and from 'Ash Wednesday VI' on page 197, and to Doubleday & Company, Inc. for permission to quote from Paul Engle's *Corn* on page 157. The lines by A.P. Herbert on page 232 are from 'Too Much!'.